# NEVER
# LET THEM
# SEE YOU
# BLEED

## Look for these exciting Western series from bestselling authors William W. Johnstone and J.A. Johnstone

*The Mountain Man*

*Luke Jensen: Bounty Hunter*

*Brannigan's Land*

*The Jensen Brand*

*Smoke Jensen: The Beginning*

*Preacher and MacCallister*

*Fort Misery*

*The Fighting O'Neils*

*Perley Gates*

*MacCoole and Boone*

*Guns of the Vigilantes*

*Shotgun Johnny*

*The Chuckwagon Trail*

*The Jackals*

*The Slash and Pecos Westerns*

*The Texas Moonshiners*

*Stoneface Finnegan Westerns*

*Ben Savage: Saloon Ranger*

*The Buck Trammel Westerns*

*The Death and Texas Westerns*

*The Hunter Buchanon Westerns*

*Will Tanner, Deputy US Marshal*

*Old Cowboys Never Die*

*Go West, Young Man*

**Published by Kensington Publishing Corp.**

# NEVER LET THEM SEE YOU BLEED

## WILLIAM W. JOHNSTONE
### AND J.A. JOHNSTONE

**PINNACLE BOOKS**
Kensington Publishing Corp.
www.kensingtonbooks.com

PINNACLE BOOKS are published by

Kensington Publishing Corp.
119 West 40th Street
New York, NY 10018

PUBLISHER'S NOTE: Following the death of William W. Johnstone, the Johnstone family is working with a carefully selected writer to organize and complete Mr. Johnstone's outlines and many unfinished manuscripts to create additional novels in all of his series like The Last Gunfighter, Mountain Man, and Eagles, among others. This novel was inspired by Mr. Johnstone's superb storytelling.

First mass market printing: February 2022
Revised mass market printing: March 2024
ISBN-13: 978-0-7860-5116-8
ISBN-13: 978-0-7860-4746-8 (eBook)

10 9 8 7 6 5 4 3

Printed in the United States of America

# CHAPTER 1

"Danged if I don't believe we could take every one of 'em," Ralph Cox commented. "It's dang near supper time and ain't nobody come to look after those cows." They counted only twenty-two cows and one bull, a number easily handled by two drovers.

"I don't know, Ralph," Jed Tubbs replied, thinking of the extra trouble that might cause them.

They had a couple of regular buyers for their stolen beef, but these customers only wanted two cows at a time. It made it fairly easy to ride in and cut out a couple of cows, throw a lead rope on them, and ride away again. The owner of the cattle generally never knew he'd lost any cattle until sometime the next day. Even then, he couldn't know for sure they had been stolen. Unlike a cattle rancher, the small farmer was generally raising only a few cattle primarily for food and not for sale. So most of his time was spent working the farm's money crops, which in that part of Texas were cotton and corn.

"I know what you're thinkin'," Jed continued. "We could drive that whole bunch up outta that bottom. But we ain't got no place to keep 'em while we're waitin' to sell 'em. I druther we just keep pickin' off a few cows at a time."

Ralph shrugged. "I reckon you're right. You're too blamed lazy to look after those cows, anyway. We'll just let this ol' sodbuster that's workin' this farm look after 'em for us till we're ready to sell a couple more. Let's get at it. There ain't nobody comin' to see if these cows are all right." He got up from the bank of the river and climbed up into the saddle.

Jed followed suit and climbed up onto his horse. He took another look back toward the first of two farmhouses built close to the riverbank some three hundred yards away before he followed Ralph down to the cattle bunched at the water's edge. As he rode, he fashioned a noose in one end of a rope he carried on his saddle.

Their form of cattle rustling was a far cry from the stampeding of a frightened herd, driven recklessly to escape the sounds of the pistol shots scattering them across a dark prairie. In contrast, the rustling of Tubbs and Cox was a casual affair. They rode their horses among the cows and selected two prime winners, dropped a noose over each one's head, and gently led it away into the night.

"Did you make sure you got a good one?" Ralph asked. "Eli complained last time. Said one of 'em was skinny."

"Hell, they was both skinny," Jed said. "'Cause those two we sold him last time came from that family that just took up homesteadin' that old deserted farm." He pulled up then when he realized Ralph had suddenly stopped.

"I expect it woulda been a better idea if you had robbed that place again tonight, instead of comin' here."

Startled, Ralph jerked back on his reins, unable to see where the voice had come from. "Hold on, now!" he blurted. "This ain't what it looks like." He tried to back his horse up, but the cow he was leading was forced to back into Jed's horse, jamming them all up against a pine thicket. "Let's talk this over. This ain't what it looks like."

"Is that right?" the voice responded. "It looks like two cattle rustlers fixin' to lead two of my cows up the river. What does it look like to you?" The next sound they heard was the cranking of a cartridge into the chamber of a rifle. "In case you're wonderin' about that," the voice explained, "that was the sound of a Henry rifle gettin' ready to go to work."

"Now, hold on, feller!" Jed exclaimed. "You got us dead to rights, but there ain't no sense in shootin' anybody over a little misunderstandin'. Why don't you come on outta them trees, so we can talk this thing over?" Like his partner, Jed was craning his neck, frantically searching for the source of the voice.

"There ain't nothin' to talk over. Cattle rustlin' is a crime in this county."

Both outlaws jumped at the sound that came from behind them, and Ralph automatically reached for his six-gun and swung his arm around to fire into the bushes behind him. His hand was smashed by a .44 slug from the Henry rifle before he could pull the trigger.

"Don't shoot!" Jed yelled and stuck both hands in the air, looking frantically at the bank of bushes from which the shot had come. But he was surprised once again when the command came from the other side of them, as before.

"Take your left hand and pull that handgun outta your belt and drop it on the ground."

Jed did as he was told, not certain now how many were surrounding them.

"Buster, if you'll keep your rifle on the fellow I shot, I'll tie his partner up."

"What are you fixin' to do?" Jed asked.

"That's up to you," Flint Moran answered. "We're gonna shoot you down if you'd rather have it that way. But if you don't give us any trouble, we'll just take you into town and let the sheriff decide what to do with you. Either way, I want your hands behind your back. Keep your eye on his partner, Buster." After tying their reins to a tree, he quickly took the rope from around the cow's neck and used it to bind Jed's hands together behind his back.

When he had him securely tied, he said, "This one's all right, Buster, you can keep your eye on him now and I'll see if I can give this other fellow some help." He picked up his rifle and stepped over beside Ralph, who was holding his wounded hand by the wrist. "You got any rags or an extra shirt or something in your saddlebags?" Flint asked.

Ralph said he had nothing but his extra shirt.

"That'll do." Flint opened the saddlebag, found the shirt, and wrapped it around the bloody hand, then tied Ralph's wrists together behind his back. He picked up the two handguns from the ground and whistled two sharp blasts. In a few seconds, a buckskin horse came trotting up from the riverbank and Flint climbed up into the saddle.

"Lemme guess," Jed smirked, suspecting they had been tricked. "That'll be Buster, right?"

"That's right," Flint answered, as both men realized then that they had been captured by one man, moving around in the dark like a jackrabbit. "We've got a six-mile ride into town, but at least it looks like it's gonna be a nice night for a ride."

Not much was going on in the tiny town of Tinhorn, Texas, when Flint Moran led his two captive cattle rustlers down the short main street. The few shops on the street had already closed for the evening. The only activity seemed to be in the saloon where two horses were tied out front. Flint rode past the saloon to a building a little farther up the street. The sheriff's office and jail occupied the major portion of the building, with the sheriff's private quarters built on one side.

Flint pulled his prisoners up before the sheriff's office and helped them dismount. Since a light was on and the door unlocked, he marched them into the office and called out, "Sheriff Jackson."

There was no answer.

Not at all surprised, Flint sat his prisoners down on a bench against one wall and walked over to look through the cell room door. No one was in there and the room was dark. He turned back when he heard someone come in the front door of the office, and a moment later, he recognized Roy Hawkins, an old man who did odd jobs for Sheriff Buck Jackson in exchange for a place to sleep and a little money now and then.

"Flint Moran, ain't it?" Roy asked when he saw the rangy young man cradling the Henry rifle. "Whatcha got here?" He nodded toward the two men seated on the bench.

"That's right, Roy," Flint answered. "I got a couple of cattle rustlers I caught tryin' to ride off with some of my cows. I thought about shootin' 'em, which woulda been a whole lot less trouble, but I decided to turn 'em over to the sheriff and let him do whatever he does with cattle rustlers." He paused while Roy took a closer look at the two prisoners, then asked, "Where is Sheriff Jackson?" He asked the question even though he could pretty well guess where Buck Jackson was.

It was a commonly known "secret" that the town's once feared sheriff was fighting a losing battle with the bottle. It was a contest that began with the death of Buck's wife some four years ago. But it was not until the last year and a half that it became obvious that the town's law officer was no longer capable of maintaining law and order. The Tinhorn town council had met several times to discuss the termination of Buck Jackson's services, since the evidence was clearly against the chance that he would ever give up the bottle completely.

Two things kept the council from ordering Buck to turn in his badge. Number one was the fact that he was the original sheriff since the town was born. And in the early years, it was the gun and the courage of Buck Jackson that kept the lawless out of the little town. In appreciation for that, the town was reluctant to fire him. Among the most loyal to Buck Jackson was Harvey Baxter, the president of the bank. It was Buck Jackson who'd squashed an attempted robbery of the bank by the Slocum brothers on its official opening day. Buck killed one of the brothers, Zack. The other one, Jesse, was wounded and sent to the Huntsville Unit of the Texas state prisons.

The second reason the council was content to retain Buck Jackson was because of the first. Tinhorn was now a peaceful little settlement with no real criminal element. The fact that Buck was no longer patrolling the streets of the town after dark seemed of little concern to the citizens of Tinhorn. It was peaceful on the main street of town at night. There no longer seemed a need for a steely-eyed fast gun to protect the citizens.

"Where's the sheriff?" Flint repeated the question. "Is he next door in his house?"

Roy fidgeted for a few seconds before answering. "Well, yessir, he took to the bed a little while ago. His rheumatism's been actin' up a little bit, so he thought he'd best lay down for a while."

"Right," Flint responded. "There's a lotta that goin' around this time of year. I expect we'd better let him rest up. And we won't bother him with the likes of these two thieves tonight. I reckon you and I can fix these fellows up with a bunk for the night."

Roy looked surprised, as if expecting to simply let Ralph and Jed go free. "Well, I don't know about that. I ain't ever done that before. I just clean up and run errands for the sheriff. I ain't got no authority to do anything else."

"Ain't nothin' to worry about," Flint assured him. "I have the authority to make a citizen's arrest, so we'll just help the sheriff out. Why don't you start with lightin' another lamp and put it in the cell room, so we can see what we're doin'?"

"Hey," Jed Tubbs called out, "that feller's right. You ain't got no authority to arrest us. You ain't the sheriff."

"I need a doctor," Ralph piped up then. "You can't leave me to bleed to death here."

Their complaints caused Roy to hesitate.

Flint said, "Go ahead and get that other lamp, Roy. You let me worry about these two." Back to them, he said, "As the injured party in your cattle rustlin', I have the right to arrest you. I also have the right to shoot you down like the lowdown outlaws you are. So if you'd rather have it that way, you'll save me and Roy, and the sheriff a lot of trouble. As far as that hand of yours, that's the price you paid for thinkin' about shootin' me while you were in the process of stealin' my cattle. The sheriff will get the doctor to look at it tomorrow, right, Roy?"

"I reckon," Roy answered, not at all sure what the sheriff would do when he showed up in the office in the morning to find he had two prisoners in his jail. He was tempted to go next door and try to awaken Jackson, but he had seen how hard that was when the sheriff was in a drunken stupor like the one he was in tonight.

Roy lit the second lamp and took it in the cell room and set it on a table outside the cells. He looked around to see what needed to be done to get the cells ready for an occupant then went back to the office. "I need to fill the water bucket. The slop bucket ain't been used, so it's all right."

"Good," Flint replied. "Sounds like you know what to do. You probably didn't need me a-tall."

"Shoot!" Roy exclaimed and took the water bucket to the pump to fill it.

Flint sat on the corner of the desk, his rifle across his thighs, and watched his prisoners while Roy put the fresh water in one of the two cells in the cell room.

Roy picked the larger one, which had one wooden wall with a small vent window near the ceiling. "All right," he called out when he came back in the office. "You can put 'em in the cell."

"All right, gents. Your room is ready," Flint announced. "Get on your feet." He stood back to give them room, his rifle leveled at them. "Stop right there," he ordered when Ralph approached the cell door. "Roy, untie his hands."

Roy responded as quickly as he could, then stepped back when the ropes were off. Ralph entered the cell to sit down on one of the two cots and unwrapped his wounded hand.

"Okay, Roy, untie his partner's hands. Stand right where you're standin' now. That way, I've got a clear shot right between his shoulder blades, if he decides he wants to show us some tricks."

The message was not lost on Jed. He stood perfectly still until he felt the ropes fall away, then he waited until Flint told him to go into the cell.

When the prisoners were inside the cell, Roy commented, "Sheriff usually locks 'em in the cell first, then has 'em back up and stick their hands through the bars to untie 'em."

Flint smiled and said, "That woulda been a lot easier,

wouldn't it?" He asked Roy where he could find the key to the cell.

Roy pointed to a single key on a large ring, hanging on a nail just inside the cell room door. Flint took the key and locked the cell door.

"You better hope they hang us," Jed Tubbs snarled. "'Cause if they don't, your life ain't worth a nickel."

"'Preciate the warnin'," Flint said. He took the key back into the office and closed the cell room door. "I'll leave the key on the desk," he said to Roy. "I don't like the idea of it hangin' on a nail where they can see it. Gives 'em too much to think about while nobody's watchin' 'em. Now, who locks the office for the night? You don't leave it unlocked all night, do ya?"

"No," Roy answered. "I lock up most nights."

"Where do you sleep?"

"On that bench where they was settin'."

"Damn," Flint exclaimed. "That's kind of a hard bed, ain't it?"

"I usually take the mattress off one of the cots in the cells when I sleep out here on the bench. Most of the time, there ain't nobody in the cells, so I sleep in there."

"I see," Flint said. "Reckon you'd best go back in there and get you a mattress. When you come out, shut the lamp off and tell 'em good night." He waited while Roy did that, and when he came back, he asked, "You all set till mornin' now?"

"I reckon," Roy answered. "I ain't ever done it like this before. I don't know what the sheriff is gonna say when he comes in to get his coffee in the mornin'."

"Well, I suppose he'll just take over, won't he? He's sure as hell been sheriff long enough to know what to do. I mean, like fix 'em up with some breakfast, things like that."

"Oh, sure," Roy replied. "He'll take care of all that. I just don't know what he'll think when he finds out somebody has arrested some rustlers and put 'em in a cell without him even knowin' about it."

"You just tell him that I'll ride back into town tomorrow as soon as I finish my mornin' chores, and I'll explain the whole thing and give him all the details. All right?"

"I reckon," Roy replied. He walked to the door with Flint.

When Flint stepped outside, he hesitated when he saw the three horses tied at the hitching rail. "I swear I forgot about their horses. We can't leave them tied at the rail all night. You reckon Lon Blake has locked up the stable for the night?"

"I expect that he has," Roy replied.

"Well, that ain't no problem," Flint decided. "I'll just take 'em back home with me, and I'll bring 'em back tomorrow. We can put 'em in the stable then." In an effort to relieve Roy's obvious bewilderment, Flint remarked, "Tell the sheriff I won't even charge him for waterin' and feedin' the prisoners' horses." When that failed to ease some of the tenseness in Roy's face, Flint asked, "You're gonna lock up as soon as I leave, right?"

Roy nodded.

"Good, you oughta be all right then, and I'll see you tomorrow." Flint climbed aboard Buster, took the reins of the other two horses, and started for home.

# CHAPTER 2

Katie Moran went into the kitchen when she heard someone come in the back door. She had a pretty good idea who it might be. "There's a plate of supper that might still be warm in the oven, but there ain't no coffee left." With hands on hips, she stood watching her youngest son as he hurried to the stove to get the plate she saved for him.

"Thanks, Ma," Flint said. "I knew you wouldn't let me starve to death."

"Where were you," she asked, "if it ain't anywhere you're ashamed to say?" She took particular delight in teasing him because she trusted his judgment completely.

He took a big bite of a biscuit before he answered. "If I told you where I was, you might not believe me."

"Try me," his father said as he walked in from the hallway. "I saw you go into the barn leadin' two saddled horses."

Flint was surprised. It was his father's common practice to retire to the front porch to smoke his pipe after supper when the weather was mild. But he didn't sit out there this late.

"Those two horses are just here for the night," Flint explained. "I'll be takin' 'em into town in the mornin'."

"What happened to the two fannies that were settin' on those saddles?" Jim Moran asked, concerned about just where his son had been for most of the evening.

"I arrested 'em," Flint said, and went on to tell his father what had taken place on the riverbank not three hundred yards north of the house, while neither he, nor Flint's two older brothers, Nate and Joe, were even aware of it. This, in spite of the fact that a single rifle shot was heard while the family was seated at the supper table. Only one remark was made at the time when Nate's thirteen-year-old son, Jack, had speculated that they might be eating venison tomorrow night, since the shot sounded like one from a Henry rifle.

"There was one shot," Jim Moran said, remembering. "How bad?"

"Nothin' a-tall," Flint said, aware of the look of concern on his mother's face. "One of 'em took a notion to go for his gun, so I put a round in his hand. There wasn't any more trouble after that." He looked at his mother and apologized. "I'm sorry I couldn't tell you I wouldn't be here for supper."

"And tomorrow, you're gonna go into town to tell Buck Jackson about his prisoners he got while he was dead drunk." Jim said. "Why bother? Roy can tell him what happened."

"I reckon," Flint allowed, "but I've gotta return two horses. I don't want Sheriff Jackson to come after me for horse stealin'. And he can still do his job pretty well as long as it's daylight."

Jim shook his head impatiently. "Yeah, I reckon." He looked at Katie and said, "He can't help it. He's got too much of that Bradshaw blood in him from your side of the family."

"Guilty," Flint sang out, having heard the accusation

many times. "Me and Ma are the wild ones in this family. Ain't that right, Ma?"

"That's right," she responded at once, knowing that her youngest son was nothing at all like his older brothers, who seemed to have come from the womb looking for land to farm. But unlike his brothers, Flint showed no interest in finding a mother for his future children, then watching them grow up to till the soil. To complicate the future of the Moran farm, Jim's holdings amounted to little more than three hundred and fifty acres. And the family was growing rapidly. Soon it would be too little land to support the families. Flint had talked the problem over many times with Nate and Joe. They knew it would be easier on them all if Flint didn't find that special woman and bring her home. Flint appreciated the fact that his brothers hadn't come out with a suggestion that he should explore different parts of the country, but he knew it was time for him to move on.

It had become the custom for all of the family to eat breakfast together in the Big House. That was the name they called the original house Jim Moran built on the farm. When Nathaniel, whom everybody called Nate, got married, there was plenty of room for him and Margie to move in with his parents. When Joe married Peggy, however, it was obvious that there would soon be a shortage of space. Consequently, the Moran men built Joe and Peggy their own home. The big family breakfasts were continued because it served to set the work schedule for the day ahead of them. The three Moran women, Katie, Margie, and Peggy, all pitched in to prepare the big breakfast, with help from Margie's eleven-year-old, Mary, and Peggy's ten-year-old, Janie.

On this morning, there were many questions and much discussion about Uncle Flint's arrest of two cattle rustlers. Thirteen-year-old, Jack, and Joe's twelve-year-old, Jody, volunteered to do some of Flint's usual chores for him, so he could go into town early. Flint didn't comment on it, but it further emphasized the fact that they could do his chores in addition to their own with very little bother.

When breakfast was over, Flint left them to return the two horses that belonged to the outlaws.

As was usually the case, the little settlement of Tinhorn was quiet, even though it was Saturday. Flint expected there would be wagons in from the farms later to trade at Harper's Feed and Supply and maybe make a visit to Jake's Place for a drink of whiskey. He led the two horses to the jail but found the office door was locked with a padlock on the outside. He considered leaving the horses at the hitching rail but decided it best to take them to the stable and led the horses to the end of the street and Lon Blake's stable.

"Mornin', Flint," Lon greeted him when he rode up in front of the barn. "Whatcha got there?"

"Mornin'," Flint returned. "I've got a couple of horses that belong to some guests in Sheriff Jackson's jailhouse. I woulda left 'em here last night, but it was late and you were already locked up. Did the sheriff say anything to you about 'em?"

"I ain't seen Buck this mornin'," Lon answered. "But if they belong to somebody he's got in jail, he'll be by to tell me about 'em, so I'll take care of 'em for you. How'd you happen to end up with the horses, anyway?"

Flint told him about his arrest of the two cattle rustlers and expressed his desire to give his story to Jackson as soon as possible. "I just came from the jail and it was locked up. I didn't even see Roy."

Lon reacted with half a chuckle. "Did you look in the saloon?"

Flint said that he didn't, assuming it was a little early for that possibility.

"Buck most always goes there to get a little breakfast," Lon went on. "Jake's wife, Rena, will fry him up some bacon and eggs."

Flint shook his head, amazed. "Why doesn't he go to Clara's Kitchen where he could get a good breakfast at a fair price?"

"'Cause he can't get any of the hair of the dog that bit him at Clara's," Lon said. "Roy's most likely there with him. He says Buck never has more than one shot. Says he just needs it to get his brain right-side-up in the mornin'."

"You think he'd still be there?" Flint asked, thinking it was late in the morning to be eating breakfast.

"Probably so," Lon replied. "That's another reason he goes to Jake's Place. It don't matter how late it is, Rena will cook him up something. You go along, if you want to. I'll take care of the horses and work it out with Buck when I see him."

"Much obliged," Flint said and turned Buster back toward the saloon.


"Yonder he is now," Roy Hawkins said, alerting Sheriff Buck Jackson that the man he had been telling him about had just walked in the door. "He said he'd be back this mornin' and here he is."

"Flint Moran, huh?" Buck reacted. He knew of the three sons of Jim Moran, but there had never been an occasion to come into contact with any of them. He made it a point to take a good look at the young man who had paused inside the door to look for him. Since the saloon was almost empty, it didn't take but a second. Buck took note of the expression of purpose on the young man's face as he headed straight for the table. He walked with no hint of a swagger or the heavy foot of the farmer. Buck was reminded more of a mountain lion padding effortlessly.

"Sheriff Jackson," Flint nodded. "Roy," he acknowledged. "Mind if I join you?"

"Not at all," Buck replied. "We were just talkin' about you." He waited while Flint pulled a chair back and sat down, then continued. "I'm interested to hear your version of the arrest of two men who are settin' in my jail. I had to take one of 'em to see Doc Beard first thing this mornin' to get his hand fixed up. Did you bring their horses back?"

"Yep, I left 'em with Lon Blake just a few minutes ago," Flint answered. "As far as my arrest, there ain't much to tell. I caught the two of 'em stealin' two cows from a little herd I take care of. I thought it would be the right thing to arrest 'em, instead of just shootin' 'em, although shootin' 'em woulda been a lot less trouble. I figured, if you had arrested 'em, you'da probably stood 'em up in front of a judge or something. That fellow with the wounded hand, I wouldn't have shot him if he hadn't drawn his handgun."

Buck nodded his understanding. Then before commenting on the arrest, he said, "Roy and I are havin' a little bit of breakfast, you want something to eat?"

"Thanks just the same," Flint answered. "I already had a pretty big breakfast."

"Just for the record," Buck continued, "who helped you capture these two men? Was there a posse or a group of vigilantes from some of the other farms? I've had complaints from several other farms about stolen cattle just like yours, takin' two or three at a time."

"Ah, no sir," Flint answered. "There wasn't anybody there but me. And I don't know about any vigilantes, if there are any." He nodded in Roy's direction and said, "Roy was a lotta help when I took 'em into the jail."

At the lull in the conversation at that point, Flint began to feel a little uncomfortable with the slight grin that seemed to be fixed on Buck Jackson's face. He was beginning to get the impression that something amused the sheriff about the arrest.

When the talk appeared to have stalled, Flint asked, "What will you do with those two men?"

"You did the right thing, bringin' 'em in," Buck replied. "We'll keep 'em in jail till the first of the month when the circuit judge hits town. And that's day after tomorrow, so you picked a good time to make your arrest. We won't have to feed 'em that long. He'll decide what to do with 'em. I expect you'll be needed at the trial. Any problem with that?"

"No, sir," Flint answered. "I'll just come back to town day after tomorrow. What time do you want me here?"

"They'll hold court at ten o'clock in the mornin', so why don't you show up here at my office about half an hour before ten."

"I'll be there," Flint said. "Anything else you need from me today?"

"Well, yes there is one more thing," Buck said. "Won't take long. You in any hurry to get back to the farm?"

Flint said that he was in no particular hurry.

Buck told him he needed to have him sign a paper accusing the two of stealing his cows. "Somebody's got to charge them with the crime, or there ain't nothin' for the judge to try 'em for, and I might as well turn 'em loose right now."

Flint shrugged indifferently. "I reckon that makes sense," he allowed, unaware that the sheriff was making it up as they sat there.

"Good," Buck said. "I think we're through with breakfast. Come on, and we'll walk back to the office." He got to his feet and called out to Jake Rudolph over behind the bar, "Put it on my bill, Jake, and tell Rena thanks for me." He motioned for Flint to go ahead, then followed him out.

Roy picked up the two biscuits left on the plate and put them in his pocket, then followed the sheriff.

When they walked out the door, Buck commented, "I see you're wearin' a Colt Frontier Six-Shooter. Mind if I take a look at it?"

Flint turned and frowned. The sheriff seemed to have a strange way about him. "I reckon not, unless you're gettin' ready to arrest me for shootin' that fellow's hand."

Buck Jackson, bigger than most men, reacted with a belly laugh suitable for a man of his size. "No, I swear I ain't arrestin' you. I just wanted to take a look at that handgun you're wearin'.'" He drew his weapon and offered it to Flint. "Here, you can hold mine while I look at yours." He held it out until Flint took his gun, then pulled his six-shooter and handed it to the sheriff. Buck looked it over only briefly before commenting. "Four-and-three-quarter-inch barrel. Are you pretty fast with this weapon?" he asked, as they traded weapons again. The shorter barrel was a common feature on the weapons of fast-draw gunslingers.

"Not particularly," Flint replied while he dropped it back into his holster. "I like the shorter barrel because I can get it out quicker when I need to. Sometimes you don't see that rattlesnake till he's fixin' to strike. And that's a time when I don't want a seven-inch barrel slowin' me down." He took Buster's reins from the hitchin' rail and led the buckskin away from the saloon.

"Is that six-shooter the gun you shot that one feller's hand with?" Buck asked then.

"No," Flint answered. "I shot him with my rifle."

Buck stepped over next to Buster, reached up, and pulled Flint's rifle out of the saddle sling. "That's an 1864 Henry," he announced. "Looks like you keep it in good shape. You any good with this thing?"

Flint, certain that the sheriff must have had more than that one drink with his breakfast, glanced at Roy, who wore an expression of total confusion.

"If there's anything to hunt, I don't ever go hungry," Flint answered.

The sheriff nodded, apparently satisfied with that answer. "I remember when your pa bought that piece of land over by the river. I thought at the time that he had enough sons to make that land produce. You like to work the farm?"

"Nope," Flint replied without hesitation.

Buck responded with an expression of surprise. "You don't? Then how come you're still on the farm? You're the only one of the boys that ain't married yet, right? Maybe, when you find the right woman, she'll change your mind about stayin' on the farm."

"She'd have to be a mighty big woman," Flint remarked, causing another chuckle from the sheriff.

When they went inside the sheriff's office, Buck hurriedly searched through his desk drawers until he found a piece of paper. There was something written on the top portion of the paper, so he tore that off and laid the remainder on the desk. He produced a pencil then and laid it on the paper. "Can you write?" he asked.

Flint said he could.

"Good. Set down there and write down why you arrested those two in the cell. Then sign it, and that'll do for what the judge needs."

Flint sat down at the desk and wrote a very short report

on the confrontation with the two cattle thieves on the family farm, signed it, and handed it to the sheriff, who only glanced at it before putting it in a drawer.

"Is that it?" Flint asked.

"Yep, that's all I need," Buck answered. "You gonna be goin' back to your farm now?"

"I thought I would," Flint answered, still confused by the sheriff's whimsical attitude, half expecting to be stopped again when he headed for the door.

But the sheriff walked to the door and held it open for him. "I'll be talkin' to you again before long," Buck said as Flint walked past him.

"Right," Flint responded, although he was thinking, *I should have just shot those two.*

The sheriff stood in the doorway of his office and watched Flint climb aboard the buckskin. When Flint loped off toward the end of the street, Buck looked back at Roy and said, "Keep your eye on the office. I'll be back in a few minutes." He walked out the door and headed toward the bank.

"Howdy, Sheriff Jackson," Robert Page, one of the bank's two tellers greeted him.

"Howdy, Robert," Buck returned. "I'd like to talk to Mr. Baxter if he ain't too busy. Is he in?" He looked across the lobby and noticed Baxter's office door was closed. "If he's talkin' business with somebody, I can wait till later."

"He's in," Page said, "and there ain't nobody in there with him. He's just got his door closed while he has his coffee. I'll tell him you wanna see him."

Buck stood there and watched Page walk across the lobby to tap lightly on the president's door. Then he stuck his head in to deliver his message, and in a few seconds, the door opened wide and Harvey Baxter signaled Buck to come on over.

Page asked if he would like a cup of coffee when they passed each other, but Buck said no.

He refused another offer of coffee from Baxter when he walked into his office. "I just drank about a gallon of it before I came up here. I'll just take a minute of your time, Mr. Mayor." He paused a moment to let Baxter know this was official town business, then he made his announcement. "I've found him, Harvey. I've found the very man we've been lookin' for."

Baxter's eyebrows raised and his face lit up in anticipation.

"He just dropped in on me this mornin'. Flint Moran."

"Moran," Baxter echoed. "Flint. That would be the youngest of the three brothers, right?"

"Right." Buck went on to tell the mayor all about the incident with the two stolen cows that played out during the night. The would-be rustlers were sitting in his jail as they talked. "Young man's a crack shot with a rifle, but instead of just shootin' those two birds when he caught 'em with his cattle, he arrested them and brought 'em to the jail last night."

"How do you know he's a crack shot?" Baxter asked.

"He was out there on that dark riverbank and one of the rustlers drew his handgun. Moran shot the gun outta the rustler's hand with a Henry rifle. I had to take the man to see Doc Beard this mornin'. Hell, even after the man drew on him, Moran still brought both of 'em to jail, instead of pumpin' a .44 slug in each one of 'em. I'd say that shows some determination, and it also tells me he ain't tryin' to make a name for himself with the Colt six-shooter he wears. Four-and-three-quarter-inch barrel tells me he's most likely pretty quick with it, if he needs to be."

"And you're sure you want to offer him the job as your deputy?" Baxter asked. He and the sheriff had already had several discussions about Jackson's problem, which was bound to become the town's problem in the event a criminal element might decide Tinhorn was prime for the taking. Since there were no candidates for the sheriff's job, the council, with the mayor's direction, had decided the answer, at least temporarily, might be to hire a deputy. Their thinking was that the town might not attract the outlaw trouble some other towns were subject to, simply because of Sheriff Buck Jackson's reputation. If the deputy was good enough to watch the town at night and jail any troublemakers, the message should go out to all drifters and hell-raisers that they wouldn't be tolerated in Tinhorn. For Buck Jackson would be very much on the scene every day until after suppertime when his demons visited him. An added plus would be the potential for Buck to train the deputy to eventually take his place.

"Are you sure?" Baxter repeated his question, knowing how important it was, not only to Buck, but to the entire town.

"Yeah, Harvey, I'm sure," Buck answered. "I don't think we will ever find anybody as qualified for the job as Flint Moran. I just know what he's got inside him that makes him a fighter, but he's got a calmness about him that makes you think he ain't gonna go off half-cocked."

"He's a farmer, Buck," Baxter reminded him. "He's a member of a farm family. A lawman might be the last thing he'd consider. And what about his wife? What will the little woman think about him leaving the farm?"

"Take my word for it," Buck insisted. "He ain't a farmer, and he ain't got a wife. He'll be leavin' that farm pretty damn soon now, I guarantee you, and I'd just like to catch him before he heads out of this part of Texas."

"Well, I believe you're sold on this young man, so I'll give you my backing when I talk to the council members tonight. And I'll let you know in the morning what the decision is. All right?"

"All right," Buck replied. "I appreciate it, Harvey." He turned and left the office, nodding to Robert Page on his way out.

The sheriff knew Harvey Baxter would push for his decision. He also knew that in an earlier day, before his wife, Beca, was taken home to the angels, Baxter would have requested his presence at the meeting, so he could answer the members' questions. It sickened him to know he could not function after dark without his whiskey to drive away the demons until he finally slumped into a comalike sleep. On some nights, he was lucky not to have the recurring dream of his wife being crushed beneath the team of runaway horses pulling a freight wagon loaded with barbed wire.

# CHAPTER 3

Two days later, Flint pulled Buster up at the sheriff's office and dismounted at exactly nine-thirty, having judged his estimated time to ride the six miles right on the nose. He had suffered a fair amount of good-natured ribbing from his brothers about his need to be in court this morning.

"We might have to cut his food rations, if he ain't gonna give us a full day's work," his elder brother, Nate, had japed.

"Maybe so," Joe had responded. "'Course, I reckon we oughta cut him a little slack for that deer he killed this mornin' while the rest of us was still in the bed."

Flint couldn't help smiling when he thought about the fat doe and he knew how the family enjoyed some fresh venison. With both Jack and Jody standing by to watch and learn, Flint had gutted and skinned the deer before he turned it over to Joe, who was happy to take over the butchering job when Flint had to leave.

As he rode into town, Flint couldn't help smiling when he remembered the faces of the two young boys. Like himself at that age, they were a lot more interested in hunting than planting corn.

His thoughts darted quickly back to the present when

Buck Jackson opened the door and offered a cordial howdy.

"Howdy," Flint returned. "Am I on time?" He knew that he was.

"Sure are," Buck answered. "You can leave your horse here, if you want to, and I'll walk over to the saloon with you and meet the judge. We've got a few minutes before I have to take Mr. Cox and Mr. Tubbs over there for their trial, and I wanna make sure His Honor's courtroom is set up to suit him."

By Buck's voice inflection when he referred to *His Honor*, Flint got the impression that something was wrong. "Didn't he know you'd be usin' the saloon for a courtroom?"

"Oh, sure, he knew," Buck answered. "This ain't his first time tryin' a case in Tinhorn. He's a little put out because he had to ride all the way down here from Tyler to try two small-time cattle thieves. See, he druther have a full day of cases to try when he comes down here, since he's paid by the case. He gets his room paid for in the hotel, and it's up to him how long he stays in town to get the job done. 'Course he gets his meals free at Clara's Kitchen, and he don't pay for any whiskey he drinks, courtesy of Jake Rudolph. So he's grumblin' a little about ridin' down here for one case. He would have druther had me wire him that we only had one case, and we'd just hold those two rustlers in our jail till next month, when we might have more to try."

"But that ain't but a twenty-six-mile ride," Flint remarked. "He could try 'em and ride back to Tyler this afternoon, if he wanted to."

"You know that, and I know that," Buck said with a chuckle, "but I don't think he wants his boss to know that, whoever his boss is."

"Oh, right," Flint said. "I wasn't thinkin' about that."

They had reached the saloon, so Flint followed Buck

inside, passing a sign propped up on a chair on the porch that said, Court Today. In the saloon, several tables were set up end to end to form the bench where the judge would sit. A couple of tables and chairs were pushed together on one side of the bench where the sheriff would sit with his prisoners. More chairs were arranged in a couple of rows for spectators. At the end of the bar, talking to Jake Rudolph, stood a tall, thin man with white hair and beard. He wore a black robe, and he was holding an empty shot glass.

"Just thought I'd check with you to see if you're ready to get started, Judge," Buck said when he and Flint walked over to the bar.

"Who's this with you?" The judge asked at once. "And why is he armed? I don't want but one armed man in my courtroom, and that'll be you. You understand?"

"I understand, Judge," Buck hurried to respond. "This is Flint Moran. He's the feller who caught the prisoners stealin' his cattle. He won't be wearin' that gun when we come back for the trial." He turned to Flint. "Flint, this is Judge Graham Dodge. He comes down to handle our legal business once a month, if we've got anything."

"Pleasure to meet you, Judge Dodge," Flint said.

"You're the one who brought them to the jail, right?" Dodge asked. "Citizen's arrest, I think you called it." He took another long moment while he studied the young man standing before him, then he suddenly looked at Buck. "All right, Sheriff, go get your prisoners and let's get this thing started."

Hearing the judge's order to Buck, Jake walked back to the middle of the bar and announced to a few early spectators standing near the door, "Bar's closed, gentlemen, till after the trial. If you hurry, you have time for one more drink before we get started." He then poured three shots of whiskey for the three customers who ordered one, plus one more for the judge.

Outside, walking back to the jail, Flint remarked, "It sounds to me like he means business. He's got plenty of time to ride on back to Tyler before supper."

"He might make short work of the trial," Buck said. "What is there to argue, even if they had a lawyer? They were stealin' your cows and you caught 'em. But ol' Dodge ain't in any hurry to get back to Tyler tonight. He'll be stayin' in his hotel room, with a bottle courtesy of Jake, and maybe a lady to keep him company." Buck chuckled when a thought struck his mind. "If Jacob Trehorn had been right ten years ago, Judge Dodge mighta been livin' here, instead of Tyler."

"Why do you say that?" Flint asked.

"Jacob Trehorn was a gambler, and not a very good one, so they say. Said he was a genuine Tinhorn Gambler. But he was lucky enough to win a piece of property on the Neches River, south of Tyler. Right where we're walkin' now. There was talk about the railroad buildin' a line through the county and everybody figured that meant Tyler. Everybody but Trehorn, that is. He figured he could make the railroad a deal that would cost them next to nothin', and he would make his money as the town grew. He was gonna call it Trehorn and he got it registered with the county under that name. Then he built the first buildin' in Trehorn."

When Flint appeared to be interested, Buck continued. "Jake's Place, the saloon. That was the business Trehorn was gonna run." Since they had arrived at the jail, Buck said, "To make a long story short, the railroad didn't build the spur line, and Jacob Trehorn came in second in a gunfight over a card game. The railroad did run the telegraph into Tinhorn before they decided not to run the spur line here and that's still here. The town didn't have but two buildings for about two years—a telegraph office and the saloon with nobody in it, till Jake Rudolph took it over. The town started attracting more businesses as more and more folks discovered this part of the county."

Flint paused while holding the door to the office open. "When did they change the name to Tinhorn?"

"I reckon Trehorn didn't sound right to most of the first folks that came here. And since *Trehorn* don't sound a whole lot different from *Tinhorn*, I guess it was the natural name to call it. And ol' Jacob Trehorn was pretty much a tinhorn gambler," Buck said, "so it just seems to fit.

"I know for the first couple of years it wasn't much of a town. A group of citizens eventually petitioned the governor to change the name to Tinhorn, so he did, and the post office made it the official designation for the town."

"I never heard that story before." Flint wondered if his father knew the origin of the town's name. It seemed he would have mentioned it, had he known. Flint looked forward to enlightening him as well as his brothers when he got back to the farm.

Roy stood in the cell room doorway and watched Buck rouse the two prisoners out of their cell. The sheriff tossed a set of cuffs to Flint and said, "Cuff his hands behind his back," referring to Jed Tubbs. "I'll cuff this one with the wounded hand." Then, making an effort not to be conspicuous about it, he watched Flint to see his reactions.

Flint caught the cuffs and gave them a quick look to see how they worked, then he slapped one cuff on Jed's wrist and captured the other behind Jed's back.

Buck smiled, satisfied. Harvey Baxter had told him of the results of his proposal to offer the job of deputy sheriff to Flint. He didn't give him an outright okay on the hiring, but he said the idea of hiring a deputy was met with favorable reactions from most of the council. There was some hesitation on the part of a few of the merchants due only to the fact that they didn't know much about Flint Moran. Buck was counting on Harvey Baxter's help to get Flint's hiring accomplished.

"Come on, boys," Buck ordered. "Let's go to the saloon." He led his prisoners outside. "Flint, you gotta get rid of that gun."

Flint removed his gun belt, rolled it up, and stuck it in his saddlebag.

"Keep an eye on his horse, Roy," Buck said, and Roy nodded.

Along with Buck, Flint marched the two defendants across the street to the saloon.

The trial of two unknown outlaws was not of sufficient interest to most of the citizens of Tinhorn to produce more than a dozen spectators. All were men, as was the case in most trials of this nature, with the exception of one woman. A stranger to the town folk of Tinhorn, Ada Tubbs, a tall, plain-looking woman, dressed in a faded gingham dress and carrying a heavy shawl, walked into the saloon. After a quick look at the way the court was set up, she seated herself at the end of the front row of chairs, close to the table where the defendants sat.

Jake Rudolph was tempted to ask her if she had wandered in by mistake, for she just sat there, looking straight ahead, her expressionless face a journal of hard times. He was not quick enough, however.

Judge Graham Dodge came in from the back room at that moment, carrying a black valise and a coffee cup.

"Everybody stand up," Buck ordered, acting as bailiff.

Those who were already seated did as he instructed, with the exception of the one woman.

The judge sat down and so did everyone else, except

those watching from the bar. He placed his cup of spiked coffee on the table, then opened the valise and took out his gavel, a Bible, and a notebook. "This court is now in session," he announced. Looking at the defendants, he said, "Jed Tubbs and Ralph Cox, you are charged with attempted robbery of two cows from"—he paused to look at his notebook—"the James Moran farm. How do you plead?"

"Not guilty, Your Honor," Ralph Cox responded. "It was all a big misunderstandin'."

"Is that a fact?" Dodge replied. "Well, maybe we'd best hear what the witness has to say about that." He looked at Buck. "If you think you can hit the defendants with your pistol at that distance, you can take the handcuffs off 'em." He waited while Buck did so, then said, "Call your witness to the stand, Sheriff."

Buck motioned to Flint to sit down in the witness box.

When Flint sat down, the judge slid the Bible over to that end of the table. "Place your left hand on that Bible and raise your right one. When Flint did so, Dodge asked, "You swear the testimony you are about to give is the truth and nothing but the truth?"

"Yes, sir," Flint answered. He went on to tell of the circumstances in which he came upon the two defendants as they were in the midst of leading two of his cattle away from his herd. As Buck had commented to Flint earlier, it was plain rustling and they were caught red-handed.

When Flint had finished, Judge Dodge looked at the defendants and asked, "You still gonna try to tell me you're not guilty?"

"That's right, Your Honor," Jed answered him. "We didn't know we was stealin' nobody's cows. Like Ralph said, it was all a big misunderstandin'."

"What did you think you were stealing?" Judge Dodge

shook his head impatiently. "A big misunderstanding, huh? Please enlighten me."

Jed hesitated, obviously unsure what the judge meant.

Dodge said, "Tell me what the misunderstanding was."

"Oh, right," Jed replied. "Well, me and Ralph bought two cows from a feller here in town last week, and he said we would have to go get 'em." He turned to look at his partner. "Ain't that right, Ralph?"

Ralph nodded vigorously while Jed continued. "Well, sir, that feller told us where they was and gave us directions to the place they was grazin'. We followed them directions and they took us right to that little farm on the river where we was attacked. The feller that sold 'em to us said to pick out any two we wanted. We was takin' our time pickin' the two we wanted when that feller, there"—he pointed at Flint—"shot Ralph. He'd been hidin' in the bushes, waitin' for us."

Judge Dodge didn't say anything for a few moments, but his facial expression conveyed a message of total disbelief. "The man who sold you the cows, is he here in the courtroom this morning?"

"I don't see him, Your Honor," Jed replied.

"What was his name?"

"I don't recollect him tellin' us his name," Jed answered, then looked at Ralph. "Do you remember him tellin' us his name?"

Ralph shook his head.

The judge shook his head in time with Ralph, then continued to stare at Jed for a long moment. "You could probably describe the man, whether he was short or tall, old or young, what kind of clothes he wore, whiskers or mustache, couldn't you?"

"Oh, yes, sir," Jed responded at once. "I can do that, right down to the boots he wore."

"Good," Dodge said. "We can take you in the back room and let you describe the man. Then we'll take Mr. Cox into the back room and let him describe the man. And I expect we'll get two descriptions that are just alike, right?"

Jed didn't respond right away while he tried to decide what to say.

After a handful of moments with no reply, Dodge said, "I didn't think so. I've got to compliment you for your creative imagination, though. I think I'm ready to make a ruling now." He referred to his notebook briefly before writing his sentence, then nodded a signal to the sheriff.

Buck instructed both defendants to stand up to receive the verdict.

"Jed Tubbs and Ralph Cox," the judge pronounced, "this court finds you both guilty of attempted cattle rustling and sentences you to two years confinement at Huntsville Unit, Texas State Prison. You will remain in the custody of the sheriff of Tinhorn until transportation is provided."

"What does that mean?" Jed demanded.

"It means you'll be held in the Tinhorn jail until a jail wagon comes to transport you to Huntsville," the judge replied. He banged his gavel on the table and declared, "This court is adjourned."

"I'll be damned," Jed protested and stepped from behind the defendant's table, causing the plain expressionless woman to get to her feet.

She pulled a .44 revolver from the shawl she had folded in her lap and tossed it toward her husband.

Jed, however, was knocked backward by Flint's shoulder as he dived in front of him to intercept the tossed revolver. Landing on the floor with the natural grace of a mountain lion, Flint did one somersault before ending up on his feet to stand holding the revolver on Ada Tubbs, in case she had another one in the shawl. He was not concerned with Jed or Ralph, since he could see that Buck already had his pistol covering them.

"Ma'am, do you have any more guns hid on you?" Flint asked.

She didn't reply but shook her head slowly.

"All right, then, why don't you just sit yourself back down until the sheriff's ready to talk to you?"

She nodded obediently and sat down again, the weary expression she wore during the entire trial never changing. He shifted his focus back to the two prisoners to cover them while Buck handcuffed them.

"Thank you, Flint," Buck said. "Now, if I can ask one more favor, could you escort the lady over to my office? And after we make Jed and Ralph comfortable again, I'll have a little talk with her to decide what I'm gonna do with her."

Before he started the prisoners toward the door, he was stopped by Judge Dodge. "You might want me to stay over another day for another trial," he said, nodding toward Ada Tubbs.

"Maybe so," Buck replied, knowing Dodge was looking for an excuse to extend his stay in Tinhorn. "I'm gonna get the whole story on this woman, and I'll let you know before supper tonight." He walked Jed and Ralph out of the saloon.

Behind him, Flint watched the woman's reaction when seeing the two men marched off in handcuffs. As with everything else that had happened in the courtroom, the expression never changed. He told her he was ready for her now, and she got to her feet obediently and walked with him to the door.

He walked at a casual pace across the street to accommodate her stride, and when they walked into the sheriff's office, Buck already had the prisoners back in their cell. While he waited for the sheriff to come back to the office,

Flint pulled the one side chair back away from the desk and asked her to sit down.

When Buck returned, he asked her, "Which one are you married to?"

"Jed Tubbs," she answered.

"What's your name?" Buck asked, his tone patient and not at all abusive.

"Ada Tubbs," she answered.

"How'd you know Jed was in jail?"

"A friend of Jed's told me," she replied, "and said they was gonna try him this mornin'."

"Didn't you know what kinda risk you were takin' when you brought a gun into a trial?"

"I don't know," she answered. "Jed told me to bring him a gun, if he ever got arrested and held for trial. So, I reckon I didn't have no choice. Are you gonna put me in jail, too?" She sounded almost hopeful when she asked.

Flint imagined she was thinking of three meals a day and a bed to sleep in, if she went to jail.

"No, I ain't gonna put you in jail," Buck told her. "In the first place, I ain't got room to keep men and women in jail at the same time. And I don't think you're gonna cause any more trouble, if I just let you go." He felt pretty sure that what she attempted to do was out of fear of her husband. "Have you got a place to go?"

"I reckon I'll go back to my daddy's house," she said. "That's where I was while Jed was gone."

"Where is that?" Buck asked and was told it was halfway between Tinhorn and Tyler. "How'd you get here this mornin'?"

She told him she drove a mule and wagon.

"All right," he decided. "I'm gonna let you go if you'll promise to get on your wagon and head back to your daddy's right away."

"Thank you, sir. I promise."

"I'll give you a little time to visit your husband before you go. That is, if you want to," Buck said.

"Yes, sir," she replied at once. "I'd like to talk to him. I ain't seen him in a while."

He took her to the cell room door and told her to go on in and talk to Jed.

Back in the office, he sat down at his desk and looked at Flint, who was leaning against the wall. "You have to feel sorry for a poor woman like that, who just got herself hooked up with a no-account man like Jed Tubbs." He changed his expression to a grin when he was reminded of something else. "That was some trick you pulled back there when she tossed that gun to her husband. You looked like you was waitin' for her to throw it. How'd you know she was gonna do that?"

"Well, I didn't know for sure what she was gonna try, but I just thought it was kinda funny for her to be carryin' a heavy shawl rolled up like that in weather this warm. It struck me that it might be a good idea to keep a close eye on her." Flint shrugged indifferently. "I just had a good perch to jump from. If you'da been standin' where I was you'da probably had the same idea."

"Like hell, I would," Buck snorted. "If I'd dived across there to catch that gun, I'd probably still be layin' on the floor in the saloon. I wouldn't have even tried it if I was your age again." They both chuckled over the thought of it, then Buck said, "You were a lotta help today and I'd like to buy your dinner at Clara's Kitchen. Whaddaya say?"

"That's mighty sportin' of you," Flint replied, "but it weren't no trouble. I expect I'd best get on back to the farm before my pa and my brothers throw my mattress out of the back room."

"Shoot," Buck said, "it ain't that much longer till Clara

will be open for dinner. By the time you got back home, it might be too late for dinner there. Besides, your folks don't know how long a trial is gonna last."

"I expect you're right about that. I reckon it'd be in my best interest to accept your generous offer, and I'll thank you kindly. While I'm thinkin' about it, I better go see if my six-gun is still in my saddlebag. And I'd better give Buster a little attention since he's been standin' at that hitchin' rail all this time."

Outside, he strapped on his Colt Frontier Six-Shooter then stroked Buster's neck and face for a few minutes before deciding the buckskin needed some water. Stepping back up on the porch, he stuck his head in the door, and told Buck, "My horse needs some water, so I'm gonna take him to the trough."

"Take him down to Lon Blake's," Buck replied. "Turn him in the corral with the other horses. Tell Lon I said I'd take care of it."

"Oh, there ain't no need for you to go to all that trouble. I can get my horse a drink at the pump."

"It ain't no trouble," Buck insisted. "I'll meet you at Clara's in about half an hour, all right?"

"All right." Flint japed, "You're the sheriff. I'll see you at Clara's."

Ada came from the cell room and headed straight for the front door.

He waited and held it open for her. "You need any help with your mule and wagon?" he asked politely. "Where is it?" He looked up and down the street but saw no mule or wagon.

"No thank you," she answered him. "I left it behind the hotel by that little creek."

"I'm goin' to the stable. I'll walk with you, if you don't mind."

"I 'spose you can walk where you want to," she said. "Ain't for me to say whether you can or can't walk up the street."

He was taken aback a little by her attitude. He had halfway expected her to be grateful to the sheriff and the town for pressing no charges against her. "Sounds to me like you'd prefer to walk alone. I'll let you go on ahead." He stopped and she kept on walking toward the hotel without even a glance back at him. *Strange woman*, he thought. *There ain't no telling what she's liable to do.* He turned around, since the stable was at the south end of the street.

Sheriff Jackson came out of his office and fixed the padlock on the door. When he turned around to leave, he was surprised to find Jim Rakestraw and John Harper waiting for him. He had seen both of them at the trial. "What's goin' on?" Looking at Jim, he said, "I was just on my way to your wife's place."

"Hire that young man before he ends up in Tyler or someplace else," Harper blurted.

"We need a man who can handle himself like that," Rakestraw declared. "We're on our way to the bank right now to tell Harvey Baxter the council votes to hire Flint Moran."

The sheriff couldn't help chuckling. These were two of the council members at the meeting who were not sure Flint was a wise choice for deputy.

After they saw his reactions when Ada Tubbs tried to toss her husband a gun, they were convinced the sheriff knew what he was talking about.

# CHAPTER 4

It was a rare occasion when Flint ate a meal at Clara's Kitchen, which served as the dining room for the hotel. Dinner today would be the first time in at least six months. He was always well satisfied with the food Clara and her cook, Margaret, prepared. And it was cheerfully served by either Bonnie or Mindy.

After leaving his horse with Lon Blake, Flint walked in the outside entrance to find Buck Jackson already there. Walking back to join him, he was intercepted by Mindy Moore.

"Whoa, Moran." She recognized him as one of the Moran brothers but couldn't remember which one. "Leave your weapon on the table, please."

"I'm sorry. I forgot." Flint immediately stepped back and deposited his Colt on the table by the door. That had always seemed a senseless practice to him, for it offered weapons right by the door for anyone entering the dining room with evil purpose. And it left anyone in the dining room unable to defend themselves against such an attack, unless the sheriff happened to be there, as was the case on that morning.

"I'll forgive you just this one time," Mindy joked. "Sheriff Jackson said it was all right to let you in. He's waiting for you. Are you gonna have coffee with your dinner?"

"I hope so," Flint answered.

She gave him a little chuckle, turned about, and went to fetch his coffee.

He walked on back to join Buck. "Hope I didn't keep you waitin'." He sat down.

"Nope," Buck replied. "I just sat down about two minutes ago. We've got one more that's gonna join us, and I see him comin' now."

Flint looked back over his shoulder, surprised to see Harvey Baxter, the president of the bank, striding toward them.

"Mr. Baxter," Buck greeted him. "Glad you could join us."

"Buck," Baxter returned his greeting, then smiled at Flint. "Mr. Moran."

"Mr. Baxter," Flint returned. Harvey Baxter was the last person he could have imagined having dinner with. *Wait till I tell Nate and Joe*, he thought, holding back a smile.

Mindy brought three plates of food and three cups of coffee and placed a separate plate of biscuits on the table.

Baxter waited only a couple of minutes more before revealing that his presence at the table was in his capacity as mayor. "Flint, I won't beat around the bush on this. I wanted to meet with you and the sheriff to make you an offer."

That captured Flint's attention at once, and he glanced from the banker's serious face to the sheriff's grinning one.

"The town of Tinhorn has arrived at a point where we need a deputy sheriff. You are Sheriff Jackson's personal pick as the man best suited to fill that position."

Flint was stunned by the mayor's offer to the extent that

he stopped momentarily with his mouth wide open and a fork loaded with meatloaf stalled halfway to it.

Baxter continued. "Working under Sheriff Jackson, you'd have full authority to make arrests and protect the people of Tinhorn."

Finding his voice at last, Flint replied. "I don't know what to say, Mr. Baxter. I don't know the first thing about being a lawman."

Buck interrupted then, laughing. "You knew all about makin' that citizen's arrest on those two rustlers sitting in the jail right now."

"That was just the first thing I could think of," Flint said.

"You don't need to worry about that part of it." Baxter went on. "Sheriff Jackson will show you the ropes. You'll be paid a salary of twenty dollars a week, but that's not all you'll get. You'll get a small room, rent-free at Hannah Green's boarding house, and Jim and Clara Rakestraw have agreed to make you a special rate to eat here. There are other things, too, like an allowance for ammunition for your weapons and no charge to stable your horse." He paused to gauge Flint's reaction to the offer, concluding Flint was so surprised by the unexpected proposal that he was trying to decide what he thought about it. "Maybe you need to think it over before making a final decision."

"Just from the little bit I've learned about you in the last couple of days, I don't think it takes you long to make a decision," Buck remarked. "Why don't you go on home and think it over. If you show up for work tomorrow mornin', we'll get started with your trainin'. If you don't show up, we'll know what your answer is. All right?"

"All right," Flint answered. Then he laughed and said, "It ain't every day you get a chance to have a job where folks shoot at you. My brothers would tell you that's what I'm probably best qualified for."

"Good," Baxter said. "I know you'll make the right decision. Now, let's eat this meatloaf before it cools off."

The food was good, but it was difficult for Flint to give it his full attention. He had been stunned by the mayor's offer, having never in his life ever given any thought toward the possibility of becoming a lawman. He took another look at Buck Jackson, who was concentrating on the plate of food before him. The expression on his face seemed to convey the notion that he was confident Flint would accept the offer.

Buck had to be in his forties, but he showed no signs of aging. Bigger than the average man, he conveyed the image of strength. Like most of the people in Tinhorn, however, Flint was aware of the one chink in Buck's armor, his losing battle with rye whiskey. Realistically, Flint told himself that he would be expected to deal with any trouble that occurred after supper. He would have to decide if he wanted that responsibility.

The conversation shifted back to the trial by the time Mindy was filling their cups for the final time.

"How about that woman, Ada Tubbs?" Baxter asked. "She took a helluva chance, smuggling that gun into the courtroom. Are you gonna hold her for trial?"

"No," Buck answered. "She's gone. I sent her home. I figured she's caught enough hell from her husband to make up for any punishment we would give her. Besides, it'd be more trouble to hold her than it's worth." He was thinking about the only place they had to hold a woman prisoner apart from the men. Little more than a windowless box, it was actually an empty storeroom at the rear of Harper's Feed and Supply. Forced to use it only a couple of times, it was the only way a woman could have any privacy.

With dinner finished, the three men walked out of the dining room. Baxter paused long enough to light a cigar before telling Flint he hoped he would decide to accept the town's offer. Then he split off to head back to the bank.

Buck walked with Flint as far as the stable, then left him with a cheerful, "I'll see you in the mornin'," and strode on back to the jail.

It was really only then that Flint realized the full significance of the decision he was determined to make on the six-mile ride back to the farm. He wanted his final decision made before he got back home. He had no desire to include the entire family in the discussion.

Flint's decision did not come as a surprise to Jim Moran. He knew it was only a matter of time before his youngest son told them he was leaving the farm. Jim was not sure that taking the deputy job was a wise move for Flint, but at least he was not riding off to Indian Territory and beyond, looking for his future. Tinhorn was just six miles away, so he didn't have far to come home if things didn't work out as he expected. Jim also knew that a large influence on Flint's decision was the fact that the farm wasn't big enough to support another family. He respected Flint's decision and forbade the rest of the family to try to talk him out of it.

The next morning, Flint was up early as usual, but instead of going hunting, he saddled Buster and packed up his belongings. It didn't take a great deal of time, since he was not one to accumulate things that didn't have a practical purpose. Ready, he attended his last big breakfast, which resembled a farewell service for only a short time before the natural tendency of his brothers to taunt each other playfully took over.

"Are you supposed to take a bottle of rye to bed with you after supper every night?" Joe japed.

"No," Flint replied. "It don't have to be rye. Buck said I could drink corn if I wanted to."

"You know," Nate cracked when the laughter dried up, "they might be thinkin' about retiring ol' Buck Jackson, and they hired you to be deputy for Sheriff Roy Hawkins. He's already got enough experience to know how to do the job." That crack generated a general round of good-natured cackles.

Enough so, that Katie Moran decided the boys were being too insulting to her youngest. "You oughta be ashamed of yourselves for talkin' about Sheriff Jackson like that and be proud that he sees the good in your brother."

"Don't let 'em bother you, Ma," Flint told her. "You know, they ain't got a lot to work with up there between their ears." He got up from the table. "I expect I'd best get goin'. I don't wanna be late for work on my first day on the job." He went to the end of the table to give his mother a hug. "Don't be too hard on my brothers, or I'll come back and arrest you."

She squeezed his hand real tightly and said, "You be careful, you hear?"

He nodded in response.

The men and the boys got up from the table and followed him outside where Buster was waiting.

Serious now, his brother, Nate, said, "If things don't look like they're gonna suit you, you come on back home, all right?"

Flint nodded. "I will."

"Damn it, Flint, you be careful," Joe insisted.

"You can count on it," Flint said as he climbed up into the saddle. "I'll be seein' you from time to time when you come to town." He wheeled the buckskin and left the yard at a trot.

"I hope to hell he ain't takin' that job just because we're gettin' a little crowded here," Nate said.

Even as he said it, his daughter Mary was hurriedly moving her things into Flint's room before Jack tried to claim it.

"Mornin'," Flint said as he walked into the sheriff's office.

Startled until he saw who it was, Roy said, "Sheriff Jackson ain't come in yet, but he oughta be here pretty quick when he smells this coffee workin'." He looked at the big pot sitting on the little stove, then asked, "Did he know you was gonna be comin' by here this mornin'? He told me to make a full pot this mornin'."

Flint snorted half a chuckle. "I reckon he knew." He decided he'd wait and let Buck tell Roy that he had a deputy now. "Have you got any extra cups?"

Roy didn't answer right away while he waited for his brain to catch up. When he did answer, it was with a tone of confusion. "We didn't have no extra cups till last night after supper. When I took the prisoners' dishes back, Buck took one of 'em off the tray. He said we needed an extra cup here." He went to a shelf on the wall near the stove and got the extra cup. "Here you go. I washed it with Buck's and my cups."

"Much obliged, Roy," Flint said, amused by Buck's complete confidence that he would take the job.

The sheriff walked in the door at that moment. "I swear I could smell that coffee boilin' all the way over in my bed," Buck announced. "Good mornin', Flint. I see you got all your belongin's on your horse out front. We'll go take your stuff to Hannah's place after we have a little coffee." He looked over at Roy then, who was lost in a fog of confusion. "Did you tell Roy about your new job?"

"No," Flint replied. "We hadn't got around to that yet."

Buck got to it right away. "Well, Roy, Flint here has accepted the town council's offer to take the job as my deputy. He'll be on the job here every day from now on."

Roy blinked his eyes rapidly, looking as forlorn as a lost puppy, while Buck waited for a verbal response. Finally, Roy asked, "You won't be needin' me no more?"

"What?" Buck reacted. "Won't be needin' you no more? Flint's job ain't got nothin' to do with your job. You're still gonna be doin' what you've always done. Flint's just gonna help me maintain peace and quiet in Tinhorn. Right, Flint?"

"That's a fact," Flint answered.

There was an immediate show of relief in Roy's face, but then another thought struck him. "You gonna sleep in the office?"

"Nope," Flint replied. "I'll be stayin' in the roomin' house. Ain't nothin' changed for you except you'll have to get used to havin' me around."

Roy grinned. "Ain't no problem with that." He grabbed a dishtowel to wrap around the handle, took the coffeepot off the stove, and filled the three cups with coffee. All was right in his world once more.

Buck sat down at his desk and started rummaging through the drawers. "I know I've got an extra badge in this desk somewhere," he insisted when he gave up on one side of the desk and started searching the other. After no luck there, he was ready to admit it was gone, but decided to look in the one middle drawer where he kept his pens, pencils, reading glasses, and things he used every day. "Well, I'll be. That's where I saw it."

"Good thing you found it," Flint japed, 'cause I wasn't gonna take the job, if I didn't get a badge to wear."

"Well, you're officially hired now," Buck said and tossed the badge to him. "There ain't much to show you here, since you've already seen the cell room. It's about time for Roy to go up to Clara's to get our prisoners' breakfast. I always wait till he gets back with that to make sure there ain't no trouble passin' the food into the cell. Then I usually go across to the saloon to get my breakfast from Rena. After that, we'll go take your belongin's to Hannah's house and get you fixed up with your room."

"I've already had breakfast," Flint said. "Why don't I take my things to the roomin' house while you're eatin'? Hannah knows about the room, doesn't she?"

"Oh, yeah, Hannah knows you'll be checkin' in," Buck replied. "That'll work out. You just go get that set up with her and come on back when you're done. I'll be back here or at the saloon." He appreciated Flint's suggestion. He would be more comfortable taking his morning shot of rye whiskey with no one but Roy to witness it. He knew he was going to have to be honest about it with Flint. Just didn't want to do it on Flint's first day on the job.

They finished off another cup of coffee while Roy went up to Clara's Kitchen to fetch Jed Tubbs and Ralph Cox's breakfasts. When he returned, Flint went into the cell room with Buck to put the tray inside the cell.

"Well, lookee here," Jed smirked when he saw Flint. "Look who's back, Ralph. It's the feller that busted up your hand for ya." He pointed his finger at Flint and said, "You might think this business between us is over, but it ain't, not by a long shot."

"I didn't know we had any business between us," Flint replied. "I don't do business with common cow thieves."

"Look there, Jed," Ralph exclaimed. "He's wearin' a badge now."

"That don't make no difference." Jed sneered. "He's a

walkin' dead man. The badge is just there to give you somethin' to aim at."

Flint looked at Buck. The big man was grinning as he watched Flint's reaction to Jed's taunting.

"I don't know, Sheriff," Flint speculated. "You reckon we could add on a couple more years to Jed's sentence for threatenin' the life of an officer of the law?"

"There's that possibility, I suppose," Buck replied. "We'll look into it when the deputy marshals get here to pick 'em up."

Jed made his hand like a pistol and pointed it at Flint. "Dead man," he declared and pretended to pull the trigger.

They left the two prisoners to eat their breakfast and bolted the cell room door. Buck said he wasn't concerned about leaving them unguarded while he was just across the street. If they somehow managed to get out of the cell, they would find the heavy cell room door another problem to break through. The only other option was a small window for ventilation, about five inches by sixteen inches close to the ceiling, impossible for anyone to squeeze through. The office door was locked as well.

"If I'm worried about it, I sit at a table by the window and I can see the front of the jail from there," Buck said.

Flint climbed up into the saddle and turned Buster toward the south end of the street. The jail was on the west side of the main street, and behind the jail, the Neches River ran north and south, some seventy-five yards away. Hannah Green's rooming house was also on the west side of the street, past the stables, which were on the east side, as were most of the businesses in the town. Hannah was a widow. Her husband, Frank, built the two-story house, and he did a fine job of it. According to Buck, Frank loved to fish, and in fitting with the craftsman he was, he built himself a small rowboat. The day after he drove the last nail in the picket fence across the front yard, he celebrated by taking his boat down the river to do some fishing.

"He told Hannah not to hold supper for him because he might be late," Buck had said. "That was four years ago and Frank ain't come back yet. Hannah's a fine-lookin' woman, still young enough to try it again. She's got a little more tote to her than she did four years ago, but most every woman adds some weight as they get older. I reckon she's still thinkin' Frank might show up 'cause she don't seem inclined to hitch up again."

Flint was thinking about what Buck said when he pulled Buster up by the front gate and stepped down. He looked at the picket fence. It still looked sturdy. So did the house. He had to wonder if maybe Frank might have been knocked in the head by somebody who admired his boat. He stepped up on the porch and rapped politely. No one answered his knock, so he rapped a little harder. Pretty soon, he heard a woman's light step coming down the hall-way, so he stepped back away from the door and waited. "Miz Green," he greeted her when she appeared in the doorway, and would have removed his hat, but he rarely wore one.

"Can I help you?" Hannah asked, looking him up and down. Then she smiled and said, "You must be Flint Moran, our new deputy sheriff."

"Yes, ma'am, I'm Flint Moran. How'd you know that?"

"Sheriff Jackson told me I'd know who you were when you showed up," Hannah said and laughed.

That only served to confuse him. How could she know who he was? But he elected not to ask. Instead, he said, "I've come to move some of my stuff into that room you're holdin' for me."

"Of course," she replied cheerfully. "Why don't you

come on inside and I'll give you a little tour of the house first. All right?" She held the screen door open for him.

"Yes, ma'am," he said and stepped inside an entry hall.

She led him down the hall, calling out the rooms. "This is the parlor on the right, which you're welcome to use anytime." They passed other rooms, some with the doors closed and she explained that they were guest rooms. "Dining room and kitchen," she ended up. "Now, I expect you'd like to see your room." He nodded. She led him past the kitchen and a guest washroom, past the back steps, to a room standing alone, attached to the main house by only a covered walkway. She handed him a key and motioned for him to proceed, then she stood back to judge his reaction.

He turned the key in the lock and walked into the room. It was small, but it was clean, with a good bed and a side chair. The floor was solid oak and there was a rug beside the bed. The one thing that was a must for him was a window. There was only one, but it was sizable, and he could see the outside. As he stood there, he could feel her silence, and knew she was waiting to see his reaction. He turned to look at her.

Before he could speak, she said, "I know it's a very small room, and it looks like it's not even part of the house, but the allowance the town gave you for your room wasn't even close to what I rent the nicer rooms for. And that includes your meals." He was glad to hear her say that, for he wasn't certain if he had room and board. He had figured, he would be spending most of his twenty dollars a week on meals at Clara's Kitchen, even though he was to be given a discount there as well. She told him what time the meals were served each day, giving him something else to think about. He figured he was going to have to try to make it there for her meals, since he didn't have to pay for them.

He hoped she was a decent cook, so he wouldn't wind up eating at Clara's Kitchen every day.

Finally, bringing his mind back to the little room, she asked, "Well, what do you think of it?"

He stepped over to the window and looked out, then turned back to answer her. "I think it's perfect," he said, bringing a sunny smile to her face along with a small sigh of relief. "There's most likely gonna be times when I have to leave real early, or I might get in real late. With this room, I can come and go in the back without disturbing your other guests."

"That's certainly true," Hannah agreed, "but I want to remind you that as a paying guest, you have a home here, just like the other guests. You don't have to knock on the front door to come in." She stepped forward and extended her hand. "Welcome to my home, Mr. Moran."

"Thank you, kindly, Miz Green. I'll go bring my horse around back and put my stuff in my room."

She walked back through the house with him to see him to the door. She couldn't help smiling to herself when she pictured the young man in the room, much like the mountain lion that Buck likened him to when he told her she would recognize him. She almost chuckled aloud when she thought, *his hair is tawny, just like a lion's.*

# CHAPTER 5

Most of Flint's first day on the job was spent calling on all the shops and businesses with Buck to introduce himself as the deputy sheriff. His reception was, in general, one of genuine welcome. He was not a stranger to many of the people, having traded with them for supplies or blacksmith services. Some of the merchants had witnessed his acrobatic response to Jed Tubbs' attempted escape at the trial and saw a sharp contrast in the two lawmen. Hopefully, the two would prove to work well together and the peaceful reputation of Tinhorn could continue.

On this first day of Flint's employment, he and Buck ate dinner at Clara's Kitchen to introduce Clara and her staff to the new deputy.

"Well, you sure went to a lot of trouble just so you wouldn't have to leave your gun on the table," Mindy Moore had joked.

As before, the food was excellent, but Flint told Buck he would go back to the boarding house for supper to see how the food compared. That comment brought to mind another subject that Flint wondered about. "What about tonight? I mean, since we've got prisoners there in the jail, do you want me to bunk in the office tonight?"

"No," Buck replied. "There ain't no need for that. I'll be

right there on the other side of the wall from the cell room."
He laughed and added, "And Roy will be sleepin' in the
office, so he can handle any attempted jail break. No, Roy
and I will guard the prisoners. I want you to keep an eye on
the town until all the businesses have closed. That is,
except Jake's Place. Sometimes he don't close until it's
damn-near mornin'. But there ain't no use in you hangin'
around for some of the town's old drunks and card players.
The only time you might wanna stick around later is if
there's some drifters or saddle tramps you ain't seen before
suddenly showin' up."

Flint understood the general nature of his responsibility,
so at supper time, he rode Buster back to Hannah's for
supper. He tied the buckskin at the back steps, then removed his gun belt and left it in his room before going into
the house.

"Good evening, Flint," Hannah greeted him when he
walked into the dining room. "Sit anywhere you like."

Three men were already seated. One was smiling at him
broadly and Flint recognized him as a clerk he had met in
Harper's Feed and Supply that afternoon. He nodded to
him and pulled the closest empty chair back and sat down.

"I hope you like pork chops," she said.

"Yes, ma'am, I do," he replied.

"We want to welcome our new guest tonight," Hannah announced then. "This is Flint Moran, our new deputy sheriff."

He received a friendly nod and a couple of comments
wishing him luck. Then Hannah went to the kitchen door
and said, "I think we're ready to serve, Myrna. Mr. Arthur
hasn't come down yet. He's havin' one of his bad days. We
might have to put a plate in the oven for him to eat later."

Myrna went to the door to get a look at the new boarder
then turned around and went back to work.

It was a pleasant supper, and the food was good. Flint

wished everyone a good evening and excused himself. When he got back to the office, Roy had just returned from Clara's after leaving the prisoners' dirty dishes. Buck announced that he was going to retire to his room to study the latest Wanted notices.

"No problem," Flint said. "I'll drop my horse off at the stable, then I'll keep an eye on the town and we'll see you in the mornin'."

"Right," Buck said, "I might just turn in a little early." He had a feeling that Flint already knew about his need for his *medicine*, but he was reluctant to own up to it. So he took the easy out Flint offered him.

Flint's first evening on patrol was an uneventful one as he exchanged pleasantries with several shop owners as they locked up for the night. One of them went to Jake's Place, instead of home, and Flint walked down there with him, where he politely refused the offer of a drink. He hung around the saloon for a while, talking to Jake then took a walk around town, checking the locked doors.

He could not avoid a question that kept trying to capture his thoughts, until finally, he spoke it aloud. "Is this what you want to do for a living?" *I swear*, he thought, *farming is more exciting than this*. He told himself the deputy job was only temporary until he decided what he was going to do for the rest of his life. In the meantime, he would be the best deputy he could be.

After even Jake's Place closed for the night, he went back to the office where he found the door locked, but not with the padlock on the outside. He took his key, unlocked the door, and went inside where he found Roy asleep on the bench. Moving quietly to the cell room door, Flint unlocked it and took a quick look inside. Both Jed and Ralph appeared to be sleeping, so Flint quietly closed the door and locked it again. Still moving quietly to keep from disturbing Roy, he went out the door and locked it. Everything seemed to be quiet in the jail and in the town, so he figured he could call it a night.

It was a clear night with a half moon shining over the Neches River, and he permitted himself to enjoy it as he walked down the street toward the boarding house. His nine-pound Henry rifle was propped across his shoulder. He had considered leaving the rifle in the office when he made his rounds, but it somehow seemed more official if he was armed for whatever might happen.

No lights were burning in the house when he got there, but he wouldn't have gone in the front door, anyway. He walked around to the back steps and went inside his room, a little surprised to find that he felt tired. Deciding it was simply because he normally went to bed much earlier, he propped his rifle against the chair, unbuckled his gun belt, and dropped it onto the chair, then sat down on the bed to take his boots off. A few gentle bounces on the bed pleased him to find it comfortable. Lying back, he was asleep before he could help himself.

It would seem the entire town of Tinhorn was fast asleep, but that was not the case. Rodents and varmints of various types were taking advantage of man's need for sleep at night, one of which was standing in a wagon behind the jail. Tall and thin, Ada Tubbs was able to easily reach the little iron grill that fit inside the tiny window of the cell. Her problem was how to affix the stick she was attempting to tie securely to the grill.

"How much you got?" Jed Tubbs whispered from inside the cell.

"Half a stick," Ada answered.

"Half a stick? You sure that's enough?"

"Vike said it was," Ada responded. "Keep your voice down, or you might not get the chance to find out."

"You don't have to worry about that," Jed came back. "You could shout and do a little dance on the bed of that wagon and ain't nobody gonna hear it. The sheriff's passed out drunk and that old fool, Roy, is asleep. He wouldn't do nothin', anyway. So hurry up with that thing."

"I'm hurryin' as fast as I can." A few moments later, she said, "There, that'll do. It's as good as I'm likely to get it. Are you and Ralph ready?"

"Near 'bout. Wait till I say when," Jed replied, still not sure about the half stick. "I hope to hell you got enough."

"Vike said it was," Ada repeated.

"I wish he was in here with us," Jed muttered as he and Ralph hurried to turn their cots over and wrap the mattresses around themselves for protection. "Go ahead!"

Outside on the wagon, Ada tried a couple of matches before she was able to strike one. Cupping her hands to keep it burning, she lifted it up to the fuse. As soon as the fuse sparked into life, she dropped the match, picked up the reins and yelled, "Mulc!" punctuating it with a sharp slap of the reins across the mule's croup.

The mule responded at once, lunging away at a gallop with Ada barely able to slow it down before it had run almost forty yards. She was able to turn the wagon around in time to see the success of her endeavor. Vike was right, it was more than enough dynamite to do the job.

Jerked out of a sound sleep, Flint wasn't sure what he had heard but knew it was something big. And he assumed, since he was the deputy sheriff, he'd better go find out what had happened. He strapped his gun belt back on, grabbed his rifle, and headed for the jail.

At the scene of the breakout, Jed and Ralph were trying to recover from the explosion that had tossed them against the bars of the cell.

"Dang!" Ralph exclaimed, shaking his head in an effort

to stop the ringing in his ears as small pieces of the wall, shattered studs, and siding fell in a smoky fog around him. "You think she used enough dynamite?" On his hands and knees, he stared at the night outside through the opening where half the back wall used to be.

Part of that wall was the corner post that the barred cell wall had been bolted to. The result was not only a casual walk out the back of the jail, but a simple opening around the end of the cell wall to get into the general cell room area. The only problem would be the heavy door that was locked. Their plan had called for the little ventilation window to be blown out, leaving a hole in the wall they could possibly climb up then crawl through. They would jump on the wagon and Ada would drive them to a couple of horses tied near the riverbank.

That plan was suddenly changed. The inconvenience of the heavy locked door was solved for them when they heard Roy frantically trying to unlock the door to the office to see what had caused him to be thrown from the bench in the office. That was a bonus. Although it had not been part of their escape plan, they realized they could now get their weapons. They slid around the loose wall of bars and positioned themselves on each side of the door.

Holding a short length of iron bar that had been pulled loose when the outside wall was blown away, Jed yelled, "Hurry, Roy, we're dyin' in here!"

In a few seconds, the door opened, and Roy rushed through, not expecting them to be out of their cell. As he ran past, Jed swung the iron bar as hard as he could swing it, catching Roy on the back of his head, knocking him unconscious.

"Hurry!" Ralph blurted. "Let's get our guns and get outta here!"

"I wanna make sure this old buzzard is out," Jed replied

and hammered Roy's head over and over. "He ain't gonna bother nobody now."

He ran into the office to find Ralph pulling their weapons out of a cabinet drawer. They strapped on their gun belts, picked up their rifles, then ran back through the destroyed cell room and out the gaping hole in the wall.

"What were you doin'?" Ada asked. "Another minute, and you wouldn'ta found no wagon waitin' for you."

"Shut up and get us to those horses," Jed told her.

She whipped the mule again and drove across the rough ground between the jail and the river.

"Wait a minute!" he yelled. "My hat! I ain't got my hat."

"To hell with your hat," Ada responded. "If you wanna go back to look for it, you can go back by yourself. I'm not goin' back."

"She's right, Jed, we'd best cut outta here while we still can," Ralph said. "You can buy another hat. With the mess that dynamite made of that cell, you most likely wouldn't find it, anyway."

Jed cursed in response but knew they were right. He and Ralph jumped down from the wagon and ran to the horses. Ada whipped the mule and drove it toward the north road out of town. Jed and Ralph passed her on their horses before she reached it.

Behind them, a half-drunk and totally confused Buck Jackson stumbled to the front door of his office and fumbled with his keys in an effort to unlock the door. He was still trying to fit the right key into the lock a few seconds later when Flint arrived.

"What happened?" Flint asked, but upon seeing immediately that Buck wasn't sure what was going on, he stepped up to the door beside him. "Here, let me get it." He inserted his key in the lock and opened the door. Stepping inside, he was met with the smell of gunpowder and a black mist that drifted through the open cell room door. "Oh, hell," he muttered and cocked his rifle as he headed for the cell room.

"What the—" Buck was forced to struggle in an effort to sober up. "What the hell happened? Are the prisoners okay?"

"We ain't got any prisoners," Flint called back. "They're gone and the whole back side of the jail went with 'em." He paused, hesitant to report the rest. "That ain't the worst of it."

"What is it?" Buck was rapidly being compelled to sober up as he walked through the cell room door to discover Flint kneeling beside a body in the dark ruins, partially lit up by the moonlight coming through the missing wall. "Roy?" Buck asked, knowing it could be no one else.

"It looks like they beat him to death with something heavy," Flint replied. "It's hard to tell with it bein' so dark in here, but that's what it looks like."

That was enough to clear Buck's mind of his drunken state, leaving him with a throbbing headache as he grieved over the unnecessary killing. "There weren't no call for that," he mumbled. "Roy wouldn'ta caused them no problem."

"I wonder how they got him to open the door to the office?" Flint said. "He might notta got hurt at all if he hadn't unlocked that door." Like Buck, he was sickened by the vicious murder of the harmless old man. He had only known Roy for a few days but felt the loss of the simple soul just the same, and wanted to make the two responsible for his brutal death pay for it.

Flint got up from his knee, walked through the debris left by the dynamite, and stepped down on the ground through the opening in the wall. He studied the ground behind the building in the faint light provided by the moon.

"Whaddaya see?" Buck asked when he walked back to the open wall.

"Wagon tracks," Flint answered.

"Ada Tubbs," Buck muttered. "I shoulda locked that witch up for that trick she pulled at the trial. Shoulda known she weren't the poor victim of her husband's abuse, like she made out to be."

"Ralph and Jed jumped on the wagon and she drove it off that way." Flint pointed toward the river. "Accordin' to the tracks, she drove that wagon up behind the buildin' more than once. She musta lit the fuse on that dynamite and drove away, then came back after it went off."

"Most likely," Buck agreed. "I don't know why I didn't hear all that goin' on. I musta been really sleepin' hard." He felt a sharp pang of conscience, knowing exactly why he hadn't heard anything right outside the wall of his quarters. It took a blast of dynamite to wake him from his drunken slumber. And he hadn't even been in bed. He'd been asleep sitting at the table, his head down on his folded arms.

Flint could readily speculate on Buck's failure to hear the beginnings of the jailbreak but was not inclined to say so. He'd known what the sheriff's problem was when he'd decided to take the deputy job, so his immediate feeling was one of frustration. He wanted to give chase, but his horse was in a stall in Lon Blake's stable, and even if he had his horse, he would unlikely be able to pick up the tracks of Ralph and Jed's horses in the trees by the river until daylight . . . if even then.

He looked up at Buck standing in the open section of the wall and appearing to still be fighting his demons. "Whaddaya wanna do?" Flint asked. "I can't do much till daylight, but I can go after them then."

Buck didn't answer immediately. When he did, he was really thinking out loud. "As sheriff, I've got no jurisdiction outside the town of Tinhorn, so I'm supposed to report their escape to the U.S. marshal, and it's his job to catch 'em. Him or the Texas Rangers." He turned to look at Roy's body lying back near the door. "But it's a different story now. Now, it's a case of murder."

"You can send me to track 'em," Flint said. "I'll bring 'em back, one way or another."

"There are two of 'em and the woman makes three," Buck replied. "I expect we'd both better go after 'em."

"Might be best if I just went alone," Flint said. "As sheriff, you're hired to watch the town. It might not be good if both of us are gone. And, like you said, you ain't got no authority to make arrests outside the city limits of Tinhorn."

Buck knew Flint was right. He shouldn't leave the town without a lawman, but it was such a senseless slaying of a harmless old man nothing short of a hanging would satisfy him. He looked at his newly hired deputy he thought of as a young mountain lion. Although he had no knowledge of Flint's skill as a tracker, he would not be surprised if tracking was one more of his talents.

Buck hesitated. "I don't know, Flint. They might be more than one man can handle."

"I'll bring 'em back," Flint said again. "I did it when they stole my cows. They won't all three stay together. Ada will go home to her daddy's, and we can worry about her after we catch up with Jed and Ralph."

"All right," Buck said after a short pause. "You're gonna be too early to get anything to eat, but Lon will be openin' the stable right at sunup. You can get your horse then. You got anything at all to eat?"

"I've got some deer jerky in my saddlebags," Flint recalled. "That'll be enough to hold me for a while."

With nothing else for them to do until daylight, they

turned the cots back up and returned the mattresses on top. They carried Roy's body into the exploded cell and laid it on a cot. Buck said he would get Walt Doolin, the town undertaker—and resident barber—to come pick up the body. He could push his little handcart around back and load the body out the back of the cell.

They lit a lamp and began picking up anything usable after the explosion, but little was salvageable in the outside cell.

"Here's what they used to kill Roy," Flint declared as he held the short length of iron bar up to show Buck.

It still had blood and patches of gray hair on the end of it. The sight of it was enough to raise the temperature in the veins of both men.

"We're gonna need a new jail," Flint said as if to remind Buck, in case he hadn't thought about it.

"I reckon I'll get Nolan Carson over here this mornin' and have him work up a price to build a solid wall across the back. One without a window," Buck decided. "That'll give the town council something to complain about. Good thing we got you hired before this happened. At least the inside cell didn't get tore up. Any arrests we make till we get this fixed, we'll have one cell to lock 'em up in. They'll have a great big view out the back till Nolan gets a back wall built, but they'll be locked up. If we get too many for that one cell, we'll have to put 'em in the storeroom behind Harper's."

They started back to the office and Buck took one more look at Roy's body on the cot. "Reckon I'll have to make my own coffee from now on."

# CHAPTER 6

Flint was waiting for Lon Blake when he opened the stable at a little past sunup.

"Mornin', Flint. You're gettin' an early start this mornin'. Have anything to do with that boom that woke me up?"

Flint told him about the jail break and Lon remarked, "I declare, I thought it mighta come from that direction. I thought about gettin' up to go see what it was, but I decided it might be best to wait till daylight, since there weren't no more booms."

"That was smart thinkin'," Flint told him. "You coulda run into some trouble. Roy Hawkins was killed."

"Oh, mercy me. Roy Hawkins. I swear, that's a shame. I never had any dealin's with the man, but he always seemed pleasant enough. You and the sheriff are all right, though, right?"

"It happened too fast for either one of us to get there before they had gone," Flint said, as he tightened the cinch under Buster's belly. He wasted no time after that, climbed aboard, and rode the buckskin over behind the jail.

Buck was waiting for him with a cup of coffee. "Here, it might not be as good as Roy's coffee, but it'll help you get started." He pointed to the tracks in the soft dirt behind the building. "Just like you said, she pulled it up behind the building while she lit the fuse, took off to wait for it to go off, then came back to get Jed and Ralph. Ain't no trouble followin' her when she left with them. You can see the trail she left through that knee-high brush"—he pointed to the river—"headin' straight for that one big oak tree by the river."

Flint gulped the last swallow of coffee from his cup and set the empty cup on the cell room floor, just inside the plate the back wall once rested upon. Buck held on to his own cup and walked beside him as he led Buster down to the river. There was no question the getaway horses had been tied there to a couple of lower limbs of the big oak. In addition to the tracks, the two horses had been considerate enough to leave fresh droppings behind to make sure someone found the place they were tied. Both lawmen studied the tracks carefully, although they were fairly obvious in their intended direction—upriver. If that wasn't sign enough, Ada had driven her wagon right along the same path.

Buck shrugged. "Even I could follow that trail, but I expect they're gonna take some pains to hide their tracks once they get clear of Tinhorn. Wish I could tell you where Ada's pappy's place is, but I ain't got no idea." He stood back and waited for Flint to climb up into the saddle. "You be careful you don't ride into an ambush. I don't wanna have to look for another deputy before I get a chance to find out what kind I just hired. Good huntin'."

Flint nodded in response and nudged the buckskin into motion.

As Buck had pointed out, the trail Flint followed was easy enough to see, making it unnecessary to even slow down. It led along the riverbank for at least a mile before it took an abrupt turn to the left and went directly to intercept the road to Tyler. Flint took extra care to make sure they'd turned onto the road. He could see no evidence of hoofprints or wagon tracks on the other side of the road. Since he was willing to bet they had not turned to the south and headed back to Tinhorn, he was satisfied they started north toward Tyler. The question was whether or not they were really headed for Tyler. Of the opinion they would leave the road somewhere short of Tyler, Flint recalled someone had said Ada's father's house was halfway between Tinhorn and Tyler. Maybe Jed or Ralph had a place near there.

Flint followed the road for a distance he estimated to be about ten miles before coming upon the first sign of departure. Where the road crossed a shallow stream wagon tracks indicated that Ada had pulled the wagon off the road a dozen feet or so and stopped to let her mule drink. Flint assumed Ralph and Jed had stopped to let their horses drink, too, but he couldn't be sure. With too many tracks in the road, it was not easy to tell which tracks were the freshest and therefore belonged to the men he sought.

He looked at the road ahead of him and saw it appeared to pass through a low ridge covered with trees. *Good place for an ambush*, he thought, and it occurred to him that he should be alert for the possibility of one. Common sense told him it was unlikely the two men would do anything but put Tinhorn behind them as soon as they could now that they had escaped, but he recalled the threats made by Jed Tubbs. Flint was not willing to discount the possibility that Jed might waste those hours of freedom he had already gained just for a chance to kill him.

When Buster had had enough water, Flint returned to the road and crossed the stream. On the other side, the wagon tracks left the road and followed the stream to the west. Seeing only one set of hoofprints—the mule's—indicated that was the place where Ada had left the two on horseback and headed for her father's house. Of course, that was assuming the three of them had traveled at the pace set by Ada's mule pulling the wagon. More likely, he decided, Ada was far behind the two on horseback by the time she'd reached the stream.

He turned to take another look at the road up ahead, particularly at the narrow notch where the road cut through the ridge. "Good place for an ambush," he repeated out loud. Maybe he was being overcautious. Maybe Jed and Ralph were already in Tyler, or wherever they were heading. But Flint still had a feeling about a possible ambush, and when he had a feeling, it was hard for him to ignore it. With that in mind, he turned Buster off the road and followed the wagon tracks to the west, continuing to follow them until he was satisfied he could turn back without being seen.

"Where the hell's he goin'?" Jed blurted. "He's followin' Ada." He turned to Ralph and demanded an explanation. "It's us he wants, and he knows blame well we're gonna be a helluva long way ahead of that wagon." Genuinely upset, Jed was so sure of what the young deputy's reaction to their escape was going to be. "He'd have to be blind not to see the trail we left. And it was pretty plain to see that we got on the road to Tyler." He had taunted Flint so much he was certain the new lawman would come after them. "Why would he break off and go after the wagon?"

"Maybe he's smarter than he looks, and figures he druther arrest Ada, than take on the two of us," Ralph suggested. "In the meantime, we've been settin' around here for hours, waitin' for him to show up when we coulda been a good piece up the road."

Jed wasn't ready to admit he was wrong about the cocky young man who had made his *citizen's arrest* with the help of his unseen partner, Buster. "I'll tell you what I think.

I think the fool figured we took the wagon, and Ada went on with the horses. He thought we'd do that to throw him off our trail."

"Well, I don't care why he followed the wagon, but he did," Ralph said. "And we coulda been to Tyler by now. So whaddaya say we go back to get the horses and clear outta here?"

"I swear, I wanted to kill that man as bad as I've ever wanted to kill anybody," Jed declared. "But I reckon you can't have everything you want, can you?" He thought about it for a moment more and said, "I might ride back down this way one day." He stepped out from behind the two small trees he had been using to shield his body and followed Ralph down toward the base of the ridge to the tiny spring where they had left their horses.

At the bottom, he found Ralph standing by the spring, looking one way, then the other. Hearing Jed come down the hill behind him, he turned to face him. "Ain't this the place where we left the horses?"

Jed said it was.

Ralph asked, "Well, where are they?"

Realizing Ralph was serious, Jed moved past him to stand by the spring to see for himself. He turned around and looked back up the ridge to make sure they were in the right place. "That's where we climbed up that slope. Same place we just came back down."

"Well, the horses ain't here," Ralph stated.

"How the hell could they wander off?" Jed asked. "I know I tied mine good enough."

"I did, too," Ralph insisted. "Tied his reins on a lower limb—that one right there—and gave him enough slack so he could reach the water. He didn't have no cause to wanna pull his reins offa that limb."

"They sure as hell wandered off," Jed declared, pointing

to a couple of hoofprints. "Went back thataway." He started after them, following a small game path the horses had evidently decided to explore. He and Ralph continued along the path for about twenty yards when it led into a clump of oak trees surrounding a small pond. "There they are," Jed announced. "They found 'em a little waterin' hole."

"Ha!" Ralph snorted. "I reckon they weren't happy with that little spring where we left 'em." He walked on down to the pond and took hold of his horse's reins, becoming distracted by a movement of some kind a little deeper in the clump of trees. At once alerted, he reached across with his left hand to draw the six-gun riding in the holster on his right side. He hesitated then when he got a better look through the branches. "I swear, Jed, there's another horse back there in the trees. That's what drew our horses down here."

"Are you sure?" Jed asked. "Somethin' ain't right here."

"That'll be Buster," announced the voice behind and now familiar to them. "He didn't wanna startle you, so he's hangin' back in the trees aways."

Both men spun around to discover Flint sitting cross-legged on a small ledge partially covered by the branches of the trees. His Henry rifle lay across his thighs, his Colt six-gun in his hand. He didn't bother to tell them to raise their hands because he did not expect them to surrender peacefully.

Although fumbling awkwardly with his left hand, Ralph already had his gun drawn, so he received Flint's first shot. Struck in his right shoulder, he automatically dropped his pistol and fell to his knee. Jed's six-gun was halfway out of the holster when he was slammed in the shoulder, as well. The force of the shot backed him up a couple of steps, but he reached for his six-gun again.

With the Henry rifle aimed at Jed, Flint cautioned him.

"You pull that weapon, and my next shot will be a kill shot. Your choice."

Jed hesitated for only a moment before releasing his pistol to let it fall back down in his holster. Flint got up from the ledge, picked up two pairs of handcuffs that had been lying on the ledge beside him, nodded toward Ralph, and ordered him to back away from the pistol on the ground by his knee. Ralph did so immediately.

"Now, Jed, stick your hands behind your back." When he did, Flint clamped the cuffs on his wrists. Then he lifted the .44 out of Jed's holster.

Finally finding his voice, Jed said, "You ain't got no authority out here. This ain't the town of Tinhorn."

"You know, that's right," Flint replied. "I am out of my jurisdiction, so I don't know if I even wanna bother with takin' you into town to get those wounds took care of. It'd be a lot easier to just put a bullet in your head right here. Or maybe I'd get more satisfaction outta just beatin' you to death, like you did for poor ol' Roy. I ain't got an iron bar, like the one you used, but the barrel of this Henry rifle would work just as well. Which one of you brave desperadoes was the one who beat the life out of that helpless old man?"

"He musta tripped and hit his head," Jed replied. "We was in a hurry. We didn't have time to bother with that old coot."

Holding his gun on Ralph, Flint said, "Put your hands behind your back."

"I didn't have no part in beatin' that man in the head," Ralph insisted as Flint clamped the cuffs around his wrists.

"I wouldn'ta thought so," the young deputy said. "Not with your right hand bandaged up like that. No, I expect Mr. Tubbs here is the one most likely guilty of that murder. But don't worry, there's plenty to charge you with— breakin' outta jail and tryin' to ambush a deputy law officer.

That oughta be enough to get you a few more years down at Huntsville. Too bad we'll have to wait till next month to find out, 'cause Judge Dodge has already gone back to Tyler. Hopefully, we won't have too many chilly nights, since there ain't no back wall between the cell you'll be in and the whole outdoors. If you're lucky, we won't have any big storms hit for a while."

"Why you snivelin' dog," Jed bellowed out at Ralph. "Everything we done, we done it as partners. You got just as big a part in killin' that old fool as I have."

"I didn't have no notion about killin' Roy," Ralph insisted. "I didn't know you was gonna knock him in the head with that bar. All I wanted to do was run." He lowered his voice to keep Jed from hearing him tell Flint, "He was the one who kept beatin' him to make sure he was dead. I didn't even know he was doin' it. I was in the office lookin' for our guns."

"Maybe I can help you out on that," Flint said. "Maybe go a little easier on you. Where was Ada goin' with that wagon? Her daddy's house?"

Ralph nodded.

"Where is his house?"

"Right up that stream about a mile."

*About a mile*, Flint thought. If they were that close to her father's house, anyone at the house would surely have heard his two shots. And since he didn't know what the situation was with Ada's family, he thought it best for him to get his prisoners back on the road to Tinhorn. He would come back to look for Ada when he didn't have Jed and Ralph to guard.

"All right," he said to Ralph, "put your foot in that stirrup and I'll boost you up." To Jed, after Ralph was in the saddle, he said, "Let's go."

"I can't lift my foot that high," Jed complained. "I need my hands free so I can grab the saddle horn."

"I don't have the time or the inclination to mess around with you, Jed," Flint told him. "Stick your foot up in that stirrup, or I'm gonna put a bullet in your brain and take you back lyin' across that saddle on your belly."

Something in the tone of the deputy's voice told Jed Flint was deadly serious.

"All right, damn it." Jed surrendered and Flint boosted him up.

Then he grabbed the reins of their horses, climbed up on Buster, and led them out to the road for the ride back to Tinhorn. He let the buckskin set the pace for the ten-mile ride back to town.


It was close to dinnertime when Flint led his two wounded prisoners into the north end of town. Since Doc Beard's office was the last house north of Tinhorn, and the first house you came to from that direction, Flint decided to stop on the way in. He found the door locked and a sign saying Doc would be back after dinner. He knocked on the door, anyway, and after a few minutes the door opened.

Doc stood there with a napkin tied around his neck. "I reckon you don't have to be able to read to be a deputy."

"Sorry to bother you, Doc," Flint replied. "I read your sign, but I just wanted to let you know I've got two gunshot wounds here, and I was hopin' you could treat 'em after dinner sometime. And I wanted to know if you druther I bring 'em back here, or will you come to the jail to treat 'em."

Doc looked beyond Flint at the two men on the horses. "Lemme see how bad they are." He went out the doorway, walked up beside Ralph's horse, and took a quick look at the bloody hole in his shirt. "You again. Your hand ain't even well yet." He turned then and looked at Jed. "Both shoulder wounds. How long you been riding to get here?"

"Ten miles," Flint answered.

"Ten miles, huh? Well, they don't look like they've done a helluva lot of bleeding. They'll be all right for a little while longer. I'll finish my dinner, then I'll come down to the jail." He turned around and went back inside without waiting for a response from Flint.

"You heard him, boys. He'll see you later." Flint climbed back up into the saddle and wheeled Buster back toward the road into town.

"Well, I'll be. I never doubted he'd catch up with 'em. I just didn't expect he'd do it so soon." Sheriff Buck Jackson was standing at the back of the jail talking to Nolan Carson about rebuilding the back wall when Flint rounded the end of the building, his two prisoners trailing behind him.

"I figured it'd be just as easy to bring these two in our new back door," Flint declared. "Especially since they had so much to do with buildin' it."

"Good thinkin'," Buck responded. "We'll relieve them of some of that extra weight they're totin' and show 'em right to their new quarters. I see you had to shoot 'em, once in the shoulder of both of 'em."

"I didn't have to, but they insisted," Flint replied. "I stopped at Doc's on the way in. He's gonna come here and fix 'em up, soon as he gets through eatin' dinner."

Buck walked up to the horse closest to him, which happened to be Jed's. He reached up and grabbed him by his shirt and jerked him roughly off the horse. "I reckon I oughta apologize for bunkin' you two in the cell smaller than the one you were in before. There's been quite a few folks comin' by to look at your handiwork on the jail. Now that you and your partner are back, I expect there'll be more comin' to take a look at you. "Whaddaya think, Flint? We could call it the Tinhorn Zoo."

Flint turned to help Ralph off his horse, but he didn't wait. After he saw the way Jed was dismounted, the cow thief swung a leg over and slid off the horse and might have fallen to the ground had not Flint caught his elbow.

Using a section of a broken bench as a step up to the floor, they led the two men inside the building, into the back of the cell room, and put them in the one intact cell.

"Sorry, there ain't no water bucket or slop bucket in there yet. Roy always took care of that," Buck said. "Maybe one of us will get around to it directly."

When the prisoners were locked inside the one remaining cell, he returned to continue his talk with the carpenter, who had found the procedure quite interesting. "Nolan, I think you know what we want. Just build us a wall so we can get it back the way it was."

"I'll get right on it, Sheriff," Nolan said. "It'll take me a couple of days after I get the lumber. You want me to hang a piece of canvas on that cell where you've got the prisoners? I know Lon Blake's got a pretty big one he used to cover some hay he had outside."

"That's a good idea," Buck answered. "Maybe that would cut out the spectators."

Almost an hour later Dr. John Thomas Beard arrived at the jail, his medical bag in hand, his stomach sufficiently full after the stewed chicken dinner his wife, Birdie, had cooked for him. The chicken, a fat pullet, came to Doc in the form of payment for the treatment of a farmer's eight-year-old daughter's sore throat.

"Howdy, Doc, Miz Beard," Buck greeted them when

they walked in the front door of the office. "'Preciate you takin' care of these two prisoners."

"You sure you want me to treat those gunshot wounds?" Doc responded. "Just walking down here from my office, I passed some folks in front of Harper's. When they asked me where I was headed, and I told 'em, they asked me why I was wasting my time. They said most of the men in town were talking about a hanging for those two."

"Is that a fact?" Buck asked. "To tell you the truth, Doc, I feel like that's exactly what we oughta do with 'em, after they beat poor Roy Hawkins to death. Flint tracked 'em down and captured 'em. I'll be honest with you, if I'da been with him, I mighta just strung 'em up right where he caught 'em. But I got to thinkin' about my job as the sheriff, and what rights I have and don't have. What I'm hopin' is for the mayor and council to try the two of 'em for what they done, and then I'll hang 'em."

"Waste of my time," Doc said, with a shake of his head. "You know, if that happens, it won't be recognized as a legitimate court. It'll be a vigilante court." He looked at Flint and said, "You coulda told me you were thinkin' about hanging them when you stopped in before."

"I didn't know about it then," Flint replied. "My job was to find 'em and arrest 'em. They didn't wanna be arrested, so I had to shoot 'em. Now they need a doctor."

"You need to treat their wounds, anyway," Buck said to Doc. "There ain't no tellin' if the mayor and council will decide to try 'em or not. It might take a couple of days to decide. If they decide to let Judge Dodge try 'em, that might be a month before it happens. Whichever happens, there ain't no use to let 'em bleed to death or something. Even if we hang 'em right after you fix 'em up, I'll see that the council pays you your fee."

Properly incensed, Doc responded. "Hell, I'm not worried

about my fee. My job is to treat the sick and the injured. It just doesn't make sense to treat a dead man for a bullet wound." He was sincere in his loyalty to his oath as a physician, and the town, for the most part, appreciated that quality. He had not completed four years in a university, but he had graduated from Jefferson Medical College, a two-year medical school, as a Doctor of Medicine and found his way to Tinhorn, a town in need of a physician's services.

His wife and nurse, Birdie, a full-blooded Cherokee, waited for him the entire two years he was away studying to be a doctor. She didn't normally accompany him when he went to the jail to treat a patient, but on this occasion, since there were two patients, she'd come along to help.

"I'll go take a look at the patients now, and you can tell the council I'll send my bill as usual."

"Flint and I'll go in the cell with you while you're workin' on 'em," Buck said, leading the way into the cell room where Jed and Ralph were sitting on their cots, waiting.

"Damn!" Doc swore when he walked through the door to the cell room. "They weren't lying when they said the whole back wall was gone!" He was one of the few folks in town who had not gone to look at the back of the jail. Standing out back of the building were half a dozen spectators who had come to gawk at the prisoners while Doc worked on them.

He looked at the gawkers, then back at the prisoners. "This won't do. I'm not here to put on a show to entertain those idiots. It's too chilly out here, anyway. I'll treat them inside the office, one at a time, if you prefer, but not out here."

Buck shrugged indifferently. "Whatever you say, Doc. Okay, come on, Ralph. You're first."

# CHAPTER 7

Flint pulled Roy Hawkins' bench away from the wall to use as Doc's operating table, and they sat Ralph down on it. With Birdie's help, Doc removed Ralph's heavy shirt and underwear top. Birdie spread them on the bench, and they laid Ralph down on them.

"I'm gonna need to clean that up a little," Doc said after he looked at the wound.

Birdie looked at Flint. "Pan?" she asked. When he didn't understand what she meant, she repeated, "Pan, for water."

"Right," he responded then looked at Buck.

There was one in his quarters and he went to get it.

"I reckon you'll want the water heated, right?" Flint asked Doc.

Doc nodded.

"Then I'd best stoke that fire up a little in the stove," Flint said, "but I'll have to wait till Buck gets back. One of us has to watch the prisoner."

"I fix the fire," Birdie said, and went to the wood box beside the stove where there was a good supply of firewood. In a few minutes, she brought the fire back to life again.

Flint was impressed with her no-nonsense approach to

the job to be done. He was even more impressed when Doc was digging for the bullet in Ralph's shoulder and she anticipated Doc's every move. They were quite a team. In no time at all, it seemed, the bullet was out of Ralph's shoulder and Birdie was completing the bandaging. Flint took Ralph back to the cell and brought Jed back for his turn.

The procedure went pretty much the same for Jed as it had for his partner, with doctor and nurse working together until the bullet was removed, and soon Jed was ready to be bandaged. Unlike Ralph, however, Jed had not surrendered. During the procedure, he watched every move Doc and Birdie made. His attention paid off when the operation was over, and Doc laid a scalpel down for Birdie to pick up and wash. Jed seized the opportunity. He snatched up the scalpel just as Birdie was about to reach for it. When she jumped back, startled, he grabbed the tiny woman around her waist with one arm, and held the scalpel against her throat with the arm she was just about to bandage.

When all three men reacted, he warned them, "Make one move toward those guns and I'll slit her throat wide open. Don't think I won't kill her. You think you're gonna hang me. Well, I think that ain't gonna happen. Now, with your left hands, I want them guns dropped on the floor. You first, Sheriff."

Buck hesitated, and Jed told him, "Even if you get off a shot, she'll be dead."

Feeling he had no choice, Buck pulled his pistol out and dropped it on the floor.

"That's a good boy," Jed taunted. "Now, kick it over here."

Buck did so.

"Now, it's your turn, hotshot," he said to Flint. "You do the same as he just did." He grinned at Flint and taunted, "You know, you've caused me one helluva lot of pain.

I'd still like to get it on with you, just the two of us with two six-guns. Too bad I ain't got time to stay today, but I might look you up some other time."

"You ain't got the slightest chance of gettin' outta here alive," Buck said. "You ain't got a horse. You've still gotta pick up those guns and that ain't gonna be too easy with two of us waiting for a wrong move."

"There ain't but one wrong move, and it would be if you tried to stop me. I've got this little Injun by the throat," Jed gloated. "I don't need anything else."

"You need this," Birdie said, turning suddenly and planting her knee in a place he didn't want it.

Jed's involuntary reaction of sheer pain caused him to jerk the scalpel away from Birdie's throat for a couple of seconds while he tried to keep from doubling up. It was enough time for Flint to draw his Colt six-gun and put a round in Jed's forehead. It happened so fast that no one could speak but Birdie, who said, "Good shot."

Finally able to find his voice, Doc reached for Birdie. "Are you all right?" She nodded, and he turned to face Flint. "You could have killed her!"

"I reckon I could have," Flint calmly replied. "But I didn't aim at her. It was Jed that was causin' the problem, so I shot him instead."

"I'll go get Walt Doolin to take the body outta here," Buck said. "I swear, I'm tempted to hang him anyway. Even though you didn't finish bandagin' Jed up, I'll see that you still get paid for rcmovin' thc bullet from his shoulder," he said to Doc.

"Help me pick up my instruments," Doc said to Birdie, disgusted with the way the procedure had developed into a life-or-death catastrophe. "Let's get the hell outta here. We'll sterilize the instruments when we get home." He grabbed them up and dumped them into his bag, and hustled Birdie out the door.

"Thanks, Doc," Buck called after them. Then back to Flint, he said, "I think that was a little too close for Doc's comfort. He must think a lot of that little Birdie." He laughed then as he recalled her defiant response to Jed's demands, which had given Flint the opportunity for a shot. "I declare, she sure is a spunky little thing, ain't she?" He paused. "She's right. That was some shot you made."

"When I arrested him and Ralph back on the Tyler road, and had to put a round in his shoulder, I warned him that the next one would be in his head," Flint declared.

Buck shook his head, amazed by his deputy's honest demeanor. He suddenly realized there was more to learn about the young man he had hired to do a simple deputy's job. "I suppose we oughta go check on our other prisoner," Buck said.

They found Ralph standing at the cell wall closest to that door, holding on to the bars. He asked, "Jed?"

"That's right," Buck answered. "He took a chance and it didn't pay off."

"I figured," Ralph declared sadly. "I was afraid he was gonna try something stupid and get hisself shot. I heard that shot and I knew he'd made his move. Who shot him?"

"That don't matter," Buck said quickly, thinking it never a good idea to name the killer of a man's partner. "There ain't no doubt he tried something stupid, all right. He never had a chance of makin' it outta here alive. I hope you've got better sense."

"I do," Ralph said at once. "You ain't gonna have no trouble outta me. I know I done the crimes, and I'm willin' to pay for 'em. I just hope you remember that I had no hand in killin' poor old Roy."

"I'm beginnin' to believe you," Buck said, "so I'm

gonna see if I can still get you some dinner." He turned to address Flint then. "Clara might still be servin'. One of us can go up there and eat and bring a couple of plates back."

"Why don't you go eat," Flint suggested, "and tell Clara you need two plates for your prisoners. If you don't tell her one of 'em is dead, I won't get charged for my dinner."

Buck chuckled. "That sounds like a good idea to me. I'd best get goin', or she'll be throwin' it out to the hogs. If I see Walt Doolin, I'll tell him to pick up Jed." He went out the back of the cell room then and told a couple of spectators to move along. "There ain't nothin' for you boys to see now, so you might as well go on back to the saloon." He told Flint that Nolan Carson was going to hang some canvas on the cell wall, and he hoped that would eliminate the gawkers.

The next thing on Flint's mind was the problem going by the name of Ada Tubbs. The woman was guilty of multiple crimes, not the least of which was dynamiting the jail. He was hoping Ralph Cox's desperation to save his own life would inspire him to be even more cooperative than he had been so far. He had told Flint how to find Ada's father's house. Hopefully, he would tell him something about Ada's family, so Flint would know what to expect, if he went looking for the woman.

Back in the office, he made a big pot of coffee then carried it out to the cell. "You want some coffee to hold you till the sheriff gets back with our dinner? I think we picked up a cup and stuck it in that cell. You want some?"

"I sure do," Ralph answered. "I could sure use some right now." He picked up the cup he saw on a small stool near one of the cots and held it through the bars.

Flint filled it with the fresh coffee.

"Thank you kindly," Ralph said. "That's mighty decent of you after what we did to the jailhouse."

"I expect you didn't plan to do as much damage as you did," Flint said. "It was Ada Tubbs who did the damage, anyway." He went back in the office, filled his own cup, put the pot back on the edge of the stove, and carried the full cup back out to the cell. "How long have you and Jed Tubbs been workin' together?"

"Two years about," Ralph answered with no evidence of hesitancy. "I knew him a few years before we teamed up to steal cattle."

Flint could sense Ralph's tendency to resist had faded, and figured it was because Jed was gone. "Did you know Ada before Jed married her?"

Ralph shook his head. "No, I didn't know her. Jed didn't know her very long before they got married." He snorted a short chuckle. "He said he met her at a square dance. Said he was dead drunk. Woke up the next mornin' and she was in the bed with him. Her pappy and two brothers were standin' at the foot of the bed, and they had a preacher with 'em. I figure her marriage prospects musta been mighty slim. Jed said her old man asked him what his intentions were toward his daughter, so he claimed he was wantin' to marry her."

"Well, that's a helluva love story," Flint commented, confident that Ralph was not reluctant to tell the story. "So, did Ada ride with you and Jed when you were doin' business?"

"No, Jed told her it was too dangerous for her, so she stayed at her papa's house most of the time while he was away on business. He went back to be with her from time to time, just to keep her papa and brothers from comin' to look for him. As long as Jed played like he was married, they didn't have no quarrel with him. He said they wanted her to stay home, anyway, 'cause Ada's mama was dead, so Ada did the cookin'."

"Papa was kinda easygoin' on him, wasn't he? Do you know his name?" Flint asked.

"Yeah, Trask. Liam Trask, and she has two brothers, Vike and Kyle," Ralph answered. "I heard plenty about them. They're in the horse-tradin' business."

"They raise horses?"

"I don't know about raisin' any horses," Ralph said. "They just traded horses."

"I'da thought Papa Trask mighta wanted his son-in-law in business with him," Flint said. "Didn't Jed ever think about that?"

"Jed didn't want no part of it with Trask, and I think Trask felt the same way," Ralph replied. "I'm pretty sure Ada's brothers didn't want anything to do with Jed. Just wanted to make sure he treated ol' Ada all right."

With a fairly good picture of Ada's family situation by the time Walt Doolin came to pick up Jed's body, Flint left his friendly little visit with Ralph to help load Jed onto the handcart Walt used to pick up his customers, and he was gone by the time Buck came back from Clara's Kitchen with two plates of food.

Flint poured Ralph another cup of coffee to go with his dinner, then went into the office to eat his. "I reckon we need to decide what we're gonna do about Ada Tubbs, don't we?" Flint asked as he worked on a tough piece of beef.

"Yeah, I was thinkin' about that while I was eatin' dinner," Buck said. "Whether we oughta go after her or not, I ain't sure. It's the same case as Jed and Ralph's was, out of our jurisdiction, and whether we should turn it over to the marshal service and let them go find her. I feel like that crazy woman oughta have to answer to us for her part in blowin' up the damn jail." He cocked his head to one side and grimaced. "Trouble is, we don't know what we're liable to run into, if we do go to find her."

"She went to her papa's place about a mile east of Tyler road. Her pa's a horse thief, near as I can figure. His name's Liam Trask. He's got two grown sons, Kyle and Vike."

"Whoa," Buck exclaimed. "How do you know all that?"

"I make good coffee," Flint answered. "It put ol' Ralph in a chatty mood, I reckon."

Buck paused to picture what might happen to any lawman intent upon arresting Ada. "That ain't very encouragin'. Sounds like we could be facing four guns, countin' Ada, and I expect we'd better count her."

He paused again, apparently thinking through possible problems if he and Flint decided to make an attempt to arrest Ada Tubbs. To begin with, as sheriff of Tinhorn, he had no jurisdiction outside the city limits to make arrests. In addition to that, he had a prisoner in his jail, and he would be leaving the sheriff's office and jail unattended. And that he could not do. It was a frustrating situation he found himself in. He looked up to find Flint watching him, waiting for his instructions.

"I don't know what I'm thinkin'. We can't go ridin' off outta town and leave a prisoner locked up with nobody in charge. It really gets my goat to have that crazy woman get away with her part in that escape, blowin' up my damn jail. I wanna have her locked up right here and tried by Judge Dodge. Might even put her in the same cell with Ralph and let the gawkers stand back there to watch 'em. Let people know that just because you're a woman, don't mean you ain't gonna get punished for the crime." Buck hesitated, realizing he was getting himself too worked up over an issue he was not going to be able to confront. "I'll contact the Texas Rangers office in Tyler and turn the arrest over to them. That's what I'm supposed to do."

Flint could understand how the whole issue was tearing Buck up. And while he agreed with the sheriff's feelings that Ada should be punished for her crimes, he was not as impassioned for her arrest. He knew Buck could picture Ada laughing at the sheriff's helplessness in this situation, but Flint didn't care if she was or not. He figured you catch some crooks, and some get away, but maybe the deputy marshals or the Texas Rangers would catch up with Ada.

To help relieve some of the strain on Buck's conscience, however, he made a suggestion. "You know, if you want me to, I could take a ride up there where those wagon tracks left the road and see if I can find the Trask place. If I do, I could just scout around there a while to see what was goin' on. Maybe Mr. Trask and his two sons ain't there all the time, and if I was lucky, I might see if Ada is there. 'Cause she mighta gone somewhere else to hide. It wouldn't hurt to know for sure, so you could tell the Rangers."

Buck didn't answer at once, but Flint could tell he was giving it some thought. Finally, he spoke. "You'd have to be mighty damn careful. Thinkin' about what Ralph told you, Trask and his boys might just take a shot at you, if they saw you snoopin' around."

"Oh, I know that's a possibility," Flint replied. "I ain't thinkin' about takin' any big chances. But if I was to just get a glimpse of Ada, then we'd know for sure she didn't think she had to take off somewhere to hide."

"That might be some good information to give the Rangers, all right," Buck agreed.

"There's still plenty of daylight left today, and my horse needs the exercise. I'll go throw a saddle on him and see if I can find that place."

"I don't know about this," Buck said, but he was obviously all for it. "You be damn careful nobody sees you."

"I will," Flint replied, picked up his rifle, and headed for the door then the stable.

"How do, Flint," Lon Blake greeted him. "You want your horse?"

"Yes, sir, I need my horse, and I need to take another horse with me. I need him saddled. Can you fix me up with one that's halfway gentle? I know we've got some horses here that our prisoners rode in on, but I need one a woman can ride with no trouble. I'll bring him back tonight and you can just tack it onto the sheriff's regular bill." He decided he'd take a horse just in case he found the men all gone from the place and he might be able to go in and arrest Ada. He didn't care for the thought of the two of them on Buster for the ten-mile ride back to town. She might be too much to handle.

"You betcha," Lon answered and pointed toward the corral. "You can take that sorrel mare in the corner." Sensing that Flint was in a hurry, he said, "I'll throw a saddle on her right quick."

In a short time, Flint was in the saddle, leading the sorrel. He left the stable and rode north, behind the buildings on the main street, just in case Buck might be looking out the window. He thought it less worrisome to the sheriff if he didn't see him leading an extra horse. When he passed behind the hotel, he swung back to strike the road to Tyler.

Reaching the stream where Ada left the road, he saw the wagon tracks were still obvious, there having been no weather to erase them. As he followed the tracks along the stream, he wished he had asked Ralph if there were any other houses farther up the stream. He had gotten the impression Trask had a farm or a small ranch, and after a short ride, he found that to be the case. He spotted the house just as he was coming to a small rise, so he stopped to look the situation over. He figured he was about a hundred yards short of the house and barn. The terrain was sparsely covered with runty oak trees, but due to a heavy growth of trees all along the stream, getting closer was no problem. From the rise, he could see pastures beyond the house and about forty or fifty horses grazing there, as near as he could estimate.

He guided Buster and the mare into the heavier cover of the trees lining the stream and moved closer to the house until he thought it too risky to take the horses any farther. He could see very well from there but still moved a little closer on foot before he settled himself to watch the house and barn beyond it. There was no one to be seen for what he figured was almost an hour, so maybe he had been lucky, and the men were off somewhere stealing horses or something else against the law. The problem was, he had no evidence that Ada was in the house.

While still trying to decide if he should approach the house or not, a man came out the back door of the house and walked to the barn. A couple of minutes later, another man came out the door and went to the barn. Flint decided the two men had to be Ada's brothers, Kyle and Vike. He was further convinced when an older man followed them out of the house. He stopped when someone from the back door called after him. They exchanged words for a minute or two, too far away for Flint to understand, but the voice from the kitchen door was definitely female. He assumed it was Ada because her mother was dead. Then Trask continued to the barn.

*Well, I brought the extra horse for nothing*, he thought, for the men of the family were definitely not away. *And I'm not dumb enough to go against these odds*. He also reminded himself that, even if the men had been gone, he might have been shot on sight by the woman herself.

It had been an unrealistic idea in the first place. He wished he could have gotten a look at the woman in the house to verify it was Ada, so it wouldn't be a total loss. He got up from his kneeling position beside a tree to move back to the horses, a dozen yards behind him, but he stopped immediately when the back door of the house opened again, and Ada Tubbs walked out. He froze in his half-kneeling position as he watched her.

Instead of following her father and brothers into the barn, she turned and started for the outhouse located in the trees by the stream on the opposite side of the house from the barn. He had paid very little attention to it when he first set up to watch the house, but it was actually closer to him. As far as he was concerned, instead of an arrest, he was going to perform a kidnapping.

Afraid she might detect his presence, he didn't move while she continued toward the outhouse. As soon as she opened the door to step inside, he ran back to his horse to replace his rifle in the saddle sling. Knowing he was going to need both hands, he grabbed his handcuffs out of his saddlebag. Thinking ahead, he took his rope off his saddle and laid it over the saddle horn on the mare's saddle.

Hurrying through the bushes, he took his bandana off and rolled it into a gag intent upon muffling her. If he just held a gun on her, she'd scream, and he'd be a dead man before he could put her on the horse and get out of there. He slowed down before reaching the outhouse, otherwise, she would hear him approaching. Reaching it, he stopped to listen, and he could hear her murmuring something he couldn't understand. *So far, so good*, he thought.

His next concern was the cracks between the boards on the side of the outhouse, one so large he could peek through it. He did and was relieved to get just a glimpse of her head. She appeared to be looking down. It occurred to him that, had she been seated and looking straight ahead, she might have noticed him passing by the cracks. As it happened, however, he'd managed to get to the corner at the front of the outhouse on the same side as the hinges on the door. When she opened the door, he would be behind it.

It was difficult to be patient, but he could do nothing but wait. Evidently, she was making a major visit to the facility, for she was taking her time. *Come on, woman, push*, he thought, *before somebody starts looking for you.*

Finally, he heard sounds of cleanup and he braced himself to strike, for he expected her to be strong, no less than a man. She pushed the door open and took one step beyond it when he struck. He kicked one of her feet into the other, tripping her. When she reached out to break her fall, he sprang on her, pulling his bandana gag over her head and into her mouth, drawing it up so tight she couldn't scream loud enough to be heard. Landing on the ground, he pulled a hard knot in the bandana and pulled her hands behind her back and clamped them together with his cuffs. In spite of her fierce struggling against him, he jerked her to her feet, turned her roughly around to face him, then picked her up and over his shoulder.

Realizing who had attacked her, she wiggled and struggled as hard as she could. But it was to no avail with her hands behind her back and her legs held tightly together in his arms as he carried her through the trees to the horses. He took her to the sorrel mare and lifted her up into the saddle. When she tried to kick her foot up to jump off, he grabbed it and tied one end of his rope around it, threw the coil of rope under the horse's belly, and hurried around to grab her other foot. When he had both feet tied securely together, he threw the rope back over her thighs and under the horse again until he was satisfied she was not going to be able to jump off the horse. He climbed aboard Buster and led the mare out of the trees. He could hear her attempts to scream around the gag he had fashioned, so he asked Buster for a lively lope to put some distance between them and the Trask family. He was afraid she might chew his bandana in two and let out a scream heard all the way to the barn.

# CHAPTER 8

O nce it was clear to Ada that she was helpless to resist her arrest, she reverted back to the same sullen-faced woman of few words and deadpan expression. Flint felt sorry enough for her to stop when they were halfway to Tinhorn, and he removed his bandana from her mouth. As he was pulling it out, she managed to spit on it, but she said nothing.

"I was gonna have to wash it anyway, since it had been in your mouth," he told her and stuck it into his saddlebag. As he had hoped, they were back to Tinhorn before supper-time.

And they did not go unnoticed as he led Ada down the main street. Clara Rakestraw happened to come out of the dining room just as he and Ada were passing. He told her they would need two suppers for the prisoners that night. Clara stared wide-eyed at the woman bound to the horse and didn't reply but nodded her understanding. Her reaction was much the same for most of the other folks who stopped to stare, most of them wondering what could possibly happen next at the jail.

Flint rode around to the back of the jail. A large sheet of canvas hung over the back wall of the one cell in use, taking Ralph off display for the gawkers. Flint dismounted, stepped up onto the floor of the cell room, opened the office door, and found Buck sitting at his desk.

"Hey," Buck greeted him. "I thought you'd be gettin' back about supper time. What did you find out?"

"I need a hand out back," Flint replied, instead of answering the question.

Buck got up and followed him out the door. "Well, I'll be damned!" That was all he could say, and he looked openmouthed at Flint for an explanation. Finally, he said, "You musta found nobody home but her."

"No, her pappy and brothers were there, but I didn't much wanna tell them she was under arrest, so I kidnapped her," Flint said.

"Well, I sure wanna hear the whole story on that." Still unable to believe it, Buck walked all the way around the sorrel mare, looking at the ropes holding the sullen woman in the saddle.

"She didn't much wanna come with me," Flint explained, "so I had to make sure she didn't jump outta the saddle and hurt herself."

Buck nodded, then shook his head in disbelief.

"I saw Clara Rakestraw when we came into town, and I told her we'd need two suppers for our prisoners," Flint informed him.

"Let's get her down off that horse," Buck said. "We've got a little problem, though. We ain't got but one cell. If I'da known ahead of time, I coulda had that room behind Harper's ready for one of 'em. But for tonight, at least, they're gonna have to share our one cell." He turned to cast an eye at Ada. "Of course, you've got yourself to blame for that, ain't you, Dynamite? I don't know if Ralph will object to you invadin' his space, but the two of you will just have to respect the other one's privacy for tonight, anyway."

Flint started untying the ropes holding Ada in the

saddle, and when he untied the last one, Buck reached up, took her by the shoulders and lifted her off the horse. "Hope you don't mind goin' in the back way, Dynamite. Flint, gimme the key to these handcuffs."

Flint gave him his key and said, "If you'll take care of her, I'll go on down to the stable and put these horses away. Then I'll be right back, so you can go to supper first and I'll stay with the prisoners."

"No, why don't you just go on to supper after you take your horses," Buck said. "I'll go eat when you come back, and you can bring their suppers back with you."

"Whatever you say." Flint headed back outside for the horses.

He knew Buck liked to retire to his quarters right after supper and was surprised when he didn't take the suggestion to eat first. Maybe the big lawman was trying to push his drinking back to a little later in the evening. Flint knew Buck had been thoroughly shaken by his inability to function properly on the night of the explosion and suspected he blamed his drunkenness for Roy Hawkins' death.

After he dropped the horses off at Lon Blake's, he walked to Clara's Kitchen for supper. "Why, howdy, Deputy Moran," Bonnie Jones called out cheerfully when he walked in the door. "Clara said you'd been out hunting, and it looked like you caught a woman."

Flint didn't respond with a comment, only smiling in reply.

It wasn't enough to discourage Bonnie. "Clara said it looked like that crazy woman that tried to throw Jed Tubbs a gun at his trial."

"That's right. Ada Tubbs."

"The same woman who dynamited the jailhouse," Bonnie continued, fishing for details of the arrest.

"That's a fact," Flint responded. "Reckon I could get a

little supper? And I'm gonna need to take two plates with me for the prisoners."

"All right," Bonnie conceded. "I reckon you want coffee."

He said he did and sat down at one of the small tables while she went to fetch it.

When she came back with the coffee, she resumed her interrogation. "Nolan Carson said you don't have but one cell you can lock up till he builds the wall back, and you've got that one fellow in there. Where you gonna put that woman?"

"Buck's reserved a room for her in the hotel," Flint answered, weary of her questions.

"You don't mean it!" Bonnie exclaimed and stopped Mindy on her way to deliver supper to another guest. "That woman he had tied up on the horse is gonna be stayin' in the hotel." Seeing the look of disbelief on Mindy's face, Bonnie hesitated, then looked accusingly at Flint. "Kiss my foot. She is not!"

Flint merely shrugged.

"I oughta make you go to the kitchen and get your own plate."

"The dinin' room would come out on the short end of that deal," Flint replied.

She turned on her heel and went to get his supper. He was aware of the awkward problem their single-cell jail might cause with some of the more genteel citizens of the town. For the time being, he couldn't see any alternative. After his short history with Ada Tubbs, he was not overly concerned for her sensitivity. He would wager the situation would be the more awkward for Ralph. Maybe Nolan Carson could come up with another piece of canvas to hang in the middle of the cell. That might help the situation for the present.

\* \* \*

The concern for Ada Tubbs was of a different nature some ten-plus miles north of Tinhorn. It began a little before suppertime when Liam Trask went back to the kitchen and found no evidence of supper on the stove.

"Ada!" He called out several times but received no reply. He went to the back of the house to see if she was in her room but found that she was not. Irritated more than alarmed, he continued to call her name as he went through the whole house, looking for her. It was suppertime and no sign of supper being prepared. "Damn it, girl!" he swore as he tried to think where she could be. She wasn't in the barn because he just came from there.

Then it occurred to him—the outhouse. He went out the back door and walked toward the outhouse, calling out, "Ada, are you in there?" Still no answer. "Are you all right? Answer me," he demanded. When there was still no answer, he stepped up and opened the outhouse door. Completely confused, he looked at his eldest son, Vike, who had come from the barn to see why his father was yelling. "Ada's gone!"

"Whaddaya mean, she's gone?" Vike asked. "Gone where?"

"That's just it," his father replied. "She's just gone. I don't know where the hell she is. She ain't in the house nowhere, and there ain't nothin' on the stove cookin'." Still standing in front of the outhouse, he motioned toward it. "And she ain't in the outhouse."

Vike was not concerned yet. "She don't always use the outhouse."

"Yeah, but she sure as hell coulda heard me yellin' for her."

"Look at that." Vike pointed toward some scuffmarks on the path in front of the outhouse. "Reckon what made them marks like that?" He dropped down on one knee to take a closer look. His eye was attracted to some trampled weeds beside the path and he moved over to get a look at them.

In a second, his father was down on his knees beside him.

"Look yonder, there's more back that way," Vike said, pointing toward the stream. He rose to his feet and looked in that direction. It didn't take a close inspection to determine something had left a definite trail back toward the stream.

"I swear, you think a bear or somethin' grabbed Ada when she came outta the outhouse?" Liam asked, half serious.

"No, it weren't no bear. Look here." Vike pointed to a footprint in the soft sand near the stream. "Somebody snatched her!" He hurried to follow the direction the footprint was pointed in and soon exclaimed, "Here! They had horses tied right here! Somebody rode in here and waited till they could snatch her when she came outta the outhouse."

"Who the hell would wanna snatch Ada?" Liam demanded.

"Ain't but one I can think of. Big Buck Jackson, sheriff of Tinhorn."

"What about Buck Jackson?" Kyle Trask walked up to join them. "What's goin' on? What are you two doin' out here? I went in the kitchen and there ain't no sign of supper, or Ada, neither."

"That's because she's been took," Liam answered him, "right out from under our noses. And you're right, Vike, it was Buck Jackson that took her."

"He sure as hell didn't do much of a job of coverin' his trail," Vike commented. "Kyle coulda followed this trail."

"I can track good as you," Kyle declared, "maybe better."

"He weren't tryin' to hide his trail," their father said, having given it more thought. "He was out to arrest Ada for her part in bustin' her husband outta jail. And he knew damn well, if he came ridin' in here to try to arrest her, he woulda got shot for his trouble. He sneaked in here like an egg-suckin' dog and snatched her up when she went to the outhouse. I shoulda known better 'n let Ada stay here. Jackson ain't got no right to arrest anybody outside Tinhorn, but I shoulda knowed he'd try to arrest her, anyway."

Vike was still standing over the hoofprints left by the horses Flint had tied there. Vike shook his head, finding it hard to accept. "And he done it while all three of us was right there in the barn. It couldn'ta been that long ago. What are we standin' around here for? Maybe we can catch him before he gets her back to town."

"I doubt it," Liam said. "Sneakin' in here like he did, I expect he knew he was gonna have to wear his horses out to keep from gettin' caught. But one of you go get a horse and see if you can pick up his tracks after he rode outta here, so we'll know for sure he went to Tinhorn. I'm pretty dang sure it was the sheriff, but I might be wrong. And if it was somebody else, we need to know which way to go to find him."

"I'll go, Pa," Kyle quickly volunteered. "I won't take time to throw a saddle on, in case I do catch up with him. Ada mighta been able to slow him down some way."

Vike hadn't thought of that possibility. "I'll go with you, in case you're right."

Even though they didn't take the time to saddle their horses, it was still five minutes or more before they galloped out of the barnyard. Liam didn't think they had much chance of catching up with the kidnapper. He went back to the kitchen to put on a pot of coffee and see if he could find something to eat.

He was right in his assumption. When his sons rode out of the barnyard, Flint and Ada were already halfway back to town.

And when they returned to report what they had found, it was the same time that Flint stopped to tell Clara Rakestraw to fix two prisoner suppers that night.

"We found his trail back to the Tyler road, all right," Vike reported when they walked into the kitchen. "But we couldn't say for sure if the tracks turned north or south."

"Yeah"—Kyle nodded in agreement—"he rode straight into the road, like he didn't want nobody to know which way he headed."

"And there was so many tracks goin' both ways, you couldn't tell for sure which ones mighta been his," Vike continued. "You reckon he coulda took her to Tyler, instead of Tinhorn, so he could put her on trial right away?"

Liam paused to consider that possibility. He hadn't thought of that, but he decided that, if he was right, and it was Buck Jackson who had taken his daughter, he'd take her to Tinhorn. "I was thinkin' we'd best take a little ride into Tinhorn tonight, but I changed my mind. We're already too late to do much of anything tonight. We'll do better to go there tomorrow, so we can see where they've got Ada locked up. Then we'll figure out what we can do to get her outta there."

"Since that's settled, let's see about fixin' somethin' to eat," Kyle said. "There's a pot of beans cooked. We need to stick some more wood in the stove. I reckon you could do that, Vike, while I slice off some bacon to go with 'em. 'Course, that is, if you ain't too busy."

"Just go ahead and put the bacon on to fry," Vike replied. "The stove was hot enough to cook beans, weren't it?"

"I swear, if you ain't the laziest son of a gun," Kyle said. "Pa, tell him to put some more wood in the stove."

"I ain't too lazy to kick your butt for you," Vike responded.

"You two save your cat-fightin' for some other time," Liam scolded. "It hurts my ears when I'm thinkin' about my poor little Ada gal locked up somewhere. I shouldn't have ever let her hook up with that damn Jed Tubbs. I shoulda knowed he weren't nothin' but trash." He shook his head sadly. "But she was so derned afraid she weren't never gonna get married. I let her go to them square dances in Tyler till she finally caught Jed just right."

"Just drunk enough, you mean," Vike said with a chuckle. "Trouble with Ada is she's just too plain and bony. A man likes a little cushion once in a while."

"Shame on you, Vike. Talking about your sister like that," his father scolded a little more.

"I don't mean no disrespect to Ada, Pa," Vike replied. "I'm just callin' a spade a spade."

Flint finished his supper and took two more plates back to the jail with him for Ada and Ralph. Stepping into the cell room, he found it unnecessary to suggest his idea of a sheet of canvas to divide the cell, for Buck had evidently had the same idea. Nolan Carson was in the cell installing some hooks down the center of the ceiling. Buck sat outside the cell keeping an eye on the prisoners.

"Sorry, Nolan," Flint joked, "I didn't bring but two plates. I didn't know you were here."

Nolan assured him that he was going to get some supper just as soon as he finished hanging the canvas.

Buck unlocked the cell door and Flint stepped inside. "I'll set this tray down on the stool there. You and Ralph be careful when you take your plate, so you don't tilt the tray," he said to Ada, then returned to the cell room.

As Buck relocked the cell door, Flint said, "Maybe we can get Nolan to nail a couple of legs onto the end of that bench that got broken up the other night. On the way back here I thought about doing that"—he nodded toward the carpenter screwing hooks in the ceiling—"but I see you thought of it first."

"I didn't think of it," Buck admitted. "Nolan got hold of another sheet of canvas and came by to see if we wanted it. I think it's gonna be a big help." He pointed to the doorway leading to the office, indicating conversation should continue farther away from the prisoners and the carpenter.

Flint nodded and they moved away.

"The prisoners gonna be all right with it?" he asked quietly. "Or are you gonna move one of 'em to that room behind Harper's?"

"I don't think I'm gonna move either one of 'em over to Harper's," Buck answered. "At least not until there's trouble over this arrangement. Ada didn't even blink when I put her in that cell with Ralph." He chortled. "Ralph looked like he was gonna faint, though. I told 'em it was up to them whether or not they shared that cell. And I told 'em, if they didn't get along, I was gonna have to put one of 'em in a room with no windows a-tall. Ada said she didn't have a problem sharing the cell with Ralph, and Ralph said whatever she wanted was fine with him. So we're gonna try it for a while and see how it works out."

"You wanna go on up and get some supper now?" Flint asked.

"Nolan's gonna be finished with that canvas in a few minutes," Buck answered. "I'm gonna wait for him and then he and I'll go up to Clara's. It's a while before she's supposed to close. There won't be anything you need to do for the prisoners. I got Ada her own water bucket and slop bucket, just the same as if she was in a separate cell. She ain't never mumbled a thing ever since she got here. She'll answer your question, usually with a yes or no, but not much more. That woman spooks me a little bit. You know, you ain't told me yet exactly how you managed to steal her right out from under their noses."

"I caught her comin' out of the outhouse," Flint said and went on to give him the detailed story of the kidnapping.

"I swear," Buck marveled. "You know, you're lucky you're still alive. I don't know anything about her pappy and her two brothers, never had any dealin's with 'em a-tall. But if they're anything like Ada, you'da never got outta there alive." He raised one eyebrow to give Flint an accusing look. "You wasn't listenin' too close to what I was tellin' you about takin' no chances, were you? And you brought her back on a horse of her own. I reckon you stole that from her pa, too."

"No, I didn't steal one of their horses," Flint said.

"So when you left here, you took an extra horse with you, even though you were just supposed to scout around to get a look at the place. Is that right?"

"Well, yeah, that was the plan," Flint admitted. "But when I went to get Buster, Lon Blake asked me if I was goin' far. I told him about ten miles and back. So he said he had a sorrel mare that needed the exercise real bad, and he'd appreciate it if I took her along for the ride. It was a little extra trouble, but Lon treats us pretty well, so I figured I'd do him the favor."

Buck continued to prod him. "I'm surprised he went to the trouble to put a saddle on the horse, if he was just exercisin' her."

"I was too, but I figured he must know what he wanted, and I don't claim to be an expert on horses."

"You best not claim to be a good liar, neither, 'cause you're one of the worst ones I've ever run into." Buck gave him a big chuckle.

"Hell," Flint said, "I just wanted to be ready for anything, in case I got lucky. And it turns out I did." He was saved from more razzing when Nolan finished hanging his canvas privacy curtain and told Buck it was time to go eat supper.

Buck unlocked the cell and relocked it after Nolan had stepped out. Flint took a good look at the new partition from the outside of the cell. There was nothing to keep either party from looking or walking around the canvas, if they were inclined to. But, somehow, it served as a wall, and he felt sure it would serve its purpose with little or no problem.

He might have been surprised to know Ada wasn't the first woman criminal to be locked up with male prisoners. But she might be the first to have a privacy curtain hung for her.

# CHAPTER 9

Flint was a little more than concerned for Buck's obvious attempt to change his evening habits, so he was especially anxious to see how he was holding up after delaying his usual hour of retirement. He heard him when he came back from supper, but instead of coming straight to the office, he stopped in his living quarters first. Flint was not surprised. He could well imagine how badly Buck needed a drink. When he came back into the office, Flint guessed that he had taken a couple.

"Everything all right?" Buck asked as he walked in the door.

"So far, everything's fine," Flint answered. "As far as I can tell, there hasn't been any contact between the two of 'em, or if there has, they've been mighty quiet about it."

"I don't see any reason why they don't get along all right," Buck said, his voice steady and calm. The quick stop at his quarters seemed to have given him confidence. "I reckon you might as well go on home for the night."

"I was wonderin' if you might want me to bunk here in the office tonight, since it is the first night of the new arrangement."

"No, ain't no need for that, with me sleepin' right on the other side of the wall from 'em," Buck insisted. "You go on to your room at the boardin' house and I'll see you back here in the mornin'."

"You're the boss. I'll take a walk around town first, since that's one of the things you hired me for." Flint laughed then japed, "I'll see what's goin' on at the saloon, in case they've heard about us havin' a woman in the cell with Ralph, and there's somebody tryin' to raise enough hell to get thrown in there with 'em."

Buck chuckled and suggested, "Tell Jake we're throwin' everybody we arrest in his place into that dark room back of Harper's."

"That ain't a bad idea," Flint said as he walked to the door. "That's what I'll tell him."

As he said he would, Flint took a walk up one side of the main street and back down the other, checking the locks on the doors of those businesses with no lights on. The town seemed as peaceful as it had been before it crossed paths with Jed Tubbs and Ralph Cox. He had to admit that he was the cause of Tinhorn's recent problems, and he couldn't help feeling some guilt because of it. The trouble began when he'd decided to arrest the two cattle thieves and he wondered if there might not have been any further trouble if he had just taken a couple of shots at them to scare them off. But he had wanted to put a stop to their rustling, minor as it was, and he had not wanted to kill two men over the theft of two cows. So he arrested them. *What is, is,* he told himself. *I can't go back and do it different.*

His last stop was Jake's Place, and it was quiet like the rest of the town. He paused momentarily to see who was there. Walt Doolin and Lon Blake were sitting at a table playing cards with Paul Roper and the postmaster, Louis Wheeler. Jake Rudolph was standing at the end of the bar, but a new face was behind the bar. Flint walked over to join them.

"Howdy, Flint," Jake greeted him. "Want you to meet my new bartender, Rudy Place. Rudy, this here's Deputy Flint Moran."

Flint shook hands with Rudy and Jake continued. "Rudy was pourin' whiskey in a saloon up in Tyler. I hired him 'cause his last name is Place, so he fits right in at Jake's Place. Trouble is, now when folks talk about Jake's Place, you won't know if they're talkin' about the saloon or the bartender." He punctuated his story with a full chuckle.

Rudy smiled, evidently having heard Jake's story more than once already. Rudy, a pleasant-looking middle-aged man, bald except for a ring of hair around the sides and back of his head, nodded at Flint. "Jake's already told me you have a special arrangement with him for your whiskey."

"No," Jake quickly corrected. "That arrangement is with Sheriff Buck Jackson. Flint's just another customer." He caught himself then. "I don't mean he's just another customer. I mean he don't have no special needs. And he ain't ever asked for any special deal." He looked at Flint, knowing he was in a corner and thinking he was about to lose some more money to the sheriff's department.

Flint laughed, then put him at ease. "I don't drink that much. Just a shot once in a while if I feel the urge for one. I'll just pay for mine like any other customer. Right about now, in fact. So why don't you pour me a shot."

"And we'll sure as hell make this one on the house," Jake said. With that settled, he was quick to change the subject. "How are you and Buck makin' out over there at your open-air jail? Nolan Carson said he's fixin' to build your wall back for you. Said he'd already hung some canvas so the folks can't look at the prisoners anymore."

Flint drank the whiskey Rudy had poured then said, "Yeah, that's about the size of it, right now. We had to do something to protect the prisoners from the town folk, instead of the other way around."

That brought a chuckle from Jake and Rudy.

"Hey Flint," Walt called out. "I got a complaint I wanna talk to you about."

"Thanks for the drink," Flint said to Jake then walked over to the table to hear Walt's complaint. "What do you wanna complain about, Walt?"

"Your shootin'. That last body I worked on, that Jed Tubbs. That bullet hole was dead center his forehead. You could draw a line straight up from the bridge of his nose and it would run right through the center of that bullet hole." It was obvious Walt just wanted to impress the others at the table with the accuracy of Flint's shooting.

Flint was not comfortable with that. He was not interested in making a name as a gunslinger.

Walt continued. "I would appreciate it if you'd just aim for the heart. A head wound like that is hard to cover up, so it ain't so obvious." He looked around at the others and grinned.

"Is somebody havin' a funeral service for Jed Tubbs?" Flint asked him. "If you dig a hole and throw him in it, nobody will see the hole in his forehead. But I'm sorry about that. I was aimin' at his foot. My gun shoots a little high sometimes."

"Hey, Flint, Hannah Green said you have a room at the boarding house, but we ain't ever seen you there. Are you still stayin' there?"

He recognized the man as Paul Roper, one of Hannah's tenants who worked for John Harper at the feed store. "Sometimes I wonder, myself. The way some things have been happenin' at the jail, it hasn't been easy to get on a regular schedule. But I've still got my room, and I'll be back there tonight."

"Mr. Harper had me cleanin' up that empty storeroom behind the store," Roper said. "He said, if you arrest any more folks, you're probably gonna put 'em in there."

"I'll tell the sheriff that it's ready for use, if we need it. Thanks," Flint said. "You'd best watch your cards real close 'cause it looks like you're playin' with some real sharks here."

"We told him to ask John Harper for a raise, so we could get a little more money in the game," Lon Blake japed. "We've got room for another hand, if you wanna sit in."

"I'm surprised you invited me to play," Flint replied. "You're a member of the town council, so you know I don't have any money to gamble with."

"I forgot about that," Lon said. "Never mind, then."

They all laughed as Flint went out the door.

He paused in front of the sheriff's office and wondered if he should go in. Buck thought he was gone for the night and Flint would not want to catch him in an embarrassing state. Buck's drinking problem was common knowledge among the leaders of the town, but Flint was not certain of the severity of it. Thinking about it, he wasn't sure he wanted to find out. But ever since the cell room explosion, he felt sure Buck was trying to do something about his drinking problem.

Still undecided if he should check in with the sheriff once more, Flint stepped up to the office door and looked through the two glass panes. A light was on and Buck was still there. Sitting at his desk, his chin resting on his chest, he appeared to be asleep. Flint slowly turned the doorknob and found the door locked. He paused to think it over. Good, he decided, he's right there in the office and the door's locked. It should be all right At least better than Buck being unconscious in his quarters.

He turned around, stepped back down into the street,

and took a slow walk down to Hannah Green's boarding house. Lights were on in the parlor, so he walked around to the back steps. As he walked up the steps to the porch and turned to go to his room, he heard someone behind him call. "Flint?"

He turned to discover Hannah coming from the washroom. She was in her robe and carrying a chamber pot. "I wasn't sure that was you. We've seen so little of you."

"Yes, ma'am, that's a fact. We've been pretty busy with all the trouble we've had with explosions and jail breaks. I'm sure hopin' things will settle down, so I can take a meal at your table for a change." He nodded toward the chamber pot in her hands and asked, "Is everything all right?"

She glanced down as if she forgot what she was holding. "Oh, Mr. Arthur is having an upset stomach and I was on my way out back to empty this for him."

"You want me to do that for you?" he asked, thinking it the polite thing to do and greatly relieved when she said no.

"Gracious, no," she exclaimed. "This isn't the first time I've had to help him out. You're coming home too late for supper again. Are you hungry?"

"Ah, no, ma'am," he said, still looking at the chamber pot. "I'm needin' a good cleanin' up, though. So, if there ain't anybody usin' the washroom, I'd like to."

"Nobody's in there now. I'll build that fire up in the stove and you can heat some hot water, all right?"

"Yes, ma'am, that would be nice."

She went to empty the chamber pot then and he went into his room at the end of the back porch. A short time later, she knocked on his door to let him know his bathwater was hot, then left him to his privacy while he gave himself a good scrubbing and changed into his spare underwear and socks. Then he washed the underwear he had just removed, dumped his bathwater, and went back to his room. He crawled into bed feeling content that Tinhorn was going to enjoy a peaceful night.

After a good night's sleep, Flint was the first to arrive at Hannah's breakfast table when Myrna pulled the first pan of biscuits out of the oven. He had almost finished his breakfast when the other guests came in to eat, and soon excused himself to go to work. He was eager to see what kind of night Buck had had, or he might have been inclined to linger a while over breakfast, since Hannah seemed to want him to become one of the family. Being honest with himself, he didn't care to know any of them too well, thinking of the chamber pot Hannah was carrying last night.

At the office, the door was unlocked and Buck was at his desk, drinking coffee. Walking inside, Flint wondered if he'd been there all night.

"Well, good mornin'," Buck sang out. "I was startin' to think you were takin' the day off."

"I ate breakfast at Hannah's this mornin'. Did you stay here in the office all night?"

"Hell, no," Buck replied. "I went to bed a little while after you left. I told you, there weren't no use to set up with those two all night. I ain't heard a peep outta them this mornin' either. They're both stayin' on their side of the curtain, and I don't think they're even talkin' to each other."

"I saw Paul Roper in the saloon last night. He said John Harper already had him cleaning up that storeroom behind his store. So if the two of 'em can't get along, he's gonna have the room ready for us."

Buck nodded as if considering that possibility.

"You want me to go up to Clara's to get their breakfasts?"

Flint asked. "You don't usually go to Jake's till a little later in the mornin'."

Buck hesitated a few moments before answering. "No," he finally said. "I think I'll have breakfast at Clara's this mornin', and I'll bring their breakfasts back."

Flint thought he detected a hint of serious determination in his tone.

"You can tell 'em it'll be just a little later than usual." Buck got up from the desk at once, plopped his hat on his head, and went out the door.

Out of curiosity, Flint stood near the door and listened. He heard Buck go into his private quarters and come back out within a couple of minutes' time. *Just enough time for another shot of determination,* he thought. He felt compassion for the man's problem and could only guess how hard it was for the task Buck seemed determined to do. *I'll help any way I think I can,* he thought as he walked to the cell room door.

Although Buck had told Flint there had been no conversation between Ada and Ralph, that was not entirely the case. He had been right in thinking Ralph not likely to communicate, though, for it was Ada who broke the silence.

"Were you there when my husband was shot?" she had asked very quietly, and Ralph had said that he was.

"How did it happen?" she'd wanted to know.

"The doctor and his nurse was in here to treat our bullet wounds," Ralph had explained. "They was ready to bandage Jed's wound up when he made his move." He had gone on to relate the incident with Doc's wife, and her aggressive move that caused Jed's death.

"So, it was Moran who killed Jed?" she had asked. "The man who jumped in between me and Jed at the trial when I tried to throw him a gun?"

Ralph had responded with a quiet, "Yes."

"So that's why they made him a deputy sheriff," she had said.

That conversation with Ralph was still on her mind when the door to the office opened and the man who had killed her husband walked through.

"You two gettin' along all right?" Flint asked as he walked around to the end wall, so he could see both of them. "The sheriff just went up to the dinin' room at the hotel to eat breakfast. He'll bring your breakfast back with him."

"Won't be a minute too soon to suit me," Ralph said in reply.

Ada got up from her cot and walked toward him but stopped when she reached the end of the canvas curtain, leaving her close to five feet short of the cell wall. "You are the one who killed my husband." She said it accusingly but spoke softly while showing no emotion.

Her tone was so ordinary he wasn't sure how to answer her accusation, if that's what it was but responded to her statement as he did to most statements. He answered truthfully. "That's a fact, ma'am, but he didn't really give me a choice, since he was fixin' to cut an innocent woman's throat. I was the only one with a chance to save her. I could tell you I am sorry I shot your husband, but that wouldn't be true. I was just the unfortunate one who had the only chance to save the lady's life . . . and maybe that of the sheriff and myself. I could say I'm sorry that I was the one in that position, but I'm glad my aim was true, and I stopped him."

She continued to meet his gaze as she paused to think about his response to her accusation. She could not really accuse the man of blatant cruelty or murder for his actions. He admitted that he had reacted just as Ralph had related, so she shifted her accusation to her own person. "If killing my husband wasn't enough, you had to sneak in like a hungry dog, and attack me in my father's house."

"Would you have come peacefully, if I had knocked on the door and said you were under arrest?" Flint asked.

She didn't answer the question.

"I didn't think so either. Besides, I didn't attack you in your father's house. I attacked you outside your father's *outhouse*."

She seemed lost for a moment.

So he said, "I was a little bit sorry I had to capture you that way, but I couldn't take a chance on you alertin' everybody."

She gave up on the aggressive assault on his authority, and asked simply, "What are you gonna do with me?"

"I'm sure Sheriff Jackson musta told you. We're gonna hold you for trial, same as Ralph."

"In that saloon?"

"I expect so," Flint answered, "unless the captain sends some Rangers to take you to Tyler for trial."

"Ain't killin' my husband enough punishment for anything I've done?"

Perplexed by the simple logic generated in her mind, Flint couldn't believe the woman's childishness. "Ada, don't you know dynamitin' the jail is against the law?"

She didn't answer at once, and when she finally did, she said, "It ain't as bad as killin' somebody."

"I suppose you're right," Flint said, totally aware now of the level of intelligence he was trying to reason with. "Killin' is about the worst crime, like what your husband did when he beat an old man to death with an iron bar. You'll be punished for what you did, and that was dynamitin' the jail and causing the escape of your husband and Ralph. Your breakfast oughta be here before long." With that, he did an about-face and went back to the office, feeling as if he had been trying to reason with a coyote.

Diagonally across the street, three riders pulled up to the hitching rail in front of the saloon. When they dismounted, Liam Trask looped his reins over the rail, then turned to look up and down the street as if he were scouting the town.

"Yonder's the jail," Vike said, pointing across the street.

All three turned to stare at it and the big man walking toward it carrying what appeared to be a food tray.

"We'll go inside and get a drink of likker," Trask said. "See if we can't find out if anybody's seen Ada. Maybe get us somethin' to eat, too, if they've got a cook."

That was enough for Vike and Kyle to lose interest in the jail, even though they had discussed the likelihood it was the sheriff who kidnapped Ada.

Since they didn't know much about Tinhorn, Trask declared, "If you wanna know anythin' about what's goin' on in a town, the saloon's where you go to find out." Whenever they made trips into town, it was Tyler they went to.

"Howdy, boys," Rudy sang out. "Whatcha gonna have?"

"Give us a shot of whiskey," Trask answered. "What's that you're pourin'?" He pointed to a bottle Rudy had just poured a drink from."

"That's pure corn whiskey," Rudy told him.

"That'll do," Trask said.

Rudy poured three shots and the two young men tossed them back immediately.

Trask took a couple of sips before downing the rest of his. "Just hold your horses," he said when both boys pushed their empty glasses toward the bottle again. "Let's get some food in us before we drown in that likker bottle. You sell any food here?" he asked Rudy.

"Yes, sir," Rudy replied. "I think we do. I mean, I know we do, but I ain't sure about breakfast." When Trask gave him a suspicious look, Rudy quickly explained. "I'm new here. I just started yesterday, and I know Rena, the cook, fixes some dinner and supper, but I ain't sure about breakfast. Lemme let you talk to the owner." He threw up his hand and waved to Jake, who was sitting at a table in the back, drinking coffee with Lon Blake.

Jake came to the bar and introduced himself. "You boys are new in town, ain'tcha?"

Trask said that they were, and they wanted to know if they could get some breakfast there.

"Yes, sir, you sure can," Jake answered. "Rena will fix you up with a good breakfast. We only have one or two customers who come here for breakfast, so we don't try to push it. But Rena will cook you up some eggs and fried potatoes, with some ham or bacon. How's that sound?"

"Suit's me," Vike said.

"Me too," Kyle said.

"Set yourself down wherever you like," Jake said. "I'll tell Rena to bring you some coffee." While they selected a table, Jake went into the kitchen to tell the cook she had three customers for breakfast.

Rena looked at him and asked, "Where's Sheriff Jackson?"

"You know, I was wonderin' that, myself," Jake said. "It ain't like him to be this late. Maybe he'll show up directly. Anyway, all three of these boys want those eggs fried hard."

He went back to the table and told Trask, "Rena's already workin' on it." He stepped aside then to let her have room when she came up behind him carrying a tray with three cups of coffee. "You fellows are new in town, ain't you?" Jake asked again.

"Matter of fact," Trask answered. "We don't get down this way much. We do most of our tradin' in Tyler."

"You oughta give Tinhorn a lookin' over," Jake suggested. "This ain't the dead little town it used to be."

"I heard somebody tried to blow the jailhouse up," Trask said. "Any truth to that?"

"You heard about that, did ya?" Jake answered. "Well, they sure did. Used enough dynamite to blow the whole back wall off the jail."

Vike reached over and gave Kyle a playful punch when he heard that. Trask fixed a fierce frown on Vike.

Jake went on. "The real funny part about it was that it was a woman who blew it up. She was married to one of the men in jail, so she was tryin' to spring her husband."

"A woman?" Trask played along while warning his sons with a deep frown.

"Yep," Jake answered. "This ol' gal was crazy as hell. Like I said, she was married to one of 'em. They had a trial for them two fellows, right here in this saloon. And she tried to throw a gun to her husband then. They let her go home after that, but she came back and dynamited the jail. The deputy sheriff caught the two fellers again. I'm tellin' you that woman is plum crazy. She's settin' in the jailhouse right now."

None of the three could pretend to be indifferent after Jake said that.

After a moment while he tried to be calm, Trask asked, "She's in jail right now?"

"Yep. They locked her up in the same cell with her husband's partner," Jake replied, obviously enjoying the telling of the tale. "After she dynamited the place, the sheriff only had one cell that didn't get blown apart, so they're both in it."

"What about her husband?" Trask asked. "Is he in the cell with 'em?"

"He's dead."

"Dead!" Trask exclaimed, surprised.

"Yeah," Jake said. "When the doctor was in there patching up a bullet hole in his shoulder, her husband made a move to escape and the deputy plugged him right between the eyes."

All three of the strangers reacted in shocked silence upon hearing that.

After a long moment, Trask finally spoke. "So after they shot her husband, they stuck Ada in the same cell with his partner?"

"That's right, 'cause they ain't got but one cell they can lock up," Jake answered, then paused when it occurred to him. "How did you know her name is Ada?"

"She's my daughter," Trask answered, "and these two boys is her brothers."

His simple statement was enough to render Jake speechless for a long awkward moment. When finally able to regain his voice, he was quick to apologize. "Damn, mister, I'm awful sorry. I wouldn'ta gone on like that if I'd known you were family."

"It ain't your fault," Trask said. "At least, we know where she is now. Somebody came onto my property and snatched her when she came outta the outhouse last night. We didn't have no idea what happened to her. Now, come to find out, it was the sheriff that snatched her. He ain't got no right to arrest anybody if they ain't in this town."

Jake didn't know what to say about that, so he started off on another track. "I reckon you'll be goin' over to the jail to visit your daughter, now that you know where she is." He was saved at that moment when Rena arrived with three plates of food. Seeing an opportunity to get a little bit of his foot out of his mouth, he said, "On account of this sad occasion for your family, I won't charge you anything for your breakfast."

Trask hesitated from getting up from the table when Vike remarked, "We might as well eat our breakfast, since she already cooked it."

"Yeah, Pa," Kyle added, "we need to eat, and there ain't no charge."

"I reckon you're right," Trask said. "We do need to eat." He looked at Jake and nodded. "Much obliged."

"You're welcome," Jake returned. "I'll leave you in peace to eat your breakfast now. Rena will check on your coffee." He returned to his table in the back of the saloon and sat down again. He looked at Lon Blake, who was looking back at him and slowly shaking his head. "Did you hear all that?" Jake asked. "That's her father and brothers."

"I heard it," Lon answered. "Most of it, anyway. You reckon they're likely to cause trouble? Maybe they'll just wanna visit her in the jail."

A big grin suddenly bloomed on Jake's face. "Did you hear him say Flint snatched his daughter outta the out-house?"

They both tried to keep from laughing.

# CHAPTER 10

"Good," Lon Blake said when he walked in the door at the sheriff's office. "I'm glad you're both here. I wanted to let you know you might have some trouble comin' your way. I just came from Jake's Place and Ada's pa and her two brothers are settin' over there right now, eatin' breakfast." As he suspected, the news was enough to capture the attention of both sheriff and deputy. So, he went on to tell them what conversation he had heard between Trask and Jake. "No," he answered when Buck asked if they had made any threats of any kind. "They didn't know for sure that you had Ada locked up 'cause they looked pretty surprised when Jake told 'em. But they didn't throw no fit or nothin'. They even sat there and ate their breakfast."

"'Preciate you lettin' us know," Buck said. He looked at Flint. "I reckon we'd both best hang around here for a while, since jailbreaks seem to run in that family."

Lon jumped. A loud thud suddenly came from behind the jail.

"That's just Nolan Carson unloadin' some lumber for the wall back there," Buck assured him. "I'll be damn glad when he gets it built, too."

Flint walked over to the door and looked across the

street to get a look at the three horses tied at the rail. He wanted to be able to recognize them, just in case they showed up somewhere later where they weren't expected.

"Well, I just wanted to let you know they were in town," Lon said. "I guess I'd better get back to the stable now." He hurried past Flint, who was still standing in the doorway.

"'Preciate it, Lon," Flint told him as he went by him.

Although in a hurry to leave the jail, Lon couldn't resist one question of Flint. "Ada's pa said you snatched her right outta the outhouse. Is that right?"

Flint shook his head. "I snatched her on her way back from the outhouse. It wouldn't have been polite to snatch her out of the outhouse." He closed the door after Lon left then went back to talk the situation over with Buck.

Ada and Ralph were just finishing up their breakfasts, and Nolan Carson was ready to start on the reconstruction of the wall.

"Should we tell Nolan to hold off for a while till we see if there's any trouble from Trask?" Flint asked. "Nolan might not like the idea of gettin' caught in the middle of something."

"I reckon we can tell him what's goin' on, and he can make his choice," Buck said. "Trask and his sons ain't broke any laws in Tinhorn, so we ain't got any reason to bother 'em. It might be that they'll decide to visit Ada, and there ain't no law against that." He couldn't resist japing Flint. "'Course, they might be in town to make a complaint against you for kidnapping."

They decided it best to at least let Nolan know of the possibility of some form of trouble, if Trask and his two sons came to the jail to visit Ada. Nolan thought it over for a few minutes, then said that maybe, if he stayed, it might let them think the numbers were equal and discourage any notions of attempting to spring Ada.

"That's up to you," Buck told him. "I'm just sayin' we ain't got no idea what's on her pa's mind. Accordin' to what Lon said, they didn't even know for sure that Ada was here in jail. If I had to take a guess, I'd say they won't try anything this mornin', since they ain't had time to plan anything. If they're thinkin' about bustin' her out, it'll more likely be at night. And if they do, I hope they ain't gonna try it with dynamite again."

"Amen to that," Flint responded.

Nolan continued the work he had just started that morning, and began nailing his corner posts together. Flint collected the breakfast dishes from the cell to return to Clara's Kitchen whenever he or Buck felt it wise to go to dinner then stood by the front door, watching Jake's Place through the glass panes.

It wasn't long before Flint said, "Okay, they're leavin' the saloon now. They're not climbing into the saddle. They're leadin' their horses over here." He remained there until he saw them tie their horses in front of the sheriff's office and start for the door. Then he moved over to the front corner of the office where he would be behind anyone standing in front of the desk talking to Buck.

Trask opened the door and walked in cautiously as if entering an enemy camp. He glanced at Flint standing in the corner, then back at Buck sitting behind the desk. Vike and Kyle filed in, as wary as their father, nervously looking from Flint to Buck. Flint speculated that any little spark would set them off like the dynamite their sister had planted.

Trask stopped a few steps short of Buck's desk and asked, "Sheriff?"

"That's right," Buck said. "I'm Sheriff Jackson. What can I do for you?"

"You're holdin' my daughter in the jail," was all Trask said in answer.

"Well, that's a fact, if your daughter is Ada Tubbs," Buck told him. "She's being held on a charge of dynamitin' this jail and creatin' the jailbreak of two prisoners. That's against the law, so she was arrested for it."

"I come to take her home," Trask said. "'Cause you snuck into my home and kidnapped her. You broke the law. You ain't got no right to do that outside this town."

"That's not entirely true," Buck came back with a ready answer. "Every town sheriff or marshal is lawfully permitted to form a posse to go after people who have committed crimes in their town. Don't matter where they are. So, I'm afraid your daughter will have to answer for her crimes."

"There weren't no posse that came to my home," Trask objected. "It was one man that snuck in and grabbed my daughter and ran off with her."

"I'm sorry, but I have to disagree with you, Mr. Trask. It was a posse that came across your daughter and arrested her. It was just a one-man posse, but it was a posse."

Trask started to sputter a little at that, especially when the sheriff called him by name. He didn't think the sheriff knew his name. Buck got up out of his chair then, well aware of the intimidating factor of his big powerful body, especially in close quarters like those in the small office. His shoulders seemed as wide as the desk. Flint was impressed as well.

"Is there something else I can help you with, Mr. Trask?" Buck asked.

"Can I see my daughter?"

"Why, sure you can," Buck said at once. "You and your sons, too. It oughta make your daughter happy to know you came to visit her. You can go right through that door there." He pointed toward the cell room. "'Course, you'll have to take those guns off and leave them here in the office until you're ready to go."

There was a moment of hesitation on the part of all three of the Trask men.

"That's just standard procedure in any jail," Buck said. "The deputy and I will go in to watch you while you're visitin' with Ada. Nothin' against you. Just standard procedure."

After a long pause, Trask finally started unbuckling his gun belt. "I reckon it'll be all right, boys," he said to his sons, who were equally nervous about giving up their weapons. "Just standard procedure," he repeated.

Once they were disarmed, Buck led them through the cell room door, announcing, "Ada Tubbs, you've got some visitors."

Like everyone else entering the cell room for the first time since the explosion, Trask and his sons were stopped in their tracks upon seeing the tremendous opening where a wall once stood.

Amused by their reaction, Buck said, "That's a sample of your daughter's handiwork."

In shocked surprise, Ada, still sitting on her cot, got to her feet, having before ignored Buck's announcement that she had visitors. She hurried to meet them, stopping once again at the edge of the dividing canvas. "Papa, what are you doin' here?"

"We come to see you," Trask answered. "You give us a terrible fright when you disappeared. It took us a little while to figure out what happened, but we finally found you." At that moment, Ralph walked out to stop even with the end of the curtain as well.

Trask recoiled and demanded, "Sheriff, what's he doin' in the cell with my daughter?"

"Ask her," Buck answered. "She's the one who used

the dynamite on the back window and left us with only one cell."

"It ain't fittin' to put a woman in a cell with a man," Trask charged, genuinely upset. Even though Jake Rudolph told him in the saloon that both prisoners were in the same cell, it had evidently not really registered in his brain. Seeing them in such close quarters had a much stronger impression. "Somethin' oughta be done about this," he complained.

"Something is being done about it," Buck said and pointed to Nolan out back. "Just as soon as we get that wall built, we'll have two cells again. Until then, we've done the best we can to give your daughter some privacy."

Ada left the edge of the curtain then and walked all the way over to the cell wall where her father and brothers were standing. "There ain't nothin' to worry about, Papa," she said, trying to calm him down. "That's Ralph Cox on the other side of the curtain. He was Jed's partner and he ain't had nothin' but respect for me. Matter of fact, it's almost like I'm in a cell by myself."

Trask calmed down a little then.

"Besides, I can handle myself when it comes to men."

"You be extra careful. He might be nice right now, but most men start to lose their good manners when they're locked up close with a woman as pretty as you are," Trask said, obviously not seeing her through the eyes of other men.

"How you makin' out, Ada?" Kyle asked, no longer able to keep silent.

"Are you makin' out?" Vike asked with a chuckle before she could answer.

"Watch your mouth!" Trask scolded. "Show some respect for your sister." Starting to become riled up again, he mumbled, "That damn over-sized sheriff rides right into my yard and steals my daughter."

"It weren't the sheriff, Pa," Ada whispered. "It was that deputy, Flint Moran, that come and took me. It was him that killed Jed, too. He was the one that ran Jed and Ralph down when I busted 'em out of here."

Standing closer to the back edge of the old cell room floor, Flint had a feeling that his name had been mentioned when Trask suddenly turned and glared at him for several long seconds.

When he turned back to his daughter, Trask whispered low, "I ain't gonna stand for this. I'll get you outta here, if I have to use some more dynamite to do it. You just do the best you can till I do. It might be best to wait a couple of days to let 'em get to thinkin' I ain't gonna do nothin'. We'll take care of that deputy while we're at it. Come into my yard and steal my daughter. That'll be his last mistake."

Buck gave them another twenty minutes, then announced, "All right, visitin' time is over. If you come on back to the office, you can have your guns back."

"Don't you worry, honey," Trask whispered to his daughter. "I'll take care of you."

"We miss you, Ada," Kyle said in leaving. "Can't none of us cook worth a damn."

Flint brought up the rear and followed them out of the cell room. He was aware of Liam Trask's accusing stare at him as he buckled on his gun belt. Then both Flint and Buck stood by with a watchful eye until the Trasks had filed out the door, got on their horses, and rode toward the north end of town.

"Well, that was downright homey, weren't it?" Buck said. "A family reunion right here in the jail. I think they're gonna plan another one and they ain't gonna invite us. What do you think?"

"I think the three of 'em are crazy as hell—make that the four of 'em—and they're gonna try to bust her out of here. I'm thinkin' I might better bring a couple of blankets from my room and bunk here at night. I think it's best for both of us to be here. I'm gettin' damn tired of these people breakin' outta jail. If Ralph goes with 'em, it'll be the second time for him."

"I'm afraid you're right," Buck remarked. "Maybe we'd better move Ada to that storeroom behind Harper's. It's a helluva place to shut somebody up in, but if they find out she ain't here no more, maybe they'll give up."

"If they make a raid on the jail and she's not here, not only do they fail to free her, but they'll give us reason to go after them and clean 'em out for good," Flint suggested.

"We ain't got a jail big enough to hold 'em," Buck reminded him.

"I forgot about that," Flint admitted. "I reckon we're gonna have to work with the U.S. Marshal Service, or the Texas Rangers."

"We shoulda been in touch with them before this," Buck said. "I think I'll at least let 'em know what we're dealin' with, so if they wanna give us some help, they would know what is goin' on." He shook his head as if perplexed and frowned. "Why the hell didn't you just let Jed and Ralph have those two cows? I swear, I need a drink of whiskey."

Flint realized it was the first time he had heard Buck make that statement. He hoped it was further proof that Buck was making an effort to gain control of his dependence upon alcohol. The big man was doing a commendable job of hiding the agony he was evidently suffering. Flint was sure the constant hammering underway by Nolan Carson was not helping Buck's condition.

"Looks like Trask and his boys rode on outta town,"

Flint said, "so I guess we don't have to worry about 'em for a little while. I think I'll take the breakfast dishes back to Clara's and then I'll get my horse outta the stable, just in case I need him in a hurry."

Buck thought that was a good idea, so Flint took the tray of dirty dishes and headed for the dining room. Once they were returned, he went back down the street to the stable.

Seeing him, Lon Blake went out to meet him. "I didn't hear no gunshots, so I reckon that fellow Trask and his boys didn't cause no trouble."

"Nope," Flint replied as he went to the corral gate. "They just visited Ada for a little while, then rode outta town."

Seeing Flint, the buckskin gelding ambled over to the gate to greet him. Flint slipped his bridle on the horse, then opened the gate and led him out.

"You reckon they'll be back to break that woman outta jail?" Lon asked.

"Hard to say," Flint answered as he threw his saddle on Buster, "but I expect we'll deal with it, if that's what happens."

Back at the sheriff's office, he found the door locked and no sign of Buck when he looked through the glass. His first thought was that the sheriff might have gone to his quarters to get that drink he had sworn he needed earlier. Instead of unlocking the door and going inside, he went around to the back where Nolan was working and asked, "Did the sheriff say where he was goin'?"

"Yeah," Nolan answered. "He said to tell you he's gone to the telegraph office."

That was good news. Anywhere other than his quarters for any reason, meant Buck was still putting up a fight against the bottle. "How's the construction comin' along?" Flint asked Nolan, just to pass the time of day.

"Well," Nolan answered, "like I told Buck, there's gonna be some delay on account of the sidin'. I'll finish the stud wall today, but I can't get the heavy sidin' to close it up, for maybe a week is what they told me."

"You can't get regular sidin' at the lumber mill?" Flint asked, finding it hard to believe.

"Well, yeah," Nolan replied, "regular sidin', like you'd put on your house, but the sidin' that went on the jail was heavy, almost twice as heavy as regular sidin'."

Flint nodded, thinking he had a pretty good idea why Buck went to the telegraph office. He had mentioned the possibility of advising the Special Ranger Company's office in Tyler of the situation in Tinhorn. Stepping up onto the cell room floor, Flint walked past the prisoners, and went into the office. He unlocked the front door then sat down to wait for Buck to return.

It wasn't long before the sheriff walked in the door. "Did Nolan tell you about the sidin'?"

Flint said that he did, so Buck continued. "I wired the Rangers office in Tyler and told 'em about our problem with the jail, and I asked if they could send a couple of men down here to transport our prisoners back to Tyler. I waited around a while, and they came right back to me. They said all their Rangers are out after a gang of cattle rustlers over near Fort Worth and said if we transport them to Tyler, they'd take 'em into custody and hold 'em for trial." He shook his head and bit his lip. "I wanted them to get that woman outta my jail. The two of us could transport her and Ralph to Tyler. It ain't but a one-day trip, but we can't both be gone from here."

"I expect I could take 'em to Tyler," Flint suggested. "And I expect I'd better do it right away, so I can be back here by the time Trask and his boys decide to make another visit."

"I don't know, Flint, those two might be hard to handle

for one man. Maybe we oughta just send Ada up there and leave Ralph where he is."

"I'm just thinkin' how much easier it would be, if the cell was empty," Flint said. "We'd take those canvas curtains down, so anybody could see that it was empty and there wouldn't be any reason for anybody to try to blow it up again." He could see that Buck was thinking it over, so he added, "I could even bed down in there to take care of anybody snoopin' around at night."

"You know, we still have the option of lockin' Ralph up in that storeroom behind Harper's. Then you wouldn't have anybody but Ada to transport," Buck suggested. "We can bring him back here after Trask finds out Ada's gone."

"That sounds like a good plan to me," Flint said. "But we'd better get Ada ready to go. It's almost dinner time already and it's twenty-six miles to Tyler. I don't wanna get there too late to turn her over to the Rangers."

"Tomorrow mornin'," Buck decided. "I'm willin' to bet Trask ain't gonna show up here tonight. I'll tell John Harper we're gonna get that room ready with a cot, some water, and a slop bucket today. You pick up the horses in the mornin', and we'll get Ada ready to ride. Start you off with plenty of time to get to Tyler. They'll want some papers with my signature, listin' the charges against her, and I'll write them this afternoon. You still up for the job?"

"Oh, yeah," Flint answered casually. "Ada and I have traveled together before, and I'm sure this ride will be just as pleasurable as our first trip."

"I reckon I don't have to tell you to be careful. You know she'll be lookin' for the first opportunity to make an escape."

Flint agreed. "Matter of fact."

# CHAPTER 11

Flint ate dinner and supper at Hannah's house, but he took a couple of blankets with him when he went back to the jail, in preference to using the blankets at the jail. He took the mangled mattress that had been on a cot when Ada dynamited the jail and made his bed outside the back cell. He figured if the Trasks did happen to show up, he'd be there to welcome them.

It was as Buck had figured, however, and no one showed up behind the jail that night. Flint was at Clara's Kitchen as soon as it opened, had his breakfast, and went back with breakfasts for the prisoners. While they were eating, he went to the stable to pick up the horses.

After the prisoners had finished their breakfasts, Flint told Ada to use the slop bucket because it was going to be a while before she would get the opportunity again. She asked why, and he told her, "Because you're goin' for a little ride this mornin'."

Automatically assuming this was not going to be a good thing, her first thought was that she was going to a hanging—hers. "Where am I goin'?" she asked in her usual stoic manner.

"I'm takin' you to Tyler. They've got better facilities for

women there. You'll be more comfortable while you're waiting for your trial."

"You're worried about Papa and my brothers, ain't you? You can take me off to Tyler or someplace else, but you still better worry about yourself. Papa knows it was you that sneaked onto our property to get me. You were too scared to ride in and face him, weren't you, Deputy Moran?"

"Scared half to death," Flint answered sarcastically. "Get yourself ready to go."

Standing nearby, waiting to give Flint a hand, Buck laughed, then said to Ralph, "You're goin' for a trip, too, Cox, just not as far."

That was enough to make Ralph nervous. Already concerned when Flint was telling Ada to get herself ready to leave, he had thoughts about a hanging as well. And maybe when Buck said the trip was not as far, he was referring to the nearest tree.

Flint opened the cell door and motioned for Ada to come forward.

She did not respond, still deciding whether or not she was going to fight.

"Come on. You might as well make it easy on yourself 'cause you're goin' one way or another."

She moved out the door then, watching him carefully. When he reached down to lock the cell again, she suddenly took a swing at him with a closed fist.

With catlike reflexes, he caught her arm by the wrist, twisted it around behind her, grabbed her other arm, and clamped her wrists together in his handcuffs. "I was hoping you'd learned something the last time I took you for a ride, but I see you haven't. Let me explain this trip we're gonna take.

"I'll make it as easy on you as I can. It'll be up to you

how hard it'll be, but I'll give you an idea. You took a swing at me, so your hands are gonna stay in those bracelets the whole trip. When I let you get off your horse, for whatever reason, I'll keep a rope on you, so you don't go wanderin' off. If you somehow get off the rope and try to run, I'll warn you to stop. If you don't stop, I'll shoot you down. I may, or may not, bring your body back for burial. It'll probably depend on how mad you make me. You understand?"

She didn't reply, but the searing look of hatred in her eyes told him that she was calling him the vilest of creatures under her breath.

"Good," he said, "Now let's get goin'." He handed the cell door key to Buck and escorted Ada out to the horses.

As they walked past the damaged cell, Flint reached over, took a wide-brimmed Montana Peak hat from a nail sticking half out of the wall, and pulled it down squarely on her head. "Here. This'll give you some protection for your fair skin. I never wear one, myself. You oughta like this one, though. It belonged to your late husband. When you dynamited the jail, it landed on that nail. Been there ever since. Nobody bothered to take it. I reckon it knew you might be comin' this way."

When they got to the horses, he said, "Put your foot in the stirrup and I'll help you up. This is the same horse you rode into Tinhorn." Remembering how roughly she had been thrown in the saddle before, she did as he said, and he boosted her up. With a short piece of rope, he tied one end around her ankle, walked around the horse, and pulled the other end of the rope under the horse's belly, and tied it to her other foot. "I won't tie you down to the saddle, like I did the last time we took a ride. I just tied your feet on the horse, so make sure you grip with your knees pretty strong. If you slide off sideways, that rope around your ankles will hold you on the horse, but you'll probably be upside down. Your head and shoulders will get beat to death by the horse's back hooves. So, it's best you keep your feet in the stirrups."

She made no reply, but her expression told him she would kill him if she was given the opportunity.

He climbed up into the saddle. "Well, Sheriff, I expect to see you back here. Maybe not in time for supper, though."

"Be careful," Buck replied. "That ain't no different than haulin' a rattlesnake."

"It's a fine day for a ride. Even for a rattlesnake. I'm hopin' she'll relax and enjoy it." Flint winked at Buck and wheeled the buckskin around to head for the street, turned north, and headed for what he hoped would be an uneventful ride to Tyler.

Once he was on the Tyler road, he started Buster out at a comfortable walk, planning to alternate the gait with a trot. Buster trotted about twice as fast as he walked, and by alternating the trotting with the walking, the horse could rest while he was walking and still keep moving. They would get to Tyler a lot quicker than if he just walked the horses all the way. He wasn't sure about the sorrel mare that Ada rode, but it was a routine Buster could maintain all day.

Ada might find the trotting part a lot less comfortable than the walking, but she was not likely to complain, since she was reluctant to speak to him at all. They reached the little stream where Ada had turned her wagon off the road after dynamiting the jail in a little less than two hours. Since they were now past the turnoff that would take them to the Trask farm, Flint was no longer concerned about a chance meeting with the Trasks on their way to town.

A little farther past the place where she had left the road, he came to the notch that cut through the long ridge where Jed and Ralph had waited so long to ambush him. He heard the first sound out of her.

"Deputy," she yelled at him.

He turned halfway around in the saddle to see what she wanted.

"I gotta pee," she said.

*Here we go,* he thought, surprised that it had taken this long. "You can hold it a little longer, can't you?"

"I gotta pee now. I've been tryin' to hold it, and I can't hold it no longer."

"All right. We'll stop in that bunch of trees up ahead on the left. You can go in those bushes near the spring." He guided Buster over where the trees were the thickest and dismounted, then took his coil of rope off his saddle and walked back to untie her feet.

After he helped her down, she stood waiting for him to unlock her handcuffs. "I can't pee without my hands."

"I know that," he replied. "I'm gonna unlock 'em, but I told you back in town that if you had to go off where I can't see you, I'm gonna tie a rope around you."

"I can't go, if you're lookin' at me."

"I ain't gonna be lookin' at you. This coil of rope is about twenty-five feet long. That's plenty of length to hide you down in those thick bushes yonder. Now, hold still." He looped one end of the rope around her waist and tied it with an extra hard double knot behind her back. "Now, I'm gonna hold this end of the rope just like this." He wrapped it a couple of times around his wrist to demonstrate. "When you get to the end of the rope, you'd better keep it pulled tight so you can't go any farther without pullin' me with you. You understand?"

She said she did.

"'Cause, if I feel that rope go slack, I'm comin' after you."

Again, she said she understood, so he unlocked the handcuffs on one hand. He looped his end of the rope around his arm and said, "I better not feel any slack after this rope gets tight."

She immediately headed into the thickest of the bushes.

Moving as fast as she could manage, she kept going until the rope became taut, almost pulling her over backward. With no time to lose, she turned her body in the rope around her waist, so she had the knots in front of her. *Damn him!* she thought as she worked feverishly to untie the first knot, leaning back to keep the rope taut. The first knot free, she was almost ready to panic before she untied the second one. *She was free!* She gave one more tug on the rope, dropped it on the ground, and turned to run, only to collide with him standing there. The collision knocked her to the ground. She laid there for several seconds, totally confused as he stood over her.

"Did you pee?" Flint asked.

"Go to hell," she replied, furious to think he had tricked her.

"I'm beginning to think I can't trust you," he said, as he rolled her over and locked her wrists back together, then picked her up onto her feet.

Taking her by the arm, he walked her back to the horses where he settled her in the saddle again and tied her feet together. Then he tied her horse's reins to a tree limb while he untied his end of the rope from around a little tree and wound it up in a coil. Furious, she stared at the tree as he untied the rope, and she realized how he had tricked her. Suspecting an attempt to escape, he had quickly tied his end of the rope around that tree as soon as she disappeared into the bushes, then he had circled around the bushes to be in front of her when she turned to run.

He climbed back onto his horse and led her back out to the road. Glancing back a couple of times to see how she was doing, he could only see the broad brim of the hat she wore, since her head was bowed, still in a furious rage. He heard nothing more from her all the way to Tyler, some two and a half hours after her attempted escape.

Going by the directions Buck gave him, he rode down the main street until he reached the post office. Taking a side street that ran past the post office, he came to a large two-story building that held a sign saying it was the office of Company F, Texas Rangers. Behind the building was another building, this one of stone—where Buck had been told to take prisoners.

Flint pulled the horses up to a hitching rail and took some papers out of his saddlebag. Then he took a seemingly subdued Ada down from the mare. Holding her by the arm, he walked her into the building and up to a counter.

"I'm Deputy Flint Moran from Tinhorn. I've got a prisoner to turn over to you," he said to the man behind the counter. "Sheriff Buck Jackson talked to a fellow named Ron Black yesterday about her, and Black said to bring her here." It was about fifteen minutes past noon. He hoped Black hadn't gone to dinner.

"Right, Deputy. Wait right here and I'll get Corporal Black." He went into a room behind the counter and called, "Ron, I got a prisoner out here for you."

The man came back to the counter with Black right behind him.

Black saw Ada and knew who she was. "This'll be Ada Tubbs, right?"

Flint said that she was.

"Dynamite Tubbs, Sheriff Jackson called her. He said he'd send some paperwork with her to list all the charges against her."

Flint handed him the papers. Black quickly scanned them, then took another look at the seemingly restrained woman. Tall and thin, plain as a mud fence, her wide-brimmed hat sitting squarely on her head.

"Sister," he addressed her, "you've been a busy little woman, haven't you?" He turned his attention back to Flint. "All right, Deputy, we'll sign her in to the women's section, and I'll give this list of charges to the court. They'll schedule her court date for trial. They'll be in touch with Sheriff Jackson." He turned to speak to Ada again. "The deputy got you here in time for you to get a little dinner."

When Flint remained standing there, Black asked, "Is there something else you need?"

"I'd like to have my handcuffs back," Flint said. "All right if I take 'em off her?"

Black laughed at that and told him to take them.

Flint pulled out his key and unlocked the cuffs from Ada's wrists.

As he was removing them, Ada threatened softly, "I ain't gonna forget you, Moran. They can't hold me in here forever."

"Why, I'll always remember you, too, Ada. It's been right interestin' knowin' you. I hope you enjoy your stay here." He remained at the counter to watch Ron Black lead her through the door to the office behind the counter. "Much obliged," he said to the man behind the counter and turned to leave.

It was a real feeling of relief to be done with Ada Tubbs, but Tinhorn's trouble was not finished until her father and brothers knew she was no longer there.

* * *

It had taken only a few minutes to turn Ada over to the Rangers, so he thought there was a chance to get back to Tinhorn before Clara quit serving supper. He had to water and rest the horses before he started back, but he planned to make the twenty-six miles without another stop. His concern was for Buck's condition after supper, knowing the battle he would be fighting by that time of night. He had no idea what they could expect from Liam Trask, but Flint knew he needed to be there when it happened.

Without asking too much of the horses, he made it back to Tinhorn just as it was beginning to get dark. Coming in from the north, the hotel and Clara's Kitchen were two of the first establishments he came to. Since the lights were still on at Clara's, he stopped there first.

"Howdy, Flint," Clara greeted him when he opened the door. Since he took a quick look to see how many customers were still eating, she said, "If you're looking for the sheriff, he just left here about fifteen minutes ago."

"To tell you the truth, I was just stickin' my head in to see how much time I had before you closed off the supper. I haven't had anything since breakfast, and I could sure use something."

She looked at the clock. "We normally start dumping everything and start cleanup in about twenty minutes. But if you don't get back by then, I'll fix you a plate and keep it in the oven for you."

"That would be mighty nice of you. I'll be back as quick as I can." He jumped back on Buster and asked for one last lope down to the stable, noticing the light was on in the sheriff's office when he rode past. At the stable, he told

Lon why he was in a hurry, and Lon took the horses and told him he'd take care of them.

"Give 'em both a portion of oats," Flint called back on his way out. "They earned 'em."

The next stop was the jail, but at least it was on the way to the dining room. Inside he found Buck sitting at his desk.

"I was wonderin' when you were gonna show up," Buck greeted him. "Have any trouble?"

"Nope. Ada was turned over to the Rangers, so we don't have her to worry about anymore. Everything all right here?"

"Yep, nothin' goin' on here a-tall. I transferred Ralph to Harper's Feed and Supply. He ain't too happy with his new accommodations. I reckon he was real worried a while ago 'cause I went to Clara's to eat supper, and I swear, I forgot all about his supper till Bonnie asked me if I wanted two plates to take back with me."

"I stopped by Clara's on my way here, and she said she'd hold a plate for me, if I could get back pretty quick, so I'm gonna get up there right away. Then I'll come right back here. Is that all right with you?"

"Yeah," Buck replied. "Go get you something to eat. Take your time. If there was gonna be any trouble here tonight, I expect it would come a lot later when they think we'd be asleep. So, go on and get you some supper, then you can tell me how things really went on that trip to Tyler."

Flint had to laugh. "What makes you think anything happened?"

"Hell," Buck snorted. "'Cause you were transportin' Dynamite Tubbs. And I know she weren't gonna go peaceful."

Flint hurried out the door and back to Clara's Kitchen. The closed sign was turned to the outside, and only one customer was still there finishing up when he walked into the dining room.

Mindy Moore saw him come in and she sang out, "Uh-oh, here he is. Too bad we threw it all out."

Flint Moran was still somewhat of a mystery to most of the citizens of Tinhorn, but the women at Clara's had learned that he could respond in kind to their teasing.

"Well, in that case, just bring the slop bucket and set it down here. And bring me a spoon with it."

She responded with a chuckle. "I'd like to see the look on your face, if I did. Do you want some coffee with your bucket of slops?"

"Yes, ma'am, please," he replied.

Clara walked over to the cash register to accept the last customer's money, then wished him a good evening and locked the door after he went out. "Mindy," she called out, "bring me a cup of coffee, too," then went over to the table Flint had chosen and sat down with him. "How was your day, Deputy Moran?" Like her young waitresses, she had some curiosity about him.

"Nothin' special, I guess," Flint answered. "Like every day, just tryin' to stay outta Sheriff Jackson's way."

"You said you didn't have anything since breakfast. Why didn't you have dinner?"

"Oh, well, I had to go to Tyler. Buck sent me up there to deliver some papers to the Rangers office. And I never found time to eat dinner, I reckon. I was tryin' to get back here to get supper. And it looks like I just made it. So thank you for that." It struck him that Clara was asking him a helluva lot of questions about his day, which he couldn't believe she was really interested in.

Her interrogation was interrupted when Mindy arrived with two cups of coffee. "Did you tell him anybody who gets this special service has to help clean up the kitchen and dining room?" she japed.

"She already told me if I finished everything in that slop

bucket, I don't have to do any of the cleanup, so hurry up and bring it in here."

Mindy giggled and returned to the kitchen, and Clara resumed her interrogation. "When the sheriff was in here for supper, he almost forgot the plates for your prisoners. When I asked him if he wanted them, he said just one."

"Is that a fact?" Flint replied.

"I asked him why he only needed one plate, and he said one of 'em didn't want any supper tonight. Is one of the prisoners sick or something?"

He was sure now that she was really probing for some inside information about Ada Tubbs. The whole town was curious about Ada Tubbs and the fact that she was locked in a cell with a male criminal. He guessed there wasn't much else for the town to gossip about. But he wasn't certain that it was wise for people in town to know where Ada now was, in case someone of her family might come asking.

"I don't know," he answered her question. "Like I said, I was out of town all day, and I haven't talked to Buck about anything." He shrugged his shoulders as if in the dark, just as she was.

"Here's your slop bucket," Mindy said as she placed a plate piled high with food before him. "Margaret said you better eat every bit of it, or you're washin' dishes." It was enough to put a halt to the questioning by Clara.

"I guess I'd better close up my register for the day," Clara remarked and got up from the table.

"Here, let me pay you for mine, so you can close out your books, or whatever you do," Flint said and reached in his pocket for the money. After her insistence that he should take his time, he tried to finish his supper in a timely fashion, so he could get out of their way.

Clara walked him to the door to let him out. He thanked

her again and she locked the door after him. As soon as she turned around, she was met by Mindy and Bonnie.

"What did you find out?" Mindy asked at once. "One of 'em is gone. I bet you it was that Ada monster."

"He wouldn't say," Clara told them. "I don't know why they want to keep it a secret, but I know they don't have but one prisoner now, and it's not Ada. Flint rode up to Tyler today, he admitted that. I know it was to take that woman there. He said he had to take some papers to the Rangers office. Why didn't he mail the papers? Because he delivered her with the papers, that's why. That other prisoner, that Ralph Cox, he's not the trouble the woman would be because she's got family that might try to break her outta the jail. Cox can just sit there till the judge gets down here again to try him."

Feeling smug and satisfied that they knew the latest news before anyone else in town, they went back to work, cleaning up the dining room.

# CHAPTER 12

Back at the jail, Flint found Buck still seated at his desk, apparently never having moved since Flint left to go to supper. With the one cell empty, Flint supposed there was really nothing for Buck to do but wait.

"You think I oughta go back there and take those two canvas curtains down, so anybody lookin' in can see there's nobody in the cell?" Flint wondered.

"You know, that probably wouldn't be a bad idea," Buck said. "I'll help you." He got up from his chair and they went out to the cell room. "Brrr," he shivered. "It's startin' to get a little chilly at night. Nolan better hurry up and get that wall finished." He nodded toward the stove sitting outside the two cells. "Won't do much good to build a fire in that with that wall out." In the winter, it was the heat for the whole cell room.

With Buck at one end and Flint at the other, they took down the canvas that divided the one cell into two. When they met in the middle, they folded the canvas.

Starting on the other canvas, Buck said, "We'll take it down for now, so anybody lookin' in can see it's empty. If Nolan doesn't shake a leg, I reckon we'll have to put it back up for Ralph. Now you can tell me how many times that witch tried to escape on the way to Tyler."

"Only once." Flint went on to tell him about the episode with the rope and the tree. "I don't know," he said in conclusion. "I think it just kinda took the starch out of her. I know she didn't pee all the way to Tyler, and neither did I."

"If we're lucky, we won't have any trouble with Trask and his sons when they find out Ada's gone from here," Buck speculated.

"I've still got a couple of my blankets here, so I'll make a bed back there by the office door. They'd have a hard time seein' me that far back. If they take a notion they wanna cause some damage after they see the cell is empty, I might be able to change their minds. I reckon you can just go to bed in your room."

"No," Buck answered at once. "You'll be out here in the cell room. I'll sleep in the office, in case they come right at the front door. When you're ready, I'll turn the lamp out in the office. I figure they ain't likely to come if there's a light on."

"That sounds as good a plan as any," Flint said. "You in the front and me in the back."

"Whaddaya think, Pa?" Vike Trask asked. "You figure they don't think we're comin' back, since we didn't show up last night?"

"I don't know what they think," Trask answered, "but we're goin' back. I promised my little girl I'd take care of her. I'm just tryin' to figure out how to get her outta there. It ain't like it was when she put that dynamite in the window and blew the wall out. That wall was wood and Jed and his partner was in that cell. The cell Ada's in now is iron bars all around. Even if we could get enough dynamite to tear that wall out, it would most likely kill Ada."

"What if we could fix it so Ada can get herself out?" Kyle wondered.

When his father asked him what he was talking about, he explained. "If they ain't got the wall boarded up yet, one of us could crawl through them studs, slip up to the cell and pass a gun to Ada through the bars. She could moan and groan and make out like she was sick or dyin', and get the sheriff or that deputy, whoever's guardin' her, to come in the cell to see what's wrong with her. Bang, she puts a hole in his head, and we'll be out back of the jail with the horses."

Trask and Vike looked at each other, impressed.

"How'd you ever think of a good plan like that?" Vike asked. He looked at his pa again. "Whaddaya think, Pa?"

"Sounds like a good idea to me. I can't think of no better way to get her outta there."

"You think Ada will be able to shoot whichever one it is that comes in the cell?" Kyle asked.

"Hell, yes," Vike declared immediately. "She weren't squirrelly about blowin' up the whole damn jail."

"All right, then," Trask decided. "It won't be tonight, though. "Tomorrow, we've gotta pack up everythin' we need and move that herd of horses down to Nacogdoches. That's liable to take all day. And we've gotta move everything outta here 'cause there's liable to be a posse here the day after we break Ada out. We can't get caught here. As soon as we get the horses to that camp, we'll go from there, straight to Tinhorn and break Ada outta that jail tomorrow night."

"Are we gonna give up our place here?" Kyle asked. "This house, the barn, the pasture? That ain't much more 'n a shack down in Nacogdoches. What if somebody else has found that shack and took it over?"

"Then I reckon it'll just be their bad luck. Just like that

old man and his wife who used to live here. It's the strong that survive on this earth, and it's the weak they survive on." Trask gave his son a solemn look. "I think that's wrote in the Bible somewhere. Besides, it's the only way we're gonna save your sister from hangin', or whatever they plan on doin' with her. We'll see, maybe after they can't find us for a while, things will die down and they'll give up lookin' for us. Might be we could come back here to this place.

"If that don't work out, we'll just find us a better place— way the hell away from Tinhorn. As long as we keep the family together, that's the important thing. We'll get everythin' packed up and ready to go today, so we can get an early start in the mornin'."

"It's gonna take all day, just to drive them horses down there," Vike complained. "And that's if we keep 'em movin' as fast as we can. We can't go no faster than the horses we're ridin' and the packhorses we'll be leadin'. I don't see how we're gonna be able to get there, then turn around and ride back up to Tinhorn, and it still be dark. Hell, Pa, we'd be lucky to get back to Tinhorn by dinnertime the next day."

Trask listened to his son's argument and had to admit he made sense. "I reckon maybe you're right," he said after thinking over the plan he had proposed. "I s'pose I'm just too anxious to get your sister outta that jail to think straight."

"Why don't we just go ahead and break her outta that jail tonight?" Kyle asked. "Leave the herd of horses here. After we get her out, we could just go on down to Nacogdoches instead of comin' back here. When they come lookin' for her, they'll come here. When they don't find us, they'll just have to decide where to look next—most likely up toward Tyler. They ain't likely to wanna mess with that little herd of horses. In a couple of days, we can come get the horses."

Trask and Vike exchanged glances again.

"I swear, Kyle," Vike commented, "you keep comin' up with these ideas. I never figured you to be the brains of this outfit. I reckon it's fair, though, since I'm the handsome one." He turned back to look at his father again. "Whaddaya think, Pa? You wanna go get Ada tonight, and take a chance on losin' them horses?"

"Kyle might be right," Trask said. "That the sheriff and that deputy might come lookin' for us here. And they ain't gonna wanna fool with no herd of horses. Even if they got up a posse, it'd likely be shopkeepers and such, and none of 'em would know the first thing about movin' a herd of horses."

He waved his fist in the air and proclaimed, "Boys, we're goin' after your sister tonight!"

The rest of the day was spent packing up everything they thought they would need at the camp in Nacogdoches. They ate one last supper of bacon, coffee, and biscuits that Trask made before packing up the flour. Then they saddled the horses and the mule Ada preferred.

"It matches her personality," Vike always commented.

Well past the hour of darkness they rode out of the barnyard, leading the packhorses and Ada's mule. A little over two hours brought the faint lights of Tinhorn into view. Not willing to risk meeting anyone leaving the saloon at that late hour, they headed toward the river that ran parallel to the main street at a distance of over one hundred yards.

They halted the horses close to the same spot Ada had left the horses for Jed and Ralph before blowing out the jail wall. Once the horses were taken care of, the three Trask men moved to the edge of the trees to look at the jail.

"Well, there ain't no lamps on." Vike stated the obvious. "The place is dark as hell."

"They didn't get no sidin' boards nailed on yet," Kyle noted. "Won't be no trouble squeezin' through them studs." He looked back at his father. "I expect you'd best watch the horses, Pa. Me or Vike can crawl in through the studs easier 'n you."

"Me and Kyle will both go," Vike said. "You got the gun we're gonna give Ada?"

His father handed the gun to him. "Now, don't forget to tell her what she's supposed to do. Tell her not to shoot him before he unlocks the cell."

"She knows that, Pa," Vike responded. "She ain't dumb."

"You tell her," Trask snapped. "Her bein' a woman, she might get too excited and won't be able to wait till the time's right."

"You ain't talkin' about Ada," Kyle said.

"You just be careful," Trask scolded. "Tell her where we'll be when she runs out the back of the jail."

Impatient, Vike said, "Come on, Kyle. Let's go." He jumped up and took off.

With Kyle right behind him, they crossed the one hundred yards of high grass and weeds that separated the river from the buildings, trying to be as stealthy as possible.

"What the—" Vike gasped when they reached the back of the cell room, for there were no curtains. They could see very little in the darkness of the cell room, but it appeared the cell was empty. "You reckon she moved back with the other prisoner?"

"If she did, we better not tell Pa about it," Kyle answered. "I'm crawlin' in to find her. You stay here in case somebody comes around the side of that buildin'." He turned sideways and easily slipped through the studs. Inside, he moved quickly to the cell wall, whispering, "Ada, Ada." Able to see a little better, he turned and whispered loud enough for Vike to hear him, "There ain't nobody in here."

"Nobody but you and me." The voice came from a dark corner just beyond the door to the office. "And we've got room for a couple more."

Kyle's reaction was instant. With a gun already in hand, he fired two rapid shots toward the corner where the voice had come from. Flint, also with his gun in hand, returned fire, one shot that struck Kyle in the chest. As soon as he pulled the trigger, Flint rolled out of the corner, knowing a shot would come from the other brother, aimed at his muzzle flash.

It came in less than a second. Lying on the floor, Flint fired at the figure outside the stud wall, catching him in the side as he turned to retreat. Vike staggered when the shot struck him but managed to stay on his feet. Not sure how badly he was hurt, he was determined not to fall, so he forced himself to run.

Immediately alarmed when he'd heard the gunshots, Trask had untied the horses. He saw Vike running drunkenly for his life, and climbed up on his horse and led Vike's horse to meet him. "Kyle?" he shouted as Vike forced himself up into his saddle.

"Kyle's dead!" Vike cried. "Run for it!"

Flint stopped to make sure Kyle was no longer a threat and decided he was dead. He jumped down from the cell room floor just as Buck came running around the corner of the building. "Buck! It's me!" he shouted.

The sheriff looked a little wobbly and he was holding his six-gun ready to shoot.

"At the river!" Flint shouted as he saw muzzle flashes when Trask fired back.

At that distance, and using his pistol, Trask's shots were wild.

Running ahead of Buck, Flint reached the river in time to see the man and his son cross over to the other side, leading packhorses behind them.

When Buck caught up to him, Flint said, "They left a mule and one packhorse behind. I reckon they didn't have time to get 'em all. The mule's got a saddle on him. That musta been for Ada. Probably the same one she hitched up to the wagon."

"I couldn't see but two of 'em," Buck said.

"The other one's layin' back there in the jail, dead," Flint told him. "He got all the way back to the cell and when I let him know I was there he took a couple shots at me. I didn't have much choice. I shot him. The other one threw a shot at me, but he missed. I got one in him, but it didn't stop him. He ran all the way over here."

"I'm sorry I didn't get here soon enough to help out," Buck said. "Tell you the truth, I got a little sleepy, settin' in the office. I didn't hear anything goin' on until the shootin' started."

"They weren't makin' any noise, so I don't see how you coulda heard 'em," Flint assured him. "That one fellow that got all the way back to the cell didn't make any noise at all till he was right on me almost. One thing for sure, though, they know Ada ain't in the jail anymore."

"Yep, that's what we were after," Buck said. "'Course, now we've gotta worry about whether Trask and his son are gonna be bound to settle with us for killin' one of 'em. I hope they're smart enough to know that, if they set foot in this town, they'll be arrested for this little shindig they put on tonight. It was an obvious attempt at another jail-break." He shook his head as if perplexed. "Whaddaya suppose they were tryin' to do? Slip Ada a gun?"

"That's what I figure."

"Well, might as well leave the body where it is, and

we'll get Walt Doolin to pick it up in the mornin'. That is, if you don't mind sleepin' with it for the rest of the night."

"No problem. As long as he doesn't start snorin'. Then, I might be inside with you." Flint walked back to the edge of the river where the mule and the packhorse had wandered. "I'll take these two back to the jail and tie 'em to the stud wall till mornin'. When Lon opens up, I'll take 'em on over to the stable."

He waited for a while to let them drink some water, then he led them back to the jail where Buck was looking at Kyle's body with the help of a lantern. "I'll bet he never knew what hit him. You got him dead center in his chest."

"I think that's the younger son, ain't it?" Flint took the packs off the horse and the saddle off the mule. "You see Ada again, you be sure and tell her I didn't make you stand here wearin' this saddle all night," he said to the mule under his breath. He started thinking about Liam Trask, and whether or not Tinhorn might see him again. *Helluva blow on a father*, he thought, *lose your daughter and one of your sons the way he did. Just all of a sudden, and he might lose the other son, depending on how serious that wound in his side is. Something like that could drive a man crazy.*

"You know, Buck, all this excitement has got me wide awake. I don't think I'll go back to bed tonight. It can't be too much longer before mornin', anyway."

"Not me," Buck declared. "I was sleepin' pretty good when this party started. If you're really gonna stay up, why don't you sit in the office? I'll go to my room and get a couple more hours' sleep."

"That'd be a lot better than sittin' back there against the wall," Flint said. "I'll take you up on that. Then, if you feel like an early one, we can go to Clara's in the mornin' for a big breakfast."

Buck said that appealed to him, so he retired to his quarters for the balance of the night, while Flint got one of his blankets from the cell room, just in case he got sleepy before dawn. He lit the lamp in the office and turned the wick down low, locked the front door, then made himself comfortable in Buck's big desk chair.

While he sat there, he began to think about the dramatic changes his ordinary life had taken in the short time he had agreed to be a deputy sheriff. It seemed like a lot longer than it had actually been. He hadn't even been back to see the family. *I wonder if this is what I want to do with my life? What the hell, I never was much of a farmer. This'll do till I find something I like better.*

After a while of random thinking, some important, some trivial, he decided, "This is a comfortable chair." He propped his feet up on the desk and leaned back. "No wonder ol' Buck got sleepy."

He glanced down then and noticed the cabinet door on the desk sitting ajar, so he reached down to close it, but it didn't close. It was hitting something. He opened the door wide and discovered an almost empty whiskey bottle. "I reckon you were sleepy." He thought of Buck seeming to wobble when he showed up around the back corner of the building and wished there was some way he could help him. But that was a personal battle a man had to face by himself.


One of the two men who had been in Flint's thoughts was trying to decide if a posse, or at the least, the sheriff and his deputy might be on his tail. Sick inside over the death of his youngest son, he was now concerned with giving some attention to Vike's wound. On top of that, his daughter was gone, who knew where? Finally, when it appeared that Vike was barely staying in the saddle, Trask had to stop. He pulled the horses over when he reached a stream that emptied into the river some thirty feet from the path, helped Vike off his horse, then tied all the horses on a rope he stretched between two trees. He took a blanket out of one of the packs and spread it for Vike to lie on while he took a look at the wound in his side.

After examining the bullet hole in Vike's side, he got a rag from the packs and soaked it in the stream, so he could clean some of the blood away. Noticing blood forming on the blanket under Vike, he rolled him over onto his side and discovered another hole.

Encouraged by what he saw, Trask told Vike, "You was lucky, son. That bullet went clear through and come out the other side. I ain't gonna have to dig no bullet outta ya. You're gonna be all right. You'll just have to give it a little time to heal. We get to Nacogdoches, there's a woman that does some doctorin'. We'll go see her, and she'll take care of it. I'll slap a bandage around your belly to keep you from losin' any more blood and you'll be fine."

After he bandaged the wound, and there was still no sign of pursuit, he decided no one had come after them. "You rest a little and then we'll ride the rest of the way to Nacogdoches. We'll have to stop and rest these horses about halfway, so we ain't likely to get there before tomorrow afternoon. You think you can make it?"

"I reckon I'll have to," Vike groaned.

# CHAPTER 13

Flint made a pot of coffee, just in case Buck showed up as early as he had said he would when he left the office in the middle of the night. Flint didn't expect it, since Buck had apparently worked on the whiskey bottle in his desk. But just as Flint pulled the pot off to the side of the hot little stove, the big lawman walked in the door.

"Good for you," he sang out. "I need a cup of that."

"I thought you might," Flint returned, but refrained from telling him why. "After last night, so did I." He poured a couple of cups and handed one of them to Buck. "I was thinkin' about Trask and his boy. Are you plannin' to see if we can cut their trail away from here?"

"No." Buck made a face when the hot coffee burned his tongue. "Damn! No, I ain't even thought about it. Shoot, he got outta town and he ain't likely to show his face in Tinhorn again. So, I think we're done with the Trask family, and well off for it. Matter of fact, I think we'll bring Ralph Cox back here to the jail today."

They replayed the scene that went on there the night before for a short while before Buck announced, "I'm ready to have my next cup of coffee with some pancakes at Clara's. How 'bout you? You ready?" Flint confirmed that he was, so Buck continued. "We can stop by the barbershop on the way up and tell Walt he's got a body to pick up."

They locked the front door and the cell room door and started toward Clara's.

Walt Doolin was just opening up when they walked in. "Mornin'," he said. "I was wonderin' if that was some business for me when I heard those gunshots in the middle of the night."

Naturally, he wanted to hear the cause of the shooting, so Buck told him what had happened and the name of the body he was to pick up. "Me and Flint are goin' to breakfast right now, and we've got a couple more things to do before we get back to the office. If you wanna get it before we get back, the office is locked, but you can walk through the studs in the back. That's where the body is."

Walt said he might do that, and Flint and Buck continued up to the top of the street to Clara's Kitchen.

When the two lawmen walked into Clara's, the eyes of the three women working the dining room immediately lit up, and Flint knew he and Buck were in for another interrogation.

"We heard the shooting down at the jail in the middle of the night," Clara started in without so much as a, "Good morning." She was joined by Mindy and Bonnie, and the three of them escorted Flint and Buck to Buck's favorite table.

Buck gave Flint a puzzled look. "I didn't hear any shootin' in the middle of the night. Did you hear any shootin'?"

"Nope, seemed kinda peaceful to me," Flint answered.

"Liar," Clara chided. "It was that Trask bunch, wasn't it? Tryin' to break Ada out of jail, but she wasn't there, was she? 'Cause Flint took her to Tyler yesterday. Lon Blake just left here. He said he counted five shots close, like in the jail. And some more shots that sounded farther away."

"Damn," Buck snorted, astonished. He looked at Flint as if asking if he was the source of her information.

Flint shrugged and shook his head. "Whaddaya askin' me for?"

Looking back at the women confronting him and Flint, Buck said, "Sounds to me like you already know what happened. Maybe you can fill us in on some of the details we overlooked."

"Just tell me I'm right," Clara said. "We still don't know if anybody got shot."

Knowing when he was licked, Buck gave in. He had no reason not to give her the information. It wasn't necessary to conceal anything after Flint transported Ada out of Tinhorn. "Yeah, it was Trask," he confirmed. "Two of 'em got shot, one of 'em dead, the other one wounded. That was the end of it. Trask and his wounded son got outta town. End of story. Now, I got a question. Can I get Margaret to fry me a stack of pancakes, or do I have to go to Jake's Place to get 'em?"

They were halfway through the pancakes when Flint suddenly uttered, "Damn."

Buck looked at him inquisitively.

Flint confessed, "I forgot about the horse and the mule I left tied behind the jail." He made as if he was about to go at once to get them.

Buck stopped him. "They ain't been there that long, and you gave 'em water at the river before you tied 'em back there. It ain't gonna hurt to let 'em wait a little bit longer till you finish your pancakes. I expect they'd want you to finish your breakfast 'cause you was thoughtful enough to unload 'em," he japed.

"I reckon you're right," Flint conceded. If anything, he had always felt a responsibility to take care of the animals that took care of him.

"I thought we'd go by Harper's when we leave here and let Ralph outta that room. If you're worried about the horse and the mule, you can go on back and take 'em to the stable. I'll go pick up Ralph. You can take his breakfast to the jail with you and he can eat it back in his cell."

Flint left the dining room while Buck was still teasing the girls about their nosiness. "Some things go on around this town that young women like yourselves don't need to know about."

"Like what?" Bonnie asked.

"See," Buck teased. "Just like that, right after I got through tellin' you that you don't need to know about 'em."

Bonnie gave him a playful slap on the shoulder, but Mindy made a request. "You'll probably tell me I'm too nosy again but tell us something about your deputy."

"Whaddaya wanna know about him?" Buck asked.

She shrugged. "I don't know. He just popped up all of a sudden. Nobody knew him, then he was suddenly your deputy and part of everything going on."

"Whaddaya talkin' about?" Buck responded. "A lot of people knew him and his family. Jim Moran and his family have been trading here in Tinhorn for quite some time."

"Oh, I know a few folks in town knew his name, but I mean nobody really knew him. Do you know what I mean?" She was having a hard time communicating her request.

"No, I reckon I don't," he confessed.

Grinning mischievously, Bonnie said, "Well, I do. Has he got a wife or a gal somewhere? Does he ever talk about any women? Is that about it, Mindy?"

"Kiss my grits, Bonnie," Mindy exclaimed. "I was asking no such a thing."

Buck had to chuckle. "I can't help you there, Mindy. Flint don't talk about them kinda things. But I can tell you this, hiring Flint Moran as my deputy was the best decision

I ever made, except maybe when I asked my wife to marry me. And it was the smartest decision the town of Tinhorn ever made."

"Well, don't make anything of it," Mindy said. "I was just curious, so don't tell him I asked about him."

"I won't," Buck said as he went out the door, and to himself, he thought, *I rather not have his mind cluttered up with thoughts about women.* As he had said he would, he went to Harper's Feed and Supply to pick up his prisoner.

"Howdy, Sheriff," John Harper greeted him when he walked in the front door. "You come to check on your prisoner? All I can tell you is he hasn't gotten out of that room. There ain't been a sound out of that storeroom since you brought him his supper and locked the door."

"Glad to hear it," Buck said. "I didn't want him to be disturbin' anybody. I'm gonna take him off your hands now."

"Gonna put him back in the jailhouse, huh?" Harper asked. "The word's pretty much all over town already about the shoot-out you and Flint had at the jail in the middle of the night. I saw Walt Doolin coming from there a little while ago totin' a body. One of that Trask fellow's sons is what I heard."

"That's a fact," Buck replied. "I reckon I'd best get my prisoner, so I can get him over to the jail before his breakfast gets cold."

"Paul's back there, if you need any help," Harper said.

"Much obliged, John," Buck said. "Usin' that room sure has helped us." He went on to the back of the store then, where he found Paul Roper tearing some crates apart with a crowbar. "Paul," Buck acknowledged.

"Howdy, Sheriff, come to check on your prisoner?"

"Come to take him outta there and put him back in the jail." Buck went directly to the storeroom door, inserted his key in the heavy padlock, and unlocked the door. He didn't expect any trouble from Ralph, but he knew it wise to always use precaution. He opened the door wide. The room was totally dark. The one candle provided for light had either gone out, or burned up, which was unlikely in such short a time. He stood for a minute or two, waiting for his eyes to adjust to the darkness inside the room. When his eyes dilated enough to make out forms in the total darkness, he didn't see Ralph anywhere.

"Ralph," he called out, but there was no answer. "What the—" he started, knowing Ralph hadn't broken out of the room. "Paul, bring me a lantern, will ya?" He was beginning to wonder if he had a second body for Walt to pick up today.

"Here ya go, Sheriff." Paul handed the lantern to Buck and stepped back right away, not sure what might be awaiting the sheriff.

Buck took the lantern and walked into the middle of the room. Ralph was not on the cot or the little bench with his supper tray. Holding the lantern out in front of him, Buck slowly turned in a circle. He stopped when the lamp light found a form sitting in a corner near the door. He was sitting next to the slop bucket, his legs pulled up tightly to his chest, with his arms wrapped around them, his eyes closed tightly.

"Ralph, what's the matter? I came to get you outta here."

Ralph's eyes opened, and he immediately squinted in response to the lantern light.

Impatient with the prisoner's weird behavior, Buck demanded, "What the hell's the matter with you? Get up from there."

"I don't like the dark," Ralph muttered as he untangled his arms and legs, then crawled around the slop bucket before he tried to get to his feet. He staggered and might have fallen if Buck hadn't caught him by his elbow. Ralph frowned. "Is it mornin'?"

"Yeah, it's mornin'," Buck answered.

"Are we goin' to a hangin'?" Ralph asked as Buck walked him out the door, where Ralph opened his eyes wide and looked all around him in the daylight.

"Nope, that ain't on the schedule today."

"I don't like the dark," Ralph repeated.

"That's why I gave you the candle in there."

"After I ate my supper, I blew my candle out and went to sleep," Ralph went on. "I didn't know it could get so dark in that room. When I woke up, my candle was gone. I couldn't find it. I felt all over the floor for it, but it was gone. I started crawling, feelin' for it, but I couldn't find it. I got to thinkin' maybe I was dead, then I bumped my head in the corner. It was too dark. So I quit crawlin'."

Buck wasn't quite sure what to make of Ralph's crazy story. Maybe that dark room drove him out of his mind. He wondered if he should take some extra precautions with the half-loony prisoner. "Just to go along with standard procedures, I'm gonna have to cuff your hands behind you till we get to the jail."

Ralph dutifully put his hands behind his back.

Paul Roper watched in amazement and when they came out of the room, he volunteered, "I'll empty those buckets for you."

"I 'preciate it," Buck told him, then remembering, he said, "I reckon I'd better take that supper tray with me, or Clara will start makin' me furnish my own dishes."

They got back to the jail in time to see one of the men from the sawmill driving an empty lumber wagon away from the jail, and Nolan Carson behind the jail, standing beside a stack of heavy siding.

"I'm fixin' to close the back of your cells up," he told

Buck in greeting. "It won't be long now." Nolan pointed toward the packs piled up inside the stud wall. "Flint said he'd do something with those packs when he got back. He took a horse and a mule down to the stable."

"Me and Ralph will be damn glad when you close it up," Buck declared. "Ain't that right, Ralph?"

The prisoner nodded vigorously.

Buck gave him a nudge. "Come on, let's go around to the front, so I don't have to carry this tray through the stud wall." As they rounded the building, they saw Flint coming from the stable. "I swear, it's good to see things workin' out the way you want 'em. Unlock the door for me, Flint. I've got my hands full."

Inside, Buck put the tray on the bench Roy used to sleep on. "Your breakfast might be gettin' pretty cold by now. I'll heat up some coffee and maybe that'll help a little bit."

"It don't matter," Ralph said. "It'll be good. Don't matter if it's stone cold."

Flint took him back to his cell after the handcuffs were removed. Back in the office, he said, "I believe ol' Ralph is glad to get back in his cell."

"Boy, you don't know just how glad he is," Buck said. "He had me spooked for a while back there at Harper's."

"I noticed you had the bracelets on him to walk him back," Flint commented.

Buck told him about Ralph hidin' in the corner of the storeroom and how crazy he was talkin'. "He said he woke up in the dark and thought he was dead. Said he crawled all over the floor lookin' for his candle. I saw it layin' right under the bench when I went back in to get the supper dishes."

"Maybe I shoulda took him to Tyler with Ada," Flint said. "But he seemed to be right at home here in that cell, gettin' fat on Clara's food."

"It won't be for almost a month before Judge Dodge comes through here again," Buck said. "I believe Ralph will be happy as a lark here in the jail. Shoot, he's such a good prisoner, I might make him a deputy by that time. At least, I might give him Roy's old job."

Both lawmen winced when they remembered how Ralph's partner had killed Roy.

"I'm sorry I said that. Anyway, Ralph won't give us any trouble, and it'll be nice to have everything peaceful in the town for a change. The only danger I see is you might get so lazy you won't show up for work half the time." Buck grinned at Flint.

Things were not as comfortable for the two riders leading a string of packhorses when they pulled into the yard of a log cabin sitting on the bank of the Angelina River about sixteen miles from the little settlement of Nacogdoches.

Liam Trask remained seated in the saddle when he called out, "Aunt Minnie Brice!"

After a few minutes, the door of the cabin opened and a skinny old woman, with long gray hair that looked to have never met a hairbrush, hobbled out on the porch. "Who calls me?" she asked, squinting in an effort to see who it was.

"It's Liam Trask, Aunt Minnie. I got my boy with me. He's needin' your doctorin' for a gunshot wound."

"How bad is it?" Aunt Minnie asked. "Can he walk?"

"Yes, ma'am, he can walk, although it pains him to. I can get him on the porch, if you'll take a look at him."

"Who told you to bring him here?" She wanted to know.

"Nobody," Trask answered. "I brung him here 'cause you treated his mother when she took sick with the pox."

"Did she get well after I give her the potion?"

"No, ma'am. She died," Trask answered.

"And you brung your son back to me to be treated when I didn't help your wife? Why?"

"'Cause I heard you was better at treating wounds than you was at treatin' the pox," Trask said.

"Well, bring him on up here, and I'll take a look. Have you got any money to pay me?"

"Yes, ma'am," Trask replied as he stepped down from the saddle. "I've got a little money and some things to trade, if the money ain't enough." He went back to Vike and helped him off his horse then up three steps to the porch, while she pulled a canvas sheet off a cot on one side of the porch. "He was lucky where he got shot," Trask told her. "It was in his side, and the bullet went in the front and out the back. I'm worried about the bullet holes gettin' infected."

"Lay him down there and get his shirt off him." She removed the bandage Trask had wrapped around Vike and studied the two bullet holes. "He ain't hurt much a-tall. You coulda treated them wounds, yourself." She looked up at Trask accusingly. "If you hadn't tried to clean 'em in the hog lot, or wherever. I'll clean 'em as best I can, then we'll see how bad they are. I'll go heat some water."

She washed the wounds with soap and hot water, cleaning the dried blood away in a not too gentle fashion, which restarted the bleeding. "Hold still, young feller," she scolded when Vike flinched. "We wanna get that bad blood outta there, anyway." She felt his side, between the entry and the exit wounds, and nodded her satisfaction. "Don't feel like no fever in your side, so I reckon the bullet didn't tear nothin' up too bad inside ya. We'll treat 'em with some germ killer." She took a jar she'd brought with her from the kitchen. "Hold still, now. This might have a little bite."

She splashed some of the liquid onto the entry wound, causing Vike to yell and arch his back in an effort to escape. As if ready for that reaction, she remained poised with the jar in hand, grabbed his back while it was arched, and turned him enough to splash the exit wound. He responded with a yell equal to the first one.

Watching the treatment, Trask commented, "That looks like moonshine likker in that fruit jar."

"It does a little, don't it?" Aunt Minnie responded. "Wouldn't hurt him none to take a drink of it to help kill any poison left inside him."

"Hell, yes," Vike exclaimed. "I need somethin' after you poured that stuff on them holes." He took a healthy swig out of the jar. It rendered him speechless.

"It's got a kick, ain't it?" she commented with a chuckle and wrapped a rag around him to catch the bleeding. "That's just gonna hold you till I make up some poultices to cover them wounds."

Back inside the cabin all she found to make the poultices were some pine and gooseberries. She chopped them up and mixed them with some flour, thinking the wounds would heal up, anyway. She took the poultices back out to the porch, applied them, then bound them tightly to his waist. "Don't take that bandage off for two days, three, if you want to. Then them wounds oughta dry up, and you'll be good as new, ready to go get shot again."

Vike shook his head, more than a little skeptical.

"How much I owe ya?" Trask asked.

"Three dollars," she replied. "Two for the treatment and another dollar for the poultices."

"Fair enough." Trask paid her then asked her a question while Vike put his shirt on. "Maybe you could tell me something. Does Malcolm Fletcher still have that place down below Nacogdoches?"

"Far as I know," Aunt Minnie replied. "I ain't heard nothin' about him leavin'."

"Much obliged." Trask followed Vike, who was walking cautiously down the steps.

"You keep that bandage dry, boy," Aunt Minnie called after them as they rode out of the yard.

They rode their horses back up the river trail and followed it to the south. "How you makin' out, son?" Trask asked.

"All right, I reckon," Vike answered, although without convincing enthusiasm. "As long as we hold the horses back to a walk, it ain't too bad."

"I expect you're about to starve to death. I know I am," Trask said. "We can stop and cook some bacon, if you want to. But if you can hold on a while longer, it's about a two-hour ride from here to your Uncle Malcolm's place. Your Aunt Melva will fix us up with somethin' to eat. You can count on that."

"That'll be better 'n anythin' we cook right now," Vike said. "That swig I took outta that fruit jar hit my empty belly like a rock. I know that weren't nothin' but moonshine whiskey. We coulda poured whiskey on them wounds, instead of givin' her three dollars."

"I expect so," his father said, "but we got them poultices, too, and we wouldn'ta knowed how to make them."

"Look comin' yonder," Harley Fletcher suddenly exclaimed. "Who the hell is that?"

"Where?" his father asked, alerted by his son's tone.

"Comin' off the river road," Harley answered. "Couple of riders, leadin' a bunch of horses." That was enough to bring his father out of the barn to see for himself.

They stood watching while the riders drew closer.

"Well, I'll be . . ." Malcolm muttered. "It's your Uncle Liam and one of the boys. It's been so long that I can't tell which one it is." He hadn't seen Liam since his wife, Malcolm's sister Lorena, died. "Well, I'll be . . ." he muttered again. "Go tell your mama."

Harley ran to the house to pass the word.

The unexpected reunion that followed was tragic in nature again, with the news of Liam's son, Kyle, shot dead in Tinhorn, and his daughter, Ada, arrested and imprisoned somewhere. Malcolm's wife, Melva, was quick to rustle up some supper for the weary travelers. Her daughter, Nelda, made it her responsibility to make Vike as comfortable as possible. Malcolm's sons, Harley, Willy, Justin, and Cody were all gathered around the big kitchen table to hear Trask's account of the whole bloody story that began with Jed Tubbs and Ralph Cox's arrest.

"That damn Buck Jackson," Malcolm declared. "He's the reason I, and most ever'body in our business, make sure we stay clear of Tinhorn."

"I was stayin' clear of Tinhorn, too," Trask said. "But when they killed Ada's husband, we got dragged into a fight with that town. And if you ain't been there lately, let me tell you, it's worse than it was, because Jackson got himself a deputy that don't know when to quit. He's the one who killed Kyle and put them holes in Vike. He rode onto my place one night and kidnapped Ada and threw her in the jail. Me and Vike and Kyle rode into Tinhorn to set her free, but they were settin' there waitin' for us to show up, and we were lucky to get outta there alive. Least me and Vike were. Kyle weren't so lucky." He went on to tell them how they happened to show up at Fletcher's, instead of returning to his own place north of Tinhorn.

"Well, you're welcome here," Malcolm said. "You and

Vike can stay right here and work with us. It'd be like old times when we used to ride together."

"That's mighty generous of you, Malcolm, but that ain't the reason me and Vike showed up on your doorstep," Trask declared as sincerely as he could manage.

In fact, that was exactly what he was hoping to hear. One look at the small ranch Malcolm and his boys had evidently built as a result of their lawless endeavors, told Trask he might have been better off had he not decided to split off on his own.

"We worked pretty good when we was partners, didn't we? There's been a lotta days when I thought about it. But that's just the way things turn out, I reckon. I'm sure you knew it was Lorena who wanted us to be on our own. And you remember how I'da done anythin' in the world that sister of yours wanted me to do." Trask made a show of pausing then. "You folks'll have to excuse me. There are some things that cause me to get melancholy once in a while. Anyway, we were down this way to get Vike some doctorin', so I thought we'd surprise ya, and maybe get a good supper at Melva's table. I see she's still the best cook in Texas."

His little performance had a compassionate effect on everyone at the table, with the exception of one. Vike was astonished to hear his father's confession of servitude to his mother. If anything, he had ruled over her like she was a slave, put on earth to cater to his every whim. Vike had no idea what *melancholy* was, but he was sure his pa had never had any.

Before the night was over, his pa and his uncle were talking about banks that were easy targets, stage lines where there were no trains, and cattle and horses that were not that heavily guarded. After supper, Trask remarked that he and Vike had better head back up the river to see if their old camp was in shape to spend the night in. Malcolm immediately insisted they should stay with them that night, since it was already getting pretty late.

Trask graciously accepted the invitation.

# CHAPTER 14

Tinhorn, Texas was once again the dull, peaceful little town it was before the arrival of Jed Tubbs and Ralph Cox. For almost two weeks after the attempted jailbreak that took Kyle Trask's life, nothing much was required of Deputy Flint Moran. The cell wall was completed and Prisoner Ralph Cox seemed content to wait for his trial. He'd been given his choice of cells and chose to move back into the larger one with the solid wood wall.

Nolan Carson had framed two tiny windows near the ceiling that provided a little bit of light to shine through, even with the lamp out. Buck had declared that the wall would have no windows, but decided Nolan was right when he advised the windows for light and ventilation.

It crossed Flint's mind that maybe a deputy wasn't needed at all and that he might be fired just as suddenly as he'd been hired. He took the time to visit his family. His father and brothers asked if he was ready to put his stint as a lawman aside and return to the farm. His response to that was how much better things were at the farm without him. "Besides," he had suggested, "it might be an impossible job to persuade Mary to move."

His brother Nate had laughed, remembering how quickly his eleven-year-old daughter had claimed Flint's old room.

"I'd have to build another room onto the house," Flint joked. "And I ain't no better carpenter than I was as a farmer. I reckon I'll hang on a while in the sheriff's office."

There was another reason he was hesitant about giving up his job as a deputy. He had grown to appreciate Sheriff Buck Jackson and was reluctant to leave him without someone to back him in the event trouble did show up. Buck had obviously made a commitment to win his battle with the whiskey bottle, but in the couple of weeks of peaceful existence, there were signs that Buck was sliding back into his old habits. He had begun retiring to his room right after supper again and eating a late breakfast at the saloon.

In effect, Flint was the nighttime sheriff once more, as he had been when first hired. He sometimes wondered if he was now filling Roy Hawkins' old job, and that was simply to watch the office while Buck was retired for the night.

It was unrealistic for him to think the peace would last indefinitely in Tinhorn, however, and that fact was brought home to the residents when Blackie Culver rode into town. Blackie called himself a shootist, based on his ability to draw his weapon and fire it before his unfortunate antagonist could draw his. He built his reputation in the gambling houses and saloons in West Texas. In the town of Waco he'd been arrested by Sheriff Buck Jackson that resulted in a twelve-year prison sentence and the end of his fame as a shootist.

During the entire twelve years, Blackie never forgot the promise he had made to have his revenge on the man who had put a stop to his growing list of kills. After searching most of Texas for the past year, he'd found that Jackson had taken the sheriff's job in the little town of Tinhorn.

Thirteen years after his arrest, Blackie knew he was older, but Buck Jackson was older, too. Otherwise, he was not likely to have crawled into the oblivion of a small town like Tinhorn. It was time for Buck Jackson to stand up to the challenge made to him thirteen years ago—to settle the trouble between them face-to-face.

Riding a white horse, Culver entered the town at the south end, past the stable. Looking the town over as he rode up the street, he came to the saloon on his right, which would ordinarily be his first stop, but he saw the sheriff's office and jail a little farther up on his left and decided to go directly to Buck Jackson's office in an attempt to save some time.

He pulled up at the rail and dismounted. Looking up and down the street before he went up the steps, he unconsciously eased his Colt .45 up and down to make sure it was riding freely in his holster. He considered the notion to pull the weapon as soon as he walked in the door and drill Jackson as he was sitting at his desk. It would settle the debt he thought he was due, but it would not give him the satisfaction of facing the sheriff down.

He walked up the two steps to the door. Through the glass, he could see someone sitting at the desk, facing the door, but he couldn't tell if it was Jackson. Culver opened the door and stepped inside to find a young man wearing a badge seated behind the desk.

"Can I do something for you?" Flint asked, when the man said nothing.

Of average height, judging by the space between the top of his hat and the top of the door, the stranger had shoulder-length hair streaked with gray extending from under his hat. Flint noticed a Colt riding at a height convenient for a fast draw.

"I'm lookin' for Sheriff Buck Jackson," Blackie finally answered. "Is he in?"

"No, Sheriff Jackson ain't in at the moment. I'm Deputy Moran. Can I help you?"

"No, I need to see Sheriff Jackson," Blackie insisted. "Do you know where he is?"

"Nope. I'm sorry I don't. He just went out to patrol the town. If it's something to do with the law, maybe I can help you." Flint knew exactly where Buck was.

At that particular time, he would be sitting in Jake's Place, eating one of Rena's greasy breakfasts, and planning to have a shot of whiskey afterward.

But Flint was not inclined to furnish that information to the rather suspicious looking stranger. "You sure there's nothin' I can do for you?"

"My business is with the sheriff. I'll just go look for him," Blackie insisted. He turned and went back out the door.

*I wonder what that business is?* Flint thought. The man didn't look like the kind of businessman Buck wanted to deal with. *I better go see if I can find Buck and let him know this fellow's looking for him.* He opened the cell room door and told Ralph he would be out of the office for a while, locked the cell room door, and went out the front door.

The stranger had left his horse tied in front of the jail. That indicated to Flint the man would be coming back to the jail to wait if he didn't find Buck. Flint took a look up and down the street in case the man might see him go straight to the saloon. Not seeing him outside any business, Flint locked the door and walked toward the saloon.

Sitting at a small table at the back of the saloon, near the kitchen door, Buck looked up from his scrambled eggs and ham when someone walked inside. Although he didn't recognize the man, something about him seemed familiar. The saloon was dark and Buck's eyes weren't as sharp as they used to be, a fact he never admitted to anyone. The man had paused just inside the door to look over the room and squinted his eyes trying to get a better look at the man sitting at the table.

Buck continued to watch the stranger, who appeared undecided as to whether he wanted to talk to Rudy, or advance closer to the table where Buck sat. He went to the bar, talked to Rudy for a few moments, then turned to look at Buck when Rudy pointed to him.

*So far, nothing to worry about*, Buck figured. Somebody looking for the sheriff for some reason.

As the man walked toward him, it struck *him—Blackie Culver!* An older version, but there was no mistaking the confident walk and the long hair that was no longer solid black. Buck thought quick. It was too late to reach under the table for his six-gun without prompting Blackie to go for his, and he knew Blackie could draw from the holster quicker than he could get to his gun, wedged up against the arm of his chair as it was.

Deciding it best to talk his way out of a shoot-out, Buck blurted, "Well, I'll be damned. Blackie Culver! If that ain't somethin'. Served your time and now a free man. Set down, Blackie, and I'll buy you some breakfast."

Blackie was stopped for a moment by the unexpected welcome, but he quickly recovered. "You ain't buyin' me a damn thing. I come to kill you." He stood poised, hoping Buck was dumb enough to reach for his gun.

"Nonsense, Blackie," Buck continued. "All that business was over and done with years ago. Don't you want a cup of coffee, at least?"

"Hell, no!" Blackie roared. "I don't want no coffee. You ain't talkin' your way outta this. You took the best part of my life away from me in that prison. It's your turn to pay the price for that."

"Now, Blackie, you gotta admit you killed that woman when you poured that whiskey down her throat till she strangled and died. I thought it was mighty lucky the judge ruled it was just manslaughter and gave you a prison sentence. And twelve years at that. You gotta admit, that wasn't much for killin' a woman."

"You got a choice, Jackson. Stand up and face me, man to man, or I'm gonna shoot you right where you sit. You ain't gettin' outta this."

"You reach for that gun and you're a dead man." Standing in the kitchen doorway, Flint was only a few feet away, his six-gun aimed squarely at Blackie's chest. "Murder is against the law in Tinhorn."

Realizing he had no chance against the already drawn weapon, Blackie insisted he had challenged Buck to face him in a duel. "It ain't got nothin' to do with murder," he insisted. "He's got a debt to pay for somethin' he done to me, and I'm callin' him out to stand up to me."

"Duelin' is against the law in Tinhorn, too, as is threatenin' an officer of the law," Flint said. "You're under arrest. Put your hands behind your back."

"I'll be damned," Blackie blurted defiantly. "I'm not goin' back behind no bars."

Buck spoke up then. "I don't see as how you've got any choice. Do like he told you and put your hands behind your back. You were wrong thirteen years ago, and you're wrong now. You didn't learn a damn thing in prison, did you?"

"All right," Blackie finally conceded. "You win. I'll put 'em behind my back."

Flint slowly shook his head as he placed one round in Blackie's chest when he snatched his gun out of the holster while pretending to put his hands behind his back.

"Yep. Ain't learned a damn thing." Buck looked over

toward the bar where Jake and Rudy were standing with mouths agape and eyes stuck wide open. "Rudy, I think I want that shot of whiskey now." To Flint, he said, "Partner, you were a welcome sight, standin' in that doorway. I don't know if he got any of his speed back, but before I sent him to prison, he woulda put three bullets in me before I got to that gun. And the way I'm wedged into this chair sure didn't help."

Flint couldn't help thinking an evening of drinking the night before would have had a hand in his reaction time as well. He walked over and checked to make sure Blackie was dead.

"How did you know he was here?" Buck asked, especially when Flint had slipped in through the kitchen, instead of coming in the front door.

"Hell, he came to the jail, lookin' for you. I reckon he was plannin' on shootin' you right there in the sheriff's office."

"Did you tell him I was over here, eatin' breakfast?"

"No, I told him I didn't know where you were. This is just the first place he went to look." Flint shook his head as if disgusted with Buck's question. "It was the obvious first choice to look. I'll drag him out front and go get Walt." He took hold of Blackie's boots and started to pull him. "He's pretty heavy. Gimme a hand, Rudy." While he waited for Rudy to come out from behind the bar, he asked Buck, "What was his name?"

"Blackie Culver," Buck answered, still thinking how smart he was to have hired Flint Moran.

"I'll tell Walt, in case he wants to know who he's burying." He and Rudy each grabbed an ankle and dragged Blackie out to the boardwalk in front.

Flint looked back down the street and saw Walt Doolin standing halfway outside his shop. He was holding the door open and looking toward them, obviously having heard the shot and checking to see if it meant business for him. Flint gave him a wave of his hand and Walt signaled back, then went to get his cart.

Calling back to Buck, who was still sitting at the table, Flint said, "I'll see you back at the office. Ralph likely heard that shot and he'll wanna know what happened." He went across the street, telling himself that, like it or not, he was becoming a permanent part of the town.

All his thinking about quitting or being fired was nothing more than a waste of brain cells. The incident that had just popped up showed him the definite need for a deputy sheriff. And Buck Jackson was in definite need of backup. Flint only hoped he could do the job required of him. It was difficult not to wonder how many other ex-convicts were riding all over Texas, looking for Buck Jackson.

"Mornin', Deputy Moran," the postmaster's wife greeted Flint politely from the doorway of the post office. "I heard a shot. Is it all right if I walk past the saloon?"

"Yes, ma'am. Everything's all right now." He realized he didn't know her name. "You know, it would be a good idea if you stayed on this side of the street. They've got to clean up something from the boardwalk right in front of the saloon. If you like, I'll walk with you."

"Why, thank you, kind sir."

He walked her past the saloon on the opposite side of the street, trying to keep her view blocked with his body. Then he turned around and headed in the direction of the jail.

"Thank you, Deputy," she called after him.

It never occurred to him that he was met with more friendly greetings from the people of Tinhorn every day.

He stopped to talk with Walt Doolin as he came out of the alley, pulling his handcart. "His name is Blackie

Culver, one of Buck's old friends who came to shoot him. There won't be anybody comin' to claim the body unless it's the devil." He held up the gun belt he was carrying. "I took his guns. Don't know if he's got anything else on him or not."

Walt got only a modest fee for taking care of the bodies, so it was the usual policy to let him keep anything of value on the body as part of his fee. The exceptions were guns and horses, and of course, any money resulting from robberies, which was returned to the victim of the robbery.

"We heard there was a shooting in the saloon this morning," Clara Rakestraw said to Buck when the sheriff came to the dining room for dinner. "Walt Doolin said Flint shot an outlaw who came looking for you. Is that right?"

"That's a fact," Buck told her.

"Is Flint coming to eat dinner with you?"

"Flint's eatin' dinner at Hannah Green's today. He said you charge too much and it ain't as good as Myrna's cookin'."

"He did not." Clara was well accustomed to the sheriff's japing. "He has to eat there once in a while to keep from hurting Hannah and Myrna's feelings." She was thoroughly confident her Margaret was without peer in the cooking department.

"I'da bought his dinner for him today. That's for sure," Buck declared. "If it weren't for him, I might notta been sittin' here right now. I told him I owed him, but he said it'd been a while since he ate at the boardin' house. And it's included in his rent, anyway."

Mindy came to the table with a cup of coffee and glanced inquisitively at Clara.

"Flint's not coming to dinner today," Clara told her, causing an immediate frown on Mindy's face.

"Stew or meatloaf?" Mindy asked.

Buck said meatloaf without hesitation. When he saw the frown still in place on her face, he asked, "What's the matter? Were you hopin' I'd take the stew?" He laughed when she did an about-face without responding to his teasing.

As always, Clara was interested in getting a more detailed report on the shooting at the saloon that morning, but she was interrupted when Harvey Baxter came in the door.

Before she could come to greet him, he spotted Buck sitting near the back, and walked directly to his table. "Sheriff, mind if I join you?"

"Not a-tall. Have a seat," Buck replied, as Mindy came to take the mayor's order.

Baxter looked at Buck's plate. "That meatloaf looks pretty good. I think I'll try that."

"It tastes pretty good, too, but you'll disappoint Mindy if you don't eat the stew."

Unaware Mindy was being teased, Baxter hesitated, looking at her curiously. "Oh, is that a fact?"

"No such a thing," Mindy said. "That's just the sheriff with some of his teasin'. I think you'll enjoy the meatloaf or the stew."

The mayor stayed with his first pick. Mindy went to the kitchen to get his meatloaf, and Clara returned to her usual position near the outside door.

Baxter inquired about the latest incident involving the sheriff's department. "I heard about the shooting this morning at Jake's Place. Heard it was Flint who shot that fellow."

"That's right." Buck told Baxter what had actually

occurred while he was eating some breakfast at the saloon, who Blackie Culver was, and why he had come to Tinhorn.

"But it was Flint who shot him," Baxter repeated.

"If he hadn't, you'd be settin' at the table with a dead man," Buck promptly told him. "Flint was fixin' to arrest him, and Culver went for his gun. Flint didn't have no choice. There weren't nothin' I could do in time to help him."

Baxter said nothing for a few moments but nodded slowly as if he was thinking about it seriously. "I'm glad to hear your firsthand version of the incident," he finally commented. "I've had conversations with a couple other members of the council, and everybody is in agreement that we hired a truly capable deputy sheriff. One of the members raised an issue that caused some concern, however, what with all that's happened in the last few weeks."

Somewhat surprised, Buck had to ask, "What kind of concerns?"

"Frankly, the fact that it's been Flint who has done all the killing," Baxter answered. "There was speculation that perhaps Flint might be building a reputation for himself, and consequently, a reputation for Tinhorn as well. One that we certainly don't want. I'm sure I don't have to tell you that. I'd very much like to hear your opinion."

Buck hesitated for a moment before answering, lest he say something that might offend the mayor. Then in a calm voice, he said, "Mr. Mayor, a reputation is the last thing that young man wants. I guarantee that. It seems to me those members of the council are complainin' because we hired a man who's doin' just what we hired him to do. The town has been mighty lucky not to have any trouble for the past few years. And we're just as lucky we hired the right man to help me when we got hit with some real trouble. You need to tell your council members that. With Tinhorn startin' to grow a little bit, we're gonna attract more trouble down the road. Be glad you hired Flint Moran and we'll keep workin' on buildin' our reputation as a town that don't tolerate troublemakers."

"That sounds good to me," Baxter concluded. "I'm glad I heard your position on the question. Now, hand me some of that gravy."

# CHAPTER 15

Twenty-six miles north of Tinhorn, a recent inmate of the Tinhorn jail was housed in a temporary female cell block, awaiting trial before Judge Graham Dodge. In a small cell with two cots, a chamber pot, and a water bucket, Ada Tubbs lived in constant despair. Her cellmate Lucy was a prostitute who had already been to prison once. With no exercise period, the women were confined to their cell twenty-four hours a day. Lucy was a disgusting human being who delighted in telling Ada tales about life in the Huntsville Unit, where they were bound to be sentenced to serve their terms.

Ada frustrated Lucy with her lack of response to her tales, remaining as stoic and fatalistic as she had been in Tinhorn's jail. Revenge upon those who had put her there was the only passion she felt. If she had no chance for that, she would choose death in whatever form it came. Hanging, shot while attempting escape, attacking a guard—it didn't matter. Remaining incarcerated for a full term, whatever that would be, was not an option.

During the second week of her stay in the cell block the commanding captain decided he wanted an old kitchen building that hadn't been used in years put back in service. It had to be scrubbed clean of all the grease and grime that had collected on its walls and floors over the years, and he wanted the women sitting in their cells awaiting trial to do the work. It was a much-sought-after assignment.

It was Ada's fortune the guards thought she was tall and strong. In her usual custom, she made no comment of gratitude or elation when informed she had been assigned to that work detail—free of her cell for twelve hours a day, for as long as it took to complete the job.

Two guards—known to the women only as Rafer and Plummer—were assigned to watch the work detail of seven women. Both men were armed, sizable brutes, with Rafer being the bigger one.

From the beginning, the work was hard. It didn't take long for the women to realize it was unpleasant work. In some places the grease was so thick, it was necessary to use hammer and chisel to remove it from the floors and walls behind the stoves. In case any of the seven women had thoughts of fleeing, their ankles were chained together. Still it was preferable to being locked up in their cells day and night.

Rafer and Plummer evaluated the women and assigned them according to how hard they worked.

"Hey, you!" Rafer yelled on the third day. "The tall, lanky one. Yeah, you," he said when Ada turned to face him. "What's your name?"

"Tubbs," Ada said, emotionless. She was already accustomed to being identified by her last name only.

"Tubbs." A grin broke out on his broad face. "Dynamite," he exclaimed and turned to his partner. "Hey, Plummer, this is that gal Ron Black said the sheriff called *Dynamite*. Dynamite Tubbs," he said again, excited as a schoolboy. He turned back toward Ada again. "That's right, ain't it? You're the one they call Dynamite."

"If you say so," she answered, still devoid of emotion.

"You don't act like dynamite," Rafer said. "Maybe if we light your fuse you might clean this place up in about fifteen minutes." When his comments were still met with a bored reaction, he said, "Come on over here behind that stove. You're tall enough to reach that grease caked up around the stovepipe where it goes up through the wall."

She reached up with her chisel and started scraping the old grease away.

"All right. Now we're gettin' somewhere. You just keep at it. All the way around that pipe." He watched her for a while before he asked, "What was you doin' before they arrested you for dynamitin' the jail. Were you a prostitute?"

"No. I'm not a prostitute. I'm a widow."

"A widow?" He was surprised. "And now, you're fixin' to go away for a long, long time, but I reckon you're already used to not havin' a man around."

"Pretty much," she replied.

Plummer called out, "Dinner time, ladies!"

"Go get yourself somethin' to eat," Rafer said. "You got a long way to go yet."

He joined Plummer and they filled a couple of plates, then sat down at a table to watch their work crew while they ate.

"I may have something staked out," Rafer said to Plummer.

"Who, ol' Dynamite Tubbs? I noticed you spendin' a lotta time with her. You ain't particular, are you? Most of the other ones in here are better lookin' than she is."

"There's somethin' kinda strange about her, and she ain't like these other women in here. She's a widow woman. Maybe I'll make a bargain with her. I won't look at her face, if she don't look at mine."

The women had thirty minutes to eat, then it was back to work for the female crew. Rafer made a show of walking around the old kitchen, watching the different women work. No one took any particular notice of the old worn-out scrub brush he carried in his hand. Near the bolted back door, he turned to catch Plummer's eye and gave him a couple of nods. Plummer grinned and nodded back.

Rafer walked behind the stove where Ada was still using a hammer and chisel on some of the hard grease places. "Here"—he tossed the worn-out brush to her— "you need to use a scrub brush on that spot that ain't so thick."

She dropped her hammer to catch it. Took one look and said, "This brush is worn out."

"It is? I didn't even look at it. Throw it back."

She did.

He looked at it and said, "I declare, you're right. Come on. We'll go to the storeroom and get a new one."

She looked uncertain and bent down to pick up her hammer.

"Leave the hammer where it is. Come on." He walked to the storeroom at the end of the hall by the back door, and opened the door for her. When she walked in, he closed the door behind her. "Look in that big carton under the window. I think that's full of scrub brushes."

She went to it and saw that he was right, so she opened it and pulled one out, then turned to go back to the door.

He stepped in front of her. "You know, if you were smart, I could make things a lot easier for you while you're here."

"I ain't interested in makin' things easier."

"It would be just like bein' with your husband again. Make your stay more enjoyable while you're here." He stepped closer to her and took her by her shoulders, pulling her close up against him.

"No!" she cried. Still holding the chisel, she came up

under his chin as hard as she could and struck him in his throat, using the chisel like a dagger.

The newly sharpened chisel cut through his windpipe like a knife, and he could do nothing but grab his throat with both hands. Gasping for air, he backed away from her.

In a fight for her life, she charged into him. Stabbing him again and again with the chisel, she could not cut deep enough to deliver a lethal wound, but they were so painful he removed one of his hands from his throat to fend her off. She struck him again in the throat, severing his windpipe. Unable to make a sound, he sank to the floor with her on top of him.

Seeing several rags on a shelf next to her arm, she grabbed one and stuffed it down his windpipe, holding it there until he was still.

Outside in the hall, Plummer walked by and paused at the door for a minute. Hearing the sounds of bodies on the floor and the rattling of boxes, he grinned and walked on up to the other end of the hall.

Exhausted, Ada sat back on her heels and wondered what to do. Seeing his revolver in the holster, she quickly grabbed it, thinking anybody who came through that door would be her next victim. But then, she began to think rationally and set her mind to thoughts of escape. To stay there would mean to die. She reached into his pockets and pulled out everything until she saw what she searched for. Taking the ring of keys, she tried each one until she found the one that unlocked the chains on her ankles. Free to move, she pulled the gun belt out from under him, strapped it on, and took the small amount of money he had carried in his pocket. Already aware the window was the only thing between her and the outside, she went at once to inspect it. It was covered by a light metal lattice but was so old, wood had rotted in places around the frame. She used her chisel to work on the edges of the lattice and soon had pried enough of the lattice away to bend it back enough for her to wiggle through. She reached up behind the lattice and unlocked the window. Even straining as hard as she could, it had been too many years since last opened. The window wouldn't slide up.

Just before smashing it with the chisel, it suddenly cracked loose from the paint and slid up. *She was free!*

*But only free from this building,* she told herself.

Looking straight out the window, she could see nothing but a long grassy area. Very cautiously, she stuck her head out the window. Looking left and right all she saw were the backs of the buildings that made up the jail compound. She took one farewell look at the body, squeezed herself out the window, and dropped to the ground. Hearing no shouts of alarm or halts, she hurried along the back of that building and the building next to it until she reached the end— nothing between her and the buildings of the town but an open field of high grass and a scattering of stunted oak trees. She hesitated for only a moment before striking out across the field, halfway expecting a fatal bullet in her back.

Inside the old kitchen, Plummer began to wonder if Rafer and Dynamite had had themselves such a good time that they had fallen asleep afterward. The last couple of times he went by the door, there were no sounds at all. Thinking maybe he'd better check, he stopped on his next pass and tapped lightly on the door. No answer, so he knocked louder. When there was still no answer, he knew something was wrong. He drew his revolver and opened the door. The sight of Rafer's bloodied body on the floor was a sight he would never forget.

Stopped motionless for a long few seconds, he didn't know what to do. Glancing up from the body, he saw the open window and blew his whistle as loud as he could.

With no idea what they were supposed to do, the women prisoners shuffled back and forth. Pretty soon a couple of them looked into the storeroom. One was stopped cold by the sight of the body. The other grabbed Rafer's keys off the floor, unlocked the chains on her ankles, and escaped. Quickly, the stunned woman followed suit and climbed out the open window too.

Plummer was too late to stop them, but turned and stood in front of the door with his pistol out to keep anyone else from trying to escape.

On the far side of the field from the chaos she had just created, Ada was walking up a side street that ran beside a saloon. Around the front of the saloon, she saw three horses tied at the rail, strolled over to stand between the roan and the dun, and waited a few minutes to see if anyone was curious about what she was doing there. Accustomed as they were to seeing most anything in front of the saloon, the couple of people who walked past on the boardwalk paid no attention to the woman wearing the wide-brimmed hat and the gun belt. No one came to inquire about her interest in the horses. Seeing the stirrups looked about right for her legs, she untied the reins for the dun and climbed up into the saddle.

Watching the saloon door anxiously, she backed the dun away from the rail, then turned his head toward the south end of the street and urged the gelding into an easy lope until she left the buildings of Tyler out of sight behind her.

Remembering the small store at a crossroad about two miles short of town, Ada reined the dun to a walk and realized in her haste to get away she had missed an important detail—a rifle was sheathed on the side of the dun. She smiled and guided the horse toward the store. Arriving, she pulled up, and dismounted.

Donald Stokely looked up in surprise to see the tall,

lanky woman walk in the door. Wearing a tall, flat-brimmed hat squarely on her head, and a gun in a holster strapped around the waist of her gingham dress, she looked to be all business.

"What can I do for you, ma'am?" Stokely blurted.

"Where does that road go?" Ada asked, pointing toward the west.

"That way, it heads to Athens," Stokely answered.

She reached into the pocket of her dress and pulled out the small roll of paper money she had taken from Rafer. Stokely watched, fascinated, as she took a minute to see how much she had. Satisfied that she had enough, she said. "I need a box of matches and a pound of that bacon yonder." She pointed to a side of meat on the table behind him.

When she stopped speaking, he asked, "Will that be all?"

"I want you to slice it for me about this thick," she answered and held her thumb and forefinger up to show him. "I ain't got a knife with me," she explained.

"Yes, ma'am," Stokely assured her. "Be glad to. Need anything else, like coffee or flour?" Seeing her counting her money encouraged him to try to sell more.

"No," she replied. "I ain't got a coffeepot."

"I've got a little one I could sell you right cheap," he urged.

She hesitated, then said, "I reckon not."

He smiled and turned, quickly slicing and wrapping the bacon in paper for her. He placed it on the counter then reached behind him, took a box of matches off the shelf, and placed it beside the bacon.

"How much?" she asked.

He took a pencil and added two figures, then said, "Seventy-nine cents. I'll knock off the four cents and we'll call it seventy-five even." Watching as she peeled a dollar bill from the small roll she carried, he could see that she had a few dollars left. "I'll tell you what I'll do." He walked to the end of the counter and pulled a small metal coffeepot off the shelf. "This little pot will hold about four cups. Coffee sells for twenty-nine cents a pound, double that if it's ground. I'll sell you this coffeepot and one pound of ground coffee plus your bacon and matches, for an even three dollars."

"Everything for three dollars," she repeated, "and the coffee ground?"

He nodded his head.

"Done," she decided.

"You got yourself a good bargain. Won't take me but a few minutes to grind the beans." He weighed the coffee beans on his scale and dumped them into his grinder.

Strongly believing it would take the guards from the jail a great amount of time to find out what had happened, she was not overly concerned about a posse catching up with her while she waited. And they wouldn't know which way to start out after her unless they ran into the rider whose horse she had stolen. To her mind, a posse couldn't be organized that soon and know exactly which way she went. If she had known that she'd created the opportunity for two other women to escape, she would have been even more confident.

"Pleasure doin' business with you, ma'am. 'Preciate it," Stokely said as he put her purchases in a little sack.

She merely nodded, paid him the three dollars, turned at once, and went out the door.

He watched her through the open door as she placed the sack in the saddlebag on her horse, climbed up into the saddle, and rode back onto the road. He walked out on his small porch and watched as she went to the crossroad and set out on the road to Athens. "My, my, my," he muttered to himself, thinking what a strange woman she was.

"What are you my, my, mying about?" asked Sadie Stokely as she joined him.

"That woman that just left here." He pointed toward the Athens road where she was just before going out of sight. "I wouldn't be surprised if she ain't one of them women outlaws you hear about from time to time."

"I wish you'da called me to help you," Sadie said. "I'da like to seen her."

"She was somethin', all right. Big ol' tall gal. Had what looked like a Colt Peacemaker strapped around her waist." He shook his head in wonder. "And didn't have more 'n two or three dollars to her name after she left here." He looked at his wife and grinned. "I sold her that little coffeepot I've been tryin' to get rid of for I don't know how long."


Ada was as happy she'd decided to buy the little coffee-pot as Donald Stokely was happy to have gotten rid of it. She was not sure what she would find when she got home. No one should be watching the house so soon after her escape. No way anyone could know about it yet, unless someone had telegraphed the Tinhorn sheriff. Only then might he send that sneaky deputy out to watch for her. She might get an opportunity to get a shot at him, if he showed up there.

The man at the store had said the road would take her to Athens, but she didn't know anything about a place named Athens. She looked carefully at the road and saw plenty of tracks on the road. That was important for what she had in mind. She didn't claim to know anything about tracking, but she had common sense, figuring anyone who would set out to catch her might assume she would head for home. She guessed they would stop at the store she'd just left to ask the owner if he had seen her. He would certainly send them down the road she was currently riding on. That's why the tracks on the road were important.

She could see enough tracks that the dun's tracks might not be distinguishable from other horses' tracks. If she left the road, anyone on her trail might not realize her tracks were not there anymore.

Her mind made up, that's what she did. As soon as she came to a stream crossing the road, she entered the stream, turned the dun downstream, and rode in the middle of it, back in the direction of her home. She stayed in the water until reaching a grassy meadow the stream had cut right through the center of and rode to the edge of the meadow. Thinking to be doubly careful, she stopped her horse, dismounted, and tied the reins to a tree limb. Walking back to the stream on foot, she tidied up any disruption of the meadow grass where the dun had come out of the water.

With a satisfied feeling she had done everything possible to mislead a posse, she started out on a course she figured would take her back to the road to Tinhorn. After crossing through forested lowlands for twenty minutes or more, her faith in her sense of direction was justified when she once again struck the Tyler-Tinhorn road.

In the later part of the afternoon she came to the trail that led to her father's house. Still of the opinion that it was too soon to expect anyone from Tinhorn to have ridden out to watch the house, she rode confidently along the path to her home and pulled up short of the barnyard to look the place over before riding in.

It seemed strange. She saw no sign of any activity on the place and looked toward the pasture beyond the barn. The herd of stolen horses was still there, but there was no sign of her father or her brothers. *They're all off somewhere, up to something, or laying around the house*, she thought as she nudged the dun and rode across the barnyard and into the barn. Since no horses were in the barn, she knew they weren't inside the house. She got down from the dun, pulled the saddle off him, then turned him out in the corral, so he could get water.

She carried her saddle and bridle into the tack room and was startled to find it empty of the commonly used tools. It was enough to make her more cautious. Drawing the Colt .45 from the holster, she checked to make sure it was loaded then went to the house where she found even more evidence that the place was deserted. The kitchen stove was cold and appeared to have been for some time. The most commonly used dishes and cookware were missing. In the bedrooms her father's and brothers' clothes were gone.

*The house was deserted!*

Having thought all the way from Tyler that there was no reason for her father and brothers to be in any trouble with the law, she suddenly remembered the last time she'd seen them. Her father's last words to her were, "Don't you worry, honey. I'll take care of you."

That was after he'd promised to get her out of the jail, even if he had to use dynamite to do it. He might have tried to break her out of the Tinhorn jail, not realizing she had been taken to Tyler.

*What to do now?*

She could think of no way to find out. Maybe they were in jail, but she could not find that out without going to Tinhorn. She shook her head. The minute she walked into Tinhorn she would be immediately recognized.

They could be dead. She had to consider that possibility and made a promise to herself to find them. But that would never happen if the law got to her first. So, taking care of herself had to be her number one priority. And while she might be safe in the house tonight, she knew it was not a safe place for her after that. Tonight, she must ready herself for the days to follow.

In her bedroom—the only room left untouched—she removed the dress she had been wearing every day since her abduction by Flint Moran, and replaced it with heavier denim trousers since she planned to be spending most of her time in the saddle. She selected a flannel shirt and a denim farm vest to wear over it and threw her shoes in the corner. With no desire to dress for any reason other than comfort and practicality—she would possibly spend the majority of her time outdoors now—she chose socks, bandanas, and rugged underwear. She dressed then packed up only those clothes she might actually wear. She had been branded an outlaw, so outlaw she would be. Since she had killed a man, she would also be branded a murderer.

She felt no regret over having killed the guard, Rafer. The fact that he was in the process of assaulting her would be of no importance. Because she had to kill him with a cold chisel, she would no doubt be referred to as a bloody murderer. *And before I'm done, Flint Moran and Buck Jackson will rue the day they ever crossed paths with Ada Tubbs*.

In her present circumstances, the most important thing on her mind was to find her father and brothers. Again considering the possibility they had been arrested and were now in the Tinhorn jail, she realized that didn't make sense. They would hardly have packed up all their clothes and cleaned out the tack room if they had gone to break her out of jail. Or would they? It's possible they planned to break her out and not return to the farm.

But if that was the case, why didn't they take some of her clothes with them? She concluded the only answer for her had to start in Tinhorn. But she could not go to Tinhorn without being immediately recognized.

Not particularly hungry for any supper, she still built a fire in the stove and made some coffee in her new coffeepot. As the night began to descend upon the barnyard, she went out to the corral to take care of her horse. Returning to the house with the guard's pistol and the stolen rifle, she was determined to resist anyone attempting to capture her. With that thought in mind, she sat by the kitchen door with no lamps lit, and waited for anyone who might think to search the house.

It was after midnight before she drifted off to sleep.

# CHAPTER 16

Flint unlocked the office on a Saturday morning. He'd just come from Clara's with a breakfast plate for Ralph, when Marvin Williams' son, Jimmy, rushed into the office. "Here's a telegram that just came in this mornin' for Sheriff Jackson. Papa said he'd wanna see it right away."

Flint took it and said, "Thanks, Jimmy. I'll see that Sheriff Jackson sees it as soon as he comes in. That oughta be pretty quick now. Tell your papa, thanks." He gave him a nickel for the delivery, then took the plate in and gave it to Ralph.

Jimmy ran back out the door, bumping into Buck as he was coming up the steps. "There's a telegram for you, Sheriff," Jimmy announced as he bounced off the big lawman, and ran back to the telegraph office.

Coming in from the cell room, Flint was reading it when Buck walked in.

"What was that about?" Buck asked.

Flint tossed the wire on the desk with only two words. "Ada's out."

"What?" Buck blurted and grabbed the telegram off the desk. "Yesterday," he said as he read it. "Killed a guard on a work detail and went out a window and stole a horse. A three-man search party picked up her trail, headin' to Athens.

Says she might be comin' this way. Hell, if she's headin' to Athens, she sure ain't comin' this way." He looked at Flint and declared, "That's a cheerful way to start off a Saturday mornin', ain't it?"

"Well, I thought she was just teasin' me," Flint japed, "but she did promise me she'd be comin' back for me." He paused to think a moment. "I wonder if she knows anything about her pa's attempt to break her outta here. I bet she don't." He cocked his head and asked, "Where's Athens?"

"A little place east of Tyler," Buck answered. "Nothin' much there. Maybe her pa's got a camp up that way."

"Maybe so," Flint commented, "but when they left here after they tried to sneak a gun to her in the jail, they didn't head up that way. They took off straight to the south, and when I checked their trail the next day, it didn't vary for as long as I followed it. 'Course, that was only for about a mile, so I reckon they coulda circled around after that, and headed up in another direction."

"Well, Ada ain't got no more notion where her pa and brother are than we do," Buck said. "Maybe those Rangers got some notion that she was headin' for Athens, but I'll bet she goes back to her pa's house."

"Maybe I oughta take a ride up that way to see if I can pick up any sign she's been there," Flint suggested.

Buck hesitated. "I don't know, Flint. Ada Tubbs is the Rangers' problem now. She ain't our problem unless she shows up here in town. You go lookin' around up there and you're liable to get shot. She'll be on the lookout for anybody snoopin' around that place, if that's where she is. Ada's crazy, but she ain't dumb. She ain't liable to show up here in town. I expect she's on the run, so that'll give the Rangers something to do. We'll take care of Tinhorn 'cause that's what we're paid to do. Right?"

"You're the boss, Boss. We'll stay here and keep the

peace in case it turns out to get wild on a Saturday," Flint said facetiously, knowing that would be a rare occasion, the Blackie Culver incident being the exception. "Meanwhile, I'll see if our star prisoner wants some more coffee." He picked up the pot from the stove and went into the cell room. "How 'bout it, Ralph? You want some more of this coffee?"

"That 'ud be mighty fine." He got up from his cot where he was sitting while eating his breakfast, walked over to the cell door, and stuck his cup through the bars.

Flint filled the cup, then to satisfy his curiosity, he asked him a question. "When you were ridin' with your old partner, did you and Jed ever use that camp up in Athens?"

Ralph's blank expression was answer enough, but he asked, "Where's Athens?"

"You know, that camp east of Tyler. Maybe it was some place Ada's father had."

"I swear, I don't ever remember Jed sayin' anythin' about it," Ralph declared. "He told me one time Ada's pa had a camp down near Nacogdoches somewhere, but it weren't much more 'n a shack. Me and Jed didn't run with Liam Trask and his boys, anyway."

"I didn't think so," Flint said. "You might be interested to know your old cell mate escaped."

"What?" Ralph exclaimed. "You talkin' about Ada? She escaped?"

"Yep, killed a guard, broke through a window, and stole a horse. That's what Jimmy's telegram was about. We don't know all the details. That's all we were told this mornin'."

"I swear, that don't surprise me none," Ralph declared, shaking his head slowly. "I'll tell you the truth, I'm scared of that woman." He looked up at Flint and nodded. "Jed wouldn't never admit it, but he was scared of her, too."

\* \* \*

The subject of Flint and Ralph's conversation was at that moment in the process of saddling the dun gelding she had acquired in Tyler. She had planned to leave before this late hour in the morning, but had overslept, and was in the barn trying to make sure the makeshift packs she had rigged on a horse she'd selected from the herd in the pasture were going to ride all right. Satisfied, she started to lead the dun out of the barn when she was stopped suddenly by the sound of horses coming through the thicket on the lower side of the yard.

"Damn! I waited too long!" She quickly tied the dun's reins to a post, pulled the Winchester rifle from the saddle sling, and ran to the other end of the barn where she could get a better view of the lower yard.

*You found me quicker than I thought you would, but it's going to be your bad luck that you did.* Cranking a cartridge into the chamber, she stood behind the open barn door and waited. Within a few seconds, she spotted two riders and figured they had come up from the south side of the farm, thinking it best not to ride in on the path from the road on the north side.

Confident she could kill both before they had time to return fire, she brought the rifle up and sighted on the spot where they would come out of the trees into the open. The first horse appeared, and she laid the front sight of the rifle on the rider. Squeezing the trigger slowly, she suddenly jerked the barrel of the rifle up in the air as it fired, when at that moment, she'd recognized the rider as her father. Equally startled, her father and her brother jerked their horses to a stop and drew their weapons as Ada ran out from behind the barn door, waving her arms back and forth over her head and yelling that it was her.

Totally confused, Trask and Vike were not sure it was her, dressed as she was, and with the wide-brimmed hat fixed squarely on her head.

"Ada?" Trask finally blurted. "Ada, is that you?"

"It's me, Pa!" she exclaimed and pulled her hat off to let her hair tumble out, then she ran to meet them. "I almost shot you! I thought you and Vike were Texas Rangers. I got back here last night, and the house was cleaned out. I thought you had left it for good."

"We have left it," Trask told her. "Me and Vike just came back for the horses and then we're gone from here."

"Where's Kyle?"

Her father just hung his head, so Vike answered. "Kyle's dead. We tried to break you outta that jail in Tinhorn, but didn't know you was gone from there. They was waitin' for us, and we had to run for it. They killed Kyle and they shot me in the side. Me and Pa was lucky to get away." He paused while she shook her head as if unable to believe her younger brother was dead. "But what the hell are you doin' here?" Vike asked. "Did they let you go?"

"I let myself go," she answered. "I had to kill a guard to do it, but I didn't have no choice." When her father looked up again at that, she said, "He come on to me like he was gonna have his way."

Vike grinned at that and asked, "No foolin'? How'd you kill him?"

"With a chisel," she answered, then went on to explain the assault, much to Vike's delight, especially the part about the guard's windpipe being severed in two. She told them of her escape, the theft of a horse, and her fake trail toward someplace called Athens.

"So now, you've got the Texas Rangers lookin' for you," Trask commented, not particularly happy with the thought.

"Now, everyone in the family is a horse thief, except Ma," Vike said, finding it amusing. "Where is the horse you stole?"

"In the barn. I was just fixin' to leave here when I heard you comin'." She led them into the barn where the dun was waiting.

Vike immediately began a thorough looking over of the gelding. "You stole a pretty good horse for yourself," he decided. "He looks like he ain't much over four years old. 'Bout time you quit ridin' a mule. You steal the packhorse, too?"

"No," she said. "That's one of the horses that was in the pasture with the rest of that herd. I was surprised that nobody ain't stole 'em yet."

Vike laughed and told his father, "I swear, she's even stealin' from us, Pa."

Not finding the occasion as funny as Vike did, Ada asked her father, "Who killed Kyle? Do you know?"

"That deputy sheriff. He was the only one waitin' in the back of the jail when we came to slip you a gun."

"Flint Moran," Ada pronounced his name softly. She knew before asking the question that it would be Flint Moran, but hearing her father confirm it made her even more angry. "What?" she asked, realizing her father had been saying something to her.

"I said, now that you're back all right, it makes things a little better, although we ain't never gonna get over losin' Kyle. Ain't that right, Vike?"

"Yeah, that's right, Pa," Vike dutifully answered, although in an indifferent tone. "Now, I expect we'd best get those horses movin'. We've got a ways to go."

"Where are you takin' 'em?" Ada asked.

"You remember your Uncle Malcolm?" Trask asked.

Ada said she did.

"Well, me and Vike, and now you, have hooked up with Malcolm and his boys. He's got hisself fixed up pretty nice down on the Angelina River. Me and Malcolm was partners for a few years, back when you and your brothers were a lot younger. He's got some horses he's gettin' ready to move to the market in Fort Worth, so we're gonna drive our horses over and put 'em in with his. I'm just tickled to see ain't nobody found out they were just grazin' here without nobody watchin' 'em."

"Uncle Malcolm's got about two hundred and fifty," Vike said. "Ours will give him a few more reasons to drive 'em to Fort Worth. He says he's workin' on other things right now, and it looks like, whatever they are, he must be doin' pretty good with 'em. When we get to his place, you'll see what I mean. He's got a good-sized ranch fixed up real nice."

"It ain't all that much better 'n what we got right here," his father was quick to comment. He was still competitive enough with Malcolm to be irritated by Vike's remarks about his uncle's success. "I was gonna get into some bigger things, but we ran into this trouble with your husband gettin' arrested, then you gettin' arrested. Now, things as they are, it's a good idea to hook up with Malcolm again."

Vike, still fascinated by his big sister's sudden change of personality, found the new family situation much more to his liking. "Come on, Ada. We got to get this herd outta here. Now that you're a genuine outlaw wanted by the Texas Rangers, let's see what kinda cowboy you are at drivin' horses."

"About as good as you are, I expect," Ada replied.

\* \* \*

It took the three drovers a full day and a half to drive the horses to Malcolm Fletcher's ranch down below Nacogdoches, with a stop for the night by a creek running through a grassy plain. Although a bona fide outlaw and a drover, Ada was still the designated cook. And much to Vike's delight, she fulfilled the role with some pan biscuits to go with the bacon and coffee that night.

Having driven the largest part of the way on the first day, the herd showed up at Fletcher's ranch at dinnertime the next day. Malcolm's four sons mounted up to help them move the horses down near the river where his horses were grazing. Trask remained with Malcolm while they let the young ones take care of the horses.

"I see you picked up another hand when you went after the horses," Malcolm commented when they returned to the barn and dismounted. "Who's the tall skinny feller?"

Confused by the question, Trask looked to see for himself. Then he understood. "That's Ada."

Malcolm was stunned. "Ada?" The last time he had seen her she was a young girl. He felt at once that Trask might have been insulted when he thought she was a man. "Well, I'll be. Standin' way over yonder and dressed up like she is, it was hard to tell. You can see she's a young woman when she comes a little closer."

"If she takes that hat off, you'd get a better look at her," Trask said. "She wears it 'cause it was her husband's hat. Ada ain't the kinda woman to sit home, cookin' and sewin', and waitin' to take care of a man. She mighta been that way once, but not since they shot her husband. She broke him outta jail up in Tinhorn. Used dynamite to blow the whole back of the jail out." Seeing how impressed Malcolm obviously was, Trask continued to boast about his daughter. "The Texas Rangers had her in jail, up in Tyler, but she killed a guard and broke out." He realized that he may have boasted too much when Malcolm reacted with a worried look and asked a question.

"You mean she's got the Texas Rangers lookin' for her?" So far, Malcolm and his boys had traveled far from his ranch to pull off their robberies and holdups, then returned to the ranch to maintain their image as a hard-working cattle ranch.

To date, their activity was far from repetitive. Sometimes, there might be only two robbers who walked into a small-town bank. Other times, all four of them would hit a larger bank in a big town. Their numbers varied so they would not be identified as the same gang to stage the robberies. When he'd invited Trask and Vike to join him, Malcolm's initial thought had been the benefit of more variation and a bigger gang to hit the banks in large towns. But now, he felt some concern upon having a member of his gang who was being sought by the Rangers.

Trask sensed Malcolm's wariness. "I know what you're worried about, and I don't think you've got any worries a-tall about Ada and the Rangers." He went on to tell Malcolm that the woman the Rangers took into custody was wearing a gingham dress when she escaped. And how she had sent the Rangers off in search of her in the opposite direction from Nacogdoches. He refrained from mentioning the wide-brimmed *Boss of the Plains* hat she'd worn, pulled snugly down on her head at the time of her arrest. "You just said, yourself, you thought she was a man when you saw her get off her horse. Shoot, I guarantee you, ain't nobody in any town or train, gonna say they thought they saw Ada Tubbs with us."

"I reckon you're right," Malcolm conceded. "It'd be mighty long odds at that." He smiled. "We was just about to eat dinner when we saw you comin' with that herd of horses, so we waited while the boys went out to help. Melva said that 'ud give her and Nelda time to put on some more biscuits and cut up some potatoes. You go tell Ada and Vike we're expectin' them for dinner. I'll tell Melva to get ready 'cause you brought your appetites with you."

"I'll tell 'em." Trask walked down to the barn where his son and daughter were unsaddling their horses.

Malcolm went into the kitchen to give Melva the word. "They'll be up here in a couple of minutes. And don't ask who the tall stranger is. That's Ada." He got the response he expected when both mother and daughter rushed to the window to take another look.

Dinner was on the table when Ada and the men came in from the barn. Melva welcomed Ada and told her how pleased the Fletchers were to have her come to stay with them. Ada removed her hat and thanked her Aunt Melva and Cousin Nelda, while seeming to be indifferent to all the staring eyes. The determination of sleeping arrangements and bathing schedules would occur but a good deal of the conversation was about plans for the future of the two-family gang.

"I've been wantin' to knock over the big new bank across the state line over in Shreveport," Malcolm told them. "But I was a little shy about tryin' it with just the three older boys and myself. Don't want to include Cody, my youngest, yet. I believe now that we have two more hands, I'm ready to take it on."

"Three more," Ada pointed out. "You have three more hands. I expect to carry my share of the load." Her statement was sufficient to cause a long silent pause while everyone at the table stared at her.

Finally, Malcolm shrugged and said, "Three more, I reckon. We'll be big enough to take on a lot of jobs I wasn't quite ready for yet. We'll be the Fletcher-Trask gang, or maybe you prefer the Trask-Fletcher gang," he said, grinning at Trask.

"I don't give a flip what you call it, as long as it ain't the Jailhouse Gang," Trask said.

With everybody finished eating, Melva and Nelda started clearing away the dishes while the men remained at the table, still drinking coffee and discussing possible targets for bank jobs. Ada got up from the table and helped clear the dishes away, much to Liam Trask's relief. After seeing her transformation to an outlaw, he had been worried she might hold herself exempt from doing women's work. She continued helping with the dishes, even suggesting that Aunt Melva should sit down and let Nelda and her wash them. Melva, obviously pleased, insisted that she should wash, and Ada and Nelda could dry.

Although helping with the cleanup, Ada gave her attention to the conversation between the men. She fully intended to take part in any robbery plans they had.

"So, you're plannin' to hit the big bank in Shreveport. Is that right?" Trask asked.

"We've been talkin' about it," Malcolm answered. "I expect we'll be talkin' more about it now that you and Vike have joined up with us." He paused, then quickly said, "And Ada," though he wasn't completely convinced she would ride with them. "But to tell you the truth, we're lookin' at one a little closer for our next job."

"Where's that?" Trask asked.

"Tinhorn," Malcolm answered.

That trapped Trask's, and Vike's attention at once, as well as Ada's standing near the kitchen door. She immediately stepped inside the dining room to hear more details.

"Tinhorn?" Trask repeated. "I thought you told me you've been stayin' away from Tinhorn because of Buck

Jackson, same reason I had, especially now since he's got that damn trigger-happy deputy."

"Well, that's true," Malcolm replied, "but look at it this way. The Bank of Tinhorn ain't been hit but one time since it was built, and that was a helluva long time ago. That was on the day of its official openin'. Zack and Jesse Slocum tried to rob it, but Buck Jackson caught 'em comin' outta the bank, and they didn't even make it back to their horses. He shot Zack down as he stepped out the door. Jesse threw his hands up, and Jackson arrested him. Sent him to Huntsville prison. So I reckon that scared ever'body who had a notion to rob that bank away from Tinhorn, 'cause of Sheriff Buck Jackson's reputation.

"But you know what? Buck Jackson's got a little older now, just like you and me. I don't know if the bark on him is as hard as it used to be or not, but I know he felt like he had to hire him a deputy to help him. I reckon you and Vike know more about that than we do, and Ada most likely knows more than you."

"That's a fact," Ada stated. "We'd be fightin' one man. Deputy Flint Moran, and he's more than a handful. The sheriff is still dangerous when he's sober, but that ain't usually until later on in the day. If we hit the bank in the mornin', it'll be the deputy we'll have to worry about the most, but he ain't but one man. Those people in that town have been left alone so long they think they don't need anybody but Buck Jackson to protect them. If a couple of us take care of the sheriff and the deputy, then the town is ours. There ain't no vigilance committee. There ain't anybody that'll raise a hand to try to stop us."

A brief moment of silence followed when she finished, since none of the men at the table had ever heard a bank job briefing by a woman.

Malcolm looked at Trask and asked "You was in the jail to see Ada when she was locked up. Do you agree with what she says?"

"Pretty much," Trask replied. "She knows more about 'em than me and Vike."

# CHAPTER 17

Texas Ranger Matt Conway pulled his horse up to the hitching rail in front of the Tinhorn sheriff's office and dismounted. It was still fairly early on this Monday morning, so Flint was in the office while Buck was at the saloon for his usual late breakfast. Busy cleaning his rifle, Flint looked up when Conway walked in the door. "Sheriff Jackson?"

"No, I'm Deputy Moran. The sheriff stepped over to eat a bite of breakfast." He took notice of the Ranger's badge pinned to Conway's vest. "You lookin' for Ada Tubbs?"

"As a matter of fact." Conway laughed. "And it sure woulda been nice if she was locked up in your jail." He extended his hand and Flint shook it. "I'm Matt Conway and I came down to see if you folks could tell me how to get to her pa's house. We followed her trail outta Tyler all the way to Athens with no trace a-tall. So, they sent me down here to check out her daddy's place, in case she went back there."

"I'd be glad to take you out to the Trask place," Flint said. "You probably wanna talk to Sheriff Jackson, so why don't we go across the street. You musta left Tyler early to get here this time of mornin'. Do you need to get something to eat? If you do, you missed the dinin' room for breakfast. They've already closed. If you're hungry, you can get something across the street at the saloon. But I ain't recommendin' it. The sheriff eats there most days because he likes to eat later in the mornin'."

Conway looked lost in the conversation.

"I'm tellin' you all this to keep you from gettin' hoof-and-mouth disease, or something worse. But if you're real hungry, the coffee's all right, and so are the biscuits. Anything else, you've been warned."

"Well, I sure appreciate all the information." Conway chuckled. "I might try the coffee."

They walked into Jake's Place and found Buck sitting at a table talking to Jake. "Buck, this is Ranger Matt Conway from up Tyler way."

Buck nodded cordially and Jake got up out of his chair. "Here, let me get outta the way, if you boys need to talk some official business. Can I get you anything? Something to eat. Some coffee? Something stronger?"

"I believe that's the whole menu." Buck chuckled. "You want anything, Mr. Conway?"

Conway took a look at Buck's plate before he answered. "I'll take a cup of coffee and a couple of those biscuits. And throw in a piece of that ham with 'em."

Jake picked up his coffee cup and moved it to another table not quite out of earshot, then went into the kitchen to give Rena the order.

"I was wonderin' if you boys wouldn't be showin' up here in Tinhorn before much longer," Buck said. "There weren't no sign of her in Athens, was there?"

Conway shook his head.

Buck continued. "We figured Ada musta thought out some way to throw you on the wrong track."

"She stopped at a store right outside of Tyler and bought some things. It's at the crossroad leadin' to Athens. She asked the store owner where that road went and he told her. She musta figured he'd watch to see which road she took."

"Like we say here," Buck said, "she's crazy as hell, but she ain't dumb. The telegram said she killed a guard. How'd she do that?" When Conway told them of the brutal killing of the guard, Leon Rafer, Buck remarked once again, "She's crazy as hell." He paused when Rena brought the Ranger coffee and a plate and let him take a couple of sips and a bite of a biscuit before continuing. "So you want Flint to take you out to Liam Trask's place, right?"

"Yes, sir," Conway responded. "That's what I want, or at least tell me how I might find it myself if you can't spare him."

"Things are pretty quiet around here today, so we're glad to help the Rangers any way we can. He's been itchin' to ride out there, anyway, to take a look around."

"If you rode all the way from Tyler this mornin', you're gonna need to rest your horse. It's about ten-and-a-half miles out to Trask's," Flint told him. "We can throw your saddle on another horse and let yours rest up while we go up there. 'Course, if you're goin' right back to Tyler tonight, you could lead your horse up to Trask's 'cause you'll be halfway to Tyler."

"I don't know what I'm gonna do," Conway said. "It depends on what I find. I didn't bring a packhorse with me, but if I pick up a strong trail I'll get on it, anyway."

"Let me remind you, Flint," Buck declared in an official-like tone, "you've got a job here in this town. You ain't a Texas Ranger, so you take Mr. Conway to the Trask place and then you come home."


Conway decided he would lead his horse up to Trask's place, just in case he picked up a trail that took him farther west or north. Flint figured the Ranger planned to go on back to Tyler all along, and that was the reason for no packhorse. So while he was eating his biscuits and ham, Flint went to the stable and saddled Buster. Then he led Jed Tubbs' horse back to the saloon and Conway threw his saddle on him.

Rena put the rest of her biscuits and ham in a sack and gave them to Flint. "Here. It'll be close to dinnertime by the time you get where you're goin'."

"Why, that's mighty kind of you," Flint told her. "I'm beginnin' to think all those bad things Jake says about you ain't true."

"Everybody knows Jake's the biggest liar in town," Rena said.


They made the trip up to the path that led into Trask's farm in about two-and-a-half hours, taking it easy on Conway's horse. The first thing Flint noticed as they approached the house was the empty pasture beyond the barn. They pulled up to look the place over before riding on into the yard. There was no sign of anyone about, but they did not think it wise to assume that to be the case. Flint had been convinced Liam Trask and his son, Vike, had fled somewhere to the south of Tinhorn, and would not come back. The question in his mind was, did Ada come back, and if so, would she have stayed there? As a precaution, before going into the house, they rode beyond it and went in the back of the barn when they found that the back door was open. When they found no horses, and no sign of anything of useful value in the tack room, they felt pretty sure no one was in the house, either, and rode their horses straight through the barn, up to the back steps of the house, and tied them there.

Inside the house was ample evidence of the evacuation of Trask and his sons, which Flint assumed happened before they tried to free Ada from the jail. The question he and Conway came to find an answer for was whether or not Ada actually came there first. The one room that was obviously Ada's was in disarray, as were the others. But the short hanging rod on the wall had half a dozen dresses, and the dresser drawers were filled with feminine undergarments and stockings. The first impression was she had not returned to her home, but then Flint saw the definite proof that she had been there. On the floor in the corner of the room, he recognized the gingham dress she'd worn ever since he kidnapped her from the outhouse path. Lying near it were the shoes he recognized as well.

"Well, I'll be damned," Conway swore when Flint told him. "She did send us off on a wild goose chase. She set that whole thing up with that visit to the store. Now the question is which way did she go from here?"

"I've gotta believe Trask and his son came back to get the horses that were in that pasture," Flint declared. "I think there's a chance she went with 'em. But if she didn't, I think she mighta gone to the same place on her own." He looked at Conway and shrugged. "If I was a Texas Ranger, that's the trail I would follow. And a trail left by fifty horses ain't a hard trail to follow."

"If you were a Texas Ranger," Conway replied, "you woulda probably brought a packhorse with you. I was so damn sure that woman was headed for Injun Territory, I didn't bother with the packhorse 'cause I just knew she didn't come this way."

"Maybe she didn't. I was just sayin' that's what I would do."

Conway agreed. "That's what I have to do. I think you're right about those horses. Her father was movin' 'em someplace he thinks is safe. She could very well be goin' to the same place. I just made the job of followin' her a whole lot tougher on myself."

"I'd go with you, if I wanted to lose my job. You heard the sheriff when he told me to get myself back to Tinhorn. But maybe we can make it easier for you. I can leave this extra horse with you for a packhorse. I saw a sheet of canvas out there in the barn. We oughta be able to cut it up in some strips and rig you up a pack saddle. It looks like these folks were in a hurry to get outta here, so we oughta check that smokehouse on the other side of the barn. There might be some cured meat still hanging in there. We can look in the kitchen for anything you could use. Hell, they musta left something you could cook." He could see from Conway's expression that he was up for it, so they got right to it.

By the time they were finished, Conway figured his horse was rested and watered enough to start again. Flint took another look at the makeshift pack saddle they had made out of canvas strips to make sure it wasn't going to come loose and dump the load of dried beans they'd found in the pantry. The bags that held them looked suspiciously like Ada's drawers.

"I believe it's gonna hold together," Flint decided.

"Flint, I appreciate your help on this job," Conway said after he climbed up into the saddle. "I don't think I woulda thought of that canvas pack saddle."

"Glad I could help," Flint replied. "Wish I could go with you. If I was you, I'd be extra careful if you do catch up with that woman. There ain't no tellin' what she's capable of."

"You don't have to tell me that," Conway said. "Not after I saw the job she did on Leon Rafer." He gave him a little salute with his forefinger to the brim of his hat and rode out of the yard to follow the trail left by fifty horses.

"Good huntin'," Flint called after him, then stepped up into the saddle and turned Buster back toward the Tyler-Tinhorn road. He had mixed feelings about the tracking of Ada Tubbs. He had no great desire to go with Conway to track Ada and her family down. Buck was right. It was the Rangers' job now. Flint should be satisfied that he had helped put a Ranger on her trail. But the trouble with Ada started out in Tinhorn, and it bothered him to think the Tinhorn lawmen didn't take care of the whole job.

Well past the dinner hour, but not quite time for supper, Flint rode back into Tinhorn and left his horse with Lon Blake. As usual, Lon wanted to know where Flint had been, so he told him the Texas Rangers were after Ada. They briefly discussed the Rangers' chances of catching her. Since he was closer to the boarding house than he was to the jail, he decided to go by his room first to get a clean pair of socks. He had worn a hole in the heel of his right sock, and it was beginning to irritate him. He walked around to the back of the house to the back steps and his preferred entrance. He changed his socks, pulled his boots back on, and was just locking the door when he turned around to find Hannah standing in the kitchen doorway, smiling at him. "Oh, howdy, Miz Green," he blurted. "You took me by surprise."

She laughed politely. "I looked out the window and saw you sneaking around to your room," she teased. "Some of my guests think you go out of your way to avoid conversation."

"Is that what they think?" Flint asked, pretending to frown. "I reckon they're smarter than I thought." He laughed.

"No, it's just that it's quicker to go straight to my room if I walk through the yard."

"Missed you again at dinner," Hannah commented. "You and the sheriff eat at Clara's?"

"No, I had to ride halfway to Tyler to help a Texas Ranger, and I didn't get back till right now."

"So you missed dinner again. How are you gonna keep your strength up if you don't eat when you're supposed to?"

He laughed again. "I don't miss many meals. That's for sure."

"Well, I made a good guess. I had a craving for a fresh cup of coffee, but I didn't want to waste coffee on myself. So, when I saw you coming this way, I put my small pot on the stove, and it oughta be just about ready by now. I've got a couple of biscuits left from dinner and some apple butter. I'm inviting you to join me for coffee." When he hesitated a few moments, thinking he should let Buck know he was back, she said, "No, I'm insisting you join me for coffee."

"When you put it that way, I reckon I'd better say I'd be pleased to pieces to sit down and have some coffee. I am kinda hungry."

"Good," she gushed and held the kitchen door open for him. "Just follow me." In the kitchen, she pointed to a chair at the table. "Sit yourself down. We'll have our coffee at the kitchen table. It's cozier than the dining room."

He did as she instructed, realizing he could use some coffee and biscuits since he had insisted Matt Conway take all the biscuits with him that Rena had given them that morning.

However, Flint was beginning to feel a little discomfort as a result of Hannah Green's sudden special attention to him. Hannah was an attractive woman, no denying that.

She had to be a few years older than he, but not so many that it wouldn't work out. But he wasn't in the market for any permanent arrangements with a woman. And she was so doggone nice, he did not want to hurt her feelings.

She poured two cups of coffee, placed a plate before him with a couple of biscuits on it, and put a jar of apple butter beside the plate. "Do you want me to butter your biscuits for you?"

"Ah, no, ma'am. I can do it."

She took a sip of her coffee. "This is so nice. I'm glad you came home and gave me an excuse to make coffee." She gave him a sweet smile. "You know, Flint Moran, every time I see you come in the house, I can't help but think of my niece. She's about your age, maybe a little younger. Her name is Nancy. She's written me that she's thinking about coming to see me, and I just bet you two would be the best of friends."

"Whoo, boy!" Flint blurted in total relief before he could catch himself. When Hannah looked alarmed, he quickly explained. "Hot coffee. I took a big gulp, and it was hot." He grabbed the spoon beside the apple butter jar and spooned out some of it on the biscuits. "I just thought about Buck. He's waitin' for me to get back to report. If I take too long, he'll come lookin' for me. I really do appreciate you doin' this for me. I hate to be a bother."

"Not at all," Hannah said. "Like I said, I was craving some coffee for myself."

He quickly finished and thanked her again. "I'd better get goin'. I'm sure I'd like your niece, if she's anywhere near as nice as you are."

Buck was in the office when Flint walked in. "I was just about ready to go look for you, but I got my usual report from Lon Blake that you were in town somewhere. I figured you'd eventually come in to tell me what you found up there at Trask's."

"Ada was there, but she ain't now," Flint said. "Somebody went up there and took the horses. Ranger Matt Conway is following the trail left by the herd of horses, and he wants you to telegraph Ranger headquarters and tell them that. End of report." He paused, then said, "And we're now missin' one horse. Conway took it for a packhorse."

Buck naturally wanted more details than that, starting with, "How do you know Ada was there?"

Flint told him about the dress and the shoes, then told him about the making of the rig for a pack saddle.

"I bet that was your idea," Buck remarked. "I hope that Ranger knows what he's dealin' with in that woman."

"I think he does. He got a look at what Ada did to that guard." He chuckled when he thought of something else. "I don't think he'll ever go off again without takin' a packhorse."

Later that day, Ranger Matt Conway was thinking those same thoughts. He had followed the broad trail left by Liam Trask's horses until it began to get too dark to see, then stopped at the first place that looked suitable for his camp. He guided his horses to a creek bank close by the path he had followed since leaving Flint. After taking the saddle off his horse, he unloaded his packhorse, watching carefully to make sure he remembered how to put the rig back together again in the morning. He considered the dried beans he had brought, but he had no means, nor the time, to soak them properly, and he had no pan. He resigned himself to having a supper of water and the bacon he'd found in the smokehouse, saying a silent prayer of thanks for Rena's biscuits. He told himself it was a lesson he was being taught.

Breakfast the next morning was the same fare, bacon and the last biscuit, with an even stronger craving for a cup of coffee.

After putting his pack saddle back together properly, he took up the trail again, alternating his pace between walking and trotting. The trail led him eventually to a river he could only guess might be the Angelina. The herd of horses had crossed over the river, then continued south again. It was late afternoon when he saw ranch buildings up ahead, and what was most likely the end of the trail. He rode a little closer before he saw the pastures beyond a thin ribbon of trees, probably lining a stream, he figured. There were many more than fifty horses in the string of pastures. The question before him now, to ride on in to inquire, or to set up someplace to watch the house and barn.

That decision was made for him when he realized he had already been spotted. A rider sat watching him from the top of a low ridge to his left. Movement in the line of trees on his right told him another rider was on that side. Conway reached up, took his badge off his vest, put it in an inside pocket, and nudged his horse with his heel toward the ranch buildings.

Entering the barnyard, he saw a couple of men come out of the barn to meet him, so he guided his horse toward them. Off to his left, the back door to the house opened and another man walked out to stand on the small porch to watch.

"Howdy," Harley Fletcher greeted him, while his brother, Justin, walked around to the other side of him.

Conway returned the greeting. That was all that was said for a few awkward moments until Vike Trask came out of the barn to join them.

"I swear, mister, that's some pack saddle you got on that horse," Vike said. All three men laughed at that.

"Yeah, ain't that somethin'?" Conway replied. "But sometimes you gotta go with whatever you got. Somebody stole my packhorse, so I had to make one."

"Dang," Harley said. "That is tough luck. What brings you out to this part of the county?"

"Horses," Conway answered. "I was hired to find a source to buy good horses, so I came to get a look at the stock. I see you've got plenty of horses, so I must be in the right place. What ranch is this?"

"What ranch are you lookin' for?" Harley answered, a wide smile spread across his face.

"Well, you see, that's just the problem," Conway answered. "I had the name of the ranch and the directions on how to get there in a notebook that was on my packhorse. And I hate to admit it, but I can't remember the name to save my soul."

"Was it Fletcher?" Justin asked.

"That sounds right," Conway replied, "I believe it was Fletcher. Is this the Fletcher ranch?"

"What is it, Harley?" Malcolm Fletcher called out from the kitchen steps.

"Feller says he was lookin' for the Fletcher ranch 'cause he's lookin' to buy some horses," Harley answered.

"He is?" Malcolm went down the steps to join them. "Howdy. I'm Malcolm Fletcher. I own this ranch. We're fixin' to drive our horses to Fort Worth to the market. How many are you lookin' to buy?"

"Not as many as you've got out there in that pasture." Caught in his hoax, Conway was forced to continue.

"Maybe it weren't us you were supposed to find," Malcolm suggested. "Maybe you was lookin' for the Trask farm. They've got a smaller herd."

"Maybe you're right," Conway said, not at all comfortable with the situation since Malcolm casually mentioned Trask. He was afraid they were suspicious. Four of them now stood around him and his horses, and they were all grinning like dogs eating yellow jackets. "Well, it was nice meeting you folks. I reckon I'd best turn around and see if I can find the Trask farm."

Before he could turn his horse, Malcolm took hold of the bridle and held him. "What's your hurry? It's too late to find Trask today. You might as well step down and take supper with us. We don't get the chance to entertain many visitors. Right now, we got some folks from back up your way that's visitin'. I know they'd like to say hello." He turned his head toward the house and yelled, "Ada, there's somebody out here to see ya."

Conway's body went tense immediately as he looked at four drawn guns aimed at him. He felt his blood stop in his veins when he saw the tall, lanky woman step outside the kitchen door.

Malcolm called out to her. "Ada, is this your deputy sheriff from Tinhorn come to see ya?"

"No, that ain't him," Ada called back. "I ain't ever seen him before." She walked out and stood with them.

"He ain't?" Malcolm responded. He had thought for sure this was Flint Moran, the deputy who was chasing Ada, Vike, and their father.

"I coulda told you that," Vike said. "I didn't know you thought it was Moran."

Back to Conway then, Malcolm demanded, "Then, who the hell are you? Pull him down from there, boys."

Harley and Justin grabbed Conway and pulled him off the horse. Each holding one of Conway's arms, they stood him up before their father. Vike stepped behind him and relieved him of his weapon. By this time, all the Fletcher and Trask families had come to witness the action.

Malcolm started searching through Conway's vest and shirt. "Uh-oh, wait a minute, what is this? Folks, we have caught us a genuine Texas Ranger." Back to Conway again, he asked, "Mister, what in the world were you thinkin', to come ridin' in here like this?"

Since in his mind, he was already dead, Conway calmly responded, "To tell you the truth, Mr. Fletcher, since I got up this mornin', I've made one mistake after another, and I reckon this last one is the biggest."

"I swear, I kinda like this feller's attitude," Malcolm remarked, then jumped, startled when a gun went off right beside him, and Conway clutched his chest and collapsed.

They all reacted to the sudden shot and turned to see Ada standing there, the Colt Six-Shooter still pointing toward the fallen man.

"He was a Texas Ranger," she offered calmly in explanation, turned around, and went back into the house.

Her blatant act of extermination, as heartless as killing a rat in a trap, was the shock that brought a cold fact to the forefront. As Ada coldly stated, he was a Texas Ranger, and now the question to be answered was, how did he know to come here, looking for Ada? That was going to be the topic of discussion around the supper table that night, and whether or not it was to have any effect upon the plans to rob the Tinhorn bank.

Malcolm Fletcher was understandably concerned that the Trasks' arrival on his ranch had put them all in jeopardy.

It was Ada who was worried the least of all, and she offered her reasons why. "I spent enough time in the Tinhorn jail to learn how the sheriff and deputy think. Buck Jackson doesn't want his deputy working outside the town limits of Tinhorn. Jackson expects Moran to do the job he's paid to

do. That's why they ain't come looking for Papa and Vike."
She looked at her father. "They think they've run you out
of town, and for Buck Jackson, that's all he wants. Besides,
he knows he has hurt you with Kyle's death. They have
turned me over to the Rangers, so they have washed their
hands of me. As for this Ranger today, you saw that he
came alone. If they thought I was down here near Nacogdoches, there would have been more. They sent him alone
just to make sure I was not back at our farm. He saw the big
trail the herd of horses left, so he followed it. He was just
lucky, or unlucky, as it turned out for him. They don't
know where he is, and if they come lookin' for him, they'll
go to our old homeplace north of Tinhorn. They don't
know where we are, and the Tinhorn sheriff doesn't care
where we are."

A lot more was discussed on the issue, but generally,
both families agreed that Ada was probably right. And their
activities should continue as planned.

# CHAPTER 18

The days that followed the killing of Matt Conway were uneventful on the Fletcher ranch, which was reassuring to Malcolm and Liam. Some of the boys went out to check on the trail left by the fifty horses Trask brought all the way down to the ranch. It seemed to be just as Ada said it would be. The grass and brush would soon recover and there would be no trail to show the horses had been driven there. Since Ada could not know of Flint Moran's involvement in the Texas Ranger incident, and that Tyler had been notified Conway was following her trail down south of Tinhorn, it was hard to predict how long Conway had to go missing before a party was sent to investigate. And even when they did, Ada insisted they would start at the Trask farm. By that time, there would no longer be any sign of a trail left by the herd of horses. It would be extremely unlikely Conway's body would ever be found, since it was buried in a wild stretch of bluffs on the Angelina River.

In light of all this, it was decided to plan the robbery of the Bank of Tinhorn.

Malcolm and Harley would ride up to Tinhorn one day to scout the bank and the town, the location of the sheriff's office and how far it was from the bank, where to leave the horses, and which way to leave the town. It was forty-four miles to Tinhorn from the ranch, so they decided to make the trip in one day, stay overnight, and scout the town the next day. Depending on what they found, they'd start back that same day. Trask was disappointed not to go with Malcolm, but he knew he would be recognized if he showed up in Tinhorn. Malcolm and his son left the ranch early one Sunday morning for the long ride to Tinhorn.

Fred Johnson, desk clerk at the Tinhorn Hotel, looked up when he heard the front door open. Two strangers walked in, looking right and left as if they'd never been in a hotel before.

"Can I help you gentlemen?" Fred asked.

"I hope so," Malcolm Fletcher replied. "Me and my son have been ridin' all day, and we need a room for the night. Can you fix us up?"

"I sure can," Fred answered. "You want one room or two?"

"One room oughta do." Malcolm asked, "Has it got a good-sized bed?"

"Yes, sir, it's a full-size bed," Fred assured him.

"One room, then," Malcolm said. "Has the hotel got a stable?"

"No, sir, but you can take your horses to the stable down at the other end of the street, and there'll be no charge. The hotel has an arrangement with the stable. We pay for your horses."

"How 'bout the dinin' room?" Harley asked. "Are we too late to get some supper?"

Fred assured him that Clara's Kitchen would be open for another hour, and that would give them time to take their horses to the stable before they ate. So they said they would take the room.

"What are your names?" Fred asked as he started to fill out the guest register.

"We're Malcolm and Harley Smith," Malcolm said. "I'm Malcolm. He's Harley."

Fred started to write, then paused to smile at them. "You aren't any kin to the owner of the hotel, are you? His name is Gilbert Smith."

Malcolm had to chuckle. "Well, now, I don't rightly know, to tell you the truth. You know how many hundreds of Smiths there are. If we are kin, your Mr. Smith most likely wouldn't want to claim it."

"Just thought I'd ask," Fred said with a chuckle. "It would have been a coincidence."

After they put their saddlebags in their room, they took their horses to the stable, which they had passed when they first hit town. Lon Blake assured them that he would take good care of their horses.

Harley said, "Come on, Mr. Smith, let's go eat before they close that dinin' room."

Lon was puzzled to see them so amused by that.

"I'm gonna have to come up with a reason why I didn't eat supper at the boardin' house again," Flint complained. "Hannah wants to know why, every time I don't show up. I hope Myrna doesn't think it's the cookin' I don't like."

"It is hard to beat Clara's when you're talkin' about day in and day out, three meals a day," Buck remarked, and signaled Mindy for more coffee. "When is that niece of Hannah's gonna show up for the visit?"

"I don't know," Flint answered. "I don't know if Hannah really knows." He was sorry he had told Buck about his coffee with Hannah and the threat of niece Nancy. It had provided Buck with an opportunity to periodically jape him about it. He was about to tell him so when they were suddenly distracted by an issue at the door of the dining room.

They paused to see what the problem was and saw right away it was one that occurred quite regularly with strangers. They waited for a minute or two to see if Clara would be able to explain the policy and take care of the problem. But it soon appeared that she was not having much success.

"I'll go," Flint volunteered and got up from the table.

Malcolm was in the middle of a long explanation to Clara as to why there was no reason for him and Harley to surrender their weapons. "We're registered guests in the hotel, and so we oughten not have to take our guns off." He glanced up and saw Flint approaching, wearing a badge and a gun. He looked back accusingly at Clara. "What? You called the law on us?"

"No," Flint answered him. "She didn't call the law. The sheriff and I are eatin' supper, and it looked like you were concerned about takin' off your guns. I thought maybe I could reassure you that nobody else in the dinin' room is wearin' a gun but the sheriff and me. It's the policy of the dinin' room. They want you and everybody else to enjoy a nice peaceful supper. I know this table is close to that outside door, but if you're worried about somebody runnin' in and stealin' your guns, I want you to know the sheriff and I will keep an eye on 'em while you eat. Now, is there any other reason why you don't wanna do what every other customer came in here for, to have a quiet, peaceful supper? I'm willin' to bet you'll find the food good." He waited for their reaction.

The determined expression on Malcolm's face slowly dissolved to form a smile of amusement. "What is your name?" he asked politely. When Flint told him, Malcolm repeated it. "Deputy Moran, I thought so."

"Yeah? Why is that?" Flint replied. "I don't recall seein' you fellows before."

"Nothin'," Malcolm answered him. "I just heard your name mentioned somewhere. I don't remember where." He started unbuckling his gun belt, the grin even wider now. "My name's Malcolm Smith. This is my son, Harley. Harley, take your gun off. We don't wanna disturb the peace here in the dinin' room." To Flint, he said, "'Preciate the explanation."

Flint nodded. "Hope you enjoy your supper. Welcome to Tinhorn."

"Just seat yourself anywhere you like," Clara told them.

They left their gun belts on the table and walked over to a table near the window.

Flint couldn't help noticing the younger man's walk. He was not a big man, but he walked boldly, with his shoulders square and his head held high. It looked as if he was trying to look bigger than he actually was.

Clara raised her eyebrows and shook her head, then whispered to Flint, "Thanks."

When Flint returned to the table, Buck wasn't even interested enough to ask him anything about the conversation, figuring it was taken care of. But Flint couldn't forget the smile of amusement on the face of the man who said he was the younger man's father. He thought it odd that the man said he had heard of him, when he was a stranger in town, unless he had some contact with someone Flint or Buck had arrested.

Finally Flint shrugged and thought, *nothing to do about it.*

At the table by the window, a genuine smile of amusement was pasted on Malcolm Fletcher's face. He had taken a chair that allowed him to watch the sheriff and his deputy. "I can't wait to tell Ada that Deputy Flint Moran, himself, officially welcomed us to Tinhorn."

"She'll probably ask you why you didn't just take your gun out and shoot him." Harley said between large bites of roast beef. "That's how she handled that Ranger." He turned his head to take another look at Flint. "He don't look all that hellfire mean, like she talks about him. That big horse he's settin' with looks like he'd be a handful."

"A feller that size just makes an easy target," Malcolm commented. "Besides, I've heard some people say he's been on the job too long, and that's the reason they hired a deputy."

"Maybe so," Harley declared. "But I'd just as well not see him again when we come back here. He's got a helluva reputation. Put a lotta men in the ground."

"Ada says he's took to the whiskey bottle, and that'll dang-sure slow you down." Malcolm waved his hand back and forth until he got Mindy's attention. When she went over, he said, "Gimme a slice of that pie that feller over there's eatin'." He looked at Harley and told her, "Make it two."

She returned shortly with two slices of apple pie.

He took a look at it and said, "That looks pretty good. Take a couple more slices over there to the sheriff and his deputy. Tell 'em it's compliments of Malcolm and Harley Smith."

When she left to do his bidding, Harley was prone to ask, "What the hell are you doin', Pa? You tryin' to start some trouble with 'em?"

Malcolm laughed at his son's concern. "Trouble? I just bought 'em a slice of apple pie. They ain't gonna arrest us for that."

Harley could see that his father was enjoying the fact

that he knew a bank robbery was going to happen in their town, and the law had no idea they were eating pie with two of the robbers. He felt the need to correct his father's attitude. "I thought we was supposed to stay low while we scouted this town, so nobody wouldn't notice us."

"Maybe that's what we talked about doin'," Malcolm replied. "And that's what we woulda done if we hadn't got into that argument with the boss-lady and wound up with the deputy steppin' into it. So we was already noticed. The best thing to do now is let 'em know we ain't got nothin' to hide." While he talked, he was watching the lawmen's table, waiting to see their reaction to his gift. In a minute or two, Mindy went to their table with the pie. Malcolm grinned to see the looks of surprise on the two lawmen's faces as they questioned Mindy. Then they both turned to look at Malcolm and Harley and nodded their thanks. Malcolm responded with a wave back at them.

"I don't know, Pa," Harley said. "I can't decide if you're smart or crazy as a bat. Let's just finish up this pie and get the hell outta here."

At Buck and Flint's table, Buck commented, "That's mighty good pie. I swear, Flint, what did you say to those two? You sure musta made an impression on 'em."

"There's something mighty fishy about those two," Flint said. "I can't help feelin' they're up to something. Makes me think I'd better keep an extra sharp eye when I'm makin' my rounds tonight."

As he said it, Malcolm and Harley got up to leave and Malcolm nodded once again toward their table. Both Buck and Flint held up a hand to respond.

When the strangers went out the door to the outside, Flint waved Mindy over. "Those two that just left, did they say why they sent that pie over here?"

Mindy shrugged. "All they said was the pie looked

good, and to send a couple of slices to you and the sheriff. Is something wrong?"

"No, I was just wonderin'. It ain't every day a couple of strangers buy you a slice of pie. Have you got Ralph's plate ready to travel?"

"And put a slice of pie on it," Buck said with a chuckle. "Everybody gets pie tonight." Buck decided to linger for one more cup of coffee.

Mindy walked to the door and held it open. "Good night, Flint," she said as he went out the door.

"Goodnight, Mindy," he returned, his mind still occupied by the two strangers. As he took Ralph's supper, complete with a slice of apple pie, down to the jail, he decided to keep a real sharp eye out for anything that didn't look just right.

Ralph was pleased to get the apple pie with his Sunday night supper, so Flint told him how it came about. He talked for a while, knowing how much Ralph appreciated any opportunity for conversation. It wasn't long before Buck came into the office, and as usual, not very long before he said everything was quiet in the town so he'd retire to his room and do some reading.

"I'll see that the town gets buttoned up for the night," Flint told him.

After Buck left, Flint hung around the office until Ralph was through eating and had all the coffee he could hold. Then he locked the office and began his nightly rounds.

The town was already locked down pretty much, since it was a Sunday. Even the church was dark. Due to poor attendance, they'd quit having the evening services. The Reverend Rance Morehead said he could preach to himself at home as well as he had been doing at the church on Sunday nights. The only place open was Jake's Place.

Flint stopped in. While he was talking to Jake and Rudy,

the two strangers came into the saloon. Seeing Flint, Malcolm Fletcher walked over to the bar to join him, leaving Harley no choice but to follow, striding boldly as usual.

"Well, Deputy Moran," Malcolm spoke out. "Fancy meetin' you again. Me and my son was takin' a little after-supper walk around your town before we turn in for the night. We thought we'd like a little drink first. This is our first time in Tinhorn. Looks like a nice, peaceful little town."

"Mr. Smith," Flint returned. "Jake and Rudy, this is Malcolm Smith and his son, Harlan."

"That's Harley," Malcolm corrected him.

"Harley, beg your pardon," Flint continued. "They're stayin' at the hotel tonight and I owe 'em a drink of whiskey."

"That's mighty sportin' of you, Deputy," Malcolm replied. "I didn't expect anything for that piece of pie. I just thought you might enjoy some."

Flint reached into his pocket, pulled out a couple of coins, and put them on the bar. "I like to stay square on all my debts," he insisted as Rudy poured the two drinks.

"Well, if you insist," Malcolm replied. "It's always best not to have any debts, I reckon." He slid one of the shot glasses over to Harley, who was not at all comfortable with the situation. "Why don't you pour another and have a drink with us," Malcolm suggested.

Harley bit his lower lip to keep from saying anything. He knew his father was just trying to fatten up the story he was eager to tell everybody back home. He could already boast about buying the pie and the deputy buying him a drink. It would be an even more entertaining story if he could say that they even had a drink of whiskey together. Harley was glad when the deputy declined.

"Thanks, anyway," Flint said. "I'm on duty, and I don't drink when I'm on duty."

"Sorry to hear that." Malcolm tossed his whiskey back. "Drink up, son," he said when Harley hesitated. He knew Harley hated the law enough not to want to drink the whiskey.

"Where are you and Harley headed?" Flint asked.

"We're headin' up Tyler way," Malcolm answered. "There's some timber land up there we wanna take a look at. We might wanna set up a sawmill up that way."

"Is that a fact?" Flint asked. "Where's home for you?"

"Shreveport," Malcolm said. That being the only town he could think of on the spur of the moment. And that was only because that was the planned site of their next holdup after the Tinhorn bank.

"You've come a long way," Flint said.

"Yes, we have, and we've gotta get an early start in the mornin'. So instead of standin' around here, gabbin' and drinkin', we'd best thank you for the whiskey and say good night to you all." Malcolm tapped Harley's shoulder. "Come on, son." When he had safely reached the door, he called back over his shoulder, "Nice talkin' to ya, Deputy."

Downright suspicious of the two, Flint looked at the big clock on the wall behind the bar. "I gotta get outta here, too. I'll see you later." He hurried out the door in time to see Malcolm and Harley walking rapidly toward the hotel, so he went in the opposite direction. The stable had already closed, so he went around to the back where Lon's living quarters were. A lamp was burning inside the small apartment, so he rapped on the door.

It took several times before Lon called out, "Who is it?"

"Lon, it's me, Flint."

Lon opened the door immediately afraid that his barn or the stable was on fire.

"I'm sorry to bother you like this, but I need to ask you a question."

"A question?" Lon asked, amazed he had been awakened for that. "What kinda question?"

"Two strangers in the hotel left their horses with you today. Malcolm and Harley Smith they said their names were. At least that's how they registered at the hotel. All I need to know is how many packhorses did they have and were they loaded pretty heavy?"

Lon looked stumped for a moment. "They didn't have no packhorses. Just the two horses they rode in on."

"That's all I need to know, and I wanna say again I'm sorry to wake you up for that. But I really needed to know it."

"Shoot, that's all right, Flint," Lon said. "I'da probably woke up before long anyway. I forgot to turn my lamp off."

Flint hurried away from the stable and took a quick check to make sure everything was all right at the jail. Ralph was already asleep, so Flint locked up again and hustled up to the hotel. It was getting late, but the night clerk, J.C. White was still at the desk.

"Whatcha say, Flint?" White greeted him when he walked in. "You just caught me. I was fixin' to go to my room. What can I do for ya?"

"I'm just kinda curious about a couple of your guests. Their names are Malcolm and Harley Smith."

"Yeah. They just walked in a few minutes ago."

"I would just like to know how much luggage they checked in with. I mean any big bags, or funny-lookin' bags. But I'd rather they not know I'm checkin' on 'em. I know you weren't here when they checked in, so I was gonna ask if I could take a quick look in their room. But they're already back in it. It's most likely nothin' a-tall. I was just curious."

"Well, I can tell you that," White said. "I put some clean

towels in their room earlier this evenin', and they didn't have any luggage. Nothin' but two saddlebags."

"Just their saddlebags?" Flint asked to be sure.

"That's all there was," White confirmed. "Is somethin' wrong?"

"No, nothin' wrong. Well, thanks, J.C. Like I said, I was just curious."

Flint walked back out the front door of the hotel and paused on the front porch for a few minutes while he thought about Malcolm and Harley Smith, and what they might have in mind. Maybe Buck was right. He had commented that Malcolm just had a little too many wheels in his brain that weren't turning at the right speed.

"Maybe I've just got too much sawdust in my brain," Flint muttered to himself, "but I believe those two are up to something. And I doubt if it's legal." He was determined to keep a sharp eye on the town for the rest of the night, even though he couldn't imagine they could have any illegal act planned. They were checked into the hotel, and their horses were locked up in the stable. They had brought nothing with them but their saddlebags. They weren't prepared to do anything, unless they were going to meet someone else who was prepared.

His first thought for a target was naturally the bank. He was 100 percent certain they had something in mind that was against the law. The lies they told were reason enough for suspicion. They claimed to have ridden all the way from Shreveport, Louisiana, on their way to Tyler, with no packhorses and only their saddlebags. In his opinion, they weren't prepared to pull off any robbery . . . unless, it occurred to him, they'd just come to scout the town in preparation for a robbery to come. That suddenly made sense of their arrival in Tinhorn.

On the question of Malcolm Smith's—or whatever his

name was—willingness to attract attention, that could be attributed to Buck's theory of loose wheels in the brain.

The more Flint thought about it as he walked the street once again, the more he came to the opinion nothing was going to happen that night, especially with their horses in the stable. His earlier determination to watch the town all night was not necessary. He decided it more important to be in position to watch the bank when it opened in the morning. Still not convinced they would try anything, but to see if they hung around to watch it open. He would talk it over with Buck in the morning. See if he read it the same as Flint had.

He went back to the jail to check on Ralph, then sat in the office for about an hour before taking one last round on the street to make sure everything was buttoned up tight. Everything was quiet, so quiet even Jake was closing up the saloon when Flint walked by.

# CHAPTER 19

Confident in his assessment of Malcolm and Harley's behavior, Flint did not skip breakfast the next morning. He was the first to greet Myrna and Hannah at the table. Both women seemed pleased to see him, even though he showed no intention to linger over coffee afterward. He had to get to the office early, but his first stop was Lon Blake's stable to pick up Buster in case he had need of him this morning. As he saddled his horse, he asked Lon, "Those two strangers pick up their horses yet?"

"Nope. That's them right there." Lon pointed to a couple of horses in the stalls. "You seem mighty interested in them two fellers."

"Nothin' serious. I was just curious about 'em. Turned out to be nothin' a-tall. I had 'em mixed up with two other fellas. I had a drink with 'em last night and I didn't think they'd get away very early this mornin'." Flint stepped up onto the buckskin gelding and rode off. He had no desire to put his thoughts about those two into Lon's mind.

Thinking it better to leave Buster at the rail in front of the sheriff's office rather than anywhere near the bank, he looked in on Ralph and told him he'd have a late breakfast this morning. Flint took the time to get a fire going in the stove, made a small pot of coffee, and unlocked Ralph's cell long enough to set the pot inside.

Locking the cell again, he said, "Maybe that'll hold you till I can get back with your breakfast."

"Just like livin' in a fancy hotel," Ralph said. "'Preciate the service, Flint."

"You ever been in a fancy hotel, Ralph?"

"Can't say as I have, but I've heard they really treat you nice, though."

Flint laughed and shook his head. He wondered if Buck was going to be able to send Ralph to be tried at the end of the month. In spite of his past crimes, it was hard to see him as a hardened criminal. It was even harder for Flint to believe he had shot Ralph twice.

He left the jail and walked up the street. Near the top of the street, the bank sat between Clara's Kitchen and Harper's Feed and Supply, and he figured Harper's would be a good place to watch the bank without being seen. The front of the store had one window, and the side of the store had very small windows back in the feed section. Two barn-type doors big enough to drive a wagon through was the spot Flint picked to watch the bank. He told John Harper he was checking out the storeroom they used for a jail cell.

Flint walked back to the feed section and talked to Paul Roper for a while before Paul got called up front to help load a customer's wagon. Flint leaned up against the side of the door and watched the bank when it opened at nine. In less than a minute, he saw Malcolm and Harley ride slowly up to the rail in front of Clara's Kitchen on the other side of the bank.

They dismounted, but didn't go in. Rolling a couple of cigarettes, they lit up for a casual smoke supposedly and watched as Robert Page, one of the tellers, came outside to hook the outer doors open, then picked up a couple of pieces of trash near the entrance. After a short while, they flipped their cigarette butts into the street and climbed back onto their horses. Instead of riding out into the street, they rode all the way around the bank.

Flint stepped back inside when Malcolm turned to look at the feed store. Still watching, he saw them ride into the street on the other side of the bank.

Apparently satisfied, they nudged their horses into a trot, turning back toward the hotel and out the north end of the street. They were on the road to Tyler, but Flint was not convinced Tyler was their destination. Malcolm might be riding out of town to the north, simply because he had told them they were on their way to Tyler. And he didn't want to raise a question in anyone's mind, if they rode down the main street toward the south.

Flint almost forgot but remembered in time to turn around and hurry into Clara's before the CLOSED sign was turned to face out.

"We were starting to wonder if you were going to feed your prisoner breakfast, or not," Clara said.

"I darn-near forgot it," Flint admitted. "I had a job to do early, so I couldn't get here any sooner 'n this. But I did tell Ralph it would be late."

"Margaret fixed up one for him about two minutes ago and put it in the oven to keep warm. What about you? Did you get any breakfast?"

"Yes, ma'am. I had to eat real early, so I got something."

She didn't say anything, but gave him an accusing look. She knew he ate breakfast at Hannah Green's house. "Well, we expect to see you at dinner. I'll get your prisoner's plate for you." She stopped, however, when she saw Mindy coming toward them, carrying a tray.

"I saw you come in," Mindy told him, "and you didn't

look like you were going to sit down, so I figured you'd come for this."

"Yes, ma'am, I did. Thank you, Mindy. I'll see if I can get down to the jail with it before it cools off too much." He turned to leave. "I reckon I'll see you at dinner," he called back over his shoulder.

When he got back to the office, Buck had returned from Jake's Place and his own breakfast. "Where you been?" he asked as Flint went straight to the cell room door.

"I'll be right back. Let me take this to Ralph. I know he thinks we ain't ever gonna feed him."

Back in the office, he jumped right into his findings. "Like I've been tellin' you those two, Malcolm and Harley, are up to something, all right. And I'm pretty damn-sure they're fixin' to rob the bank." He immediately saw a skeptical expression on Buck's face. "Just hear me out," Flint insisted.

Buck leaned back in his chair and listened to what Flint had found out. He went over everything he had put together and pointed out all the things Malcolm said that didn't make sense. Buck soon lost his skepticism when he realized so many things didn't make sense.

"Shreveport to Tyler?" Flint blurted, "With no pack-horses? They were here to look that bank over, and there'll be more with 'em when they come back."

"As much as I hate to admit it, I believe you might be right," Buck confessed. "I swear, that older one, Malcolm, whether he's Harley's daddy or not, is one helluva per-former, ain't he? I gotta hand it to ya. You sniffed him out right from the first, so now it's a question of when are they gonna show up here again, and how many of 'em will there be? And we ain't got no way of knowin' the answers to either one of them questions. You got any ideas on that?"

"I hadn't really thought about that," Flint said. "But if I

had a gang of men, I suppose on the mornin' I was gonna hit that bank—and it looks like they're plannin' on a mornin' strike—I'd have my men break up and ride into town kinda casual-like. Get 'em set up on the street near this jail and anywhere else where trouble might come from. And when we made the robbery, we'd come outta the bank shootin'. The men at each end of the street would ride down to meet 'em, shootin' at everybody who even looked like they were gonna do something."

"That sounds like a lotta bank holdups I've seen or heard about," Buck said. "Say you're the sheriff, how you gonna fight 'em?"

"Well, we need to know as soon as we can that it's gonna happen," Flint said. "I reckon to begin with, we've gotta really watch the town in case we see more than one or two strangers ridin' into town one mornin', and at about the same time. As soon as we do, one of us oughta go straight to the bank to fight from inside. And maybe the other one go to the post office. It's right across the street from the bank and you could shoot 'em comin' out the bank door."

"So far, you've come up with a plan I can't top," Buck said. "I reckon we're both gonna be watchin' the streets every mornin' from now on. From what you've seen, it seems like they plan to hit the bank right after it opens."

"That's right. These strangers will most likely be showin' up in town before nine o'clock." Flint didn't say more about that, waiting for Buck to respond.

"Yep," Buck finally said after a long pause while he was obviously thinking about it. "I reckon I'll be changin' my regular breakfast time. I'll have to get outta my room earlier than I have been." He clamped his teeth together and grimaced then reached down into the right cabinet of his desk, pulled out the bottle, and poured a generous shot into his empty coffee cup. Before he corked the bottle, he gestured toward Flint with it, but Flint shook his head.

He wasn't sure which crisis caused Buck to need a drink so badly that he didn't try to hide it. It could have been the danger of fighting a gang of bank robbers, but Flint figured it was the thought of missing his morning ritual after a drunken night in his quarters. It would remain to be seen if Buck could do it. He had cut back on his drinking for a short time after the back of the jail was blown away. He might not be up to it again.

*In which case,* Flint thought, *I'm going to be facing a gang of bank robbers by myself.*

"From what I've heard," he told Buck, "this won't be the first time you've saved the Bank of Tinhorn from bein' robbed."

Buck looked into the empty coffee cup for a moment before placing it back on the desk and returning the whiskey bottle to the cabinet. "You know, that's a fact. I stopped an attempted robbery on the bank's openin' day. And you and me are gonna stop this attempt, too. By God, they're soon gonna learn they can't have their way in Tinhorn. We don't know where these outlaws are comin' from, and they might be here tomorrow mornin'. We'd best start our early watch first thing tomorrow."

Flint nodded his agreement.

"The bank opens at nine, so whaddaya figure? Think they'll start driftin' into town about eight to eight-thirty?"

"Sounds about right to me. Eating about seven o'clock will give us plenty of time. I don't expect they'll wanna get here too early, since they ain't thinkin' about breakin' in the doors before opening time. It'll be a lot easier for them to have the banker open the door for 'em. I'll eat breakfast at Clara's every mornin' so I can see the bank from the window there."

"That's a good idea. I'll meet you there." Buck grimaced again, then added, "If I ain't there at seven, come roust me out." He gave Flint a weak smile. "You know, at my age it ain't easy breakin' old habits."

"I'll getcha," Flint declared.

They talked about the possibility of asking some of the citizens for help, maybe as riflemen, but Buck was not sure they could count on them. "Tell you the truth, we ain't got enough men in town with any backbone to make up a decent posse. Raymond Chadwick, maybe, I can't think of anybody else we could count on."

Powerfully built, Raymond Chadwick was the blacksmith.

Flint had to agree that Chadwick would be useful in an all-out brawl, but he was untested when bullets were flying. Buck went on to say he was reluctant to tell the merchants a gang of bank robbers might come galloping down the street. When he was a much younger lawman, he had been involved in a robbery where every window had a rifle shooting out of it. The town had ended up with two of their citizens killed by stray shots from the stores, as well as half a dozen wounded. He shook his head as he thought about it happening in the little town of Tinhorn. "It sure would help if we knew how many were comin'," he finally said.

"Seems to me, we'd have one advantage over 'em," Flint suggested. "They won't know we're expectin' 'em. And if we get set up with one of us in the bank to protect the people inside, and a rifle across the street, we oughta be able to stop the ones takin' the money." He paused in his thinking when it suddenly struck him. "You know what? I've got a feelin' that Harley really is Malcolm's son. I don't know how many brothers he's got at home, but I'll bet this bank holdup is a family affair. That's why they pick smaller banks like ours. Maybe there won't be an extra large gang of men. They might not think the take would be as much as they need. I think one of the reasons ol' Malcolm did so much talkin' to you and me was because he wasn't gonna be one of the gunmen in the bank. It'll be Harley and other younger ones to do the dirty work."

"Maybe," Buck responded, having already learned that many of Flint's *feelings* turned out to be fact. "I reckon we'll just wait and find out, won't we? We'll just get ready for 'em. However many show up, we'll do what we're supposed to do. Protect the town. That's what they're payin' us all that money for, right?"

"Right," Flint answered with a chuckle. "You think we oughta have a meetin' with Harvey Baxter to let him know what we suspect? He might wanna move most of his cash outta that big safe he's got. Matter of fact, when we give him the word we've spotted the gang in town, he might wanna slip out the back door."

"Maybe you're right. We oughta let him know he and his tellers are in danger. We'll let him know, if we see it happenin', and he can decide what to do about himself and the two tellers." Buck took another moment to consider it, then decided, "I expect we'd best let him know right now what we expect, so he'll have a little time to make up his mind. We might as well go next door to the bank when we go to Clara's for dinner."


"Howdy, Sheriff, Deputy," Robert Page greeted them when they walked into the bank. "What can we do for you today?"

"Howdy, Robert," Buck replied. "We need to have a few words with Mr. Baxter, if he's available."

"Right now, he talking to a potential customer who's

moving his accounts from a bank in Tyler. I don't know how much longer that's gonna take," Page said.

Buck glanced at Flint, then back to Page. "No problem. Me and Flint are goin' to Clara's next door to eat dinner. We'll come back after we eat but tell Mr. Baxter I do need to see him. All right?"

"Sure thing," Page replied. "I'll tell him."

Buck thanked him, then he and Flint headed next door to Clara's Kitchen.

"Everybody watch yourself," Bonnie Jones japed when they walked in. "Here comes the whole sheriff's department of Tinhorn."

"That's right," Buck responded. "It takes both of us to place you and the rest of you loose women in this establishment under arrest."

That brought a big laugh out of Bonnie, which always reminded Flint of a chicken cackling.

"Well, I'm not going without a fight," Mindy declared boldly.

"I bet I can guess which one you wanna fight with," Bonnie said aside to her.

"Shut your mouth, Bonnie," Mindy whispered, then aloud, she asked, "Where do you gentlemen want to sit?"

"Let's take that table over there by the window," Flint answered, and led the way. Buck followed and when they sat down, Flint said, "This is the table Malcolm and Harley sat at. You notice, you get a pretty good view of the bank from here?"

"Well, that's the truth, ain't it?" Buck replied. "I never gave it much thought before. Maybe from now on, we oughta arrest anybody takin' this table as potential bank robbers."

"We've got pork chops today," Mindy said as she

placed two cups of coffee on the table. "If you don't want chops, Margaret will cook you a steak."

They decided on the chops, since they weren't offered very often.

When she left to give Margaret the order, Buck asked a question. "Why is it, whenever I'm eatin' in here with you, it's always Mindy that waits on us?"

"Is it? I don't know. I hadn't noticed it."

Buck chortled, truly believing he hadn't. Unaware he was being japed, Flint shrugged, wondering why Buck found it amusing. They had just started into their pork chops when Mayor Harvey Baxter came into the dining room.

He spoke briefly to Clara, then went directly to their table. "Mind if I join you?" Baxter asked as he pulled a chair back and sat down. He nodded to both of them, then looked directly at Buck. "What did you want to talk to me about?"

Before Buck could answer, Mindy came to take his order.

Baxter glanced from Buck's plate to Flint's. "I'll have the same thing."

Buck got right to the point and told him that he and Flint suspected his bank was the target of a gang of bank robbers. He went over all the signs of a planned robbery he and Flint had discussed.

Baxter's reaction was one of disbelief at first. "Oh, no. Don't tell me we're going to go through that again," he complained. "I thought they would have learned their lesson the first time."

"That was a few years back," Buck said. "Somebody thinks your bank is ripe for the pickin' now."

Baxter just sat there shaking his head, too upset to

speak for a moment. "I hope like hell we're wrong," Buck told him, "but we can't take a chance on ignorin' signs that could sure point to an attempted robbery. I stopped that first robbery, and with Flint workin' with me now, we got a better chance this time."

"All right," Baxter said, finally accepting the possibility. "What do you want me to do? When do you think it's going to happen?"

"Well, that's what we don't know," Buck said. "We suspect they'll try it within the next couple of days. There's no reason to think they wouldn't, since they sent two men to scout it yesterday. Me and Flint will be watchin' the town real close every day now for strangers." He went on to tell Baxter what he and his tellers should do when they are warned it is about to happen. "It'll be in the morning, so right after you open your doors at nine, you and your tellers need to head out the back door right away. Flint will be your new teller."

"I'm not leaving my bank," Baxter told them. "I'll send Robert and Eugene out the back, but I'm not leaving."

"I reckon that's up to you," Buck said. "But I reckon you might wanna take most of your cash outta that big safe in the back room, if you've got some other place to put it that don't look like a safe. That's just in case we don't stop 'em, and you have to open it for 'em. I hope it don't come to that." He glanced over at Flint, conscious of what that would mean if it did. Understanding, Baxter shifted his gaze toward Flint as well.

"I expect you'd better start on that pork chop," Flint remarked. "They're a lot better when they're still hot."

Baxter gave him a look of astonishment, wondering if he fully realized the danger threatening them.

"The sheriff and I won't let 'em take your bank," Flint said then.

Baxter had to laugh at that. "Good!" He looked at Flint, then back at Buck. "Good!" he repeated. "Just keep me informed on anything else you find out. I trust your judgment, so just tell me what to do."

"We'll do that, Mr. Mayor," Buck said. "We'll try to give you as much warning as we can."

Baxter got up from the table and left, his plate untouched.

"I'm afraid we spoiled the mayor's dinner," Buck said to Mindy when she came with more coffee and saw the untouched plate.

"It's not the first time he's done that," Mindy said. "We'll put it in the warmer oven for a little while, then send it over to his office. You want some more coffee?"

Buck nodded.

"Flint?"

"No thanks, Mindy. I've had about enough. Thanks just the same."

Unable to think of any other reason to stand there, she turned and went back to the kitchen.

# CHAPTER 20

Those gathering around the long kitchen table at the Fletcher ranch were enjoying a hearty supper of fresh butchered beef. Eager to hear the scouting report brought back by Malcolm and Harley they were also entertained by Malcolm's accounting of his encounters with the Tinhorn lawmen. He drew big belly laughs telling of the apple pie incident and the evening when Deputy Moran bought him and Harley a drink. Ada Tubbs was the only one who found none of the encounters with Deputy Flint Moran humorous. Her hatred of the man who had caused her so much internal pain was too great to permit anything having to do with him to be funny.

"Ain't you afraid he got to know you so well he'll recognize you on sight when you go into that bank?" Vike Trask asked.

"I ain't goin' into that bank," Malcolm corrected him. "I'll be just another rider holdin' your horse *outside* the bank. You young men will be inside the bank gettin' the cash, just like me and your pa did when we were young men. Ain't that right, Liam?"

Trask said it was.

"Harley knows what to do. This ain't his first holdup. He'll tell you what to do. Justin will go in with you and

Harley. Me and Willy will be outside holdin' the horses. Ada says she can guard the remounts with your pa. We picked out a nice little creek about three and a half miles north of Tinhorn to hold the fresh horses. The night before we hit 'em, we'll camp about a hundred yards down that creek. We'll leave that bank at a gallop and drive our horses as fast as they'll go all the way to that creek. Then we'll slap our saddles on fresh horses and be long gone before they can get up a posse to come after us. But we ain't gonna be on that Tyler road. Me and Harley looked it over, and what we'll do is just ride farther down that creek about another hundred yards where it empties into the river. We'll let the posse go to Tyler." Malcolm grinned. "They'll be ridin' north while we're ridin' south."

That sounded good to everybody and they voiced their approval.

"They have a bank guard?" Justin asked.

"No," Harley answered him before his father could. "They ain't got no guard. We saw a couple of tellers through the windows. We watched 'em when they closed the bank, and nobody came out except one man—the feller that owns it, I reckon. Couldn't be much easier. It'll be a good one for your first time, Vike."

"Ain't that a helluva lot of trouble, drivin' those extra horses up north of Tinhorn?" Ada asked. "Seems to me you'd have enough head start on a posse, anyway. And it don't seem to me like you'd want to drive a bunch of wore-out horses with you when you're tryin' to make a getaway."

"In this game, it always helps to have an extra ace in your hand," Malcolm answered. "There's right about three hundred horses out yonder in our pastures. I ain't worried about losin' seven of 'em. If you're likin' that dun geldin' you came here on, you'd best pick you another one outta the herd."

Ada didn't reply right away. She just looked at him as if she couldn't believe him. Then she said, "I'll just ride my dun up to that creek. I don't need no extra horse. Since I'm not goin' into town with you, my dun will be just as fresh as your other horses. You don't have to lose but five horses outta your herd. Pa won't need an extra one, neither."

Malcolm laughed. "I swear, you're right. I forgot about that." He looked at Trask and quipped, "Maybe Ada oughta be the boss of this gang."

His comment was a notion she'd had, but she refrained from saying so.

"Well, it seems like we know what we're gonna do," Justin said. "So when are we gonna do it?"

"I'm thinkin' we oughta drive those extra horses up above Tinhorn tomorrow and make our camp on that creek. Then we ride into the bank before it opens day after tomorrow. Whaddaya think, Liam? That all right with you?" Malcolm asked the question simply to placate Trask, so he wouldn't feel like he was being left out.

"Okay by me," Trask answered. "I just wish I could be part of the holdup."

"I know you do, partner," Malcolm responded, "but we can't take a chance on somebody recognizin' you. I'm gonna have to wear my other hat and cover up my face. Ain't nobody likely to recognize me unless I go into the sheriff's office, the saloon, or the hotel dinin' room. I ain't plannin' on goin' in any of them places."

The planning continued for quite some time, although there was little left to work out. They decided to take one packhorse but to load it with only cooking utensils, the coffee pot, some flour, and some bacon. They didn't want to load the packhorse with anything approaching the weight of a rider and saddle.

That afternoon, Malcolm and the boys went out among

the horses grazing in the first pasture to cut out a horse to ride into town. Many of the horses were not saddle broken and the operation provided a few laughs. More than one first choice was rejected due to the possibility of being bucked out of the saddle during the getaway. After the final selections were made, the chosen horses were taken to the barn and released into the corral.

Early the next morning, Melva, Nelda, and Ada served up a big breakfast to send Ada and the men off on their mission. Well accustomed to being left with only the youngest son to do the male chores till the men returned from their mischief, Melva and Nelda were just as glad that Ada was going with the men. As Nelda once confided to her mother, Ada was like having a ghost around, and she never smiled.

Thirteen-year-old Cody begged to be included in the gang, but his father had a set rule when it came to age. Justin had not been allowed to participate in the family's unlawful endeavors until he reached his fourteenth year. The same rule applied to Cody.

"You ain't got but half a year before you'll be fourteen," Malcolm told him. "Besides, I need a man to take care of the ranch and the women while we're gone. You'll be the head man till I get back."

"It ain't the same as bein' part of the gang, Pa, and you know it," Cody complained.

Malcolm ended the discussion. "But that's the way it is. Take care of your mother and sister, and we'll be back in a couple of days."


In the town of Tinhorn few seemed to notice they were seeing the sheriff and his deputy out on the street more often than the day before—especially in the morning but also in the afternoon. The change in routine was noticed perhaps the most in Clara's Kitchen when Flint, but especially Buck, was there for breakfast at seven o'clock sharp.

It did not escape comment. "Well, this is a special occasion," Clara said in greeting. "The sheriff is having breakfast with us this morning." She couldn't help adding, "I certainly hope Rena isn't ill."

"Damn, Clara," Bonnie said, upon overhearing her remark. "That was mean."

"That was kinda mean, wasn't it?" Clara replied. "I'm sorry, Buck. I'm always happy to see you, even if you think Rena's breakfast is better."

"Doggone you, Clara," Buck replied. "You know dang well I don't think no such a thing. It's just that I don't get hungry for breakfast till later in the mornin', and you're closed then."

She looked at the deputy. "There must be some reason you two are here so early this morning. What is it, Flint?"

"We were just thinking we could save a lot more of the day, if we got an earlier start on breakfast. Would you rather we leave and come back later?"

"No," she said with a look of distrust on her face. "Go sit down and Mindy will wait on you."

"What's wrong with me?" Bonnie asked indignantly.

"Or Bonnie," Clara said, knowing Bonnie was protesting just to get Mindy's goat when she came from the pump and discovered Flint in the dining room.

Bonnie hurried into the kitchen to fill two cups. Carrying them back to the dining room, she discovered Buck and Flint had taken the table by the window. "Are you gonna sit here?" she asked, standing before them, still holding the coffee cups.

Buck looked at her, then gave Flint a puzzled look. "It's kinda obvious, ain't it?"

"This ain't your favorite table," Bonnie informed him. "You always sit at that table by the kitchen door."

"Yeah, but this is breakfast," Buck replied with a perfectly serious face. "This is my favorite table for breakfast."

"Since it doesn't matter where I sit, can I have that cup of coffee?" Flint interrupted.

She gave them an exasperated frown, placed the cups on the table, and returned to the kitchen.

Flint and Buck turned their attention toward the bank next door, although it was a little early yet to expect anyone there. As they ate, they would keep a watchful eye out the window the whole while. Since it was the end of town Flint had seen Malcolm and Harley leave Tinhorn from, they figured it would likely be the end of town to watch for strangers seeming to drift in. Thinking of Buck's little word exchange with Bonnie over the table, Flint was encouraged to see that, in spite of his forced change of schedule, Buck still maintained his sense of humor.

"Those two plates ready for Flint and Buck?" Bonnie sang out when she saw Mindy come in the back door carrying two full buckets of water she had offered to get for Margaret. "Oh, Mindy," she teased, "the sheriff and his deputy came in and they asked for me to wait on 'em."

Mindy looked alarmed at once. She looked at Margaret, who was looking back at her with a slight grin. Slowly Margaret shook her head then picked up the two plates she'd prepared and handed them to Mindy.

Mindy walked by a grinning Bonnie and whispered, "You really are a witch, aren't you?"

Like Bonnie, she was surprised to see the two lawmen sitting by the window but didn't hesitate to glide right over and place the plates before them. "Good morning, gentlemen."

Both gave her a big smile in return.

"Is there anything else I can get for you?"

When they said they were fine for the moment, she returned to the kitchen and a grinning Bonnie.

In spite of the threat to their town that occupied almost all of their thoughts, Buck could not resist asking a question that had baffled him before. "Flint, it ain't none of my business, but have you ever thought about what a nice gal that Mindy is?"

No doubt, especially when heavier thoughts were on their minds, that his question surprised Flint. "Yes, I suppose I have. She is a nice gal. One of the sweetest I've ever met."

"She'd sure make some lucky man a wonderful wife," Buck remarked. "Don't you think so?"

"I sure do," Flint replied at once. "I've always thought that ever since I met her. She's the kind of woman who could make a man happy."

"It's hard to let her know you're interested, though, ain't it?" Buck pressed. "I mean, to come right out with it and tell her how you feel."

"I reckon it is, Buck. But if you're lettin' the age difference stop you from gettin' up your nerve, there's a lot of women that prefer an older man. Gives 'em a sense of security, I guess. You'll never know unless you ask her."

"What?" Buck put his fork down. "I ain't talkin' about me, you blitherin' idiot. I'm talkin' about *you* and Mindy."

"Oh," Flint uttered, then grinned. "I can't think about things like that. I can't afford to support a wife on the pay I get for this job. Even if she was interested in me in a marryin' way, it wouldn't be fair to her. I can't afford to take care of her."

"Right," Buck said when he couldn't think what else to say. "Right," he repeated. "Ain't none of my business, anyway." There was nothing he could do to solve that problem. He had to respect the young man's sense of responsibility toward marriage. Most men in his circumstances would go after the girl, whether they could afford her or not. Nothing more was said for several long minutes as sheriff and deputy concentrated on their food.

It was a relief for Buck when Clara asked if they wanted Margaret to go ahead and fix Ralph's breakfast.

"Yes, ma'am," he replied at once. "We're about done here."

They got up from the table and walked over to Clara's register and Flint paid for his breakfast. Then they waited there and made small talk with her while they waited for Ralph's breakfast.

In a minute, Mindy came out with the plate wrapped with a heavy cloth to keep it warm. She walked straight to Flint and gave it to him.

"Thanks, Mindy. I know Ralph will be glad to get this."

"Will we see you back here at dinner?" she asked.

"Yep, I expect so." Flint turned and followed Buck out the door.

Since there was no activity on the street at all, and certainly no strangers to be seen, they walked back to the jail where Ralph was eager to get his breakfast. Flint made another pot of coffee, so Ralph could have all he wanted then walked out onto the little front porch and looked up and down the street that was just beginning to show some life.

A few strangers to Flint had come into town, but they were driving farm wagons, and some had women and children with them. He and Buck walked the street in opposite directions a couple of times. At eight-thirty, they walked back toward the bank, on opposite sides of the street, both carrying rifles as well as their sidearms. With past attacks on the jail in mind, both were aware the street was not the only approach to the bank. On that side of the street, Flint was also watching the open spaces between the buildings and the river. On the other side, Buck had some small trees for cover within twenty yards of the stores' back doors, so he was able to walk unnoticed.

They saw no strangers on horseback drifting into town. At nine o'clock, teller Eugene Bannerman opened the front door to the bank, and like Robert Page on alternate days, he picked up any trash he saw lying near the bank's entrance. Buck, across the street at the post office, walked out and signaled Flint to join him at the bank's door. Going inside, they saw Harvey Baxter standing in the doorway of his office, watching the door.

He walked out to meet them and greeted them with one word. "Anything?"

"No, sir," Buck said. "We've been watchin' the town pretty close. So far, there hasn't been anybody we can't account for. But that don't mean we can afford to assume today ain't the day. They could come ridin' in here any time of day and attempt to rob you, so we'll be watchin' all day. Although, we still think it'll come in the morning at openin' time. Maybe not tomorrow mornin'," he hedged, "but it won't be long."

"Well, I can't say that's encouraging." Baxter sighed. "But I appreciate your and Flint's diligence on the bank's behalf." He shook his head and confessed, "When I was unlocking that front door this morning, I fumbled so long trying to get the key in the lock, I thought I was gonna get knocked in the head or something."

"We had our eyes on the bank," Buck assured him. "We weren't gonna let nothin' like that happen. And like I said, we're gonna be watchin' the bank all day. Even when we eat. Through a window over at Clara's is where we can watch the bank."

"I appreciate it," Baxter said.

They started to leave, then Buck thought of one more thing. "Have you told your tellers about this yet?"

Baxter said he had not.

"Good. I think it's best not to, until it happens. Then we can just let 'em out the back door, and they'll be safe."

While things were peaceful as usual in the town, a small troop of riders were making their way north with intentions to alter that state of mind. As carefree and cheerful a band of riders as you would expect on their way to a carnival or a fair, the Fletcher-Trask gang rode at a comfortable pace. Seven in number, five of them led a spare horse. Except for the ever-somber Ada, they joked back and forth with each other. Sitting tall in the saddle, her wide-brim hat pulled down squarely on her head, she felt cheated by not being able to participate in the robbery and the possible opportunity to get a shot at Flint Moran. Accustomed to her constant moody disposition, the rest of the party left her to her own hell.

Late in the afternoon Malcolm Fletcher signaled for them to stay close to the trees along the Neches River and to keep quiet. They were about to bypass the town of Tinhorn. Once they were past the town, a ride of a little over three miles took them to the creek he had told them about. Crossing over the river, they followed the creek upstream.

Malcolm pointed up the creek. "It's about a hundred yards on up before we get to the spot that would make a good camp. Another hundred yards and we'll be at the Tyler road we'll be riding outta town on when we're makin' our getaway. As thick as these trees are along the creek, we can go ahead and make a small fire. It won't be seen from the road, even if anybody's ridin' by tonight."

Reaching the spot Malcolm had picked out, they watered the horses and let them graze. Some of the boys gathered wood for the fire for Ada to cook some bacon, prepare some simple pan bread to go with it, and make coffee to wash it all down with. It was a family outing with prospects of better things to come in the morning. The only restriction was there would be no whiskey that night. Malcolm and Trask had laid down the law. They wanted no fuzzy heads riding into Tinhorn in the morning.

When it was time to roll out the bedrolls the horses were tied on a rope line between two trees, and the two-family gang of outlaws turned in for the night. They had no need for an extra early start in the morning, for they were only three-and-a-half miles north of the town. Since the bank didn't open until nine, they planned to ride in, hopefully unnoticed, a little before that time, and be the bank's first customers of the day.

"And the last customers of the day," Malcolm whispered as he thought over the plan one more time.

# CHAPTER 21

Just as the day before, Flint met Buck at Clara's Kitchen at seven o'clock for breakfast. Once again, they were to endure the taunting of the women at the dining room.

The second early breakfast convinced Clara something was up and the sheriff wasn't talking about it. After coffee was served to the two lawmen, she walked over to their table. "What's going on in our little town today?" she asked, casually but with an accusing eye.

"I reckon that's what we're waitin' to find out," Buck answered, well familiar with the woman's tendency to dig for information the rest of the public wasn't privy to. "Do you know something?"

"Come on, Buck, you know it's not the usual thing for you two to meet here for an early breakfast. Two mornings in a row? Something's going on." She glanced over at Flint, whose face remained a blank slate, then back to Buck. "What are you expecting, a bank robbery or something?" She failed to notice the sudden lifting of Flint's eyebrows when Buck answered her.

"I declare, Clara, you do beat all. Where do you get ideas like that? Me and Flint decided to eat early yesterday to get an early start on the day. We liked it so much we thought we'd try it again today."

They were saved then from additional grilling when Mindy arrived with their breakfasts. Clara reluctantly turned away to let them eat in peace, but not before casting a suspicious eye in Buck's direction.

"Sitting at their new breakfast table again. They're up to something," she said to Margaret as she walked back into the kitchen.

"I swear, that woman's got a nose like a bloodhound," Buck remarked. "Maybe we shoulda asked her if she thinks they're gonna hit the bank today."

"Nah," Flint replied. "She's just nosy. Has to have something to gossip about, and there ain't much to choose from in Tinhorn. Any little change in anybody sets her mind to wonderin'."

They enjoyed another fine breakfast with plenty of attention from Mindy, even though it would have been much nicer without the uncertainty of what might befall their little town. Consequently, they kept an eye on the clock on the wall by the kitchen, and the other eye on the bank next door. They were especially alert when Harvey Baxter unlocked the back door at eight o'clock and went inside. In a few minutes' time, both tellers showed up as well.

Deciding they'd best get out on the street again, Flint picked up Ralph's breakfast tray and Buck told the ladies they'd see them at dinner.

Flint didn't spend much time getting Ralph set up with his breakfast before he picked up his rifle, checked to make sure the magazine was fully loaded, then he stood at the door. If any of the outlaws showed up, he hoped to see them before they saw him. He had his hand on the knob to go outside when he was stopped by the sight of two riders walking their horses slowly past the bank. He did not recognize them at first.

"Buck." Flint's tone of voice was enough to make Buck go immediately to the door. "You know those two fellows?"

"Today's the day!" Buck exclaimed. "It's goin' down. We'd best get up to the bank."

Knowing it was important not to be seen by the outlaws, they remained inside until the two riders rode past the jail. Neither rider was the one who'd said he was Malcolm Smith, but they recognized one of them at almost the same time.

"Damned if that ain't Vike Trask!"

They weren't surprised Vike was in it with "the Smiths", but they didn't expect him to be that brazen. The big hat and bandana weren't enough to disguise him. When the two riders rode on down to the south end of the street, Flint and Buck hurried out the door and ran around to the back of the building.

"Did they see us?" Buck asked when Flint stopped at the back corner to check.

"Nope."

"Good."

They ran along the backs of the buildings until reaching the post office right across the street from the bank, and ducked into the building.

"Hold on," Buck said when Flint started to run out again. "There's another 'n pullin' up in front of the hotel!"

"Buck, Flint, what's goin' on?" Louis Wheeler, the postmaster asked, baffled by their sudden entrance.

"Louis," Buck roared, "the U.S. Postal Service is about to take part in the defense of Tinhorn. We've got a bank holdup about to happen and your post office is gonna be my firin' position."

"Good Lord in Heaven!" Louis exclaimed. "What do you want me to do?"

"I want you to get back there in your cage and keep your

head down. Me and Flint will take care of the rest." Turning back to Flint, Buck said, "Whenever you're ready!"

"I'm waitin' till that last fellow looks the other way." Looking back to answer Buck, Flint spotted a couple of hats hanging on hooks near the half door of the postmaster's cage and hurried over to them. "I need to borrow a hat," he said, figuring anybody in the gang who had seen him had never seen him wear a hat.

When Willy Fletcher turned his horse back toward the Tyler road and waved his arm to signal Malcolm and Harley that it was all clear, Flint didn't wait for an okay. He plopped a borrowed hat onto his head and strode across the street, holding his rifle vertically and hiding it with his body. He went straight to Harper's store next door to the bank and went in the front entrance.

"Howdy Flint," John Harper sang out, puzzled to see the deputy with a hat on.

"Mr. Harper," Flint returned without slowing down.

To the store owner's astonishment, Flint ran straight through the store to the feed section, where he ran by Paul Roper, and out the back door. Across the alley between the buildings, he ran to the back door of the bank and started rapping loudly.

"We're not open yet. Please use the front entrance," a voice he did not recognize informed him.

"It's Deputy Moran! Open the door!" He heard no answer for a few moments then recognized the voice of Harvey Baxter and heard the rattle of a key in the door lock. "It's happenin'," he said as Baxter let him in. There was no need to explain what he meant.

"What do I do?" Baxter asked frantically.

Flint looked at the big clock on the wall. "You're supposed to open in five minutes. Are you still determined to stay?"

Baxter nodded rapidly. His tellers stood gaping and confused.

"All right." Flint looked at the tellers. "You two go out the back door and over to Harper's next door. There's gonna be an attempt to rob the bank, and I don't need to take a chance on one of you gettin' shot. Go now!" Before they could move, he said, "Wait a minute! I need to borrow one of your coats. Yours." He pointed toward Bannerman, who took off his large black morning coat immediately. "Okay, now go!"

They didn't wait.

Baxter watched him put the coat on, then take off the borrowed hat and toss it behind the teller's cage. "Where do you want me?" he asked, trying hard not to show any nervousness.

"I want you in your office. Be prepared to be called out. No matter what's happenin' with me, just do whatever they tell you to do. The penalty for bank robbery ain't nowhere near as bad as the one for murder, and I'm hoping these boys keep that in mind. Just do what they say. And remember, Buck Jackson is right across the street with a rifle, so they ain't gonna get very far with the money." Flint put his rifle behind the teller's cage and removed his gun belt, then drew his Colt six-gun and stuck it in his belt.

"I'll have to open the front door," Baxter said. "It's nine o'clock."

"This mornin', I'll do that. You just unlock the door then go to your office. I'll open up and hook the doors. If I see any trash, I'll pick it up."

"Can't you and Buck just go ahead and arrest them, instead of letting them in the bank?"

"Arrest 'em for what?" Flint asked. "Loiterin'? They ain't broke no laws yet."

Baxter nodded as if understanding, went to the door

with Flint, and unlocked it. He gave Flint a look of uncertainty and said, "I'll do as you said, but I've got a revolver in my desk, and if I hear any shooting, I'll blast the first one of them that comes through my door." Then he retreated to his office.

Flint opened the front door and hooked it on the post there for that purpose, all the while trying to look inconspicuous. Relieved to find no obvious trash to pick up, in case Malcolm and Harley's gang watched every detail when they had scouted the bank, he hurried back inside and behind the teller's cage where he had left his rifle. He saw a pair of glasses and a tinted visor on top of the cash drawers, and put them on in an effort to complete his disguise.

"So far, so good," Malcolm told Harley when they saw Justin and Vike approaching the bank just as one of the tellers opened up the front door.

"Open for business," Malcolm japed and nudged his horse to lope the rest of the way. *It couldn't have been better,* he thought. *No customers were waiting for the bank to open, which meant no one to run down the street, yelling for the sheriff.*

Willy was waiting for them in front of the bank and took the reins of Harley's horse when he stepped down and quickly pulled up a full face mask made from a cloth sack to cover his entire face. It was identical to the one his father, Malcolm, pulled on. They were in real danger of being recognized. Vike Trask might have been recognized by the sheriff or deputy had they been present at the holdup. Since the plan was to strike the bank and get away before the law could be alerted, the gang didn't anticipate seeing the big sheriff and his gunman deputy. Vike, like the other two members of the party—Justin and Willy—relied on his bandana to prevent a likeness of his face from showing up on WANTED posters.

Justin and Vike pulled up and quickly dismounted, handing their reins to Malcolm and Willy.

"Go get it, boys," Malcolm said, "and let's be quick about it."

Justin and Vike followed Harley into the bank, while Malcolm and Willy held all the horses.

Through the front window, Flint could see the three men preparing to enter the bank, and he was not sure how he wanted to handle the confrontation. He had asked Buck what his plan was, to arrest them, or to kill them. Buck's answer was to shoot them all down as soon as they entered the bank with obvious intentions of robbing it.

"Even if they throw up their hands and surrender?" Flint had asked.

"They ain't likely to do that," Buck had replied. "They're most likely to shoot their way outta there, so you might as well make sure they don't. 'Cause if you do, there'll just be one more coyote out there waitin' to ambush you to get his revenge."

Flint wasn't sure he felt right about shooting a man who threw his gun down and surrendered. To him, that sounded too much like murder.

As those thoughts were running through his mind, the three outlaws pushed through the doors. With guns drawn, they swaggered into the bank, looking right and left.

Upon seeing only one man behind the cage, Harley demanded, "Where the hell are the others?"

"They went out the back door to go to breakfast," Flint said. "What can I do for you gentlemen?"

"Gentlemen! Ha!" Harley snorted and threw a large

canvas bag at him. "This is a holdup. Empty them cash drawers into that bag, no coins, and make it quick unless you want me to put a hole in your head. Where's the bigshot that owns this bank?"

"That's his office yonder." Justin pointed toward Baxter's door. "I'll bet that's where the big money is, in his safe."

Harley looked back at Flint. "How 'bout it? Is that where the safe is?" He roared, "Hey, you dumb hick, I told you to empty them drawers." He looked at Justin. "You keep your eye on him, and if he don't fill that bag, shoot him. We ain't got time to fool with nobody who's dumb as a fence post. I'm goin' to visit the bigshot." He started toward Baxter's door.

"That's as far as you go, Harley." Even with a full face mask, Flint had recognized him from his exaggerated walk to compensate for his shortness. Flint slid the barrel of his Henry rifle under the bars of the teller's cage.

The command stopped Harley cold, and he suddenly recognized the voice. He spun around and fired, too fast for accuracy it turned out. Before he could get off another shot, he doubled over in pain when Flint's shot caught him in the stomach. Caught completely off guard, Vike and Justin opened fire on the teller's cage as Harley dropped to his knees and fell over onto his side.

But Flint was no longer there. Having anticipated their response, he'd dropped down on the floor and crawled to the end of the cage. While Vike and Justin continued to destroy the teller's window, Flint pulled his six-gun from his belt. With one quick move, he came from behind the end of the cage and placed a shot in Justin's chest before ducking back behind the base of the cage. Finding himself alone against the deadly fire from the teller's cage, Vike backed toward the door, firing at the end of the counter until he emptied his gun. When the hammer fell on a spent cartridge, Flint raised up and caught him in the back with one shot as he turned and ran out the door. Vike managed only two steps outside before a slug from Buck's Winchester smashed his breastbone.

Alarmed by the first shot he'd heard inside the bank, Malcolm Fletcher's initial reaction was anger. He had planned a nice quiet holdup with no gunfire to alert the town. When it was followed by the sounds of many shots exchanged, he knew something had gone wrong. When Vike staggered out the door and was dropped by a shot from across the street, Malcolm cried, "They was waitin' for us! Run!"

He dropped the reins of the extra horses and immediately wheeled his horse and galloped away. Willy was not so lucky. Unlike his father, he had stepped down from the saddle, and Buck's second shot nailed him as he attempted to step up. With one foot in the stirrup, the impact of the shot between his shoulder blades caused him to fall across his saddle on his belly. The frightened horse chased after Malcolm's horse, along with the other horses. Willy's body slid off his horse in front of the hotel to lie still in the road.

The sheriff ran out of the post office and threw one shot at the fleeing survivor, but Malcolm was already too far away for accuracy. Buck turned and ran into the bank. He found Flint standing over Harley Fletcher who looked closer to death than survival. Reaching down, Buck pulled the sack off his face.

Harley's eyes flickered open to stare up at the big sheriff bending over him.

"You gonna make it, Harley?" Buck asked. "Your daddy took off when the shootin' started. He's the only one that made it, except you. You wanna tell me your real last name?"

"I'm gut-shot, you dumb gorilla," Harley muttered. "I'm good as dead. I ain't tellin' you squat."

"I expect you're right." Buck pulled out his pistol and put a round right between his eyes. Looking at Flint, he asked, "Is Baxter in the bank?"

"He's in his office," Flint answered. When Buck started to go there, Flint added, "and he said he's gonna shoot the first son of a gun that walks through that door."

"Glad you remembered to tell me that." Buck called out, "Mr. Mayor, you can come out now."

"My horse is saddled and waitin' down at the stable," Flint said. "I'm gonna see if I can catch up with Harley's daddy. We ain't got time to get up a posse." He took Bannerman's coat off and laid it across a chair. "Tell Eugene I'm sorry I got it a little dirty." He ran out the door just as Baxter came out of his office with his revolver still in hand.

"You be careful you don't run into no ambush," Buck yelled after Flint.

Flint ran through a small gathering of people already out in the street.

Lon Blake was standing in front of his stable. "I heard all the shootin'. You come for your horse? What was it?" he asked as Flint ran by him to the corral.

"An attempt to rob the bank," Flint told him as he led Buster out of the corral and stepped up into the saddle. "They didn't get any money. I'll tell you about it later. I ain't got time now." He started back up the street at a gallop, dodging spectators who wanted to know what was going on.

Past Doc Beard's house on the northbound road, he saw a couple of horses with empty saddles that had evidently followed Malcolm before trailing off. Flint was in a race, confident his buckskin was a fairly fast horse. But Malcolm was also riding at a gallop.

Wondering how fast the bank robber's horse was, Flint urged his horse faster. "He's got a pretty good head start on you, Buster."

"Somebody's comin'!" Trask called to Ada, who was down by the edge of the creek.

Because she couldn't hear anything, Ada called back to him, "Better be careful. It might not be them." She walked back up to join him by the horses. In a few seconds, she heard what he evidently had. "That sounds like somethin' comin' this way, but it don't sound like them comin' back. Maybe it's a stray cow or somethin'. It ain't movin' very fast." She drew her Colt .45 just in case it might be needed. Then they heard the alert.

"Get on your horses!" Malcolm yelled.

They saw him then, flailing away at his exhausted horse, which was laboring to push slowly through the bushes, barely able to remain on its feet. He slid off the horse and frantically began taking his saddle off, as if afraid the horse might collapse before he got it off.

"Malcolm, what the hell?" Trask exclaimed. "Where's the rest of 'em?"

"They're dead," Malcolm answered as he took his saddle over and threw it on his favorite horse. Working as fast as he could, he pressed them to get ready to ride. "Everybody but me, dead. It was a trap. They was waitin' for us. I don't know how they knew we was gonna hit that bank, but they was ready and waitin'."

"Damn!" Ada exclaimed. "Who was it? Rangers?"

"No, it weren't Rangers," Malcolm replied, almost panting in his haste to saddle up and flee. "Had to be the sheriff and his deputy. They had us set up in a crossfire." He paused to look at them as if he couldn't believe it had happened. "They knew we was comin'. They was there, waitin' for us," he repeated.

"Flint Moran." Ada spat the name as if it was offensive to her tongue.

"Vike?" Trask asked. "Vike's dead? You said this was gonna be a simple little job."

"Damn it, Liam, I lost three of my sons. I know how you feel. I feel as bad as you do. I lost my boys. I don't know how the hell the sheriff coulda known we were gonna hit that bank, and the day we were gonna do it.

"Don't forget I was there when all the shootin' was goin' on. Me and Willy was standin' outside in front of the bank while the boys went inside. Anybody coulda shot me and him any time they wanted to. Then when the shootin' did start, we tried to run. I made it, but they got Willy. What I'm tellin' you now is we've got to get outta here if you don't wanna get killed, too."

"Get on your horse, Pa," Ada told him when it appeared he might not do anything but stand there. "Whatever we do now is better than gettin' caught by a posse." He nodded his head sadly and climbed up into his saddle. They followed Malcolm down the creek to the river. They kept the horses in the river and turned back toward Tinhorn. Two fathers who were career criminals, now found themselves the fathers of daughters and one young son to carry on their chosen line of work.

Flint was not willing to hold Buster to a gallop past the point where the buckskin began to show signs of fatigue. Reining him back to a walk, Flint figured he must be about three miles or so from town and had to admit he was not likely to catch up with Malcolm Whoever. With his head start, Malcolm had a sizable lead and had shown he was going to get every last ounce of effort from his horse before he rested him. Flint was afraid he could never close the gap between them. And then up ahead he saw one lone horse with an empty saddle standing beside the road, drinking from a creek. It had to be one more of the horses that had galloped away after Malcolm and become too tired to continue the gallop. The horse made no move to avoid him as he walked Buster to the creek to let him drink as well.

Finished, Flint decided to turn Buster around and walk him home. As they turned, Flint noticed hoofprints in the soft sand at the edge of the road and realized they led to the creek. He drew his rifle from the saddle sling and dismounted.

Leading Buster, he walked along the creek bank where he saw many hoofprints. It dawned on him the outlaws might have left fresh horses there in case of a quick posse, and was proven right when he came to their campsite. They had camped there last night, and left in such a hurry when Malcolm returned they didn't take the rope used to tie the fresh horses.

Down at the edge of the creek Flint saw the weary horse he had been chasing. If their holdup plan had been successful, five weary horses would have been left there, while the bandits rode away on fresh horses.

*And I'm left here with a tired horse. Might as well go back and tell Buck I lost him.*

Changing his mind, he decided to follow the creek to the river. See which way Malcolm went from there. Flint led his horse for what he figured was another one hundred yards before he reached the river. He stood on the bank for a minute or two where the tracks went into the water. North or south? he wondered. He looked at Buster and said, "You ain't too tired to keep my feet dry, are you? That bank over on the other side ain't very steep."

As usual, Buster declined to answer, so Flint stepped up into the saddle again and rode across to the other side and dismounted.

Looking closely on the other bank, he could find no tracks showing any horses leaving the river on that side. There would have been some trace of probably more than one horse, he figured, because someone had probably been left to watch the fresh horses. He did see tracks, but they were left by a group of horses going into the river.

Flint had no doubt now the horses he was tracking had stayed in the river to keep anyone following from knowing which way they'd gone. It occurred to him the tracks leading *into* the river from that side should have come from the north, if the bank robbers had ridden down from Tyler, which was what he and Buck had assumed. But Flint was looking at tracks left by a bunch of horses coming from the south to cross at the creek.

*Was this another party?*

He had to find out. Walking up the river north of the creek, he found no tracks of any horses. It was pretty clear the bank robbers had gone to the trouble to always leave town to the north, but their home base was somewhere south of Tinhorn. And if they had ridden up to this creek from the south, he was bound to find their tracks where they had come out of the river this morning. He turned around and started walking downriver watching for their exit from the water.

He walked only a couple hundred yards before finding it—not very well hidden, which he attributed to their haste to escape. The tracks continued following the river south, right past Tinhorn. He could not give chase now. Unlike Malcolm and the man or men he had with him, Flint had no fresh horse. In view of that, he decided to walk the three miles back to town to let Buster walk without a load in the saddle.

He continued walking on that side of the river until he saw the buildings of Tinhorn through the trees on the opposite side of the river. Reaching the spot where Liam Trask and his son, Vike, had fled from the jail after attempting to free Ada, it registered that they had run to the south. It became obvious a hive of outlaws was operating someplace south of Tinhorn. He rode Buster across the river to the Tinhorn side, dismounted, and walked him straight to the stable.

Since Lon wasn't there, Flint took off his saddle and turned Buster out into the corral. *This would be a good time to rob one of the other places*, he thought. It appeared everyone was still up at the bank.

"I swear," Buck exclaimed when he saw Flint making his way through the group of spectators jamming up the doorway. "I was wonderin' if you hadn't got bushwhacked. Don't look like you caught up with him."

"Nope," Flint replied. "They had fresh horses waitin' at that creek about three-and-a-half miles north of town. He broke that horse's wind he was ridin' away from here." He went on to tell Buck what he had found up by the river. "If you go across the river there, you can see their tracks where they rode past the town on their way up to that creek. They went to a lotta trouble to make us think they came from somewhere north of here."

"Did you take a look at that one?" Buck pointed to the body just past the doorway.

Flint replied that he had not.

"You already shot him once. He's still wearin' a bandage around his belly. I pulled his bandana off his face. It was Vike Trask all right, just like we thought."

That was no surprise to Flint, and he wondered if one of the men guarding the fresh horses was Liam Trask. "So him and his pa hooked up with Malcolm and his gang. I wouldn't be surprised if Ada was down there with 'em. The question is where? I just think it's south of here somewhere. I expect the Texas Rangers might like to know that."

That reminded him of a conversation he and Buck had a few days ago. They were talking about Ranger Matt Conway, and wondering if he'd had any luck trailing that little herd of horses. Based on what they found out after the attempt on the bank, Flint had to assume Conway wasn't successful. Either that, or he found Ada Tubbs and took her back to Tyler. He mentioned it to Buck.

"I am surprised the Rangers didn't bother to let us know what happened." Turning back to the business at hand, Buck said, "I told Walt he could go ahead and take the bodies. Too bad I didn't get a chance to thank Mr. Malcolm Smith and his runaway mouth for causin' you to get so suspicious. If he hadn't tried to show off so much, he mighta pulled that bank robbery off with no trouble."

# CHAPTER 22

The attempted holdup of the Bank of Tinhorn gave the people of the little town something to discuss for several days after Walt Doolin had buried the bodies. Mayor Harvey Baxter did not hesitate to remind the members of the town council he had recommended the hiring of young Flint Moran as a deputy for Buck Jackson.

Clara Rakestraw was quick to remind the women working in Clara's Kitchen she had suspected something was up when Buck and Flint started having breakfast together. "I knew it was something big about to happen. But Buck wouldn't admit it."

Flint's curiosity about the fate of Ada Tubbs reared again when Buck received a WANTED notice in the mail stating she was a fugitive from the law on charges of the murder of jail guard Leon Rafer and also a suspect in the disappearance of Texas Ranger Matt Conway.

Buck looked at the notice, then handed it to Flint. "Looks like Matt Conway caught up with Ada."

Flint took the notice, read it, then reread it. "Looks that way, all right," he agreed. "I was afraid he might not take Ada to be the dangerous woman she is. I swear, that's sorry news. He seemed to be a decent man. I'da thought when he went missin' they woulda sent some more Rangers down here to look for him."

"Maybe they did," Buck commented. "They just didn't come through Tinhorn. They mighta thought we sent him on a suicide trail, and they'd pick up their own trail. Suits me. As long as they keep it outta Tinhorn, I don't care what they do about her."

It was not as easy for Flint to dismiss Ada Tubbs. By nature, he was the type who liked to see things finished, especially if he was involved with their beginning. And there was no doubt in his mind he was as much a spark as any to light the fuse that set Ada Tubbs off. Beginning with the arrest of her husband, then spoiling her attempts to free him, and finally killing him, he could well imagine the burning hatred she carried for him. If that wasn't enough, he also killed one brother and had a part in the killing of her other brother.

He felt sure he had come to know Ada well enough to be certain she would not reconcile herself to permit him to go unpunished. That she was a woman made it doubly troubling for him. He wasn't comfortable having a woman to settle with. That's why he hoped the Rangers would find her and arrest her, and why he was happy when two Texas Rangers rode into town one afternoon shortly after Buck brought Ralph's dinner back to the jail.

Time was getting along toward the middle of the month and the occasion of Ralph's trial. Ralph was beginning to realize his leisurely existence was rapidly coming to an end.

Buck tried to console him by telling him that after his trial, he wouldn't leave Tinhorn right away. "Most likely you'll serve your sentence at the Huntsville Unit, and you'll have to wait here till a deputy marshal gets here with a jail wagon to take you there."

He heard someone come into the office then, so he left

Ralph to his dinner and walked out of the cell room to find two strangers standing in front of his desk.

"Sheriff Jackson?" Ranger Henry Birch asked.

"That's right." Buck sized up him and his companion, a tendency that had become a habit after years as a lawman. "What can I do for you?" he asked the tall slim man with a considerable amount of gray in his mustache and sideburns.

"Henry Birch, Texas Ranger, Sheriff. This is my partner, Ranger John Duncan. We're hopin' to find some trace of Ranger Matt Conway, and maybe run Mrs. Ada Tubbs to ground."

"I was wonderin' why we hadn't seen you Rangers before this," Buck said. "Matter of fact, we thought Conway might show up here again, maybe with Ada Tubbs in tow. He seemed like a sensible young feller. I'd hate to think he came to harm at the hands of Ada Tubbs. You boys are here right after we had an attempted holdup of the bank. It might interest you to know one of the outlaws was Ada's brother. We have reason to think she and her father are in cahoots with the other outlaws, south of here somewhere."

John Duncan spoke up then. "We'd like to talk to this brother of Ada's."

"Sorry, he's talkin' to the devil right now. Didn't but one of the robbers get away after that holdup." Buck went on to tell them about the bank robbery and how the one survivor managed to escape. He summed it up by saying he strongly suspected Ada, her father, and her brother had joined up with the family of the one man who escaped. "And now, there ain't no brother, so it's just Ada and her pa."

The two Rangers listened with great interest, and when Buck finished, Henry Birch asked a question. "Where is that deputy of yours? The one that took Conway to Ada

Tubbs' home, where Conway started following that trail of horses?"

"Flint? Why, he oughta be showin' up here any minute now," Buck said. "He went to his boardin' house to eat dinner. What about you boys? You can still make dinner at Clara's Kitchen."

"Thank you just the same," Birch said. "We had a little somethin' when we stopped to rest the horses."

Buck was about to tell them they were missing an opportunity for some good food, when Flint walked in the door. "Here's Flint now. Flint, these two fellers are Texas Rangers and they're hopin' to find Ada."

"Howdy, Flint," Birch introduced himself. "I'm Henry Birch." He nodded toward his partner. "He's John Duncan. We was hopin' you might take us to Ada's home, so we could take a look at that trail Conway followed. You think you could do that?" He glanced at Buck then. "That is, if your boss says it's all right."

Buck didn't comment, so Flint said, "Sure, I can take you out to the Trask place, if that's what you want. But I'da thought you'd have better luck followin' a trail on the other side of the river yonder." He nodded toward the back of the office. "And it oughta be about three-and-a-half miles closer that way." He looked at Buck and asked, "You tell 'em about the bank holdup?" Buck said he did, so Flint told them about the escape route Malcolm "Smith" and one or two others had taken. "That trail is a fresher one, and I think it leads to the same place that trail from the Trask place led to."

"That sounds like somethin' we'd wanna take a look at," Birch said. "Can you take us over and show us the tracks?"

"Be glad to. We'll ride over. It ain't far, but you have to cross the river." Flint led them out the door to the horses tied at the rail.

Buck followed them out but elected to stay at the jail and let Flint take care of the Rangers. They got on their horses and Flint led them across the open field to the bank of the Neches River, where he guided Buster across. On the other side, Flint dismounted and pointed out the tracks he felt sure were left by Malcolm during his retreat.

Still in the saddle, as was his partner, John Duncan remarked, "There's a helluva lot of tracks along this bank, goin' both ways. How do you know which ones are the tracks we're lookin' for?"

"Well, you know for sure you ain't interested in the tracks headin' north," Flint answered him. "All you care about are the tracks headin' south. And there are a lot of 'em goin' that way, too. Most of 'em are old tracks from an attempted jailbreak. If you look a little closer, you can see tracks left by three or four horses, newer tracks. Those are the ones you wanna follow to be sure."

"You're pretty good at trackin', ain'tcha?" Henry Birch asked.

Flint shrugged. "I don't know. I never thought about it. I reckon anybody who's done a lot of huntin' has done some trackin'."

"And you can identify Liam Trask and Ada Tubbs, too?" John Duncan added.

"Yeah, I can identify Trask, but you won't have any trouble identifyin' Ada," Flint said.

"You're the one who brought Ada Tubbs to Tyler and turned her over to the jail there," Birch said. "How'd you like to help with her capture? I think we could use you on this job."

"I wouldn't mind goin' along with you fellas, but it'd be up to the sheriff. He's kinda strict about protectin' the town. He hired me to help him do that, so it's up to him. If he's all right with it, I'd be willin' to ride along with you."

Truth be told, he was eager to join in the hunt. "I'd have to get a packhorse. I don't have any idea how far we'd be goin'."

"All you need is a plate and a cup," Birch said. "We've got enough chuck to feed half a dozen of us."

Flint grinned. "It's up to Buck. Whatever he says is fine by me. That's where my paycheck comes from."

"Fine," Birch replied. "Let's go back and talk to the sheriff."

As Flint had suspected, Buck wasn't too crazy about the idea. He had become quite comfortable knowing Flint was keeping an eye on the town, especially when he felt like retiring to his room early in the evening.

"I know it looks pretty peaceful here in Tinhorn right now," Buck admitted, "but you can't never know when you're gonna get some half-crazy gunslinger come ridin' into town. I had to do some high-powered arguin' to get the town council to let me hire Flint, so he needs to be seen on the street all the time."

"You've got a helluva reputation, Sheriff. It sure would be nice to be able to tell my captain how you cooperated with the Texas Rangers in the capture of Ada Tubbs. He'd most likely pass it on to the governor himself." Birch paused when he saw Buck rolling that over in his mind. "Without him, we wouldn't know Liam Trask if we did bump into him. Or Ada, either, if she was wearin' a dress and wasn't totin' a gun."

"Oh, hell. You wanna go after 'em?" Buck asked Flint.

Flint nodded in answer.

Buck gave in. "All right, but you'd better not get my deputy shot," he said to the Rangers. "Flint, you watch yourself. Be careful what you walk into. There ain't no tellin' how many people are mixed up with that bunch of horse thieves and bank robbers."

"Don't worry. I have to come back. My room and board is paid up to the end of the month." Flint turned to the two Rangers waiting for his answer. "You ready to get started? I'll take a few minutes to go by my room to get my bedroll, a plate, and a cup, then I'll meet you back here."

They left Tinhorn and rode about eighteen miles before striking an old trail running east and west that had obviously been a commonly used road in years past but was rapidly being shrunk by weeds and small trees. The tracks they followed turned onto the old trail and headed east. Since it was time to rest the horses, they stopped at the first good stream and made their camp. Already late in the afternoon, it would be dark in an hour or less. They decided to stay there for the night.

John Duncan took on the responsibility for cooking supper, and Flint had to admit he did a pretty good job of it. They sat around the campfire, eating bacon, beans, and hardtack fried in the bacon grease. It was washed down with coffee strong enough to leave scratch marks on his throat.

After a couple of cups, Flint was inspired to remark, "I ain't sure I'm man enough to be a Ranger, if you have to live with coffee this strong."

Henry laughed. "That's John's idea of good coffee. It won't be so rough when I make it"—he chuckled—"hell . . . if anybody else makes it. When John makes it, he just fills the whole pot up with coffee, then adds a little water if there's any room left."

"I notice you don't ever spit any of it out," John responded in his defense.

"That's only because it's so strong you can't pucker up to spit," Henry came back.

They all got a chuckle out of that.

Then Henry asked, "Flint, is that your first name or last?"

"First name. My name's Flint Moran."

"I'll have to remember that when I'm writin' up my report on this job and sayin' as how you tracked Ada down like a bloodhound."

"I expect you'd best wait to see if we find Ada." Flint decided he liked the two Rangers. Henry, definitely the older one, seemed a patient man and one who would doggedly stay on a fugitive's trail forever. John, on the other hand, appeared restless at times, impatient to get the job done. They seemed a good match for each other and probably made a good team.

The next morning, after a ride of only a little over a couple of hours the trail led them to the Angelina River. The outlaws hadn't crossed the shallows. Instead, they'd followed the river south.

"It's been a while since I was in this part of the state," Henry remarked, "but I'd say Nacogdoches ain't but about fifteen miles east of here."

That was of slight interest to Flint because he had never been there. However, the tracks he continued to follow gave him no sign he might visit Nacogdoches any time soon. A few miles farther a small log cabin built on the bank of the river came in sight. As they approached it, they saw an old woman sitting in a rocking chair on the little porch.

"Mornin', ma'am," Henry called out when they pulled up even with the porch.

"Mornin'," Aunt Minnie Brice returned. "You fellers lost?"

"Seems that way sometimes," Henry answered, "but we

ain't lost. We know where we are, but we ain't sure where we're goin'."

"Lawmen?"

"Yes, ma'am. Texas Rangers," Henry answered.

"Then you ain't lost. You're headin' in the right direction, and you ain't but about ten or eleven miles short." She reached down to pick up her spit can and spat a stream of snuff into it.

"What makes you say that?" John asked.

"You're lookin' for the Fletcher place, ain't you?" Aunt Minnie responded. "I seen 'em ridin' north the other day. And I seen 'em when they came back, but there wasn't but three of 'em that came back. I reckon you settled with the rest of 'em. Did they get anything for their trouble?"

"No, ma'am," Henry answered. "They tried to rob a bank, but they weren't successful."

"Well, there won't be many folks around these parts that'll be grievin' over that," Aunt Minnie remarked.

Since there was nothing left to ask the old woman—she had volunteered the last name of the party they'd followed and told them how far it was to his ranch—Henry saw no need to linger. "It was nice talkin' to you, ma'am, but I guess we'd best move along. A good day to ya." He gave his horse a nudge and started out again.

Flint and John gave Aunt Minnie a polite nod as they followed Henry out of the yard.

Back on the trail, Henry pulled back to let Flint lead, even though there was no need for Flint's sharp eyes. They knew they were only a couple of hours away from the ranch of the man who now had a full name—Malcolm Fletcher.

John couldn't resist japing his partner about the brief encounter with Aunt Minnie. "It sure took a long time for you to dig that information outta that old lady. I know I was impressed at how you finally got her to come out with all that information. Weren't you, Flint?"

"It sounded to me like Malcolm Fletcher and his crew ain't too popular with the other folks around here," Flint remarked. "I would have expected her to close up like a clam if we had asked her how to find Malcolm Fletcher. Looks like you didn't need me to ride along on this trip after all. Tracks so easy to see, you don't even have to get off your horse, and an old woman who talks like a parrot— I'd better try not to get in the way."

"It never hurts to have an extra gun with you when you don't know for sure what you're walkin' into," Henry told him. "Don't worry. You'll be all right." He glanced at John and John nodded.

The Rangers had talked about the possibility of riding into a stronghold of outlaws to try to arrest Ada Tubbs. Maybe that was a question they should have asked the old lady on the porch. As it stood, all they knew for certain was three riders had escaped from the failed bank holdup. One of them was Malcolm Fletcher. They didn't know who the other two were.

The other unknown was Flint Moran. The young deputy looked so much like deputies they had seen in other towns, little more than errand boys for the sheriff. How much they could depend on him in a gunfight was hard to say. On the night just passed, when Flint sought the solitude of the bushes to answer nature's call, John reminded Henry the young deputy had been given the responsible job of transporting Ada to the Ranger station in Tyler. He had obviously successfully delivered her and was not carved up with a chisel like the guard Ada killed in Tyler.

Using the old lady's information, the two Rangers decided to go only half the distance between her cabin and the Fletcher ranch. They preferred to rest their horses before riding on, not wishing to arrive at the ranch with tired horses. Had they known how many horses were grazing on three different pastures beyond the barn, they might not have worried. Flint might have advised them there were probably fifty extra horses at Fletcher's, but he didn't know for sure Trask and his son had driven them there. Anyway, he was not inclined to offer his opinions on how they should conduct their search for Ada. He figured the Rangers had a reliable approach to an arrest, and he was just along for the ride.

# CHAPTER 23

Several days had passed since Malcolm Fletcher came back from a planned robbery without three of his sons. The cloud of mourning that had descended upon the Fletcher household was as dense as on that night when the exhausted horses of Malcolm, Liam, and Ada walked slowly into the barnyard. Melva Fletcher could not bring herself to forgive her husband for leading her sons into slaughter at the bank in Tinhorn.

"They knew we were comin'. It was a trap." Malcolm pleaded with her to understand he'd had no way of knowing.

"How did they know?" Melva demanded. "Who told them you and the boys would try to rob the bank on that mornin'?" She pointed a finger at him and accused. "You, that's who told them. You and your braggin' about how you and Harley had such a big time makin' fools outta the sheriff and his deputy. They knew you was up to somethin' and started watchin' out for you to come back. And now, who's laughin'?"

"Melva, honey," he pleaded. "That don't make no sense a-tall. There weren't nothin' I said that coulda give that sheriff any such notion. Hell, he bought me and Harley a drink of likker. At least, the deputy did. We just ran into some bad luck. You oughta be glad I was able to get away." He tried to put his arm around her shoulders, but she backed away from him. "You oughten to be like that, honey. They was my loss, too."

"You just don't come near me right now," she warned him, "or I'm liable to take this skillet and beat you to death with it." She held up the heavy iron frying pan and made a threatening motion with it. "Me and Nelda will cook for you and your no-good brother-in-law and his crazy daughter because we've got to eat." She pointed out the window at thirteen-year-old Cody coming out of the barn. "I've got to take care of him, or you'll have him ridin' off with you and Liam and Ada to rob somebody."

The spat in the kitchen between husband and wife was clearly heard in the parlor where Trask and Ada waited impatiently for Malcolm to join them.

"Sounds like Malcolm is gonna be sleepin' in one of the boys' rooms tonight," Liam Trask commented coldly.

"He needs to get his behind in here," Ada complained. "I don't know what he's thinkin', takin' his time decidin' what we're gonna do. You know that sheriff in Tinhorn ain't gonna get a posse together to try to find us. All he cares about is keepin' trouble outta his town. Besides, he doesn't know I was there and the bank didn't lose a penny. If anybody shows up here, it might be the Rangers. They've got a man missin' down this way."

"And whose fault is that?" Malcolm asked as he walked into the room in time to hear Ada's comment. "Seems to me that Ranger you shot came down this way lookin' for you."

"I did what you and your brave sons were too damned yellow to do," she hissed. "What did you think I was gonna do? Hand him my gun and surrender? The Rangers ain't got any reason to suspect you of anything. They're just lookin' everywhere for that missin' Ranger. If they come by here, I'll hide till they leave. What are you so worried about?" She glared at him, her eyes flashing with anger. "What really happened in that bank in Tinhorn? You said there wasn't but one man inside the bank. And he shot two of your brave sons and my brother, too? Where the hell were you while all that was goin' on? Ain't it lucky you got away? Everybody else got killed, but you got away."

For once, Malcolm was speechless against her outright accusations. He stood there and took it until it appeared she was never going to stop.

When he finally spoke, he turned to Trask for help. "Your daughter ain't got no right to talk to me like that. We welcomed her the same as we did you and Vike, even though I was afraid she'd draw the damn Rangers down here. And when one showed up, she shot him down."

"What did that have to do with you messin' up that bank holdup so bad you got everybody killed but you?" Ada shot back. "That mess didn't have nothin' to do with the Rangers. I really don't think you need to worry too much about another Ranger showin' up here, lookin' for me, anyway. That first one had a wide trail that fifty horses left for him to follow. That trail ain't there no more. Ain't nothin' to lead anybody to your door." She paused briefly to shake her head impatiently. "Like I said, if one did stumble across this place, I'd hide, and you'd tell him you don't know anybody named Ada Tubbs, then he'd be on his way."

Malcolm seemed flustered.

Trask spoke up. "You know, Malcolm, she might be right. Any other Ranger comin' down in these parts would just be lookin' up a tree where there ain't no coon. He ain't likely to know about that bank holdup, or even care if he does know about it. We'd just tell him we're sorry we couldn't help and send him on his way."

"Maybe so," Malcolm allowed and seemed to calm down a little. "There ain't no reason a Ranger would come straight to my place. He'd just be riding the countryside, hopin' to get lucky."

They were interrupted when Cody came into the parlor looking for his father. "Papa, there's somebody on the river trail, comin' this way."

That caught the immediate attention of the three people who had been arguing moments before.

"Who is it?" Malcolm asked. "Is it anybody we know?"

"I don't know," Cody said. "They ain't close enough to tell. But there's three of 'em."

"Might just be somebody followin' the river trail south," Malcolm said, although he was unable to hide his concern. "Cody, go back outside and see if they start up the path toward the house."

The boy left at once, and Malcolm turned to Trask and Ada. "Speak of the devil and up he pops. We might be gettin' ready to find out if what you said about the Rangers just lookin' everywhere is true." He headed for the front porch to get a look at the three riders.

Ada and her father followed him out the front door.

"Where's he goin'?" Malcolm exclaimed when they saw Cody trotting up the path. "I didn't tell him to go up there to meet 'em. I just told him to watch to see if they headed this way."

It was too late to call him back, however, for he was already halfway up the path.

"Here comes a boy runnin' up the path," Henry said to John and Flint. "Looks like he's comin' to meet us."

They pulled up at the head of the path and waited for Cody to reach the trail.

"Afternoon, young fellow," Henry greeted him.

"Afternoon," Cody returned.

"Is this the Fletcher place?" Henry asked.

"Yes, sir," Cody replied.

"Which Fletcher are you?"

"Cody."

"Nice to meet you, Cody. Is your pa at home?"

"Are ya'll Texas Rangers?" Cody asked when he noticed the badges on two of the men.

"That's right," Henry answered. "We're on our way south of here, and we'd like to talk to your pa. He might be able to tell us if we're headin' in the right direction. I don't see many people around. Who's in the house?"

"My ma and pa and my uncle," Cody answered. "That's all. And my sister." He knew they were looking for Ada, so he didn't mention her.

"We'll go down to the house with you and you can tell your pa we'd just like a word with him, then we'll have to hurry on our way. We've got a long way to go today. Hop up, and I'll give you a ride to the house." Henry reached down and took hold of Cody's arm before the boy might think to back away. "Put a foot in the stirrup and I'll swing you right up."

With no time to think about it, Cody put his foot in the stirrup. Henry shifted his butt back so Cody could sit in the saddle.

Flint smiled to himself when he thought how smoothly Henry fashioned a shield in front of himself in case someone had a rifle sighted on him. *Too bad they didn't send three kids to meet us,* he thought. He and John followed along behind Henry in single file.

"Cody got on the horse with him," Malcolm blurted in surprise as he stared at the three riders coming down the path.

"Son of a—" Ada suddenly uttered. It had just dawned

on her the third in line was riding a buckskin. "I need my rifle."

Malcolm and Trask reacted in alarm.

"Whaddaya need your rifle for?" Malcolm asked. "You try to shoot one of those riders, you're liable to hit my boy. We don't even know who they are. We already agreed on it. If they're Rangers, you just hide till they leave and that'll take care of it."

"Two of 'em might be Rangers. I don't care about them," Ada responded. "But the one ridin' the buckskin is Flint Moran, and I'll damn-sure take care of him."

"Are you sure?" Trask responded. "What would he be doin' ridin' with the Rangers?" He strained to see the riders more clearly. "I can't tell for sure if it's him or not."

"For one thing, he ain't wearin' a hat," Ada said. "Flint Moran never wears a hat."

"Liam," Malcolm implored, seriously worried now. "Talk some sense into your daughter. If she shoots Flint Moran, we'll have two Rangers to deal with. Moran can identify all three of us, but I don't believe he'll try to arrest us for the trouble we made in Tinhorn. Ada said it herself, Buck Jackson and Flint Moran are satisfied to just have us stay outta town.

"If we start somethin' now with Moran, we're gonna be dealin' with two Texas Rangers. I say we hide Ada and take our chances with Moran. If he tries to arrest us, that's when we fight. I don't know about you, but I ain't goin' to prison at this stage of my life. I'm too old to put up with it. I druther die right here."

"That suits me just fine." Trask looked at Ada, her face still twisted with rage, and gave her stern notice. "That's the way it's gonna be, darlin'. You go find you someplace to get outta sight. We'll see if we can get these Rangers on their way as soon as we can. If it comes to a fight, you'll know it and you can join in then. If they move on peacefully, you can track Moran down, if that's what you think you gotta do. All right?"

She didn't answer him for a long moment as the blood grew hot in her veins. "All right," she finally spat out. "I'll do it for you and Melva and Nelda. But when he leaves here, I'll be right behind him."

"Thank you," Malcolm said. "We ain't got much time. They're in the backyard now." He ran through the kitchen and hurriedly told Melva and Nelda what was happening. "I think there's a good chance they'll pass right on outta here when they think Ada ain't here. I'm goin' out on the back porch to talk to 'em. It wouldn't hurt if you and Nelda come out and let 'em see I got a family."

Frightened to hear there were Texas Rangers in the backyard, Melva nevertheless responded with her pledge that she would stand by him. "Nelda and I will be there, and I'll have my .38 in my skirt pocket."


Riding up to the back of the house, Flint eased his rifle halfway out of the saddle sling in case he had to pull it quickly. He watched Henry ride up near the steps and wheel his horse around in order to dismount with the horse between him and the house before he let Cody drop to the ground. John duplicated the maneuver, using his horse for cover also.

*Good idea,* Flint thought, *but I've known Buster a lot longer than I've known Henry and John.* Flint moved the buckskin up behind all of them while keeping one eye on the barn in case someone was in there.

"Tell Mr. Fletcher we'd like to speak to him," Henry told Cody.

"You wanna talk to me?" Malcolm asked, stepping out

the kitchen door before Cody went up the steps. Watching Flint carefully, waiting for an instant reaction from him, Malcolm saw none and realized the deputy really had no interest in him. He told himself what he had told Trask and Ada about the Rangers was true. The Rangers had no desire to transport him and Trask anywhere.

His self-confidence returned at once. "Always glad to help the Texas Rangers," he said as Trask, Melva, and Nelda stepped out onto the porch.

Henry proceeded to tell him they were seeking information on one Ada Tubbs, wanted for the murder of a jail guard and possibly involved in the disappearance of a Texas Ranger. Malcolm, Trask, Melva, and Nelda all shook their heads when Henry said the Rangers thought she might have come there.

"Why would you think she came here?" Malcolm asked.

When neither Henry or John answered right away, Flint said, "'Cause she's your daughter, Trask, and I doubt she's got many places where she'd be welcome."

"Ada don't know I'm here," Trask replied immediately.

Afraid things were going to get a little tense, Malcolm sought to diffuse the situation. "Nah, Ada wouldn't have no notion to come here. I'll bet you boys could use a cup of coffee right about now. How 'bout it, Melva? You reckon you could set up a pot of coffee for the Texas Rangers?"

She looked at him like she thought he had lost his mind, but she nodded and went back inside the kitchen.

To Henry, Malcolm said, "Might as well come on in and set around the kitchen table."

"Well, that's mighty neighborly of you, Mr. Fletcher, that surely is." Henry winked at John. They had decided they weren't going to leave until they searched the house.

Malcolm, almost to the point of enjoying the chance to run another bluff on the law, led them into the kitchen where Melva and Nelda were scurrying around to brew a large pot of coffee. It seemed longer than usual for the coffee to boil, but it was finally ready and Melva and Nelda served it to the lawmen.

Like Flint, Henry was interested to note the tense concern of mother and daughter. "This is a nice house you've built here, Mr. Smith."

The wide smile on Malcolm's face froze in place.

"If you wouldn't mind, I'd like to look at the rest of the house. Would that be all right with you?"

Malcolm hesitated only a moment while his brain was racing to decide what to do. Thinking his best chance was to continue the bluff, he replied. "Sure, I'll show you the house. We've got nothin' to hide, have we, Melva?"

"No," she replied at once, trying not to show her panic. "But please be quiet when you go by the back bedroom. Your sister, Alice, is still in the bed. She was throwin' up all last night and most of today. I'm afraid she's got the pox or somethin'."

"We surely wouldn't want to disturb her," Henry said. "We'll just take a quick look, so I can write on my report that we did."

Malcolm did his best to make conversation while the lawmen finished their coffee, this in spite of the tenseness of his wife and daughter.

It wasn't as long as it seemed to the women before Henry said, "I reckon we'd best get on our way. It'll be time to make camp for the night before much longer."

They all got up from the table, trying to appear casual, the lawmen as well as the outlaws.

"I wanna thank you, Mrs. Fletcher, for the coffee and the hospitality." He started for the door but stopped suddenly. "Oh, I almost forgot. Won't take but a minute, John. Come on, Flint, we'll take a quick look in the other rooms, so I ain't a liar on my report."

They walked quickly through the dining room and down the hall, guns drawn. All the bedroom doors were open except the one at the end.

"When we open this door," Henry whispered, "I want you to take a look. See if it's Ada."

Flint nodded and slowly turned the knob. He opened the door very slowly, being careful to use it for cover. The woman in the bed was propped up on the pillows, but she didn't look like Ada. This woman's long hair was hanging loose around her face, not at all the stark look of Ada Tubbs.

He backed slowly into the hall, closing the door behind him. "It ain't her," he said quietly.

"Damn." Henry cursed the wasted time. "I'd arrest those two bank robbers, but John and I were sent down here to find that woman. And I don't wanna mess with those two jaspers. I reckon there ain't nothin' we can do but just keep lookin', but I swear it ain't nothin' but a waste of time."

"I think you'll find her," Flint said. "I'd guarantee it, but I don't guarantee anything. I'm just sayin' you'll find her."

Henry snorted half a chuckle. "I'd rather you guarantee it. Let's get outta here."

They walked back into the kitchen to a tense gathering around the table.

"Thanks again for the coffee, ma'am. Hope we haven't bothered you folks."

"Not at all," replied an amazed Malcolm Fletcher. "Good luck on your hunt." He followed them out the back door and watched until they reached the end of the path and turned back the way they had come on the river trail. He turned to go back in the house and almost bumped into Ada, her hair still down and frazzled around her face. "Well, you got away with it. Did they look in the room?"

She said that Moran took a quick look.

"I can see why he didn't recognize you," Malcolm said. "If he had, he'd be a dead man right now."


The lawmen rode for about five miles before coming to a parklike grassy clearing they remembered passing on their way to the Fletcher ranch. Situated in an oak collar by the river, the clearing showed it was a popular camping site. They stopped to water the horses and decided to go ahead and make camp. With at least one more hour of daylight left, Flint could feel the loss of enthusiasm between the two Rangers. They had counted pretty heavily on finding Ada at the Fletcher ranch and were facing the prospect of losing her altogether.

To bolster their spirits, he volunteered to make some pan biscuits since they had flour. That decision pleased him when, for a change, they had actually turned out decent.

"I gotta say you make better biscuits than John does," Henry declared to Flint when they were sitting around their campfire. I've gotten kinda used to havin' you around, but I reckon Sheriff Jackson will be gettin' itchy if you don't show up in Tinhorn before long. You might as well head on back in the mornin'. I'm thinkin' maybe John and I will head over toward Nacogdoches, just in case Ada showed up around there."

"You don't have to go to Nacogdoches to look for Ada," Flint told him. "I expect Ada will show up right here later on tonight."

Following their conversation, John asked, "What are you talkin' about?"

"It's like this," Flint explained. "Ada hates all lawmen, but she hates me more than all the rest of you put together. I've had the misfortune to be the one who killed her husband

and her brothers. She's already sworn to kill me, so she'll be comin' after me tonight. I've kept this fire burnin' bright so she don't have any trouble findin' us." Noticing John automatically looking around in case she was already there, Flint added, "She'll most likely wait till we roll up in our blankets and go to sleep."

"You mean Ada Tubbs was in that bedroom when you looked in there?" Henry asked, trying to decide if he should be angry or not.

"Yeah, that was Ada lyin' up in the bed like she was sick. Had her hair down all over her face trying to look different, but it was her."

"We had her right there!" Henry exclaimed. "Why the hell did you—? He took a deep breath. "Now we've got to go back, and this time they'll know why we're comin'."

"If you'da kicked that door in like you started to do, you'da got a bullet for your trouble. When I eased that door open, I saw her propped up against the wall, covers pulled up around her. I also saw the muzzle of her rifle peekin' out from under the quilt. I figured we might as well do it the easy way. Let Ada come to us and we won't have to worry about Malcolm or Trask. Or the other women, for that matter." He paused when John and Henry looked at each other and shook their heads. "If I'm wrong, I'll go back with you. We'll arrest Ada at the house and take our chances on how much help she gets."

"I swear, Flint, I don't know if you're a genius or a damn fool," Henry told him, "but we'll go along with your idea. That all right with you, John?"

"Sounds like a helluva idea to me. If it works, and she comes sneakin' in here tonight."

\* \* \*

"Ada, why don't you let it go?" Liam Trask pleaded with his daughter. "They've come here and found out you ain't here. Now you can stay here with us and not worry about the Rangers."

"I've got a helluva debt to settle with that man," Ada responded. "It eats away at me, how much of my life that one man has took away from me. I ain't gonna know no peace till I see him dead." She climbed up on the big dun she had stolen in Tyler. "Don't worry about me, Pa. Worry about Flint Moran." She let the dun feel her heels.

She figured they would not have traveled far before making camp. Wanting to give them time to turn in for the night, she did not hurry the dun along as she watched the trees close to the river, looking to spot signs of a campfire. About five miles from the ranch she saw what she was looking for—a line of smoke and sparks rising up through the treetops. She continued along the dark road until she came even with the fire then dismounted and tied the dun's reins to a tree limb. As she made her way through the trees and bushes, she saw the horses down near the water.

*After tonight, I'll be riding a buckskin*, she thought, taking great care to make no noise.

At the edge of the clearing, she stopped to survey the campsite and saw the three sleeping forms around the fire like spokes in a wheel. Which one, she wondered, was Flint Moran? From that distance, there was no way she could tell. It didn't really matter. She intended to kill all three men anyway. Less than fifty yards from the campfire, she was confident she could fire, cock her rifle, fire a second time, cock her rifle, and fire a third time before any one of them could escape or return fire. She was also confident she would not miss. Her Winchester was deadly accurate at that distance.

To be sure of her aim, she settled herself against a small tree and laid the barrel in the crook formed by the lower limb. Feeling her heart pounding in her chest, she took a deep breath and exhaled slowly. Once she pulled the trigger, she would have only seconds to crank in the next shot, giving them no time to roll out of their blankets or return fire.

She smiled and squeezed the trigger, continuing the sequence, and putting rounds in all three blanket rolls. It was perfect. She saw no sign of anyone struggling to escape. All three were still. She rose to her feet and cranked another cartridge into the chamber.

*I hope Flint Moran is not dead*, she thought. *I want him to see me, to see my face, to know it is I who have killed him.* In a hurry to see his face before he died, she entered the clearing and ran to the bodies.

It was not until she reached the first bedroll that she understood she had been tricked.

"Drop the rifle, Ada."

The voice behind her was like a bullet to her brain, shutting down her ability to think.

"Drop it," the voice demanded again.

Still, she held the rifle.

"It'll be a lot easier on you, if you just lay that rifle down," another voice spoke to her, slightly to her side.

She recognized that voice as Flint Moran's and immediately turned toward him, raising her rifle to fire.

Using his rifle as a hammer, John Duncan pounded down hard on her forearms before she could pull the trigger and the .44 slug went into the ground at Flint's feet. Flint moved quickly to jerk the Winchester out of Ada's hands and Henry grabbed her wrists, pulled them behind her, and clamped his manacles around them.

"Damn you!" she cursed Flint directly, then looked

around at the two Rangers. "Damn you all! It took three of you to do it."

"Nice to see you again, Ada," Flint responded. "I'd like you to meet Rangers Henry Birch and John Duncan. They've taken time outta their busy schedule to come escort you to Tyler. I'm hopin' you'll be sensible enough to behave yourself. They're not gonna have time to put up with any nonsense."

"Let's get Mrs. Tubbs locked up to a tree," Henry said. "Then we'll salvage what we can outta this night." He looked at Flint and shook his head as if amazed. "What would you have done if she hadn't showed up here? After you told us you recognized her back at the house."

"I told ya. We'd go back and arrest her and hope the family didn't give her much help. "Then," Flint joked, "I'd probably try to talk you and John outta arrestin' me for harborin' a fugitive."

"What I wanna know," John asked, "is don't you think you took a helluva chance stepping right up beside her to tell her to drop that rifle?"

"Why, no. I knew you were standin' there doin' nothin', so I figured you'd make sure she didn't shoot me."

# CHAPTER 24

They headed back to Tinhorn early the next morning, planning to let Ada spend the night in the jail there. John and Henry would go on to Tyler with their prisoner the next day. Flint was dead-certain Ada had something to do with the disappearance of Ranger Matt Conway, but she'd denied knowing anything about it.

There was a reunion of sorts when Ada was put in the small cell next to Ralph, who resided in the new, larger one. News of any kind always spread quickly in a small town like Tinhorn, and news of Ada Tubbs' return spread through the town like wildfire on a windy prairie. Unfortunately for the gawkers, she arrived too late at night to go on display. Only those few who came to work before breakfast time the next day were able to get a glimpse of her as the two Rangers led her out of town on the Tyler road.

It was with a great sense of relief Buck Jackson saw his deputy return. His brief absence had caused the sheriff to realize how much he'd depended on Deputy Flint Moran. He was also tired of being asked when Flint would return. Seemed everyone from the mayor and town council members, to the women at Clara's Kitchen wanted to know. Even Rena at Jake's Place inquired about Flint.

"I reckon I've got job security," Flint told his older brother Nate when he saw him in town the next Saturday.

"Ma and the rest of the family have been hopin' you'd find time to visit a little more often. We kinda miss havin' you around."

"I was thinkin' about that, myself," Flint said. "Things are lookin' peaceful around Tinhorn now. You'd better warn Ma that I'll be showin' up for Sunday dinner."

He returned to the office and found Buck sitting at the desk. "I just told my brother I'd ride out to the house tomorrow to have dinner with the family. Is that all right with you?"

"Shoot, 'course it is," Buck responded at once. "It's about time you took a little time to see the family."

"Ma's wantin' to have a big family dinner. I might not want any supper, but I'll fetch Ralph's supper, so you won't have to bother with it." Unsure if Buck had given up on his recent attempt to cut back on his drinking, and even though Tinhorn appeared to be back to its old peaceful self, Flint didn't want to leave him alone with the town, even on a Sunday night.

"Don't cut your visit short just to get back here before dark. Hell, if I have any real trouble, I'll deputize Ralph," Buck japed. "He oughta be familiar with the way we do things."

His joking caused Flint to comment on the subject of Ralph. "Better use him while you can, I reckon. He ain't got many more days with us before he goes to trial again. I swear, I'll kinda miss him. He sure don't cause any trouble, does he?"

"Nary a bit," Buck answered. "I believe if you forgot to lock his cell, he wouldn't walk out. It's a damn shame to send him down to Huntsville just because he was with Jed Tubbs. I'd be inclined to cut Ralph loose, but I made that mistake with Ada. And he did draw his gun on you. Hell, you had to shoot him twice before it was over."

"That's a fact, but I believe Ralph really was forced to

act the way he did because he was afraid not to, afraid Jed wouldn't hesitate to shoot him if he didn't. He turned plum peaceable as soon as Jed was gone." Flint paused to watch Buck a moment.

The big man was thinking about it, obviously troubled. Flint was witnessing a side of Buck Jackson not normally on display.

"I reckon you could always say he's served enough jail time for his crimes in our town. Call off his trial and put him on probation. Leave his cell unlocked and let him do the jobs Roy used to do."

Buck's eyes lit up. "That's a helluva idea," he exclaimed. "You really think he's given up his outlaw ways?"

"I think he surely wants to. And what if he hasn't? He'll sure as hell leave Tinhorn to get in trouble again."

"Come on," Buck said. "We'll hold court right now." He started for the cell room door and Flint followed him.

Ralph looked up in surprise when the sheriff unlocked his cell door, and he and his deputy came into his cell, looking like they meant business. "What's up, fellers?" he asked cautiously.

"Get on your feet, prisoner," Buck ordered.

Ralph did so immediately, alarmed by Buck's official-like manner and confused by the grin on Flint's face.

Buck continued. "Ralph Cox, in my official capacity as sheriff of the town of Tinhorn, I'm ruling your sentence has been completed. You will be placed on probation until the end of the month."

"What does that mean?" Ralph asked, still fearful.

"Well, it means we ain't gonna lock your cell anymore and you're free to go. Or you can stay and take over the job Roy Hawkins held before your partner murdered him. So, what's it gonna be?" Buck waited for his answer.

"I didn't have nothin' to do with killin' Roy," Ralph

declared, as he always did any time the subject came up. "You fellers ain't japin' me, are you?"

Sheriff and deputy shook their heads.

"Then I'll stay here and take the job. You won't be sorry. I'll do a good job."

Leaving Ralph to ponder his new situation, Buck and Flint went back into the office. Buck sat down at his desk and was about to say more, but the office door opened, and to their surprise, Hannah Green walked in. Buck immediately jumped to his feet. Flint took hold of the doorknob and held the door for her.

"Miz Green," Buck stammered. "How can I help you, ma'am?"

"I declare, Buck Jackson," Hannah replied, "how many years does a woman have to know you before you call her by her first name?"

"Hannah, then," Buck sputtered sheepishly.

Flint could only gawk, amazed. He had never seen Buck at a loss for words, and with a woman at that.

"That's better," Hannah said cheerfully. "In all the years I've known you, I've never been in here before." She took a brief look around her. "This is where you and Flint hole up." She smiled at Flint. "Well, I don't want to take up any more of your valuable time."

"You can take all the time you want," Buck replied at once. "We're at your service. Ain't we, Flint?"

"Depends," Flint answered with a chuckle, afraid this visit had something to do with her niece Nancy.

"It's nothing really," Hannah said. "Tomorrow's Sunday and I wanted to let Flint know I planned to fix a big Sunday dinner. I came here to tell you because I wanted to invite Buck to come with you."

Flint turned at once to see Buck's reaction.

The powerful and fearless guardian of the town of

Tinhorn appeared struck dumb, his jaw hanging open. "You want me to come to dinner?" Buck responded, obviously dumbfounded.

"Doggone it, Hannah," Flint said. "I was just tellin' Buck I promised my brother, Nate, I'd ride down there tomorrow to have dinner with the family."

She gave him a pretty frown of disappointment.

"I woulda asked Buck to go with me, but both of us can't be out of town at the same time, especially with a prisoner in the jail." He turned to grin at Buck before saying to Hannah, "But since your house is in town, there ain't no reason Buck can't be there for dinner."

"Good," Hannah exclaimed. "We'll be honored to have our brave sheriff tomorrow. Myrna and I are fixing a big dinner, so we'll start a little later than usual. Can I expect you at one o'clock, Sheriff?" She displayed a warm smile for his benefit.

Seeing his boss still in a slight state of shock, Flint volunteered, "Yes, ma'am, you can."

"Good," Hannah said again and turned to Buck. "I've always wanted to see if our cooking could satisfy a big strong man like you. I look forward to seeing you tomorrow." She went back out the door with a smile for Flint.

"Well, ain't that somethin'?" Flint commented, armed with first-hand evidence of something he had not had a hint of in the short time he had known Buck Jackson—that he went limp as a noodle in Hannah Green's presence.

"This changes things." Flint pointed his finger at his embarrassed boss. "I don't wanna hear nothin' else about Mindy Moore unless you're ready to tell me how long you've been pining over Hannah Green." He shook his head slowly. "I reckon she decided you weren't ever gonna make the first move, so she had to do it." He fixed Buck with a grinning gaze. "Yes, sir, this changes things."

**TURN THE PAGE FOR AN EXCITING PREVIEW!**

# MONTANA

### Two Families. Six Generations.
### One Stretch of Land.
### A Bold New Saga Centuries in the Making.

*An exciting new series from the bestselling Johnstones
celebrates the hardworking residents
of Cutthroat County: the ranchers who staked
their claims, the lawmen who risked their lives,
and the descendants who carried their dreams
into the twenty-first century.*

Bordered by the Blackfeet Reservation to the north and
mountain ranges to the east and west, Cutthroat County
is seven hundred glorious square miles of Big Sky
grandeur. For generations, the Maddox and Drew
families have ruled the county—often at odds with each
other. Today, Ashton Maddox runs the biggest
Black Angus ranch in the country, while County Sheriff
John T. Drew upholds the law like his forefathers did
more than a century ago. A lot has changed since
the county was established in 1891. But some things feel
straight out of the 1800s. Especially when cows start
disappearing from the ranches. . . .

Intrigued, a local newsman digs up the gun-blazing tale
of the land-grabbing battles fought by Maddox's and
Drew's ancestors. Meanwhile, their present-day
descendants face a new kind of war that's every bit as
bloody. When a rival rancher's foreman is found shot to
death, Ashton Maddox is the prime suspect. Sheriff Drew
is pressured into arresting him, in spite of a lack of
evidence. So the two families decide to do what their
forefathers did so many years ago: join forces against a
common enemy. Risk their skins against all odds.
And keep the dream of Montana alive
for generations to come . . .

**National Bestselling Authors**
**William W. Johnstone and J.A. Johnstone**

# MONTANA

On sale wherever Pinnacle Books are sold.

Live Free. Read Hard.

www.williamjohnstone.net
Visit us at www.kensingtonbooks.com

# PROLOGUE

*From the May issue of* Big Sky Monthly Magazine
*By Paula Schraeder*

The best-selling T-shirt for tourists at Wantlands Mercantile in Basin Creek has an image of a colorful trout in the center circle and these words on the front.

## WELCOME TO CUTTHROAT COUNTY

### *We're Named After Montana's State Fish*

But on the back is the image of a tough-looking, bearded cowboy wearing an eyepatch and biting down on a large knife blade, with these words below.

### *But WATCH Your Back*

Yes, this is Cutthroat County, all 1,197 square miles, according to the US Geological Survey's National Geospatial Program, with 31.2 of those square miles water. According to the 2020 US Census Bureau, the county's population is a healthy 397, though the sunbaked, silver-headed lady working the counter at Wantlands Mercantile when I dropped in on a windy but wonderfully sunny June afternoon told me differently. "Oh, 'em guvment volunteers mighta missed a coupla dozen or so. Folks live here 'cause they've lived here all their lives. Or they come because—"

I waited. Finally, I had to ask, "Why do folks come here?"

"To hide," she said.

Having been in Cutthroat County for three days, I know there must be roughly 1,130 square miles (not including the 31.2 miles of water) for anyone to hide in.

It seemed like a good place to hide.

And getting to Basin Creek wasn't easy.

I left Billings early in the morning in my Toyota Camry, winding through plenty of Big Sky country, and after hitting the turnoff north at Augusta, I drove and drove and drove, with nothing to see but pastures and open country.

*Aside:* A truck driver at a Great Falls coffeeshop on my way back home laughed when he heard my story.

"Was it at night?" he asked.

"No, sir," I told him.

"You should drive through there at night. It's like you're in a [expletive] bowl." He sipped his latte. "Liked to've sent me to the looney bin a time or two."

*Back to my trip:* Finally, reaching a crossroads store, I stopped for coffee and confirmation. "Is this the right way to Basin Creek?" I asked the young Native man who rang me up.

"Yes." He took my money.

He must have read the skepticism on my face. Then he smiled, titled his head north, and confirmed it. "Just keep going that way, and drive till you reach the end of the earth."

Cutthroat County is bordered by the Blackfeet Indian Reservation on the north, the Ponoká (Elk) Mountains to the east, the Always Winter mountain range on the west, and US Highway 103 on the south. If you are driving to Glacier National Park or the Canadian entry point at Milk River City, it's a good idea to take your potty break at Basin Creek. Maybe top off the gas tank, as well. (That crossroads station I stopped at on the drive north has no gasoline for sale; and I did not have courage enough to use the outhouse.) There are only two gas stations in Cutthroat County, and both are in Basin Creek.

"That's not exactly true," I was later told.

"Roscoe Moss has a pump at Crimson Feather, [a community of four trailers and a ranch far to the east of where owner Garland Foster has brought in wind turbines]. At least when the Conoco truck driver—there's a refinery in Billings, you know—remembers to stop on the first of the month. 'Course, old Roscoe's prices are higher than a loan shark's interest rates, and his pump is slower than spring getting here."

The speaker, a handsome man of slightly above average height, dark hair flecked with gray, and the darkest eyes I've ever seen, paused to sip coffee—black ( his third cup since I'd been interviewing him)—and appeared to be counting the other gas pumps.

"And most ranchers and mining companies have their own pumps," he continued. "Though some stopped after they had to dig up their old pumps and haul them away. EPA thing, if I remember right." His smile was disarming. "But you're too young to remember leaded gasoline."

He did not appear to be flirting. But he sure was charming.

"If you run out of gas, there's a pretty good chance someone will top you off with enough to get you to East

Glacier. Maybe as far as Cut Bank." The disarming man was John T. Drew, Cutthroat County sheriff, one of those fellows *"who's lived here all their lives."*

"Well," he politely corrected, "if you don't count four-and-a-half years in Bozeman." He points to the Montana State University diploma—criminal justice—on the wall to the right of the window overlooking the county courthouse grounds.

Those four and a half years might be the only period of time when any Drew male had not dined, slept, and worked in Cutthroat County since long before Cutthroat County was carved out of Choteau County in 1891. I pointed out the first Maddox to set foot in Cutthroat County was a mountain man—perhaps *seven, eight, nine generations ago.*

Drew smiled and shrugged—"I've never figured the math"—then nodded at the diploma. "Math's why it took me an extra semester to get that sheepskin on the wall."

"Do people hide here?" I asked.

"People escape here," he said, the smile still warm. "Tourists come here to fly-fish for cutthroat trout or to pick up one of those T-shirts Maudie sells by the scores during peak season. The three hundred and ninety-seven folks who call this patch of heaven home live here because they love it. Because this country's in their blood. The air's clean. The water's pure. And if you don't mind a whole lot of winter most years, it's a good place to call home."

Sixty years ago, Cutthroat County made national headlines for being the last of the Old West towns. The sprawling Maddox Ranch, now headed by Ashton Maddox, was likened to the Ponderosa of TV's *Bonanza*. The county sheriff then—John Drew's grandfather—was called a real Matt Dillon, the character played by James Arness in the long-running western series *Gunsmoke*.

Tourists from across the world flocked to Cutthroat

County not just to go trout fishing in America but to see the
wildest Wild West. A Montana state tourism guide raved
about four guest ranches—three of which boasted to be
real, working ranches—and a restored historic hotel. Two
stables offered guided horseback rides along the county's
myriad peaks, valleys, and creeks. A plan was to turn part
of the long abandoned railroad tracks, originally laid in the
1890s, into an Old West tourism train complete with a
coal-powered locomotive and mock gunfights and train
robberies.

That boom lasted slightly less than a decade.

A few years later, Cutthroat County, and especially
Basin Creek, got statewide attention and a joke on *The
Tonight Show* [though I have been unable to confirm it
since there's no video on YouTube] as a speed trap.

Drew laughed at that memory. "Well, the town speed
limit was thirty-five, and my daddy did not like speeders.
Maybe because his daddy preferred riding a horse than
driving that Ford Galaxy. We have Ford Police Interceptor
SUVs now, by the way. But we're getting some pressure
from the state to move to hybrids. If we get another electric
charging unit, we might go for that. But that's up to the
county. And the annual budget."

Today, no 1890s train runs through Basin Creek. There
aren't even any iron rails anymore. The only electric-
charging station in the county is at my motel, though the
Wantlands Mercantile is investigating the costs and relia-
bility of adding one in the next two years. The restored
historic hotel burned down twenty-five years ago. The site
is home to the cinder block Wild Bunch Casino, where
cowboys, sheepherders, townspeople, and a few passing
tourists drink beer and play video poker, video keno, video
blackjack, video slots, while Chuckie Corvallis serves up
food. The day's special was $7.99 for Tater-Tot Casserole.

I opted for coffee and the soup of the day, cream of mushroom, probably straight from a can.

There's a NO SMOKING sign on the outside door, but Chuckie Corvallis was lighting a new filterless Pall Mall with the one he'd just burned down to almost nothing.

"It's my place," he said when he noticed my questioning, healthy-lung face. "I own this place. I can smoke if I wanna. Nobody else can. Ain't my law. It's the [expletive] feds."

*Aside:* By the time our interview was over, I had to race back to my motel room, shower twice, and find a laundromat to rid my clothes of tobacco stink.

"What happened to Basin Creek?" I asked Corvallis.

"The [expletive] government. [Expletive] feds. [Expletive expletives]. Folks stopped carin' 'bout their country. Hippies. Freaks. Now it's the [expletive expletives] and their [expletive] ignoramus politics. [Expletive] 'em." He pulled hard on his cigarette and blew smoke. "Pardon my [expletive] French."

Both town stables have been paved over. On one site sits my quaint motel.

Things, however, are changing in Basin Creek.

A month before my arrival, newcomer Elison Dempsey announced his candidacy for Cutthroat County sheriff—a position that has been held almost exclusively by Drews since the county's founding. Dempsey heads the Citizens Action Network, a quasi-military vigilante group, which MSNBC said nothing is "quasi" about. Dempsey has been getting plenty of press, statewide, regionally, and nationally.

Tan, clean-shaven, his dark hair buzzed in crew-cut fashion, and white teeth, he looks like he might have been an Olympic track star or boxer. Smiling after I told him that, he corrected me.

"I might have done well in the biathlon. I'm a great skier,

downhill or cross-country. Out here, it's good to be able to ski. Winters can be long, and skiing sure beats snow-shoeing when it's forty below zero. But I am an excellent marksman. Rifle. Shotgun. .45 automatic."

A Colt .45 was holstered on his hip. The rack behind him in his massive four-wheel-drive Ford carries a lever-action Winchester, a twelve-gauge pump shotgun, and a lethal-looking assault rifle, perhaps an AK-47. I don't know. And I don't want to ask.

"I do have a concealed carry permit," he assures me when he notices my focus on the automatic pistol. "You can ask our soon-to-be ousted sheriff." He chuckles. "All the members of C.A.N. have concealed carry permits, too. But as you can see, we *conceal* nothing."

Dempsey volunteered to take me on a tour of Cutthroat County. His truck gets eight miles a gallon, he said, but told me not to worry.

The gas container in the bed of the Ford looks like it could refill an aircraft carrier.

"The problem here," he said as he slowed down and pulled off the road, "is that two men run this county." He nods at a gate on the left. The arched sign above the dirt road reads *Maddox Cattle Company*. An encircled *M*—a brand well recognized across Montana—hangs just below the company's name.

"There's one of them. Ashton thinks he's God," Dempsey said. "Maddoxes have been gods here for too long. Maddoxes and Drews. It's time for someone to put both of those gods in their place."

Dempsey wore a camouflage T-shirt that appeared painted to his chest and upper arms. It was not a tourist T-shirt from Wantlands Mercantile, but a red, white and blue Citizens Action Network T-shirt.

CUTTHROAT COUNTY
C.A.N.!
WE WILL!
*Citizens Action Network*

He flexed his muscles and grinned, showing those white teeth. "And I happen to be Zeus, Hercules, and Apollo rolled into one."

For the record, Ashton Maddox declined my multiple interview requests.

"Who's the other god?" I asked.

He snorted. "You just spent a couple hours with him in the sheriff's office. You know that. For more than a century—two centuries really—this county has been all Drew and all Maddox. I'm here to change that. And I will. For the better."

Several miles up the road, we turned onto another two-track. An hour later, I was thinking *No one's going to find my body. Ever!*

Dempsey finally stopped, rolled down his window, and nodded at a ramshackle building. "Here's another problem nobody seems to want to fix."

Figuring it was abandoned, I stared at the *house*, if that's the right word. One wall was made of straw bales. The rest that I could see appeared to be made of anything and everything someone could throw together. Wooden crates. Driftwood. Broken two-by-fours. Cans. Cinderblocks. Dirt. The window—singular—was apparently made of Coke bottles and Mason jars.

"Someone lives there?" I finally asked.

"If you call that living," Dempsey answered.

I was about to ask what someone who lived there does. Maybe it was a line camp for Ashton Maddox. Then I remembered the lady at Wantlands Mercantile.

*They hide.*

"You've heard of folks wanting to live off the grid?" Dempsey asked.

"Sure, but—"

"You can't get farther off the grid than Cutthroat County and fifteen miles off the highway." Dempsey shifted the gear into first and we pulled away.

"He's not so bad. I mean, he likely paid money for four or five acres. Land's cheap here. This ain't Livingston or Missoula. If he's registered to vote, I like him. He can vote for me come November. I don't care what party he belongs to. See, I'm running as an independent. I like all folks, those who don't break the law, I mean. Maybe he grows a little grass. Does some illegal trapping. There's a good crick four miles northeast. Poaches a pronghorn or takes an elk out of season. I don't know. Maybe he's like you. Wants to be a real writer. A real Louis L'Amour."

I let him know. "I am a *real* writer."

A half hour later, he stopped again. "Here's another problem," he said, pointing at another rundown trailer home. "The dude that lives here is a poacher. See, that good-looking deputy that Drew got himself, she was pulling off the road a deer that got hit by a tourist on the way back from Glacier. This dude comes by in that Jap rig and asked if he could take the deer carcass. Deputy Mary Broadbent let him. That's illegal.

"This isn't deer season. She broke the law. Broadbent, I mean. When I heard of it, I told Drew. He didn't do a thing. So I called Trent, the local game warden here. He didn't do a thing. Because if Ashton Maddox isn't ruling Cutthroat County, John T. Drew is."

We drove back to the main highway, and headed back to Basin Creek. When we saw two hitchhikers, Dempsey swore, blew the horn, and floored the rig, sending the lean man and tall woman jumping over the ditch and almost falling against the barbed-wire fence.

"That's another problem," Dempsey said after he stopped laughing. "Blackfeet Indians keep coming down here, taking jobs away from folks who live here and want to work."

I didn't bring up the fact that Cutthroat County covers what once was Blackfeet country and that anyone has the right to work anyplace in America.

He had to slow down when we found ourselves behind a semi hauling cattle.

"And there's the final biggest problem in Cutthroat County. I aim to fix it once I send John T. Drew to pasture," Dempsey said.

I smelled cattle manure over diesel.

"You won't believe this, lady, but this spring, we had a report of rustling here. Cattle rustling. Just like you'd see in an old movie on Channel 16."

"Rustling?"

He nodded then named his suspects, but I left them out of this article. My editor and publisher have a policy that they don't want to be sued for libel.

Elison Dempsey said he had reached out to George Grimes, a noted Texas Ranger recently retired, and the subject of last year's action movie titled *Beretta Law*. He asked him to join C.A.N. as a stock detective, but fears the fee George Grimes demands is far more than C.A.N. can afford.

Grimes could not be reached for comment.

"Is rustling why Garland Foster put up wind turbines on his ranch?" I asked.

"Foster is a fool," was all Dempsey would say. "He won't vote for me. But he'll be the only one."

When I reach Garland Foster by telephone, he laughed

when I asked for a response to being called a fool. "Been called worse, little lady." He still reaps millions from his Florida condos and myriad business interests in Texas, many Great Plains states and in Mexico, Central and South America. He moved from southern Texas after the death of his wife four years ago.

Dempsey isn't the only person who has criticized Foster.

"Ashton Maddox hates my guts," Foster said with another chuckle. "But it's not my fault his granddaddy had to sell off part of that big ol' Circle M spread during the Great Depression. I just happened to have a few million bucks to spend and thought Montana would sure beat the heat in Florida, Texas, and Mexico. I didn't know a blasted thing about Sacagawea Pasture when I paid cash for eleven sections [7,040 acres] of real estate."

Sacagawea Pasture, according to legend once property of Maddoxes and Drews, has a name that dates to the 1840s, but the Maddox and Drew names go back even farther in Montana lore and legend and actual history.

So why, I asked, is a longtime cattle rancher turning to wind turbines?

"More sheep than cattle," he corrected. "Least for the past coupla years. Wind turbines don't smell like cattle or sheep, and while beef and wool prices fluctuate, the wind always blows in this country."

"What about rustling?" I ask.

Foster laughed. "Nobody's rustled one of my turbines yet."

Back in town, John T. Drew confirmed there had been one report of rustling on a small ranch. He and both deputies were investigating. "Not to sound like a fellow running for public office, but I cannot comment further because this is an active investigation." He smiled that disarming smile again.

"Elison Dempsey says he has offered his Citizens

Action Network volunteers to help with your investigation," I told him.

The sheriff nodded. "Elison Dempsey says lots of things. Offers a lot of things. Most of them I ignore. No, I reckon I ignore anything Dempsey says. But I did tell him and some of his C.A.N. folks they are welcome to volunteer for the county's search and rescue team.

"There's a lot of country for hikers, hunters, and anglers to get lost in," he explained, "and a lot of my time as county sheriff is spent searching and rescuing, not citing speeders who think all Montana highways are autobahns."

I asked about the controversy with Mary Broadbent, game warden Ferguson C. Trent, and the deer given to a so-called squatter.

"Deputy Broadbent told that man he could have the deer as long as he told the game warden about it the next morning, which he did." Drew smiled. "No sense in letting good deer meat rot when it could feed a family for a week. I'm partial to backstrap myself."

That was confirmed by Trent of the state Department of Fish, Wildlife and Parks. Not the backstrap part. But that the taker of the deer did call Warden Trent about taking the roadkill for many suppers.

Drew stared at me. "This place can still be the frontier."

I asked about Mary Broadbent, who, like Ashton Maddox, declined to talk to me for this article.

The sheriff's smile was gone, and the eyes again hardened. "She's a good deputy."

I looked around the office and kept looking.

"You look confused, Miss Schraeder," he said politely.

I was. "Do you have a dispatcher? I mean, where do calls come in? If you're patrolling how do you—"

"Nine-one-one calls go to Cut Bank in Glacier County.

Those are relayed here." The smile returned. "We're small. But we are efficient."

"Do you think you'll win reelection?"

"That's up to the voters."

"Are things changing in Cutthroat County?" I asked.

"Nothing ever stays the same." The look on his face tells me he's okay with change . . . unlike some Westerners I've interviewed over the years. "We've never been on CNN or *Face the Nation* or NPR till recently. That takes some getting used to. But if that brings us some tourist dollars that won't hurt us. We thank *Big Sky Monthly Magazine* for sending you here.

"Just remind your readers we indeed have speed limits. If you speed here, you'll get pulled over. And fined. And if you commit a major crime, there's one thing you need to know."

"What's that?"

There was that smile again. "The judge might not be in town for some time. Our jail holds ten comfortably. But it's like any jail anywhere. It loses its uniqueness after a few hours."

The jail is in the basement of the combination county courthouse and town hall, a rectangular two-story building of limestone that is dwarfed by Basin Creek's biggest structure, a leaning wooden granary next to the old depot in what is called Killone Memorial Park.

Abe Killone was a rancher who paid out of his own pocket for the construction of the county courthouse. He was murdered on the streets of Basin Creek in 1917.

Except for the bathrooms, the entire eastern wing of the first floor holds the county library. Several rooms labeled storage, and town-related government offices (or desks) are also on the first floor.

Mayor Sabrina Richey, Tax Assessor Henry Richey,

and the constable Derrick Taylor, though he likes to call himself the town marshal. His hours are the same as the county's justice of the peace, 9:00 a.m.-noon Mondays, and 1:00-4:00 P.M. Thursdays.

Other kiosks are scattered across the western side of the dark building for the school superintendent, clerk, and recorder, while the county's road department, treasurer, and assessor have their own offices.

"They keep the important stuff downstairs," librarian Phyllis Lynne told me. "So people don't have to walk up those stairs."

Don't worry. The building is ADA compliant. An elevator at the far corner was completed in 1992. County Manager Dan O'Riley told me, "It runs like it was put in in 1492."

His offices are upstairs, along with Sheriff Drew's and the three elected county commissioners, chairwoman Grace Gallagher, Sid Pritchard, and Mack "Yes, it's my real name. Wanna see my birth certificate?" McDonald. They are responsible for the hiring of all non-elected county officers, including the county coroner and county attorney. Cutthroat County went to a county commissioner management style in 1948.

Most of the second floor covers what's officially called the Cutthroat County Courthouse Basin Creek Municipal Building, even if the court is hardly used . . . for trials, anyway. Town hall meetings are sometimes held there, and the public school put on a presentation of *Inherit the Wind* three years ago.

The clerk, James Alder, says the last criminal case tried was six months ago. "Connie Good Stabbing stole a truck to get back to the rez. Well, she said she borrowed it. Dom Purcell pressed charges. But they reached a plea deal while the jury was deliberating. So everybody was happy.

The jurors got paid for their time, Connie had to paint the Catholic church here in town and pay Purcell a 'rental fee' and reimburse him for gas."

I stared at him, and expected to wake up in front of an *Andy Griffith* rerun on MeTV.

"It's not always this tame," John T. Drew said when I found my way back to his office. "And it's a long way from Mayberry."

There have been four deaths over the past eighteen months, two in traffic accidents (neither involving alcohol), one hiker who met up with a bear in the Ponoká range, and this past December, a cowboy on Garland Foster's ranch was killed while working alone. Apparently he was killed in what the coroner called "a horse wreck."

The coroner, George J. White, by the way, does not live in Cutthroat County. He resides in Havre, Hill County seat and "a bit of a haul" from Basin Creek. The county attorney lives in Choteau, Teton County seat and "not as far away as Havre," attorney Murdoch Robeson tells me over the phone, "but it sure ain't close."

"Does that work?" I asked Dan O'Riley, who was standing in the doorway to the sheriff's office.

"It has to. Lawyers can't make a living in Cutthroat County. Coroners don't have much to do here, either."

I asked O'Riley why Elison Dempsey was talking about the need for his Citizens Action Network in a town and county like this. "He told me Cutthroat County needs a change and a lot of illegal activity goes unreported."

O'Riley laughed. "Most illegal activity goes unreported everywhere, miss. But how much illegal activity do you think you can find in a county of fewer than four hundred people?"

Dempsey also said he would reopen the investigation into the death in one of those traffic accidents. A single-car accident that claimed the life of forty-nine-year-old Cathy Drew, wife of Sheriff John T. Drew.

Disgusted as this makes me, I have to bring that up to the charming sheriff because those charges have been flying around the state – and on some cable news networks – since Mrs. Drew was found in her overturned Nissan Rogue on US Highway 103 between 12:30 and 4:15 A.M. on Friday, December 3, 2021. She was rushed to a Missoula hospital and pronounced dead on arrival.

Drew sighed. "US Highway, so Montana State Police troopers were the primary on that. They handled the investigation. Best guess is that she swerved, overcorrected. I'm a cop. I don't like best guesses. I'd like to know for sure what happened. But I have gotten mighty sick of Elison Dempsey and one of these days, he's going to wish he kept his mouth shut."

Dan O'Riley quickly changed the subject. "You read enough history books on Montana and you'll come across lots of names you'll still find on the list of registered voters."

"Like Drew and Maddox?" I asked.

"More than that," O'Riley said. "My ancestors came here in 1881. But I'm a newcomer. You don't read anything about Dempseys."

"There you have it," Elison Dempsey yelled when I met him at the Busted Stirrup Bar in Basin Creek. "If your roots don't go back to fur trappers and cattle rustlers and Indian killers, you got no right to live in Cutthroat County. That's what I'm fighting. That's why I'm running for sheriff. And that's why the truth will come out and I will be elected."

Yet, when I left my motel, and drove down Main Street, I saw Sheriff John T. Drew getting out his Interceptor in front of the county-town courthouse. I stopped, rolled down the window, and thanked him for all his help.

His eyes were mellow again, and he leaned against the

passenger door. "You're welcome back anytime, Miss Schraeder."

"You haven't read my story yet."

His grin widened and his eyes twinkled. "Most likely, I won't. No offense. I just don't like reading about me or Drews or Maddoxes. Got enough of those yarns growing up."

Well, we heard the stories, too, read the novels, some so-called histories, and heard the schoolground rhymes even when I was a child.

> *Pew Pew*
>
> *Marshal Drew*
>
> *Killed a Maddox*
>
> *Times Thirty-two*
>
> *Pew Pew*
>
> *Marshal Drew*

"Drive safe," the sheriff said, tipped his hat and stepped back. "And watch your speed. Remember what I told you. A person can wait a long time before the judge comes to town."

As I headed out of Basin Creek to return to Billings, I made sure I didn't go a hair over thirty-five miles per hour and just to be safe, kept my Camry at sixty-five as I headed out of Cutthroat County, the last frontier in Montana.

But a frontier that is rapidly changing.

# CHAPTER 1

After opening the back door, Ashton Maddox stepped inside his ranch home in the foothills of the Always Winter Mountains. His boots echoed hollowly on the hardwood floors as he walked from the garage through the utility room, then the kitchen, and into the living room.

Someone had left the downstairs lights on for him, thank God, because he was exhausted after spending four days in Helena, mingling with a congressman and two lobbyists—even though the legislature wouldn't meet till the first Monday in January—plus lobbyists and business associates, then leaving at the end of business this afternoon and driving to Great Falls for another worthless but costly meeting with a private investigator. After crawling back into his Ford SUV, he'd spent two more hours driving only twelve miles on the interstate, then a little more than a hundred winding, rough, wind-buffeted miles with hardly any headlights or taillights to break up the darkness, which meant having to pay constant attention to avoid colliding with elk, deer, bear, Blackfoot Indian, buffalo, and even an occasional moose.

Somehow, the drive from Basin Creek to the ranch road always seemed the worst stretch of the haul. Because he knew what he would find when he got home.

An empty house.

He was nothing short of complete exhaustion.

But, since he was a Maddox, he found enough stamina to switch on more lights and climb the staircase, *clomp, clomp, clomp* to the second floor, where his right hand found another switch, pushed it up, and let the wagon wheel chandelier and wall sconces bathe the upper story in unnatural radiance.

Still running, the grandfather clock said it was a quarter past midnight.

His father would have scolded him for leaving all those lights on downstairs, wasting electricity—not cheap in this part of Montana. His grandfather would have reminded both of them about how life was before electricity and television and gas-guzzling pickup trucks.

Reaching his office, Ashton flicked on another switch, hung his gray Stetson on the elk horn on the wall, and pulled a heavy Waterford crystal tumbler off the bookshelf before making a beeline toward the closet. He opened the door and stared at the mini-ice maker.

His father and grandfather had also rebuked him for years about building a house on the top of the hill. "This is Montana, boy," Grandpa had scolded time and again. "The wind up that high'll blow you clear down to Coloradie."

Per his nature, Ashton's father had put it bluntly. "Putting on airs, boy. Just putting on airs."

What, Ashton wondered, would Grandpa and Daddy say about having an ice maker in his closet? "Waste of water *and* electricity!"

Not that he cared a fig about what either of those hard rocks might have thought. They were six feet under. Had been for years. But no matter how long he lived, no matter how many millions of dollars he earned, he would always hear their voices.

Grandpa: *The Maddoxes might as well just start birthin'
girls.*

Daddy: *If you'd gone through Vietnam like I did, you
might know a thing or two.*

Ashton opened the ice maker's lid, scooped up the right
number of cubes, and left the closet door open as he walked
back to the desk, his boot heels pounding on the hardwood
floor. Once he set the tumbler on last week's Sunday
*Denver Post*, which he had never gotten around to reading,
he found the bottle of Blanton's Single Barrel, and poured
until bourbon and iced reached the rim.

Grandpa would have suffered an apoplexy had he knew
a Maddox paid close to two hundred bucks, including
tax, for seven hundred and fifty milliliters of Kentucky
bourbon. Both his grandpa and father would have given
him grief about drinking bourbon anyway. As far back
as anyone could recollect, Maddox men had been rye
drinkers.

The cheaper the better.

"If it burns," his father had often said, "I yearns."

Ashton sipped. *Good whiskey is worth every penny*,
he thought.

Glass still in his hand, he crossed the room till he
reached the large window. The heavy drapes had already
been pulled open—not that he could remember, but he
probably had left them that way before driving down to the
state capital.

They used to have a cleaning lady who would have
closed them. One of the hired men's wife, sweetheart,
concubine, whatever. But that man had gotten a job in
Wyoming, and she had followed him. And with Patricia
gone, Ashton didn't see any need to have floors swept and
furniture dusted.

He debated closing the drapes, but what was the point?

He could step outside on the balcony. Get some fresh air. Close his eyes and just feel the coolness, the sereneness of a summer night in Montana. Years ago, he had loved that—even when the wind come a-sweepin' 'cross the high plains. Grandpa had not been fooling about that wind, but Ashton Maddox knew what he was doing and what the weather was like when he told the man at M.R. Russell Construction Company exactly what he wanted and exactly where he wanted his house.

Well, rather, where Patricia had wanted it.

Wherever she was now.

He stood there, sipping good bourbon and feeling rotten, making himself look into the night that never was night. Not like it used to be.

"You can see forever," Patricia had told him on their first night, before Russell's subcontractor had even gotten the electricity installed.

He could still see forever. *Forever.* Hades stretching on from here north to the Pole and east toward the Dakotas, forever and ever and ever, amen.

The door opened. Boots sounded heavy on the floor, coming close, then a grunt, the hitching of jeans, and the sound of a hat dropping on Ashton's desk. "How was Helena?" foreman Colter Norris asked in his gruff monotone.

"Waste of time." Ashton did not turn around. He lifted his tumbler and sipped more bourbon.

"You read that gal's hatchet job in that rag folks call the *Big Sky Monthly*?"

"Skimmed it. Heard some coffee rats talking about it at the Stirrup."

"Well, that gal sure made a hero out of our sheriff."

Ashton saw Colter's reflection in the plate glass window. "And made Garland Foster sound like some homespun hick hero, cacklin' out flapdoodle about cattle and sheep prices and how wind's gonna save us all." Holding a long-neck beer in his left hand, Colter lifted his dark beer bottle and took a long pull.

Ashton started to raise his tumbler, but lowered it, shook his head, and whispered, "'while beef and wool prices fluctuate, the wind always blows in this country.'"

The bottle Colter held lowered rapidly. "What's that?"

"Nothing." Ashton took a good pull of bourbon, let some ice fall into his mouth, and crunched it, grinding it down, down, down.

The foreman frowned. "Thought you said you just skimmed that gal's exposé." Colter never missed a thing—a sign, a clear shot with a .30-.30, a trout's strike, or a half-baked sentence someone mumbled.

Raising the tumbler again, Ashton held the Waterford toward the window. "He didn't put up those wind turbines," he said caustically, "because of any market concerns." He shook his head, and cursed his neighboring rancher softly. "He put those up to torment me. All day. All night."

A man couldn't see the spinning blades at that time of night. But no one could escape the flashing red warning lights. Blinking on. Blinking off. On and off. Red light. No light. Red light. No light. Red light. Red . . . red . . . red . . . red . . . all night long. All night long till dawn finally broke. There had to be more wind turbines on Foster's land than that skinflint had ever run cattle or sheep.

Ashton turned away and stared across the room. Colter held the longneck, his face showing a few days growth of white and black stubble and that bushy mustache with the ends twisted into a thin curl. The face, like his neck and wrists and the forearms as far as he could roll up the sleeves of his work shirts, were bronzed from wind and sun and scarred from horse wrecks and bar fights. The nose had been busted so many times, Ashton often wondered how his foreman even managed to breathe.

"You didn't come up here to get some gossip about a college girl's story in some slick magazine," Ashton told him. "Certainly not after I've spent three hours driving in a night as dark as pitch from Helena to here by way of Great Falls."

"No, sir." The man set his beer next to the bottle of fine bourbon.

"Couldn't wait till breakfast, I take it." Ashton started to bring the crystal tumbler up again, but saw it contained nothing but melting ice and his own saliva. "I figured not."

Few people could read Colter's face. Ashton had given up years ago. But he didn't have to read the cowboy's face. The voice told him everything he needed to know.

Colter wasn't here because some hired hand had wrecked a truck or ruined a good horse and had been paid off, then kicked off the ranch. Colter wasn't here because someone got his innards gored by a steer's horn or kicked to pieces by a bull or widow-making horse.

Frowning, Ashton set the glass on a side table, walked to the window, found the pull, and closed the drapes. At least he couldn't see those flashing red lights on wind turbines any longer.

Walking back, his cold blue eyes met Colter's hard greens. "Let's have it," Ashton said.

The foreman obeyed. "We're short."

Ashton's head cocked just a fraction. No punch line came. But he had not expected one. Most cowboys Ashton knew had wickedly acerbic senses of humor—or thought they did—but Colter had never cracked a joke. Hardly even let a smile crack the grizzled façade of his face. Still, the rancher could not believe what he had heard.

"We're . . . *short*?"

Colter's rugged head barely moved up and down once.

Ashton reached down, pulled the fancy cork out of the bottle, and splashed two fingers of amber beauty into the tumbler. He didn't care about ice. He drank half of it down and looked again at his foreman.

No question was needed.

"Sixteen head. Section fifty-four at Dead Indian Pony Crick." His pronunciation of *creek* was the same as many Westerners.

Ashton took his glass and rising anger to the modern map hanging on the north-facing wall, underneath the bearskin. Colter left his empty longneck on the desk and followed, but the foreman knew better than to point.

Ashton knew his ranch, leased and owned, better than anyone living. He found section fifty-four quickly, pointed a finger wet from the tumbler, and then began circling around, slowly, reading the topography and the roads. "You see any truck tracks?"

"No, sir. Even hard-pressed, a body'd never get a truck into that country 'cept on our roads. What passes for roads, I mean. Our boys don't even take ATVs into that section. Shucks, we're even careful about what horses we ride when working up there."

Ashton nodded in agreement. "Steers? Bull or . . . ?"

"Heifers."

"Who discovered they were missing?"

"Dante Crump."

Ashton's head bobbed again. Crump had been working for the Circle M for seven years. He was the only cowboy Ashton had ever known who went to church regularly on Sundays. Most of the others were sleeping off hangovers till Monday. A rancher might question the honesty of many cowboys, but no one ever accused Dante Crump of anything except having a conscience and a soul.

Ashton kept studying the map. He even forgot he was holding a glass of expensive bourbon.

Colter cleared his throat. "No bear tracks. No carcasses. The cattle just vanished."

"Horse tracks?" Ashton turned away from the big wall map.

The cowboy's head shook. "Some. But Dante had rode 'cross that country—me and Homer Cooper, too—before we even considered them cattle got stoled. So we couldn't tell if the tracks were ours or their'uns."

"Do we have any more cattle up that way?" Ashton asked.

"Not now. We'd left fifty in the section in September. Dante went there to take them to the higher summer pasture. Found bones and carcasses of three. About normal, but he took only thirty-one up. So best I can figure is that sixteen got rustled."

*"Rustled."* Ashton chuckled without mirth. The word sounded like something straight out of an old Western movie or TV show.

"Yeah," the foreman said. "I don't never recollect your daddy sayin' nothin' 'bout rustlers."

"Because it never happened." Ashton let out another mirthless chuckle. "I don't even think my grandpa had to cope with rustlers, unless some starving Blackfoot cut out a calf or half-starved steer for his family. Grandpa had his faults, but he wasn't one to begrudge any man with a hungry wife and kids." He sighed, shook his head, and stared at Colter. "You're sure those heifers aren't just hiding in that rough country?"

The man's eyes glared. "I said so," was all he said.

That was good enough for Ashton, just as it had been good enough for his father.

"Could they have just wandered to another pasture?"

"Homer Cooper rode the lines," the foreman said. "He said no fence was down. Sure ain't goin' 'cross no cattle guards, and the gates was all shut and locked."

They studied one another, thinking the same thought. An inside job. A Circle M cowboy taking a few Black Angus for himself. But even that made no sense. No one could sneak sixteen head all the way from that pasture to the main road without being seen or leaving sign.

"How?" Ashton shook his head again. "How in heaven's name . . . ?"

Colter shrugged. "Those hippies livin' 'cross the highway on Bonner Flats will say it was extraterrestrials." Said without a smile, it probably wasn't a joke.

In fact, Ashton had to agree with the weathered cowboy. The *Basin River Weekly Item* had reported cattle turning up missing at smaller ranches in the county, but Ashton had figured those animals had probably just wandered off. The ranchers weren't really ranchers. Just folks wealthy enough to buy land and lease a pasture from the feds for grazing and have themselves a quiet place to come to and get a good tax break on top of it. Like that TV director or producer or company executive who ran buffalo on his place and had his own private helicopter. There were only two real ranchers left in Cutthroat County, though Ashton would never publicly admit that Garland Foster was a real rancher. He'd been mostly a sheepman since arriving in Cutthroat County, and he was hardly even that anymore.

Ashton looked at the curtains that kept him from seeing those flashing red lights all across Foster's spread. "How did someone manage to get sixteen Black Angus of our herd out of there? Without a truck or trucks. Without being seen? That's what perplexes me." He moved back to the map, reached his left hand up to the crooked line marked in blue type—*Dead Indian Pony Creek*—and traced it down to the nearest two-track, then followed that to the ranch road, then down the eleven miles to the main highway.

Colter moved closer to the map. Those hard eyes narrowed as he memorized the topography, the roads, paths, streams, canyons, everything. Then he seemed to dismiss the map and remember the country from personal experience, riding a half-broke cowpony in that rough, hard, impenetrable country in the spring, the summer, the fall. Probably not the winter, though. Not in northern Montana. Not unless a man was desperate or suicidal.

His head shook after thirty seconds. "I can take some boys up, see if we can find a trail."

Ashton shook his head. He had forgotten about a wife who had left him, had dismissed a fruitless trip to the state capital, and then an even more unproductive meeting in a Great Falls coffeeshop with a high-priced private dick. "No point in that," he said. "They stole sixteen head of prime Black Angus because we were sleeping. Anyone who has lived in Montana for a month knows you might catch Ashton Maddox asleep once, and only once. I'll never make that mistake again. They won't be back there. Any missing head elsewhere?"

"Nothin' yet," Colter replied. "But I ain't got all the tallies yet."

Ashton remembered the bourbon and raised the tumbler as he gave his foreman that look that needed no interpretation. "I want those tallies done right quick. There's one thing in my book that sure hasn't changed since the eighteen hundreds. Nobody steals Circle M beef and gets away with it."

Visit our website at
**KensingtonBooks.com**
to sign up for our newsletters, read
more from your favorite authors, see
books by series, view reading group
guides, and more!

Become a Part of Our
**Between the Chapters Book Club**
Community and Join the Conversation

Betweenthechapters.net